THE SHOAL OF TIME

Acclaim for J.M. Redmann's Micky Knight Series

Ill Will

Lambda Literary Award Winner

Foreword Magazine Honorable Mention

"*Ill Will* is fast-paced, well-plotted, and peopled with great characters. Redmann's dialogue is, as usual, marvelous. To top it off, you get an unexpected twist at the end. Please join me in hoping that book number eight is well underway."—*Lambda Literary Review*

"Ill Will is a solidly plotted, strongly character-driven mystery that is well paced."—*Mysterious Reviews*

Water Mark

Foreword Magazine Gold Medal Winner

Golden Crown Literary Award Winner

"*Water Mark* is a rich, deep novel filled with humor and pathos. Its exciting plot keeps the pages flying, while it shows that long after a front page story has ceased to exist, even in the back sections of the newspaper, it remains very real to those whose lives it touched. This is another great read from a fine author."—*Just About Write*

Death of a Dying Man

Lambda Literary Award Winner

"Like other books in the series, Redmann's pacing is sharp, her sense of place acute and her characters well crafted. The story has a definite edge, raising some discomfiting questions about the selfishly unsavory way some gay men and lesbians live their lives and what the consequences of that behavior can be. Redmann isn't all edge, however—she's got plenty of sass. Knight is funny, her relationship with Cordelia is believably long-term-lover sexy and little details of both the characters' lives and New Orleans give the atmosphere heft."—*Lambda Book Report*

Death of a Dying Man

"As the investigation continues and Micky's personal dramas rage, a big storm is brewing. Redmann, whose day job is with NOAIDS, gets the Hurricane Katrina evacuation just right—at times she brought tears to my eyes. An unsettled Micky searches for friends and does her work as she constantly grieves for her beloved city."
—*New Orleans Times-Picayune*

The Intersection of Law and Desire

Lambda Literary Award Winner

San Francisco Chronicle Editor's Choice for the year

Profiled on *Fresh Air*, hosted by Terry Gross, and selected for book reviewer Maureen Corrigan's recommended holiday book list.

"Superbly crafted, multi-layered...One of the most hard-boiled and complex female detectives in print today."—*San Francisco Chronicle* (An Editor's Choice selection for 1995)

"Fine, hard-boiled tale-telling."—*Washington Post Book World*

"An edge-of-the-seat, action-packed New Orleans adventure... Micky Knight is a fast-moving, fearless, fascinating character...*The Intersection of Law and Desire* will win Redmann lots more fans."
—*New Orleans Times-Picayune*

"Crackling with tension...an uncommonly rich book...Redmann has the making of a landmark series."—*Kirkus Review*

"Perceptive, sensitive prose; in-depth characterization; and pensive, wry wit add up to a memorable and compelling read."—*Library Journal*

"Powerful and page turning...A rip-roaring read, as randy as it is reflective...Micky Knight is a to-die-for creation...a Cajun firebrand with the proverbial quick wit, fast tongue, and heavy heart."
—*Lambda Book Report*

Lost Daughters

"A sophisticated, funny, plot-driven, character-laden murder mystery set in New Orleans...as tightly plotted a page-turner as they come...One of the pleasures of *Lost Daughters* is its highly accurate portrayal of the real work of private detection—a standout accomplishment in the usually sloppily conjectured world of thriller-killer fiction. Redmann has a firm grasp of both the techniques and the emotions of real-life cases—in this instance, why people decide to search for their relatives, why people don't, what they fear finding and losing...and Knight is a competent, tightly wound, sardonic, passionate detective with a keen eye for detail and a spine made of steel."—*San Francisco Chronicle*

"Redmann's Micky Knight series just gets better...For finely delineated characters, unerring timing, and page-turning action, Redmann deserves the widest possible audience."—*Booklist*, starred review

"Like fine wine, J.M. Redmann's private eye has developed interesting depths and nuances with age...Redmann continues to write some of the fastest –moving action scenes in the business... In Lost Daughters, Redmann has found a winning combination of action and emotion that should attract new fans—both gay and straight—in droves."—*New Orleans Times Picayune*

"An admirable, tough PI with an eye for detail and the courage, finally, to confront her own fear. Recommended."—*Library Journal*

Visit us at www.boldstrokesbooks.com

By the Author

The Micky Knight Mystery Series:

Death by the Riverside

Deaths of Jocasta

The Intersection of Law and Desire

Lost Daughters

Death of a Dying Man

Water Mark

Ill Will

The Shoal of Time

Women of the Mean Streets: Lesbian Noir
edited with Greg Herren

Men of the Mean Streets: Gay Noir
Edited with Greg Herren

Night Shadows: Queer Horror
edited with Greg Herren

THE SHOAL OF TIME

by
J.M. Redmann

2013

THE SHOAL OF TIME

ISBN 13: 978-1-60282-967-1

This Trade Paperback Original Is Published By
Bold Strokes Books, Inc.
P.O. Box 249
Valley Falls, NY 12185

First Edition: December 2013

Credits
Editors: Greg Herren and Stacia Seaman
Production Design: Stacia Seaman
Cover Design by Sheri (graphicartist2020@hotmail.com)

Acknowledgments

You know who you are—the ones who have been nagging, begging, pleading with me for a certain plot element. Be careful what you ask for; you may get it. This has been a hard book to write—not like the others were a walk in the park. Sitting in front of a computer trying to make words turn into worlds is never easy. (Nor are the words ever as perfect as the vision we have in our brains.) I have to admit there are moments when I come home from the day job and I'm tired and want nothing more than to turn my brain off, and I wonder why I do this. But in those moments, I remember the coterie of readers and writers who keep me sane and focused. Yes, that would be you. Even when you're nagging, begging, and pleading. Thank you.

Of course a big thank you to Greg Herren for his editorial brilliance and calmness, especially as I kept sliding deadlines. And he didn't even add extra weight at the gym. (Well, not much.) I also need to thank the motley and wonderful crew who met us downtown in NYC at City Hall—one of my oldest and dearest friends, Maude Brickner; a dear new friend, Lizz; the inimitable Rob Byrnes; and in a surprise guest appearance, Greg Herren. Oh, and Gillian for suggesting it in the first place. And Greg, Rob, and Gillian for being stalwart enough to come to the Lambda Awards after.

Also a big thanks to Cherry and Beth, my friendly computer geeks and all-around fun gals. More charbroiled oysters soon. Mr. Squeaky and Arnold, because I'm a lesbian and we have to thank our cats. My partner, Gillian, for all the joy in us both spending evenings at our respective computers working on our respective books.

There are many people at my day job who keep me sane—or don't point out to me that I'm not—and are greatly understanding about the writing career. Noel, our CEO and my boss, for his tireless leadership and letting me run off to do book things. My staff is great and makes my job easy enough that I have time to write—Josh, Narquis, Lauren, Joey,

Petera, and all the members of the Prevention Department. I would love to be able to write full-time, but since I have to have a real job, I'm very lucky to have one of the best ones possible.

Also huge thanks to Rad for making Bold Strokes what it is. Ruth, Connie, Shelley, Sandy, Stacia, and Cindy for all their hard work behind the scenes, and everyone at BSB for being such a great and supportive publishing house.

To GMR
For being a fast reader and willing to drive through Illinois for me. It is the small daily things that eventually make a life and a love.

But here, upon this bank and shoal of time,
We'd jump the life to come. But in these cases
We still have judgment here, that we but teach
Bloody instructions, which, being taught, return
To plague th' inventor: this even-handed justice
Commends the ingredients of our poisoned chalice
To our own lips

Macbeth, Act 1, Scene 7

CHAPTER ONE

L ife is full of stupid moments, most of them not chosen.
You know what I mean—bitching about a coworker, not realizing
she's two feet behind you. Trying to find your sunglasses when they're
on the top of your head. Taking a turn and realizing that all the cars
are coming at you. Putting your keys in a secure place you can't
remember.

"Hey, give me your money," he muttered at me.

Dark, rainy, the deepening chill bite of winter, my head had been
down watching for wet, slippery spots and I hadn't noticed anyone else
on the street.

Occasionally stupid turns to tragic. Mostly we pay what I call
stupid tax—going back to the grocery store to get the one thing we
forgot, standing in line and paying to replace the lost license, waiting
in the rain for the friend with the spare key. There is a lot of stupid in
the world, both ours and others', and we pretty much stumble over it
every day.

Today had been stupid on steroids.

Weather was supposed to affect crooks, too. At least that had been
my theory when I decided to head out after dark to pick up food made
by someone other than myself.

It had been a long—dare I say it?—stupid day. People who
promised to call right back and hadn't. Traffic that included a car driving
over the speed limit in the left lane on Claiborne with the passenger
opening his door to upchuck into the right lane, which left me hoping
the rain would clean off whatever got on my tires. A client who changed
her mind about wanting me to follow her husband to see if he had an
on-the-side girlfriend.

I mostly avoid messy domestic cases and had only taken this one as a favor to a friend. It took a stupidly exasperating amount of time to explain to her she still owed me for the hours I'd spent on her case. Her calling-off call came just as I had returned to my office after a fruitless morning of following said husband. Annoyingly, I hadn't caught him at anything, but he was a player, too easy with his smiles and glances at anything female, handing a business card to the young chick at the coffee-shop counter. Happily married men don't prowl like that.

If the wife didn't want to know—well, wanted to know but didn't want evidence that would require her to admit knowing—that was her affair, not mine. She called back three times asking for a discount since I hadn't finished the case.

Webster's, when you update your dictionary, I have the perfect picture for *annoying*.

The day had started out in the summer, acting as if the calendar didn't say something entirely different, sunny and in the seventies, and the temps had plunged thirty degrees since I left this morning in light pants and a T-shirt that had me underdressed long before the first of the annoying wife calls. Winter here is one of the reasons people with snow phobias move to this part of the world; it rarely gets below freezing and even when it does, it doesn't stay there. Yes, Minnesota, I'm talking to you. But, as proven by today, it can be from annoyingly smug to unpleasantly cold in all too short a span of time.

New Orleans is a damp city, held between a mighty river and a large lake, exits west and east over water. In the summer, the humidity turns it to a steam bath, in the winter, a damp cold that blows through every crack in a building or clothes.

When I finally got home I was bone-deep cold, too pissed at the events of the day to be tired, and too tired to un-piss myself and get in a better mood. The house was chilly and dark. No cat, no person, nothing living to greet me. I quickly turned the fans off and the heat on—I hate days when I have to do that—threw on a ratty sweatshirt and jacket because I was too chilled to take off my clothes or to spend time finding what we call winter clothes down here.

Knowing the contents of my refrigerator would turn into a science experiment any day now, I had decided on a quick hike into the French Quarter, with its dense population of food possibilities, and hoped the house would be warmer by the time I got back.

And now I was standing on a dark patch of Esplanade Avenue with a young punk in front of me demanding my money.

He was slight, with one of those faces that could have been between fourteen and forty, shadowed as it was by the faint light at the end of the block and the brim of his pulled-low hat. Cowboys. Fucking stuck up by a Dallas Cowboys fan. His face was thin and long, a bare wisp of a beard on his chin. He was wearing a hooded sweatshirt, thin and faded, not heavy enough for the chill in the air and hadn't thought to pull the hood over his head. Guess he decided the fuckin' Cowboys hat was enough of a disguise. One hand was hanging by his side; the other was hidden in the sweatshirt pocket, outlined by a bulge that could be a gun. Or his fingers in a bang-bang pose.

It was the French Quarter; I was a woman alone. He probably assumed I was a tourist who got lost in the old buildings and forgot this was a real city and not some manufactured playland for visitors.

Most of the time stupid is random. Every once in a while we choose it.

I knew what I was supposed to do, be calm and unthreatening, defuse the situation and quietly give him my money.

I also knew I wasn't going to do it.

Instead I was going to do something stupid that might get me killed. I didn't give a damn. I was tired of being civilized and polite and wanted to kick someone, and this poor kid had just given me an excuse.

"Be cool," I said quietly. "I'm getting my wallet." Using two fingers, I tried to extract it from my front pocket, but it was chilly and damp and I couldn't get a good grip. I finally managed to get it out, but just as I was lifting it to offer to him, it dropped out of my hand onto the sidewalk.

"Sorry," I mumbled, reaching down to pick it up. I fumbled for a moment with the leather on the slick, wet street. Just like a stupid woman tourist would.

But I wasn't any kind of tourist.

I shot up, throwing the wallet at his face, following immediately with a kick to his gun hand.

My foot hit flesh, not metal. I kicked again, this time in the crotch.

The one thing I had changed was my shoes, from low-slung loafers to a beat-up old pair of cowboy boots. Much warmer than my earlier shoes, with heels and toes made for kicking.

He covered the kicked area with his good hand and sank to his knees in pain.

I yanked the hood, pulling it tight around his neck.

He coughed, said, "Hey, let me breathe."

"You try to hold me up and I'm supposed to be nice?"

I grabbed the Cowboys hat and tossed it into a puddle, landing it on top of greasy fried chicken bones.

"Hey, that's a good hat." He struggled to get up.

I kicked his foot out and he thudded back down on his knees. I yanked the hood, pulling him down, his face a few inches from his soaked hat and the rotting food.

"It was my good money you were trying to steal."

Without the hat and this close, I could see he was young and should have been home studying instead of out thieving. His small beard was probably the only hair he could grow.

I used my knee to shove him all the way to the ground, being kind enough not to put his face in the puddle. With my knee in his back, one hand holding his sweatshirt, I quickly patted him down with the other hand. Just because he didn't have a gun wasn't proof he didn't have other unpleasant weapons like a knife or brass knuckles.

There were a lot of bumps under his sweatshirt, but they were all wallet-shaped. Baby boy had been busy this evening.

Thieves—and too many other people—seemed to live by immediate experience. If they did it and didn't get caught, then they wouldn't get caught. My young thief had been pushing his luck.

As I was pushing mine. He was recovering from the kick to his crotch.

I was still a woman; worse, one with gray in her hair. His ego wasn't happy about the situation.

He suddenly struggled under me, trying to push up with his hands and legs, twisting under me. I heard him mutter, "Fucking bitch."

I yanked hard on his hood, but he pulled on the zipper, halfway opening the sweatshirt and freeing his neck. He may have been slight, but he was strong. And desperate.

I had been too nice and not kicked his pretend gun hand hard enough. He used it to grab my ankle. My other leg was planted in his back, so that was my only support.

No more being nice. I'd started feeling sorry for him because he was young. And stupid, but that goes without saying. Most crooks are stupid. The smart ones work for banks.

I slammed my weight down on him, so I was almost flat against his back, shoving his face into the sidewalk.

Maybe an effective tactic, but not a pleasant one. He smelled like an unbathed wet dog. But I didn't have time to worry about unpleasant odors. He was still struggling to throw me off. He let go of my ankle, using the hand to lever himself up.

I had wanted a fight. I just hadn't wanted one I would lose.

Don't be kind, I reminded myself. I put one hand on the back of his neck—I'd worry about cleaning the dirty-dog grime off later—hoping between that and my knee in his back I could keep him down long enough to figure out how the hell to get out of this.

Be nice, give him his hat back. I reached over his shoulder to the puddle and slapped it and a few chicken bones on his face.

He sputtered and, as I had hoped, used his hands to grab the dripping, stinking cap away.

I shoved myself up into a standing position, aiming a kick between his legs on the way up. Then another when I was fully standing.

He yelped and flopped away, enough to land in the puddle. He let the water distract him, clearly not trained well enough to know that in a fight, nothing matters, not getting wet or dirty or being hit; you have to focus intensely on winning.

I kicked him again in the crotch. This time he curled up into fetal position, not worrying about the puddle or the chicken bones anymore, pain his only focal point.

One last insult. He'd be down for at least a minute or two. I rifled under his jacket for the stolen wallets, grabbing as many as I could. One hand weakly tried to stop me.

"Don't move or I'll kick you again. And again."

His only answer was a groan.

I stuffed the wallets into my jacket as he had in his and then walked rapidly away.

As I got to the corner, I briefly looked back. He was still on the ground.

I kept walking, moving as quickly as I could without running. I didn't want to be running with a bunch of stolen wallets on me.

Okay, I'm not perfect—I had a brief argument with myself about keeping the money. There was a high probability that Mrs. I-Changed-My-Mind would be slow, *extremely* slow to pay me, but I had other cases and some active billing on my part would bring in money owed me. Maybe it would be enough to cover the bills.

There was a fire station at the corner of Frenchmen and Esplanade, near the river. But firemen would ask questions. There was a place where they provided HIV services right across the street. I threw the wallets behind their iron gate. Perfect. Do-gooders would do the right thing.

There are advantages to being a woman. No one pays much attention when you're standing in front of a closed place and shoving things through the opening in the door. At least four different groups of people walked by and none of them even glanced at me.

That taken care of, I headed into the Quarter in search of food.

Taking that kid on had been major stupid.

What scared me was that I didn't regret it.

Chapter Two

I found a quiet corner in a pizza place on Decatur. My plan had been to get something to go and head back home. But the house wasn't calling me; instead, I found I wanted the distractions of lights, watching people go by, the ritual of perusing a menu, waiting for food. I also wanted plenty of time for the stupid thief to get up and go home. Most of the other tables were couples or groups. It was boisterous, people out to party.

I was alone in my small world. Food, getting warm, that was all I'd think about. And maybe not doing anything stupid on the way home.

Usually I bring a book, but this was unplanned, so I was unprepared. I've found if I don't have something to distract me, I easily fall into PI mode, watching too carefully, trying to pick out the mark in the room. Then I have to remind myself I'm just here for a pizza, not to right the wrongs of the world.

Perusing the menu, I didn't even bother looking at the salads. Tonight was comfort food: cheese, grease, meat, and dough. I added mushrooms to the pepperoni and extra cheese. That would count as my vegetable for the evening.

I glanced around the room—three gay couples, four straight ones, one girls'-night-out party, two groups of men on the prowl, young enough to not even notice me, a couple of mixed groups. Mostly locals, as this was the far end of the Quarter, away from the tourist bustle of Canal Street. A group of five was seated next to me, taking the extra chairs from my table.

I cased them out of habit, three men, two women. A work or social group. One of the women was older than the men and wore a sensible pantsuit, the kind one wears to a conference. The younger woman sat next to her on the banquette, with her jacket marking the space between us. Not dating, nor local from their accents. The younger woman gave me a sidelong look, like I might be a threat to her nice leather jacket.

I shifted my glance slowly, as if just idly looking around the restaurant at nothing and no one in particular. Haste is noticeable. I kept her just enough in the periphery of my vision to know when she turned back to her companions.

Then I reminded myself I was only here for food and warmth. They were strangers I would never see again.

Ignoring them, I distracted myself with the toy of the modern age, my phone, as if something more vital than tomorrow's weather was there.

I have to admit after looking at the temperatures in North Dakota, I felt much warmer. Our high tomorrow would be well above freezing; they would be warm only compared to zero Kelvin.

Food was placed in front of me. Melted, gooey cheese doesn't solve all the world's problems, but it takes care of the stomach ones. I disentangled the strings of mozzarella and slid a steaming slice onto my plate.

"Wow, that smells good," said the woman at the next table. She was commenting on my pizza, but not speaking to me.

If you comment on my food, I get to look your way. I took a bite and glanced in her direction. She wasn't as young as she had first looked, mid to late thirties, maybe even well-preserved early forties. She had no gray in her hair, so I suspected dye. It was a chestnut red, probably very close to her original color. Green eyes, brought out by her olive-green sweater. A smattering of freckles across her nose and cheeks with clear, fair skin. Her small ski-slope nose didn't perfectly balance her mouth, which was a little too big for her face. It was minor, the difference between being model pretty and girl-next-door pretty.

"Sorry," I said to her. "I'll try and keep my fumes to myself."

She turned to me and smiled. She had a great smile, the wide mouth bringing her whole face with it. The laugh lines at her eyes had been earned.

"Not your fault," she said. "If it wasn't yours, it would be another pizza. And I didn't come to New Orleans to use calories on something I can get anywhere."

"This isn't exactly an Italian city," one of the younger men added.

I considered correcting him—it wasn't Cajuns who came up with the muffuletta sandwich. At one time, the French Quarter was a run-down area of town, so crowded with Sicilian immigrants it was known as "Little Italy." In a dark chapter of the city's history in 1891, eleven Italian men were dragged from the jail and lynched after being acquitted in the murder of the police chief. They were the un-American immigrants of the day.

I went back to my pizza and the oh-so-interesting weather on my phone and left them to their tourist's myths.

Just as the waitress was handing me a to-go box, one of the men at the next table said, "A shotgun to the stomach will solve that."

"Mel, keep your voice down," the older woman said. "This isn't the place to talk about things like that."

A couple of beer bottles in front of him explained his loose lips.

I concentrated on getting the pizza into the box, as if I'd heard nothing out of the ordinary.

A hand rested on my forearm.

"It's not what it seems," the younger woman said to me. "We're not plotting murder and mayhem."

"So, my leftover pizza is safe?"

"Can't promise that. The salad didn't really do it for me." She smiled that gorgeous smile of hers.

"You're welcome to a slice," I said. I smiled back; it was hard not to.

"Mel likes to think like a criminal. He says it helps him know what they might do."

"You're law enforcement?" I asked. I hadn't pegged them as pros, instead guessing something like in town for a plastics convention. If this had been anything other than eating pizza—like a real case—that would have been a major slipup.

"Immigration."

"I was born here."

She laughed. "Don't worry, I'm not working. And even if I was I'd have to have probable cause. Eating pizza next to me doesn't qualify."

Was she flirting with me? Or just falling into the friendly ways of New Orleans where you talked to people on the street like you knew them your entire life? And even if she was, that was the last thing I needed. I was way over my stupid quota for the day. And the year.

"You here for a conference?" I asked.

"No, we're working."

"But you're not from here."

"You know everyone around here?"

"No, but your clothes aren't right. Your jacket and sweater are both too heavy for the local climate. I doubt you could buy anything like that here."

She gave me an appraising look. "Amazing. You notice things like that?"

"Occupational hazard. I'm paid to notice and it's hard to turn it off."

"What's your occupation? And why is noticing things a hazard?"

I pulled out my PI license and showed it to her. She took it out of my hand, letting her fingers brush mine.

After looking at it for a moment, she said, "You're local?"

"This is the heaviest jacket I own."

"I take that's a yes." She gave me another look, less flirt and more appraising. "We could use some local help."

"Shouldn't the local border guys do the trick?"

"They should," she said smoothly, "but they don't like to think this port is the sieve that we believe it to be. Everything gets in, drugs, stolen goods. Human trafficking."

"Is that what you're working on?"

"Yeah, that's what landed us here. Willing to help?"

"I can't get places where they can."

"We'll actually pay for your time," she said with another dazzling smile. "Not asking for a favor."

"Just as well. I think I used up my quota of favors earlier today." Local cops didn't like private dicks on their territory. Especially stupid and/or corrupt cops. And it wouldn't hurt to stay away from women with nice eyes.

The waitress handed me the check. It was a busy night and she needed to turn the table over. I put enough money on the table to cover the bill and leave a generous tip.

I got up to leave.

She put her hand on my arm. "How do I get in touch with you?"

I took a business card out of my wallet and handed it to her, then made my way through the crowded restaurant.

Maybe she'd call, maybe she wouldn't.

Maybe I wanted her to. And maybe I didn't.

It was cold and the streets were deserted. I hurried through the night to home.

Chapter Three

B reakfast was cold pizza. It took two bites for me to relent and pop it in the microwave. I'd been good at the restaurant. One beer with the pizza. But by the time I'd gotten home, the night wind had chilled me and I opened the Scotch bottle that I kept promising myself I wouldn't open again, and had a drink. And another.

Cold pizza just wasn't going to cut it for the hangover. Maybe hot grease would help. Or I could pretend it would in the hope it would convince my roiling stomach.

I'd come to hate the weekends. For so long, they had been crammed to splitting open, dividing a sprint through the workweek, then a frenzy of flying or driving to Houston, only to return exhausted from cheap hotel rooms and constant, helpless waiting.

Then, abruptly, that was over. The weekends stretched to the breaking point.

The only thing I had learned is how quickly things can spiral out of control. A misstep, one mistake that cascades into consequences never intended or expected.

Consequences that left me here with cold pizza and a hangover.

So what if it was the weekend? I worked for myself, so I could still go to work. I threw on a jacket—even though I had no idea if it was still cold. Global climate change at our micro level has led to devastating hurricanes—the big issue—and winter days that could start out in the mid-seventies and drop thirty degrees or vice versa.

A blast of chilly air came through the door as I opened it to leave. And bright sunshine that made me squint even after I found my sunglasses.

No one was out, save for a small scattering of people who seemed to be dressed in every piece of clothing they owned. It's how we deal with the occasional blasts of cold that come our way. My northern friends—especially the obnoxious ones from the Midwest who seem to live only to be able to brag about how much snow they've shoveled and wearing the light winter jacket until it was below zero degrees—make fun of our winters. We rarely make it to freezing. But we live in a place designed for steam-bath summers. Most of my heat ends up at the ceiling—fourteen feet high means the top seven feet are warm, the bottom seven where I actually live, not so much. I have yet to meet a cold I hate worse than a rainy day in the low forties, and we get a lot of those during the winter months. High humidity really does make the chill seep into all the places you want to keep warm.

There was no important case calling me to the office. I just wanted the distraction of going there, getting out of the house, something to pass the time.

Out of habit I checked email and my answering machine, but I hadn't even got another begging call from the annoying wife about not paying my bill. I decided to be optimistic and hope that meant she would pay.

However, just to make sure everything was working, I called my work number on my cell phone. That helped pass a few more minutes and proved my answering machine was in fine fettle. Enough junk email had gotten through for me to know that my email was still working.

You're here, you might as well do something, I told myself. Unless something else is pressing, I've made myself devote at least one morning a week to boring, mind-numbing paperwork. It sucks, but it doesn't suck as much as trying to do catch-up after a couple of months. However, there is *always* more to do. I first caught up on all my billing—including one to Mrs. Annoying Wife. Then on to the filing.

Dusting. Cleaning the bathroom. Went out and got something for lunch. Ate it slowly while reading news online.

After I swept the stairs all the way to the bottom floor, I decided I had worked enough for the day. Time to do a grocery list. That required doing online searches for interesting recipes. What did we do to waste time before the Internet? Actually getting to the grocery store could wait. There was still a slice of pizza at home, after all.

The woman from last night hadn't called. I was mildly disappointed only because I wanted the distraction. Every other part of me thought it was stupid to get involved in something like that. Most of what I do is find missing people—from employees who've given themselves a one-time unapproved bonus and a ticket someplace warm to parents seeking their runaway kids. A few of them turn into trafficking cases, typically a runaway teenage girl who met the wrong person stepping off the bus. But my role is usually to locate the kid and do what I can to get her back to her parents. Or if the parents turn out to be part of the problem, on to some place where she can get help. I have a few social workers on speed dial. Sometimes that includes bailing a particular kid out on a prostitution charge. That's where it gets messy. If you're selling your body, you're engaging in sex work and even if you've been coerced into it, you're still breaking the law. If I bring in the cops, I risk getting the person I'm trying to find arrested and put in jail. Most of the time I've been able to work something out, especially if I can provide reasonable evidence that she didn't willingly choose this. But there are assholes everywhere, some who think any woman in that situation did something to deserve it. I've had that happen enough to be wary of involving any authorities other than the few do-good social workers.

It was probably a good thing the woman with the green eyes wasn't serious. Working with what I was guessing were the Feds and doing it around the locals just wasn't how to make friends and influence people.

Of course, since I was in wasting-time mode, I did an online search for information about any local busts that might involve trafficking. There were a few cases, but most of them were small-time (except to those involved), one man luring a teenage girl into prostitution. Louisiana had updated its laws in 2005 to give harsher penalties to anyone convicted of sex trafficking. But I couldn't find anything indicating New Orleans was a major trafficking hub. Which didn't mean it wasn't. We are a port city and that always opens the door to more vice. We're also a tourist city, with a reputation as an adult party town. Someone far less cynical than I could guess that a lot of women are brought into the city for events like Mardi Gras.

But those are messy cases and not the kind of thing for a lone private eye to get involved in.

Time to go blow this joint. I headed out the door.

Chapter Four

Sunday passed with cooking and house cleaning and working out at the gym. I didn't open the Scotch bottle. I didn't pour it down the drain either.

Monday morning required a few errands, the fun exciting things that can only be done on workdays, like going to the post office. I stopped and got myself a big cup of coffee at a local place. Mondays can't have too much caffeine. It was a little after ten when I got to my office.

I noticed the light on the answering machine was blinking. Probably Annoying Wife took the weekend off and the "I don't want to pay" calls started bright and early with the new workweek. I ignored it, instead sitting at my desk doing important stuff like mainlining caffeine and, courtesy of the blueberry-filled croissant, sugar.

I checked my email while munching and slurping. No, I don't have erectile dysfunction, nor do I want to chat with sexy Russian ladies.

Answering machine time.

"Hi, I hope I'm not calling too early," said the voice from the machine. Definitely not the Annoying Wife. Far too polite for her. The time stamp said she called a little after nine. The voice continued, "You may not remember me, we talked briefly while we were both out at dinner. The pizza place?"

"I remember you," I told the machine.

It ignored me and continued, "It would really be helpful to have someone local on our team. I'd like to get together and talk about that." She left her phone number. Then added, "Oh, sorry, my name is Ashley West. Always forget the basics."

I gulped more coffee. Call her back or ignore it? Get involved in something not so smart professionally and—potentially—personally?

I picked up the phone and dialed her number.

She answered on the first ring.

"Hi, this is Michele Knight, returning your phone call."

"Hey, great to hear from you." Her voice held the smile I remembered from the night.

"What can I do for you?"

"I have to admit I don't usually pick up women in restaurants," she said. Flirting? I wondered. She continued, "But I was impressed with what you noticed, the way you observed people. My team is good, but this isn't our backyard. We really need someone from here to make sure we don't get lost in a swamp."

"If it doesn't say Audubon Zoo and you see an alligator, run."

"No commitment, but can we get together and talk about it?"

Talk is cheap, I thought. No harm in talking to a woman with handsome green eyes. "Sure, we can meet at my office if you want. Unless you'd prefer another place." Going to her hotel room seemed a bit risky. My office has seen its fair share of lowlife scum. Given how far downtown it was, I could probably even get it cleaned by the time she got here.

"How about lunch? I don't want to miss out on any good eating while I'm here."

Despite the very recent croissant, I rallied my stomach. We could meet for lunch.

We agreed on around one, giving me time to digest my late, unhealthy breakfast. We, mostly me, picked a place in the Marigny on Frenchmen Street, close to the French Quarter. It was getting a little too hipster for my taste, but would be good to show an out-of-towner.

To pass the time, I did some more Internet searching on trafficking. Soon New Orleans would be in the chaos of not only Mardi Gras, but the Super Bowl was also being played here. I found a couple articles about the police thinking those two might cause a spike in prostitution. Yeah, does the pope wear a dress?

That added a hint of legitimacy to this. It was possible that more than the usual security types would be nosing around at this time. Plus I had to guess that running the vice end of things might not be the glamour spot—who wants to tell everyone in party town that some parties aren't allowed?

And even if it was a task I'd say no to in the end, the sun was shining and I'd have the distraction of lunch with a good-looking woman who seemed to be flirting with me.

Except I wasn't sure I wanted her to flirt with me. Maybe that was a complication too far.

Stop, I told myself. I was wasting time and energy and angst on a business lunch. *Worry about things if they actually happen. Until then, enjoy the ride. You can get off anytime you want.*

She wasn't going to flirt in front of her coworkers and it was a good bet that there would be at least a few of them along for this.

I left a little after 12:30. It should be plenty of time, but even on a cold Monday, parking in that part of town can be challenging.

The parking gods were the typical bitches I expected. A few circles of the block made me give up on free parking and plant myself at a meter. I consoled myself that it was a business expense and I could write it off.

I shook off my parking annoyance as I saw her standing at the corner. Alone.

Maybe the rest of her crew was already in the restaurant.

She smiled when she spied me. Even waved.

I smiled back. The sun was shining.

"Hey," she said as I approached. "Glad you could make it on such short notice."

"Mondays aren't my busy days. The miscreants like to sleep late from their weekend debauchery." Safe behind my sunglasses, I gave her a good look over. The bright sun was more revealing than the evening light. Definitely mid to late thirties, maybe even early forties. There were hints of laugh lines at her eyes, a slight crease to her brow. Old enough to know the nuances of how to drop hints of interest—if she was flirting it was because she intended to. She was medium height, several inches shorter than me, probably about five-six. Short hair, cut in a stylish bob to just below her ears. The sun brought out the shine in her thick reddish hair. Fair skin, the freckles highlighted by the sun, a splash across her nose. A great smile. All together interesting more than strikingly good-looking. That was my preference. Too often beautiful women—and men—think that's all they need to be.

"Then I must appreciate their laziness." The bright light brought out hints of yellow-gold in her green eyes. "What's good along here?"

"What's your pleasure?" I asked. It was a beautiful day; a little flirting couldn't hurt.

"It's New Orleans. What are my options?"

"Are we meeting the rest of your crew?"

"No, just us. They did a little partying last night and are easing into Monday."

"How come you survived?"

"Better constitution, I guess. And not so foolish in mixing my drinks."

"Smart move." I gave her a list of the possible food places. She hadn't had an oyster po-boy yet, so that decided us.

As she looked at the menu she said, "Would you think I'm decadent if I have a beer with lunch?"

"No. This is a city with twenty-four-hour bars. Even the nuns have beer with lunch." It would give me an excuse to have one as well.

She didn't seem to be in a hurry to get down to business; we meandered through talking about what to do and see in New Orleans, the surface details of our lives. Yes, I grew up around here. She was from New York state, but grew up all over, military family.

After we'd been served the food—oyster po-boys and Abita Amber all around—and eaten a good chunk of it, I asked, "So how do you think I could help you?"

"There are a lot of ways you could help me," she said, punctuating with a sip of beer, "but I suppose we should start with the professional." She reached into her bag and took out a picture. Saying nothing, she handed it to me.

It was small, black and white, of a young girl. She looked happy, smiling, on the edge between childhood and putting away her jump rope to grow up. I said nothing, asking a question with my face.

"Kimmie Fremont. Last seen by her mother when she was thirteen. She should be around seventeen by now." Another sip of beer. "If she's still alive."

"You never found her?" It wasn't really a question, more to move the conversation.

"No. Not yet. But…even when the years pass and you know it's probably hopeless, I keep her picture around to remind myself to keep looking."

"Any chance she's here?" I asked.

"No, no reason to think so. Was from around where I was born. A few towns over. Guess that makes it more personal. I recognized the streets she walked on. She could be anywhere by now, but most likely she was trafficked to one of the big cities up there—New York, Boston."

I handed the picture back to her. "So, who are you with?"

"Who am I with?"

"What agency?"

"Ah, thought you were asking who I was dating."

"Bit personal for lunch and only one beer."

"Should we get another beer?" she asked. Then continued, "Multidisciplinary team. We're with several different agencies."

"Which one are you?"

"You do like to focus on business, don't you?" She gave me a crooked smile.

I smiled back. "Get the boring stuff out of the way."

"I like a woman who can stay focused. I'm with ICE—U.S. Immigrations and Customs Enforcement. Some other team members are FBI, Secret Service, DEA, and ATF."

"Secret Service?"

"Fraud and money crimes. They were originally started to deal with counterfeit money. We're dragging a pretty big net, mainly human trafficking, but contraband often follows the same path, so we're likely to stumble over alcohol, drugs, illegal guns, and fake hundred-dollar bills."

"Sounds like a big operation. Why involve a small-fish private eye like me?"

"Like I hinted before, we're not sure how up-and-up the locals are."

"I've got some friends in law enforcement, I can vouch for them and if you'd like—"

"No," she cut me off. "This needs to be kept as quiet as possible. I'd really appreciate you not talking to anyone besides me or my team."

"Okay," I said slowly. "Explain to me why you'll let me in—a stranger you met in a bar—but not the local cops?"

She looked at me sharply, like she wasn't used to being questioned. Asking less-than-polite questions is my bread and butter, so if she wanted me around she'd have to get used to it.

"Trust me, you were thoroughly vetted before I arranged this meeting. You're what we're looking for. A good, smart PI, someone who's been working here for a while and knows the city, independent and tough-minded enough to do the right thing, not enmeshed in the local scene."

"And can deflect bullets with my bracelets." To her confused look I said, "Wonder Woman. One of her super powers."

"Ah. Been a while since I've done comics. Would be a good power to have."

"So, what do you want from me?"

She gave me a long appraising look, one that said she had more than a professional interest. "Mostly background. Show us the side of the city the tourists don't see. Where are the likely places to find what we're looking for?" She covered my hand with hers. "Don't worry, we won't put you in any danger."

"I'm not worried about that. I can take care of myself."

She pulled her hand back, took a sip of beer, and said, "Good to know. Still, you get to leave the dirty work to us."

"Sounds like a good deal."

We finished our beers and worked out the details—how much time they might need, how much I'd get paid and when to start.

Tomorrow.

Lunch was over. She had places she had to go.

We waved good-bye. I watched her for a moment as she walked away, the sun still glinting in her hair.

This one should be easy, I thought as I returned to my car. A little sightseeing of the less seen sights. The money was decent. I had no other cases needing undivided attention.

And maybe it was time to break out of my bitter, cynical, love-is-just-a-four-letter-word shell. I vowed I'd never fall in love again, never get involved with someone, never, never allow life to rip my heart out.

I wasn't planning—if a few disentangled threads of thought could be called planning—to go back on that vow. She wasn't local. We could have a pleasant little affair and then she'd go her way and I'd go mine.

Yeah, right. Cynical wasn't far away. For all I knew, her seeming flirting was just another way to get my cooperation, just part of her job and something she put away when she went home. She'd been vague about her personal life. Maybe there were two screaming kids and a husband in the background.

This is just a job, I decided. It would be her move if it became more than that.

I got in my car. At least the sun was still shining.

CHAPTER FIVE

The sun didn't hang around. Mostly winter here is what we call smug season. But there are times when the clouds come and the temperature hovers in the forties. Today was such a day. My northern friends laugh and call us wimps, but the pervasive high humidity puts a biting chill in the air and houses designed to keep you cool in the summer aren't good at keeping the cold out. Which means that you can't get warm inside or outside. Maybe in the car, after the heat kicks on.

I'd had to force myself out of bed, closing the door to the bathroom while I showered to keep the meager heat in.

Not an auspicious day to lead people on a tour of the underside of the town, I thought as I hurriedly dressed.

I dashed through the spitting rain to my car. Money was an issue. She'd left me the house—and the mortgage. Taken half of our joint account—and the cats. But I ended up in the same place, wanting desperately to be angry, and knowing at best, neither of us could have changed anything. At worst, I was the one who failed.

It was easier to concentrate on driving in the rain.

I had a job to do and people to distract me.

We had agreed to meet Uptown in Audubon Park. I didn't ask. It was their tour. Maybe someone wanted to go jogging in the rain.

I got there first. Guess the jogging had been canceled due to inclement weather.

Or maybe they had gotten lost. New Orleans is a city hewed and twisted by the Mississippi River, and its contours show in our streets.

I glanced at my watch. It was 10:15. Our meeting time had been ten, late enough in the morning that it should have counted as sleeping in for most federal agents. Or maybe they were taking advantage of being in the field, and—in the line of duty, no doubt—checking out places where sex traffickers might hawk their wares, like Bourbon Street. As far as I was concerned, I was on the clock, and sitting and waiting was earning me money.

At 10:25, a black SUV pulled up beside my car. The passenger side window rolled down and Ashley appeared. The windows were tinted and I couldn't make out the others in the car.

I lowered my window.

"Sorry we're late," she said. "Got caught in traffic."

"That's okay, I've been sitting here enjoying the weather." I summoned up a smile.

"Why don't I join you in your car and we can follow you around?"

"Whatever best suits you."

She hopped out and one of the men took her place in the front passenger seat. The older woman I'd seen at the restaurant stayed in the backseat. No introductions were made. Either it was the weather or they were impolite Yankees.

"Damn, it's chilly," Ashley said as she slid into my car.

"Drop the temperature and a wet city gets cold." She was an outsider; I decided to let her in on our secrets. "We're surrounded by water. The river on one side, the lake to the north, swamps to the east and west. Humidity is a constant. Makes it hotter in the summers and puts the chill into cold days in the winter."

She shivered. "It does blow through you," she said as she buckled her seat belt.

"What are you interested in seeing?" I asked.

"What do you think we should see?" she countered.

"Give me a clue as to what you'd like. Do you want a general city tour with my cynical commentary, or is there something you'd like to focus on?" I smiled as I said it, but sitting in my car in the cold wasn't a great start to the day.

"Fair enough," she said, smiling back with enough of a hint of apology to wipe the slate clean. And she had a nice smile. "How about the lowlights of the city? The boring, seemingly normal parts."

"That would be the suburbs."

"Ah, no interest there. How about a general cynical tour with a swing by known sex-traffic sites?"

"Do you want to include the suburban residence of one of our senators? Although the rumors are that he prefers the French Quarter brothels."

"Skip the 'burbs. Let's stick with the city for today. Be polite, they're listening in." She took her cell phone out of her purse, put it on speaker, and called someone in the other car.

Time to be a tour guide. Since we were already Uptown, I started with a swing around Tulane and Loyola, going past the frat houses on Broadway (yes, New Orleans has a Broadway). From there up Oak Street for all the restaurants. Yeah, they wanted to see the sex-traffic areas, but they had to eat, too. Plus I wanted them to see the good things about New Orleans; it's easy to see the seamy side of the city—any city—if that's all you're shown.

"This is more a drug area," I said as we turned off Oak Street and drove through Holly Grove, a poor enclave between Carrolton Ave. and the parish line.

"Wow, some of these houses are tiny," Ashley said. She was looking at a narrow house, maybe twelve feet wide at most.

"A single. At one time property tax was based on how big the front of the house was. So houses became long and narrow. Many of them are doubles—two separate houses built as one. My current house used to be ten feet by eighty feet before we converted it to a single."

"We? You have a partner?"

"Had. Over on your left is where we get our drinking water. It comes from the Mississippi."

"Should I drink it?"

"You can."

"Do you?"

"For the most part no. It has more to do with Katrina than the Mississippi. There was so much damage to the pipes that they have to keep the pressure high enough to prevent any backflow from coming in through the broken parts."

"That sounds not good."

"I got into the habit of not drinking tap water after the storm. It's probably okay now. But…anyway, back to the tour. We're just crossing Claiborne, and in a block or two it turns into Jefferson Highway at the parish line."

"Parish?"

"You'd call it a county. We go our Napoleonic Code way, so they're parishes here. This side is Orleans, that side is Jefferson."

"AKA the 'burbs."

"Yep. But don't worry, we're not going there." I cut through the back streets to give them an idea of the neighborhood.

"Lot of boarded-up houses. Wow, that one's held up by the vines," she said, pointing to a leaning house with green covering most of the roof. "Did it flood here?"

"It flooded most places. Only the area close to the river didn't flood. Neighborhoods with money came back. Ones without are still struggling."

We rode in silence for a few minutes, letting her look at the small houses, some neat and tidy, flowers in the garden. Others were falling apart, yards overgrown, paint faded and blistering. *What right do we have to observe and judge lives we'll never live*, I wondered as we drove by.

"A lot of people couldn't come back," I said quietly. "A place they lived all their lives, thrown out by the levee failures, landed someplace else, Houston, Atlanta. Found themselves barely standing there and not enough time and money or hope to get back here. If you have a job in Houston and can barely pay the rent there, the house here gets left behind."

She touched my hand. Briefly, a brush of fingertips, then switched the cell phone into that hand, as if reminding both of us the other car was still listening.

"Earhart Boulevard. It's one of the main ways through the city," I said as we came out of the side street onto a wide road. From there I hooked a left onto Carrollton, another of the main drags, being careful to go slow enough to not lose the SUV.

I pointed out the main interests, Xavier University, one of the few Catholic historically black colleges, the I-10 mess, which maps labeled an on-ramp.

I took a right onto Tulane Avenue.

"We are now officially in a sex-work location. The area is changing, mind you," I said loud enough for the folks on the cell phone to hear. "It's a development area and there are a number of new buildings, including residences, going up, but it's long been known for cheap hotels and ladies of the night plying their avocation." I pointed my finger at one as we drove past. There was too much drizzle and daylight for there to be much action.

Near Tulane and Broad I pointed out the Orleans Parish Prison and the court buildings.

"I think I've counted at least five motels," Ashley said.

"As you can see, this is not a scenic part of New Orleans."

"And I'm guessing not anywhere near the French Quarter."

"Not that far, actually. It's a bit of a hike, about two miles, but you could walk from here to there. Most of the rest of Tulane has turned into a construction site; they're building two major medical facilities here, the new VA hospital and the replacement for Charity Hospital," I explained as we continued toward the river. The low-class motels were on their way out.

Tulane Avenue is also known as Highway 61, famously built by Huey Long as a direct route from the capitol in Baton Rouge to his favorite watering hole in New Orleans. It literally ends half a block from the Roosevelt Hotel and its well-known bar.

I took a swing through the CBD, aka Central Business District, going down Poydras with its tall buildings, then turning right on Convention Center Boulevard so we could get a good look at the casino. Conventions and casinos probably touched on the sex trade, less so when the librarians were in town, more so for the Baptists—go figure. Then a quick U-turn to go back to the adjacent Warehouse District, closer to the river and a section of old, you guessed it, warehouses that had been converted to condos, trendy restaurants, and bars.

The back car had been fairly quiet—enough that I was beginning to suspect they'd turned off the phone and were talking amongst themselves—but after we passed the World War II Museum they piped up, inquiring about lunch.

I glanced at my watch. It was close to one p.m. I was starting to get hungry.

"What would you like?" I asked the cell phone.

A garbled mishmash of replies came back, ranging from hamburgers to alligator. In other words, unless they were serious about the alligator, it was up to me to pick a place that would satisfy everyone. I looked at Ashley for guidance.

She looked at the phone. Asked them to repeat. Same answers with some elaborations that ran from "not where we ate before" to "not too hot" to "something local." Helpful. Not.

She shrugged at me.

"Parking is a pain in this part of town, so let's head downtown. About ten minutes," I added for the starving masses.

Not that it mattered, but I explained why I was going around the French Quarter instead of through. Ashley nodded and even laughed at my comments about slow donkey carriages, one-way streets, drunk tourists who weren't sure where the sidewalk ended and the street began, sober tourists who seemed to think a historic district like the French Quarter shouldn't allow cars (bet they'd be upset if the beer truck didn't get through). "And don't get me started on frat boys."

Then it was time to point out another sex-work area, the Quarter edge of Rampart Street. It's the dividing line between Treme and the Quarter, with a fair number of bars and some brisk business between the blocks. It would be busy later, but a rainy day wasn't prime stroll time.

We headed downtown to a place in the Bywater, away from the hordes of tourists and the concentration of workers in the CBD. It had praline bacon; that should make everyone happy.

As we parked, Ashley briefly put her hand on my knee and said, "This is the real reason we hired you, to steer us away from the usual tourist traps." It was a light, quick touch. The big SUV pulled in behind us. It was after one p.m., so late enough that the restaurant wasn't packed.

Other than the hurried moment in the park, when Ashley got out, this was the first time I was able to see who had been listening to my narrative. The older woman, a much younger woman I hadn't seen before, and two of the three men from the pizza place.

The rain and the chill pushed us inside before anyone said anything.

As we waited to be seated, I said, "Hi, I'm Micky," mostly to the young woman, since she was the one person I'd never seen before.

She glanced at the younger man before answering, "I'm Sandy." Then she looked at him again.

"I forgot we haven't been properly introduced," Ashley said. "Micky, this is Cara, John, and Jack. Everyone, Micky Knight, the person saving us from lunch at the boring tourist places."

They all spoke at once, a mumble of "pleased to meet you" (the older woman, I think), "hi, howya doin'," to a slurred murmur that could have been anything from "great to meet you" to "I know where Jimmy Hoffa is buried." It seemed to be a habit of theirs, no hierarchy in replies.

The waitress led us to the table.

I'd been there before so I knew what I was going to get, but the others were perusing their menus. I observed them as they did. They were a motley bunch for law enforcement. The older woman was probably in her mid-fifties and looked every day of it. Her hair was ash blond, a dye job needing a touch-up. She had sad, brown hound-dog eyes, almost lost in her crow's feet and under-eye bags. Her waist had thickened, and she didn't move as if she did more than sit at a desk in the day and in front of the TV at night. Her voice was low and raspy, either a bad cold or years of smoking. I was guessing that field work wasn't her usual assignment, so maybe she had some expertise that made it useful for her to come along. Or maybe she was high up enough that she could tag along on places she wanted to go, like New Orleans.

The older man would probably be her in about fifteen years. I put him as early to mid-forties, and again, he looked like someone who needed to eat a lot more broccoli and a lot fewer burgers and fries. The muscle was starting to turn to flab, but he was still a big, imposing man, like a linebacker who played his last game ten years ago and has spent too much time in bars with his former teammates. His crew-cut hair was brown, peppered with gray flecks. His eyes were dark, small and hidden under his ridge of a brow. His voice was a low rumble, an accent that slurred and could have been anything from Philly to New Jersey. If this was a gang, he'd be the muscle.

The younger two bothered me. They almost read as a couple. Sandy was looking over the same menu as Jack (or was it John?) instead of perusing her own. Even if they were dating, they should keep it out of the workplace.

Or maybe I was just turning into the kind of person who was going to start yelling at kids to stay off my lawn any day now.

Jack (John?) was good-looking. Thick, wavy brown hair, worn a tad long and in the spiky style that takes work to achieve unless you happen to wake up looking like that. His eyes were a gray-blue, set in a face with a strong jaw and high cheekbones. He verged on being pretty. He was either a well-preserved late twenties or early thirties. I was leaning to the former because Sandy was early twenties and read as even younger. Her name matched her hair, a light, sandy brown. She was conventionally pretty, and would have been even prettier if she wasn't trying so hard at it, too much makeup, her eyes almost a black ring of mascara, hair teased and blown out in a way that didn't do well in wind and rain. Her eyebrows were too tweezed; they looked plucked, not shaped. There wasn't a single wrinkle in her face, a little baby fat still in her cheeks.

As I suspected, the praline bacon was a hit. Ashley and I were the only ones who skipped ordering it, although Sandy was just sharing an order with Jack.

Cara, the older woman, ordered a salad. And the bacon. As if she knew she needed to be better with her diet, but couldn't quite get there. John, as if to type, ordered a hamburger with fries. And a beer.

Jack ordered a couple of appetizers, oysters and fried green tomatoes in addition to the bacon. Sandy ordered a veggie sandwich, as if to prove that she would always be skinny and beautiful. Or maybe she just liked veggies.

Ashley ordered gumbo and a salad with shrimp.

I went with the oyster po-boy. I do salads at home and save the fried stuff for eating out.

I hoped they would talk about their work down here, but the conversation drifted from the weather to sports. Mostly Jack and John talked, with Sandy listening intently, while Cara checked messages on her phone. I was seated between her and Sandy and neither of them seemed inclined to chat me up.

Ashley was across the table on the other side of John. He spoke the most and the loudest, so she only managed a few comments to me, mostly about the food. Our most sustained conversation was about the weather and when it might warm up.

I reminded myself this wasn't a lunch with friends; I was getting paid. I also reminded myself I was seeing more of the social side than the professional side of these people. Maybe they were experts at what they did and quite competent when they needed to be. So far I wasn't impressed, but then it hardly mattered what I thought.

I liked Ashley. She seemed smart and personable. It was possible she was making her confederates seem dim in contrast. And it was possible that because I liked her, I wanted to be doing something besides being chaperoned by four other coworkers. I wanted to ask more questions about who they were and what their purpose was here but understood that banal talk of weather and sports might be more appropriate in a public place.

And I had to admit, I wanted to talk shop to prove I knew what I was doing, to show off. To prove Ashley had been right to hire me. Work was what sustained me, the small triumphs of solving a case, finding a person others hadn't, the compliments from my clients. I wanted to see admiration in her eyes. I chastised myself, not to care so much, to need so much. But other than the Saints, I don't much keep up on sports and we had long exhausted the weather. It was likely to rain tomorrow as well, but get drier and warmer for the weekend.

Cara picked up the check, using cash. I remembered to grab the receipt for her; she was already halfway to the SUV when I caught up to hand it to her.

She and John decided they had enough of the touring and wanted to head back to the hotel. Jack, and therefore Sandy, still wanted to see more of the city. So they and Ashley piled in my car. Given how small the backseat was, it was a good thing they were friendly.

Since we were already pretty far downtown, I took them to the Lower Ninth Ward. It's below the Industrial Canal. Their side of the levee failed during Katrina and the water from other canals lower down also flowed in, making it one of the most destroyed areas in the city. Houses weren't just washed off their foundations but flung down the street and left stewing in rooftop-deep waters for weeks.

It wasn't a sex-trafficking area, had been a working-class neighborhood before the storm, and it was still struggling to come back. I drove them there because people should see and know what happened; know that it takes years and years after the cameras have gone for things to recover.

I again played tour guide, explaining where we were, what we were seeing. Jack seemed interested, and both he and Ashley asked intelligent questions.

I did catch in the rearview mirror that he and Sandy were holding hands. Rather, Sandy was clutching his and he was letting her.

After the Ninth Ward, I took them back through Bywater into the Marigny. We drove slowly along Frenchmen Street, a drag with a lot of bars and restaurants, teeming with people on any given weekend night. It's more a local than tourist area, but even the locals have been known to buy their sex.

Then we drove through the French Quarter and Ashley got to see that I wasn't exaggerating (much) about the slow donkey carts and the drunken tourists. Sandy even started asking about the shops and bars on Decatur Street. She asked if we could drive down Bourbon and I had to say that even if it wasn't blocked to traffic, there were so many people ambling—and stumbling drunk—that it was much slower to drive than to walk.

Jack promised to take her there that evening.

They were staying at one of the hotels near Canal Street. Traffic was heavy. I had to impolitely nose my car between two taxis to be able to let them out.

"I'll call you," Ashley said as she got out. Then the taxi horn blared and words were useless.

CHAPTER SIX

It was late enough in the day that I didn't bother going back to my office and just headed home. It was closer anyway.

After I let myself in, I looked at my phone. She said she'd call me. We hadn't mentioned anything about working again. Maybe this tour was all they wanted, although I hadn't been paid for it yet. I stuffed the phone in my pocket and went upstairs to the bedroom to change into sweatpants and a T-shirt—and more importantly, no bra or shoes.

I kept the phone with me, something I don't usually do. I have both a cell and home phone. My friends know me well enough to know that, unlike the younger generation, I don't keep my cell attached to my hip and they can call on the real phone. However, Ashley only had my cell number.

I wandered to the kitchen. I should start dinner, but dawdled. Maybe she would call and want to go out to eat.

No, I told myself, *you don't know her well enough to worry like this*. If she calls, she calls. I realized it wasn't about her; it was about me. Ashley was a pleasant enough woman, but so far there was nothing outstanding or interesting about her beyond a mild flirtation. And mild flirtations are, to paraphrase, just mild flirtations.

This was me. I was between times, adrift in change, so much so that anything floating by was something to cling to. The real interest in Ashley was that she was someone new, someone with whom I could leave the past behind and pretend it hadn't happened.

If only I could pretend that with myself.

The blizzard wasn't my fault.

The alcohol and forgetting to set my alarm the night before was.

Cordelia, the woman I thought I'd be with forever, had cancer. New Orleans was still, even this many years out, recovering from

Katrina. One of the areas hardest hit was medical care. We made the hard decision that she couldn't get the best treatment here, so she transferred to Houston.

When did it change? I couldn't tell; it seemed a blur.

She had inherited money, but the treatment and distance quickly cut into it. I tried to hold on, balancing my work and traveling to be with her. She was a doctor, though never interested in being a high-paid one; she still made a decent wage when she was working. But she wasn't working, and I had to cut back on the cases I could take. Being in Houston every weekend made it impossible to take anything that couldn't be wrapped up on a nine-to-five schedule. That cut into my income.

It seems so trivial now, the money. But the truth was there wasn't quite enough to stretch to meet all our needs. The most important, getting her the best treatment, was covered. But that left the daily expenses of life, from the mortgage to cat food to flying to Houston every week. I wasn't making quite enough to cover all of those and I was loath to ask Cordelia for help because she needed her inheritance money to cover medical expenses. We were lucky, even had about a hundred thousand in the bank, our rainy day fund, but I was loath to touch that once I saw how quickly the bills added up, and the unexpected extra costs. Between my travel and her medical costs, we could easily spend ten thousand above our normal bills in a month.

I tried driving instead of flying, but that just cut into time I could be earning money and in the end saved little or nothing. I'd have to either cut my Friday hours or leave in the late afternoon for the six-hour drive to Houston, It was the same coming back, leave Sunday afternoon or very early Monday morning. Either way it was twelve hours in a car in three days. One late Sunday night I almost went off the road because I was too tired. I didn't get in until after midnight because I had to stop every hour or so to drink coffee.

The weeks and months became an exhausted blur. I worked as many hours as I could cram in while in New Orleans, often getting in at midnight and starting again at six in the morning, hustled to the airport for a late Friday or early Saturday flight, constantly searching for hotel deals to save money, eating cheap, bad food, to save money. Then on the plane again late Sunday or early Monday, making phone calls and doing paperwork in the airport because it was the only way I could keep up.

Time fled as if chased by a banshee. Cordelia had started there in a broiling July and suddenly I was in the airport shivering because the earth had turned, it was October, and the cold had come.

And now I was here. Soon it would be spring again, as if warmth and the new green of budding leaves could make a difference. It seemed impossible to have so quickly gone from scrabbling for one minute of stillness, wanting a place of rest where nothing was demanded of me, to this numb place of going through the routines of the day because what else could I do? I had savagely gotten what I wanted—everything stopped, no one needing or wanting me, no demand after demand piling up to exhaustion.

A few weeks, now a month, two, stretching into days of getting up, going to my office. It didn't matter if I had a case or not, it was the semblance of motion. Doing the work that needed to be done or finding ways to make the time pass. Winter to spring. Then spring to summer.

Ashley broke the routine and gave me something to think about other than how much I'd screwed up my life, in ways I'd never be able to fix.

It led me being a forty-something woman, with nothing more important than wondering if another woman I barely knew was going to call me.

She didn't.

A day passed. And another.

I'd given up on her, just knowing she wouldn't call with another morning staring me in my uncaffeinated eyes. I'd gotten up, again moved through the routines of breakfast, gone to my office. At this time of the morning phone calls are about business.

I was on my third cup of coffee when the phone rang.

"Hey, Micky, thanks for the tour. It gave us good insight into the city."

"You're kind. You probably could have gotten the same info from the usual tour guides for a lot cheaper."

"I doubt that. Don't think too many tours cruise down Tulane Avenue and point out the hooker hotels."

"I'm sure there are some that do, but admittedly not the ones you can book through the usual channels. How are things going?"

"Boring. Catching up on paperwork with room service. Necessary, but not my first choice in how I'd spend my time in New Orleans."

"I certainly hope you get a chance to spend time on higher choices before you leave." There, that was as much flirting as I was going to do.

"Me, too. I'm calling because we'd like your services again. I know this is late notice, but we could use you today. Something just came up."

"What do you need?" Truth was I didn't have much going on and a distraction would be welcome, but I knew better than to sound needy or as if nothing else was going on in my life.

"Mostly navigation. We got a tip about a location where some stuff is going on and we'd like to check it out."

"Shouldn't you bring in the big guns for this?"

"Hey, we are the big guns, remember? But yeah, if we thought it was active, we'd get backup. But this tip is about where they used to be. We want to take a look and see if we can get any clues that might lead us to where they really are."

"What if your tip is wrong and they're still around?"

"We can handle it. If you're concerned, we can do it on our own, just be nicer to have someone who knows which way to go."

When did I get old and cautious, I wondered. I was worried about a few bad guys with a bunch of Feds around me. And I didn't want Ashley to think I was scared. "Let me take a look and see what I have going," I said, although I pretty well knew the calendar I pulled up was empty. "Your lucky day. I need to wrap up a few things and I can be ready in an hour." I was too vain to let her know I could actually walk out the door right now—*unwanted* is not attractive.

"Great! I knew we could count on you." We agreed to meet at their hotel.

Job. It's just a job, Micky, I told myself. But she did seem to want to see me again and even if it was only professionally, I had a productive, moneymaking way to fill otherwise empty hours.

Morning on a weekday wasn't so crazy by her hotel. Evidently, the car split was our standard operating procedure—she was waiting out front and joined me in the passenger seat of my car.

"We're going out in the sticks," she said without even saying hello. "I think the boys are afraid of snakes."

"Probably still too cold. Sticks as in where?"

She showed me on her phone.

"Might want to write that down," I suggested. "Not likely to have cell reception out there." It was out in the boonies, past Jean Lafitte Park, on the other bank of the Mississippi.

The big black SUV roared up behind me as if to say *we're here, let's go*. I don't like big metal things kissing my bumper, so I took off, not even bothering to make sure the traffic gap was big enough for both of us to get out.

"Should I use my GPS to get us there?" Ashley asked.

"You can if you want, but I know the area."

Her cell rang. Her end of the conversation was "uh-huh," and "yeah."

When she finished, she said, "John wants us to take the back roads. Avoid tolls, things like that."

"Nice to know, but there aren't too many back roads across the river. I was going to go over the Crescent City Connection, it's a toll bridge, but we don't pay a toll on the way out, only on the way back."

She got on the phone.

"And he needs to decide quickly as we'll be there in a few minutes," I added.

Ashley rendered the verdict. "He wants to avoid that. Is there any way around?"

"Yeah," I muttered, mentally rerouting. "But it's a long way around."

"Long's okay," she verified.

"Hope they gassed up recently." I took that to mean they wanted to avoid 1-10. Which was fine with me as I usually avoid it as well— it's either bumper-to-bumper going eighty miles an hour or bumper-to-bumper going nowhere, and both of those are rarely worth the frustration.

The Mississippi down here in New Orleans is a big-ass river. For a long time there were no bridges over it. The swift currents, depth of the river, and how wide it was all made it hard to span. Finally in the 1930s, the first bridge in Louisiana was erected, the Huey P. Long Bridge, so named because he was assassinated shortly before it opened. That would be our crossing. It had been an old, narrow bridge, but was now cluttered with road work as it was being widened. The old lanes were nine feet across, add in workers and machinery and that made it tight for a big SUV.

But they wanted no tolls, so they would get no tolls.

"Where are we?" Ashley asked after we left the safe confines of the CBD.

"The back roads. More or less." They got to see some more of the New Orleans the tourists don't see, roads that took us through either poor neighborhoods or industrial areas. So not a scenic route.

Ashley didn't say much; she seemed to be checking messages on her phone. Or maybe she just found the scenery too uninteresting to bother.

The Huey Long Bridge is not in New Orleans proper, but out in the suburbs of the city. It took us a good twenty minutes to get there.

As we started to go up its steep ramp, Ashley looked up from her phone. "Oh, this is an old bridge." I was paying attention to traffic and could only briefly glance her way, but she looked pale. I heard her take a deep, steadying breath. All the construction and the railroad tracks in the center don't make this a good bridge to go over in the best of times.

"It's okay," I said. "The bridge isn't very long." Not really true, but she didn't need to know that.

"Why is it so high?" she said. I could hear her breathing.

"River traffic. Some big boats have to go under here."

She reached over and put her hand on my forearm. "Is this okay? I'm not great with heights."

"Not a problem," I said. It made shifting more difficult—she was holding on tightly, but that was probably better than her getting panicked or—worse—queasy.

The SUV was hugging my bumper as if they were afraid to lose me. I hoped there were no sudden stops in my immediate future.

"Close your eyes," I told her. "Tell me about a favorite vacation."

"Think it'll work?" she said with a shaky smile. But she did as she was instructed. "Hard to decide. Virgin Islands or Paris."

"Start with the beach."

We spent the rest of the bridge with her telling me about blue-green water and sandy shores.

"We're back to earth," I said as the road met the ground.

"Sorry," she said with a rueful grin. "I should have asked. I'm okay if I'm prepared to be up in the air. And thinking of beaches helped." She let go of my arm. "Hope I didn't leave a bruise."

"My hide is tougher than that." I changed the subject. "Tell me more about what you're hoping to find. And are you all Border Patrol or are there other agencies involved?"

"I can tell you, but I might have to kill you." She said it with a smile, but her message got across—she couldn't really talk about her mission.

"Not in the mood to get killed today. Plus you need a navigator. Can you talk about how you got involved in law enforcement? Or is that a killing topic as well?"

"I wish I could go into more details, but we're on strict need-to-know orders. But I can talk about myself—one of my favorite topics." She again smiled, but this time a friendly one. "Wow, how did I get started in law enforcement? My dad was a cop, two uncles were cops, so it was always on the what I wanted to be when I grew up list. I guess they thought it was cute and assumed that I'd grow out of it like the other girls. My dad wasn't too happy when I decided to major in criminal justice at college. He kept telling me I'd never get a man that way. He liked it even less when I told I wasn't interested in getting a man."

"Has he come around since then?"

"No. Or he hadn't when he died about a year later."

"That's rough."

She said softly, "I'd like to think he would have…learned to keep loving me. But it's hard to know."

"I'm sorry. I seem to be hitting all the bad subjects today. Maybe we should go back to tropical vacations."

"Even tropical waters have sharks in them."

"I'm bombing, why don't you pick a topic?"

"How did you get to be a PI?"

"Couldn't stand panty hose and nine-to-five."

"There has to be more to it than that. By the way, where are we? This doesn't look like swampland."

"We went out of our way, remember? Not many bridges across the Mississippi and not many roads into the swamps. We're paralleling the river, heading more or less south. So this is the populated area close to the riverbank. We'll turn off into the swampland in a bit."

"Okay, so give me the more than twenty-five words version of how you became a PI."

"It really is about panty hose."

"So if you had to wear female undergarments, you'd be in another profession?"

"If I had to do it every day, it's possible."

"C'mon, if we're going to spend time together, at least tell me part of your story." She playfully punched me on the shoulder.

"Okay, okay. I was young, probably foolish, but I don't like to think that. Out of college, still trying to decide what I wanted to do with my life. Tried the usual so-called good career jobs, like working at a bank. Discovered I hated it. Capital *H* hated. Got a job as a security guard.

It didn't pay much, but I thought I'd have time to read." I signaled to move into the right lane for the upcoming turn.

She glanced back at the SUV to make sure it was still following. "I'm guessing the reading didn't work out so well."

"Did get some reading done. Made it through *Middlemarch*. But one of the managers was stealing office supplies and making it look like the low-level workers were to blame. I was suspicious; he was too friendly. So I tracked when he came in and out of the building after hours, got a few pictures of him loading stuff into his truck. Eventually put things together—he was always in the building after hours whenever stuff went missing."

"Your first case."

"I guess. Anyway, the head of the security firm was impressed and hired me as his assistant investigator. He taught me a lot, helped me get a license. I found I liked the work. I had to use my brain, work varied hours. After a while I decided I wanted to be on my own." Blinker on for a right turn; we'd soon be leaving box stores and traffic behind.

"Just like that? You went solo?"

"He wanted more than a business partnership and I wasn't interested. But he thought if he kept asking I'd eventually say yes. I knew that wasn't going to happen."

"Was he a troll? Or was it something more fundamental?"

"Both," I said. "He got a little tipsy one night and told me that I needed to earn all the chances he'd given me. Plus, like you, I like men fine with their clothes on. Naked, not so much."

"Did you try telling him that?"

"Oh, yeah. That was part of the troll behavior. He let me know that he'd be cool with me having a girlfriend, if he could watch."

"Yuck. Major troll."

"His final words to me were that I'd fail in less than six months."

"I'm betting that was a long time ago."

"Long, long time. He went under long before I did."

"You're the better PI?"

"Maybe, but I was careful with money and he liked to spend it. He wasn't good at cutting back when things were sluggish." I slowed for a stoplight. "Your turn to talk. Where did you grow up?"

"Me? All over, bit of a military brat."

"Thought you said your dad was a cop."

"Oh, yeah. He was military police until I was about fourteen. By then he'd put in his twenty years. He retired and took a regular cop job."

"Where was that?"

"Ohio. Some small town outside of Cleveland."

"Interesting. I would have picked your accent as Mid-Atlantic."

"Really? And here I don't think I have an accent."

"Not much of a one, but it's there. I wouldn't have picked Midwest."

"Spent a lot of time in New Jersey when I was young. Grandparents. We'd get left there whenever Dad and Mom moved—which was a lot when he was in the military. Hey, what kind of bird is that?"

"Probably a snowy egret," I said. I'd only seen a white blur on the side of the road. "They're pretty common down here."

"How much further do we have to go?"

"About ten, fifteen minutes. Depending on the alligator crossings. Why? Tired of my company?"

"No, I like your company. It's just—wait, you're kidding about the alligator crossings, aren't you? I am not good with green scaly things."

"Unless we're going deep into the swamp, you don't need to worry about alligators. And unless there's an airboat packed in the back of your SUV, we're not going deep in the swamp."

"Okay, good to know."

"What do you want me to do when we get there?"

"What do you mean?"

"Do I stay in my car? Be a lookout? Help check the place out?" The suburban houses had disappeared, a thick strand of trees on either side of the road and few intersections were out here.

"Good question. You'd probably be most helpful with the search. You might notice things that we won't. Like alligators."

"You get close enough, you'll notice the alligator."

"That's the point. I want you to spot them before I get close enough."

"I can probably do that."

"And snakes. Try to spot the snakes before I get close to them."

"Most snakes are harmless. And they'd prefer to stay away from us."

"For my sake, do your best to enforce that rule."

"I'll do my most excellent snake wrangling." We passed a sign that said "Swamp Tours" pointing in the direction we were going. "City cops, scared of a little harmless woodland creature."

"I don't get along with any creature that has sharp teeth and might bite me."

I turned off onto a narrow two-lane road. On either side was a ditch, swollen with recent rain water, separated from the road by the barest wisp of a shoulder. The trees were lower, not the tall pines from earlier, but the truncated swamp trees, mixed with palmetto and grasses, some of the tree limbs draped in Spanish moss. They crowded against each other, a matted barrier of greens. We passed a rusted trailer; it looked abandoned. A beer can floating in the ditch was the only other sign people were here.

"Your location is somewhere along this road, so you might want to be on the lookout for it," I told Ashley.

She punched in a number in her cell phone. "We're pretty close," she told what I guessed to be the trailing SUV. "Get ready to rock and roll." She scanned the side of the road, her brow furrowed.

In the twenty minutes since we'd left stoplights and fast-food joints, we'd traveled to a different world. Trees enclosed the road, and only the thin stretch of asphalt said that humans had passed this way and claimed the land. The sun had been struggling with clouds all day and just as we passed under the shade of an oak tree, the clouds won the battle, leaving us in shadow even as we passed the trees. Rain was likely on the way back.

"Are you sure this is the right road?" Ashley asked as the trees remained unbroken.

"Not too many roads out here. This is the right road if you gave me the right directions."

She flashed me a brief smile as apology for her churlishness.

"Everything seems longer when you count the trees," I said. "We are close."

"Don't want to miss it."

"We can turn around. Not much traffic here," I pointed out.

"Not sure they could do a three-point turn," she said, nodding back at the others. She was probably right. The road had no shoulder and the rain-filled ditches on either side left little room for error.

I slowed even more. A fine scatter of mist hit my windshield and the clouds got darker.

"Is that it?" I asked, seeing a notch in the trees.

"Where?"

"Up ahead, it's a driveway." I took my foot off the gas and let the car coast to the opening. The gap was barely wide enough for a small car, the gravel driveway rutted by rain and neglect. It curved around a dense thatch of trees; there was no way to see beyond the green and gray.

"This should be it," she said, glancing from her notes to her phone to the trees. She dialed the phone, listened for a moment, tried again and then again.

"No signal out here," I said.

"Of course, you're right." She rolled down her window and did it the old-fashioned way by pointing.

Once her arm was back in the car, I turned slowly onto the gravel driveway. The first hole almost swallowed my tire. Either this place was abandoned, or whoever came here had serious four-wheel drive. There was a patch of ground at the curve, barely enough for me to pull over.

"My car is made for city driving," I told Ashley. "I don't like my chances of getting all the way up and back without damaging an axle." This was not a place I wanted to wait for roadside assistance.

"There's not enough room for both of us," she said, meaning the SUV.

"That's okay. I'll walk. It can't be that far."

"Okay," she said, sliding out of the door, carefully scanning the ground. In case of alligators, I assumed.

I got out and started up the road. The property was overgrown, weeds growing in the gravel, underbrush to waist height just off the road. I carefully picked my way along the edge of the track, where the gravel hadn't been sprayed away by tires. I stepped as far as I could into the weeds as I heard the SUV come up behind me.

As it passed me, I noticed what looked like a tire mark up ahead. But the SUV drove over it, obliterating what was there.

Whoever was driving was going very slowly, barely faster than my walking—for good reason. There were deep holes filled with the recent rains, making it impossible to tell their depth until your tire rolled into it. Even with its much higher clearance, the SUV scraped bottom a few times.

I stayed far enough behind to avoid getting sloshed when it sank into the mud holes. The curve took its time leading around the trees. It was a good fifty yards before I could begin to see a cleared area that told me something was beyond the leafy veil. Once around the turn, the SUV hit smoother ground and left me behind.

As I came around the bend, I went on alert. Hidden in the trees was a large metal building, the area around it neatly cleared and mowed, with a nicely paved parking area in front. I could think of only one reason for the disparity; they wanted it hidden, as if whatever was back here was poor and ramshackle. Now I wished I'd had a chance to examine the tire track. In the glimpse I saw of it, it seemed new, but was it new in hours or in days?

If it was just me, I would have turned around and left.

But it wasn't just me, so I trudged on, joining them at the SUV. Cara, the older woman, seemed to be in charge. Jack and John were listening to her as she talked in a low voice. Sandy was wandering around the cleared area.

Ashley met me halfway down the paved area as if to keep me out of earshot of whatever the others were saying.

"So, what do you think?" she asked.

"Conveniently hidden. This patch is mowed to the nub and the gravel road is left to look like no one's been here in years. I thought I saw a fairly recent tire track just before you drove past me."

"So you think someone might be here?"

"Probably not. No vehicle and no reason to hide one once they're back in here. But they might have been here in the last few days. Or even hours."

She nodded as if that was what she thought as well.

"And they might come back."

"We'll be quick. Just a brief look around." She rejoined the others, but I didn't feel invited to join the confab so I wandered off, walking the perimeter. I could call it alligator patrol. It was a large facility, wide at the front and deep, going to the tree line at the far edge of the property. The building itself was nondescript, a fairly new metal warehouse, painted a dull battleship gray. The color would help keep it hidden behind the trees, no glimmer of white showing through. A neatly squared patch of lawn had been trimmed around the building. At one side was a garage door, either to park something inside or to use as a loading dock. I scanned for tire tracks just in case someone was parked in there, but saw nothing. It was wet enough that there would be a mud trace for anything recent. In the middle of the front was a regular door, a small glass window opaque behind closed blinds. The few windows were high, near the top, good for light, but not for spying on what was inside.

There was a large air-conditioning unit near the back. It was also new-looking and massive enough to cool the whole building. I had to admit that I wasn't up on the latest in drug trafficking, but I didn't think cocaine had to be climate-controlled. As for humans, I doubted the kind of pimps who raped and forced woman into prostitution worried about keeping them cool in the summer.

All signs seemed to point to this being more than a neglected and abandoned storage site.

I was just going around the back when I heard a gunshot. Just one, and no shouting or return fire. I ran to the front of the building to find that John had shot the lock on the door.

"What are you doing?" I asked, although it was clear they were getting into the building any way they could.

Ashley replied, "We needed to get in. Not likely, but if they're holding people in there, we can't wait."

She was right. But as isolated as this was, there were still neighbors close enough to hear a gunshot. This place might be owned by strangers, but it seemed more likely that it was someone from around here, someone who knew about this property, and that would mean someone whose word would prevail against outsiders—even outsiders with badges.

"Better be quick. Local cops will be here soon," I said. Or the people who owned this place. They were probably smart enough to bribe the neighbors to be on the lookout. Not an out-and-out bribe, that would be too obvious, but favors like "going away, can you use these ribeyes," that kind of thing.

Each one of them had guns. I had managed to grab my flashlight from my car.

Jack led the way in, Sandy at his side even now. John was next. Cara stayed by the SUV; she clearly wasn't going inside. Ashley shrugged at me as if to say I could stay here or go with them, and went inside.

I had to admit I was curious. So I followed her.

The door led to a small office, a cheap desk and chairs. A table at one corner with a beer bottle still on it. Cheap beer at that. A couple of cigarettes had been put out in it. I touched the bottle. Cool. The cigarettes were old, not just put out as we drove up. At the far end a door led out of the office. I followed them through it.

The rest of the building was an open space, or would have been if not for the maze of pallets and boxes piled everywhere.

They had enough stuff they could have rivaled a big box store. Piles of unopened boxes promising new TVs, stereos, computers, all manner of electronics. All kinds of booze from cheap gin to expensive whiskey. Guns and ammo. Stolen. Trucks hijacked, loads diverted. Sometimes the drivers were in on it, sometimes not. Some of the stacks went almost all the way to the roof. I quickly skimmed past the piles of material goods. They had a bit of everything. I even noticed a box labeled "truffle oil." I was looking for signs that anyone human had been here. To bend victims to their will, traffickers will hold them captive, away from any hope of rescue, often repeatedly raping those they wanted to force into prostitution. Maybe these were the nice guys—a very relative term—and they simply kept them locked up out here, but there still needed to be someplace where several people could be securely held.

So far all I saw was booty of the material kind.

"Found their stash," John called from somewhere in the maze.

Bile rose in my throat. He probably meant he found where the human cargo was kept.

But I was wrong.

"Coke, smack, weed," he continued. "They got something for everyone here."

"Shit," Jack said. "Big pile of crap."

"We gotta hurry." John again.

I couldn't see them through the piles of boxes. *Hurry* was good news to my ears. If they wanted to raid this place proper, they needed a SWAT team. This much stuff, especially drugs, would be heavily guarded. The only reason it wasn't swarming with goons was the crooks must have gotten complacent and thought the hidden location was enough protection.

John said, "Grab as much as you can."

That didn't make sense. They shouldn't touch anything.

Suddenly someone touched my sleeve.

Ashley.

"Time to leave?" I asked.

"A minute. Can you take a look at something?"

She led me to the back of the warehouse. "What do you make of this?" She showed me a ledger she seemed to have pulled from file cabinets that were back against the wall.

The page she indicated was in code. One column seemed to be dates, written the European way with day first, then month, but with the numbers not separated. Once I worked that out, it seemed to be about goods received and sent out. But they were all numeric codes, no way to tell if the shipments referred to truffle oil or human flesh. I told her so.

"That's what I thought. Too bad we don't have enough time to look over everything."

"But isn't this evidence?" I asked.

She sighed. "Yes, but we didn't think we'd find anything. Now that we know this is an active site, we have to decide whether to let them continue and see if they can lead us to bigger fish or bust them now. We're not going to do that today."

"Don't you think they'll notice the shot-out door?"

"Probably. But they'll likely think that's everyday thieves, especially if we strategically remove a few things."

"Like the drugs."

"Yeah, at least we can dispose of them and keep them off the streets," she said.

"Sounds good. Someone has probably called them about the gunshot. My guess is that whoever is doing this is from around here and probably has friends who report to him."

"Let me check with the others. Give these another quick look over and I'll be right back."

She disappeared into the maze. I glanced at my watch. Right back or not, I'd give her two minutes and then I was getting out of here. They weren't paying me enough to tangle with the kind of thugs who ran this operation.

I tried to take another look at the ledger as I listened for any sound that would tell me to get out now. I quickly flipped through the pages. A lot of pages. A lot of stuff. All of it a mishmash of numbers. I glanced back at the file cabinets. The top drawer of one was ajar. Guessing that was where Ashley took it from, I put the ledger back in an empty space. There were other notebooks as well. I fanned the pages in several more of them, but they all had the same listings, most in one handwriting, a few in a different one.

Then I noticed one in back, sectioned off by a metal divider. The others were all gray, this one was red.

The drawer only opened halfway, so I had to angle my arm to reach it.

Still meaningless numbers. I could decipher the date—some were recent. Then I noticed other numbers.

5-7-36-27-38. These weren't sophisticated crooks, they hadn't done a good job of hiding the dates. Five feet, seven inches? Bust thirty-six, waist twenty-seven, and hips thirty-eight.

I stared at the figures in front of me. I flipped through the ledger. Several pages were filled, all in the same handwriting, a neat script. There were about twenty entries per page. Over fifty…women?

The numbers could mean something else. I could be convoluting them to show me what I wanted—and was afraid—to find.

The most recent date was two days ago.

"What the hell are you doing here?"

Don't look; just run. But I couldn't help glancing at the person behind the voice.

He was big enough to put fear into most linebackers and his tattoos were tattooed. His head was shaved, his nose pierced, and he had a mustache that almost reached his shoulders.

His most riveting accessory was the gun pointing in my direction.

Then I did what my animal brain was screaming at me to do. I threw the ledger at him and ran in the opposite direction as quickly as I could, skittering around a pile of boxes to be out of his sight—gun-aiming sight, that is.

I hear a bellowed "What the fuck?" from his direction and the lumbering thump of footsteps.

As I passed the box of truffle oil, I grabbed a bottle and heaved it over my shoulder, hoping to make a very expensive banana peel for my pursuer. The smash of glass told me at least the bottle had broken.

The less pleasant sound was the report of a gun.

I angled around another pile of boxes, trying to keep walls of the goods between me and any bullets. And also doing my best to head in the direction of the door. It was likely that Mr. Tattooed Tattoos wasn't alone and there might well be a non-welcoming party at the door.

But I had heard nothing—or been too engrossed in the human trafficking ledger to be paying enough attention—so it might be that he was the lone guard. Ashley and her crew must have heard or seen him. He couldn't have slipped by all of us. Maybe they had laid low to see what he was up to.

Assuming they hadn't thought he could be firing a gun at me. Certainly cause to arrest him, but I didn't like the idea that they just left me alone to deal with him. Me and my flashlight.

"Shit!" I heard behind me. Then a loud thud. Truffle Oil one, Tattoos zero.

I kept running, trying to keep my bearings in the maze of boxes.

As I heard his footsteps start up—another sharp crack of a gun—I shoved off against a big pile of TV boxes with enough force to tip them over, blocking the aisle I was running down.

Daylight.

The door.

Another gunshot.

This time I heard the bullet whiz by my head.

It was long past time for me to be out of here. The adrenaline rush from the bullet gave me extra speed as I sprinted to the door.

Just inside it, I pulled down another pile of boxes, cheap bourbon this time, to block the way to the door and slow down Mr. Tattooed Tattoos.

I heard the bottles crash behind me as I ran for daylight.

Either I was very fast or he was a poor shot or both. That and a man as big as he is just isn't going to be fleet of foot were my only advantages.

At least until I could meet up with my federal cavalry.

I slammed through the door, not even bothering to close it.

No one else was in sight.

Even more worrisome, no sight of anyone being around. The big SUV was gone. Had they left? Stranding me here with a big thug? Or were they hiding somewhere?

Now would be a great time to signal.

But I couldn't wait. I took off running, heading parallel with the front of the building. When I got to the corner, I turned as if heading to the back. After a few paces, I again turned, this time tearing across the lawn to the woods. This way I was hidden from his immediate view when he came out the door. The building itself would keep me concealed until I was most of the way to the woods, and even then he'd have to look back and not down the road to see me.

Once I was in the woods, I could outrun him. Not his bullets, of course, but weaving through the trees and the shadows of the leaves would make me a much harder target than running down the open driveway.

My idealistic plan was to lose him in the woods, then work my way back to my car and speed the hell out of here. My more realistic plan was to hide in the woods, maybe a few hours and thousands of mosquito bites, until a plethora of police showed up and I could safely get out.

I guessed that Ashley, Cara, John, Jack, and Sandy had done the prudent, by-the-book thing and removed themselves from the premises until they could secure backup. I would give them the benefit of the doubt.

If I survived, that is.

I was at the edge of the lawn, searching for a way into the dense thicket. There had to be an animal path here somewhere. I didn't want to just thrash through the undergrowth. I needed to find an opening, otherwise it would be too slow and the shaking of the branches would give me away.

Two feet away was a break in the brush. I angled myself though it, stepping carefully over fallen branches. This looked a bit like an alligator trail, but fugitives from gun-toting thugs couldn't be picky. It was the off season for alligators and they were more likely to be hibernating in a mud hole than sunning themselves in my path.

Balancing speed and stealth, I moved as quickly as I could into the underbrush.

I heard another shot, but this time it was distant and no swoosh of a bullet near me.

Another "What the fuck?" sounded like it came from the front of the building.

I moved a few more feet in, then slid behind a fallen tree, glad I had decided on gray and black clothes and not the sparkly pink.

Between the log and the leaves, I should be well enough hidden that he wouldn't find me with a quick scan. My plan—hope—was that he wouldn't know which way I went and would probably guess down the driveway to my car.

That would give me a chance to move deeper into the woods and find a secure hiding place. I would stay there until it was safe to come out. If I was really lucky, that would be sometime today.

Gym, I thought, as I listened to my heavy breathing. *Time to go to the gym more often.* It's hard to conceal yourself after a headlong sprint if you're breathing so heavily it can be heard in the next parish.

I saw a flash of blue through the leaves. His jeans. He was walking the perimeter. If I could see him, he could see me, so I couldn't stick my head up and gauge where he was going. If he was just walking around the building, I was probably okay. If he was looking closely for tracks he'd eventually find me. I hadn't stepped in any mud—that I knew of— but my running footsteps might have crushed the grass, the break in the bushes might have a bent twig. Enough clues for anyone looking.

Time for me to push my luck and keep moving.

If it worked for the alligators, it might work for me. Instead of standing, I crawled down the indentation in the brush. The main stand of trees was still about twenty feet away; I was in tall grasses and scrub bushes, ferns and palmettos. This close to the water, the ground was soft and wet, soaking my knees and elbows.

Inch by inch. I didn't dare to look behind me. This wasn't a speedy way to move, but it kept me down, not where he would probably be looking for me, and it made less motion in the brush.

When I was close to the trees I risked standing up. Crawling is hard work and I was huffing and puffing again.

"Hey," I heard Mr. Tattooed Tattoos call. "This might be a footprint."

It didn't sound like he was talking to me.

Which meant he had to be talking to someone else, and that meant two people were looking for me now.

His voice still seemed to be near the building. Maybe he had found my track, or maybe he had found something entirely different.

I didn't run; that might make too much noise. I kept moving, careful step after step, occasionally looking over my shoulder to see if they were coming after me.

"Make it quick, we need to get out of here," a voice answered him. A woman? A high-pitched male voice? I couldn't see the person.

I faded back into the trees, taking care to slide around them and keep a trunk between me and where I'd come from.

A few more feet, pause, listen, then move again. They didn't seem to be following me.

I finally came to a ragged barbed-wire fence, rusted with age. The property line.

Weaving back into the trees, I followed it as best I could. It should lead me to the road. Not that I was planning to leave the safety of the trees, but I wanted to be close enough to the road to be able to hear if people came and left. The ground here was soft and muddy, not good for running and very good for leaving clear footprints. I wanted to get to more stable footing.

I didn't have to wait long. I heard the roar of a truck, the chug of a big diesel engine from the direction of the building.

Faintly, in the distance, I also heard the sound of a siren.

Those two combined noises probably lowered my blood pressure by about one thousand points. The man trying to shoot me was leaving and the cops were on their way.

Which enabled me to move from the problems of life and death to the more mundane ones of hiding in the woods at what was clearly a den of thieves without much of a good excuse for being here without Ashley to back me up.

The roaring truck revved its engine; I could hear the motor as it left the loading area—where it obviously had been parked, the door clanked down—then it snaked down the driveway to the road.

Once at the road the engine revved again and sped off.

The sirens were louder now.

Explaining my thin story over and over again to the local cops did not sound like a good time. It was more than possible these crooks were in cahoots with the locals and they were assuming their cop buddy would give them my name. No longer needing to be quiet, I thrashed through the woods heading to where I hoped my car was.

I was in a hurry now.

Trees and plants are never gone this far south; even in January there is still something green and growing here. But this time of year, before spring bellowed into exuberant growth, was probably the best time of year to be bushwhacking through the woods.

I swung around trees, taking running steps when I could.

I finally burst from the trees to the tall grass lining the road.

It was still a slog though them, but I was near now.

The sirens were closer.

My arms were getting tired from slapping away vines and weeds, my breath rasping as I struggled to push through the tangled brush.

Get into the car, away from the mosquitoes. Just do it, I told myself.

I could see the pitted driveway.

Another step.

And another.

My car. It was about twenty feet away.

I ripped my feet free from the matted weeds, stumbled on the rough gravel, gained my footing, and raced for my car.

I didn't bother with a seat belt, just gunned it into gear, did a sloppy three-point turn, one that scraped the bottom and undoubtedly left mud in places there shouldn't be mud.

But I needed to get out of there.

I jounced around the worst of the potholes. There is never a good time to break an axle, but this would be an especially bad time.

The road loomed before me.

I paused before pulling out, listening for the sirens. They were coming from my left, which was the direction I wanted to go.

At least at some point.

I turned right.

Hit the gas.

Was at sixty mph in about six seconds. Then seventy, faster than this road allowed, but this was a straight patch and I was taking advantage of it.

I slowed as I came to the first curve.

In my rearview mirror, I saw flashing lights.

I took the curve and slowed to the speed limit. As of now, I was just someone who grew up in the bayous and was taking a drive to visit old friends.

Except I had been gone from here a long time. Taken to the suburbs when I was ten after my father died. Lived with my pious Aunt Greta and resigned Uncle Claude. It was thirty-plus years since I'd lived out here. I kept my father's shipyard, but it had been destroyed in Katrina. Now it was just a wild patch of land that I didn't know what to do with. Everything that held memories—the house, the patch of garden my mother had planted, the docks on the bayou—had all been washed away, replaced by wild debris that housed memories of strangers.

I had only a past here; I didn't have connections.

But I still drove on, a leisurely pace. This was the only highway in or out, so I would have to go back the way I came and pass right by that hidden driveway. Much as I wanted to get back to the city—and decent cell service—I also wanted to delay being that close again. I drive a nondescript gray car, a little Mazda that looks like just about every other small car, but if anyone paid attention—and I was sure they couldn't have missed it parked on the driveway—they might notice it on the way back.

I had to wait long enough for the police to have mostly cleared out, but not long enough for the bad guys to come back.

CHAPTER SEVEN

I let about forty-five minutes pass before heading back. I stopped and got gas, indulged myself with a sugared, caffeinated soda, then hit a seafood place and picked up some oysters and crabs, less because I was hungry and more as a plausible excuse for being out here if I should need one. Seafood right off the dock. Was out on the Westbank, ran down to the family's favorite seafood place.

I'd never been there before, but they didn't need to know that.

I had turned my cell phone off. I hadn't brought the car charger, and constantly searching for a signal had drained its battery.

I was more than annoyed at being left behind. If Ashley was trying to reach me—which she'd better be doing—payback was that I wasn't going to make it easy. I also didn't want to talk to her while driving, especially on a narrow, unfamiliar road.

I tried to keep my eyes on the road as I drove by the slight notch of the driveway, as if I was out here for the reasons I claimed to be with no awareness that anything had happened there. But I glanced quickly as I went by. It was a bare gap in the trees and brush, a flash of gravel and then gone. As if nothing had happened here.

I headed back via the main bridge. I didn't have a toll tag, since I didn't cross the bridge often enough to need one, so there would be no record of my car. Plus I had the seafood—and its receipt—as an excuse for being on this side of the river. Ashley and her crew's paranoia was infecting me. I hadn't broken any laws. Well, technically breaking and entering, but they had the authority to do so. I was just along for the ride.

By the time I got back to civilization, or at least stoplights and burger joints, I was starving. It was long past lunch, sliding into the early part of rush hour. Plus, I had burned up a few calories crawling

333333

333

through the woods. I ignored the siren call of orange and yellow signs promising greasy relief. I wanted to be home, safe on my territory before I could relax enough to eat.

Even though I was going against the main flow of traffic, it was still an annoying mess coming into the city and through the CBD when everyone else was intent on getting out. I saw two left turns from the right lane.

Cordelia and I used to joke that every day a new traffic memo went out—"today is jaywalking day—just meander out in traffic, if you don't see the cars, they can't hit you," or "it's wrong-way Thursday," or as today, "left turn from the right lane day." On Fridays all memos were in effect.

But Cordelia was gone and she wasn't coming back.

I laid on my horn to suggest to the person in front of me that the traffic light was as green as it was going to get.

I didn't bother going to my office, instead headed straight home.

The first order of business was food.

It might as well be the oysters and crabs. It was still cold enough to eat the oysters raw. The rule is only in months with an *R* in them. I usually skip September as well just to be on the safe side. A little ketchup, horseradish sauce, lemon, and garlic, and I had a quick cocktail sauce.

Only as I was slurping down bivalves did I turn my cell phone back on and check it.

Ashley had called four times. She left three messages.

I got a beer out of the refrigerator and finished the oysters. Never call a woman when you're hungry.

The crabs could wait. They're too messy to crack while talking on the phone.

She answered on the first ring.

"Micky! Are you all right? I've been so worried about you."

I almost smiled at her concerned tone, but I wasn't letting her off that easily.

"What the hell happened? You tell me you'll be back in a minute or two and the next thing I know a tattooed goon is shooting at me."

"Oh, my God, I'm so sorry. This shouldn't have happened."

"So how did it happen?"

"We don't know yet. Really bad luck…or they were tipped off."

"Are you accusing me?" I asked.

"No, oh, no. Please don't think that. No, we have some idea who might have done it. You're nowhere even near the list."

"Where did you go?"

"It happened so fast. I was talking to Cara, then Jack said everyone in the car, now. I started to call you to warn you but remembered you left your cell phone in your car."

That was true, I had. I hadn't stuffed it in my pocket as I didn't think I'd need it.

She continued, "We pulled out and ducked into another driveway, waiting for them to come by."

"But it was only a few minutes after you left me that Mr. Tattooed Goon showed up."

"Damn. He must have come in some other way. We saw a big truck drive up a good ten minutes after we pulled out. It left almost immediately after."

I hadn't heard the truck come in, although I had heard it leave. Of course, I hadn't heard the SUV drive away either. Maybe because I was all the way in the back. Or maybe it had arrived while I was running through the woods and I couldn't hear it over my rasping breath.

"How could he have gotten in the front door without you seeing him?"

"He probably came in the back way."

"I didn't see a back way."

"It's pretty well hidden."

"How do you know?"

"We came back. To look for you."

"Oh. Did you call the local cops?"

"Yes, I did that, Jack didn't want me to, but I did anyway. We had to scare them off and that was the only way to do it."

"Why didn't Jack want you to call?"

"He wanted to bring in our team to really check the place out. And to avoid all the repeated questions and checking and double-checking the local cops would do when we came back. That's how I found the back door, wandering around while they were questioning Jack and Cara. We only got back to our hotel a short while ago. I called you every chance when I had a signal."

That mollified me. That and the concern in her voice. "Okay, but let's try to avoid these kinds of situations in the future."

"Yes, absolutely. I'm so glad you're okay."

"I must have been a cat in a previous life. Nine lives and all that."

"I'm so glad you're okay," she repeated. "Look, I need to make this up to you."

"Not necessary. Things messed up, but that's not your fault."

"I got you into this. Besides…I'd like to. I've got piles of paperwork and meetings all day tomorrow and probably tomorrow evening, but in the next day or two let me take you out to dinner, one of the really good restaurants here."

I smiled as I hung up. Yeah, I'd be eating alone tonight, but it was nice to have an evening out with Ashley to look forward to.

I finished the crabs, eating about half and saving the rest for crab cakes. I wondered vaguely what it would be like to cook for Ashley. I contented myself with two more beers to ease into the night. After my day, I felt I deserved them.

Of course what I didn't deserve was the headache in the morning. It wasn't the beer, I decided as I looked at my sleep-tousled hair in the bathroom mirror. The seafood place had put a little too much cayenne in the crab boil. Or maybe it was the changing weather. Or that I hadn't slept well. Even three beers hadn't been enough to keep me from waking at every noise wondering if some tattooed giant was breaking in.

Back to real life, I told myself as I stepped in the shower. Today would be a nice, relaxing day of boring paper chases. Nothing more strenuous than filing.

As I got out of the shower, I noticed that my knees and elbows were bruised from my crawl in the woods yesterday. Proof that it had really happened.

And that Ashley wanted to make it up to me.

I didn't bother with breakfast, instead grabbing a big travel mug of coffee, a bagel, and a banana. I'd eat at my office while checking email.

I had slept a little late, so I didn't get to my office until around 9:30.

As I pulled up, an unmarked car pulled in right behind me. It had that look to it. A big black boxy car. It could be mob, but I checked in my rear view mirror and made out the radio and some official-type parking sticker.

Good times. I took a sip of my coffee, then dialed Ashley. I angled my head slightly to conceal the cell from them.

"Hey, Micky, what's up?" She sounded far more awake than I did.

"Some of your compatriots have joined me outside my workplace. An unmarked car just pulled in behind me." They could want something unrelated to our adventures yesterday, but my money was on the most obvious.

"Not our team. You might want to be careful. We're pretty sure we have a mole. Do your best to not reveal anything."

"If I need, will you come bail me out?"

"Of course, but I doubt you'll need that. It's your word against a bunch of crooks that you were even there."

The driver's door opened.

"Gotta go. Time for the third degree."

"Good luck," I heard her tinny voice say as I shut my cell phone.

I quickly stuffed it into my pocket and took a leisurely sip of my coffee. Using my side mirror, I looked at the person stepping out of the car.

Hot. Not my coffee. The woman staring at me in the mirror. She'd caught that I was checking her out and she was looking right in the mirror and therefore at me.

She was tall, broad shoulders that indicated muscles and time working out. Her hair was dark, almost black, cut short and in the spiky style favored nowadays. Her eyes were hidden by sunglasses and her skin was pale, that of someone who worked overtime in the office instead of heading out to the beach early on Friday. Her clothes were as unmarked as the car: tailored black slacks, a conservative blue button-down shirt, and a gray blazer large enough to easily hide the gun I knew she had to be packing.

She stared at me in the mirror. It was my turn.

I considered sitting in my car, forcing her hand, but that wouldn't improve what would undoubtedly be a less-than-fun experience.

I shoved open my door and got out.

"Top of the morning to you," I said.

"I'm looking for Michele Knight. You her?"

Her voice was definitely in the dyke range and her accent from somewhere not at all local. It sounded Mid-Atlantic newscaster, as if she'd taken speech lessons.

"Who's looking?" I asked.

"I ask the questions."

I wondered if she knew how clichéd that line was. To make the point I glanced at my watch.

I was silent long enough—about two seconds—for her to ask, "Can I see your ID?"

"You'd have to show me your ID to prove that you have the authority to ask to see my ID." I took a sip of my coffee.

She took off her sunglasses and stared at me. Stunning blue eyes.

"You're going to make this hard, aren't you?" she asked.

"I'm going to make this legal. Right now we're just two strangers standing on a public street."

"Your car," she pointed at my license plate, "was seen at the location of a crime."

"We haven't even established I'm the person you're looking for."

"You're either Michele Knight or her evil twin."

"She's back? I thought she'd left for Eastern Europe about a decade ago and agreed to never return."

"You want to talk in the street or somewhere more private?"

"Actually I don't want to talk. You have a good day." I turned and headed for my building.

Of course she followed. Of course I had to fumble with my key, almost dropping it, giving her plenty of time to position herself to push through the door behind me.

"I take it your answer is more private," she said as I started up the steps.

"Wrong. My answer is that I don't want to talk to you."

"That, I'm afraid, is not an option."

I ignored her as I hastened up the stairs. Maybe three flights would slow her down.

Her long, athletic legs easily kept pace.

I tried not to huff and puff as I put the key in my office door. *Gym, every day next week*, I vowed.

After catching a breath but before opening my door, I said, "I have not committed any crime. If my car was in the vicinity of a crime scene, it was coincidence. I'm sorry you had to waste the gas to come down here, but that's the whole story."

"Mind if I ask a few questions?"

"Yes."

"Why don't we go in your office and make ourselves comfortable?" She smiled at me. Of course, she had perfect white teeth. "This is going to take a while."

Do it. Jump through the hoops. Get it over with. Resigned, I sighed as I opened the door to my office.

"Sorry, I don't have any coffee. Except for this," I said lifting the travel mug in my hand. "Ran out last week and haven't had time to get more." Not true. I never run out of coffee. I had some tucked away in the cupboard. I drink good coffee and I didn't want her to feel welcome.

"Not a problem. I prefer tea anyway."

"Don't have any of that either." Also a lie. A friend brought me back tea from Australia with kangaroos on the box. So cute. That was also stuck somewhere in the cupboard.

I crossed my office and sat at my desk, leaving her to find her own seat. I was trying to decide how to play this. Clearly someone had tipped off the crooks that law enforcement had been sniffing around their hideout. Was this dark and handsome stranger part of that? No way to know. The way to play it was safe. I knew nothing, saw nothing, heard nothing, and forgot it even if I did.

"So what's this about?" I asked as she made herself comfortable in the chair closest to my desk. "Oh, and before I answer questions, can I see some ID? Can't be too careful these days."

"You are Michele Knight, aren't you?"

She probably had already reviewed my driver's license and passport photo, so I said, "Yes, I am." I didn't tell her most people call me Micky; she'd have to earn that. "And you are?"

"Special Agent Emily Harris."

"ID please?"

She pulled out the fancy FBI badge and waved it under my nose. Could it be a fake? Yeah, but even if she'd let me look at it for ten minutes I probably wouldn't be able to tell. It's not like I've spent a lot of time examining FBI papers.

"So, what's an important FIB like you doing tracking down a peon like me?" I smiled as I said it. We both knew she was probably low on the totem pole and been assigned the grunt work. I rarely crossed paths with the FBI, but I knew they didn't like their initials inverted to FIB.

Her look told me she knew exactly what I was up to. I reminded myself she didn't get to be an FBI agent by being dumb.

"Following up on leads. Where were you yesterday?"

"In the morning I met a client over on the Westbank."

"Can you give me the name of the client?"

"No, I can't."

"We can subpoena, you know."

"Yes, I know. My clients pay me for confidentiality. That means I'm legally obligated to make it as hard as possible. Even if it's a total waste of your time."

She nodded, not agreement, just acknowledgment, then said, "Where on the Westbank?"

"Over in Harvey, past the canal."

Another nod, but it didn't look like she knew where I was talking about. "And then what?"

"We drove around for a bit. She wanted to show me the places she suspected her husband was hanging out with other women."

"I thought you did mostly missing persons, not divorce."

She had done her research. "True. I agreed to this one for a friend. Someone who is less of a good friend now." I was using my recent annoying client as my cover story. The more truth you have in your lies, the better.

"Why is that?"

"Not my favorite client. She wants to know, but doesn't want to know, so I'm getting jerked around. No good deeds go unpunished."

She smiled at that one. She had a great smile. "Did you come back here after that?"

"No, it was past lunch when we got done and I had no more pressing cases, so I decided to take a drive down to bayou country."

"Really? Just like that?" She made her skepticism apparent.

"No, not just like that. I grew up out there."

"Where?"

"Bayou St. Jack. You have to look pretty hard on a map, it's a small little hamlet."

"You went there because you were hungry?"

"Yeah. I could scarf down a greasy burger or go get a fried shrimp po-boy with shrimp just harvested from the Gulf. And pick up some crabs and oysters for dinner as well." Then I had to add, "But you're a Yankee, you wouldn't understand how seriously we take our food down here."

"I've been here long enough to take food seriously. So how did a po-boy get your car parked off the road near a crime scene?"

"What kind of crime?"

"Why don't you just tell me what you did the rest of your day?"

"Oh, wait, I know what happened. There aren't a lot of places to stop to relieve yourself. So I found a little abandoned driveway to pull off the road and went into the bushes to take care of business."

"That would take you, what, five minutes?"

"It would have, if I hadn't got distracted. The first promising location has something that could have been poison ivy, so I moved on. I found an appropriate spot and when I was finished noticed what looked like an alligator track. It's too cold for them now, so I followed it as far as I could down to the bayou."

"Why'd you do that?"

"I find a beauty in the swamp. Land that's not meant for humans, with its stark splendor of scrub pines holding to the few solid places, the waves of grass a border between land and water."

"Kind of cold to be wandering around outside."

"Yeah, but I was out there and didn't know when or even if I'd ever get back to that spot."

"So what happened?"

I could see she wasn't going to let it go. Stick as close to the truth as possible. "As I was heading back to my car, I heard a couple of gunshots. Decided it was time to get out of there."

"You didn't call the police?"

"No, I had no idea why they were shooting. Could have been a snake. Or just target practice. It's a rural area. People shoot guns."

"You didn't check it out?"

"I'd just been peeing on someone's private property. I wasn't going to inquire why they were firing a gun. I got in my car and left. Oh, wait, I got a glimpse of the shooter through the trees. A big man, tattooed, bald or shaved head, and a big droopy mustache. I know you shouldn't judge people by their looks, but he didn't look friendly and I had no desire to meet him. I hurried back to my car and left as quickly as I could." Mr. Tattooed Tattoos was there; I had no problem giving him up.

"That was it?"

"That was it. Who told you my car was there?"

She shook her head. "I'm just the peon who talks to peons. I don't always know where the tips come from." Then she added, "I hope you're telling the truth, because if you're not, you could be playing a very dangerous game."

"What was out there that I almost stepped in?"

She looked down at the floor, then directly at me, as if making a decision. "Drugs and gray-market goods. Basically anything they can make money with. Maybe even sex trade."

"Out in the middle of the bayous?"

"It's fairly close to the city, close enough to do a lunch run."

"It was a very good shrimp po-boy," I defended myself.

"Yeah? Maybe you should take me sometime."

"If we're ever around there together, I will." Not likely, but I knew a couple of places around Bayou St. Jack's I could take her. I just needed to check they were still open. "Are you saying they might be doing human trafficking?"

"Certainly possible. Anything for money. But we didn't see any evidence of it there."

I couldn't tell her about the red ledger. I'd have to leave that to Ashley's team.

She looked down at the floor again, then back at me. "Look, I know sometimes the money can be tempting. It's just an easy favor—"

"I've done nothing illegal. Do I call you guys every time someone makes an illegal left turn? No." (I'd be calling every hour on the hour with the way people here drive.) "But if I stumble over something big, like drugs or forced prostitution, you wouldn't have to find me, I'd find you. I'm not a saint, but I've never needed money enough to cross the line where people get hurt."

"People do get hurt. They get hurt every day." She said it quietly, almost sadly.

"Anything else you need to know?"

"Not at the moment." The quiet voice was gone. "I hope you're telling the truth. I hate it when women I really want to be on my side turn out to be the ones I have to arrest." She smiled, making it clear there was a compliment in her words.

"Don't worry, you and I will never play with handcuffs."

"That's good because I'm not that kind of girl. Put them on too many crooks to think they're fun anywhere else." She smiled again.

I smiled back. Emily Harris was a smart and attractive woman. I hoped we were on the same side.

She gave me her card and I agreed to call her if I remembered anything else. Or if I stumbled over any crimes.

Once she was gone, I called Ashley, but only got her voice mail. I left a brief message, "So far so good. If you want the details, give me a call."

After that I busied myself with the flotsam and jetsam of the day, checking email, checking the weather, all the little distracting things that make time pass. Filing, sending out reminders about unpaid invoices.

After lunch, I was left with cleaning the bathroom. Cleaning toilets is one of my least favorite chores. I usually skipped over it by reasoning I was the only person who used this particular one, so it had to be germs I was already exposed to. Or that a healthy immune system needed an occasional challenge. Those covered most of the bases.

Then I remembered Ashley talking about why she did this. She had mentioned a lost young girl who had never been found. I have an odd memory, and it tucks away little pieces of information. Ashley said her name was Kimmie Fremont, age thirteen when she disappeared and would be around seventeen now.

Four years is a pretty cold trail and it didn't happen around here, but I could look. If the police had done a thorough job of searching for her, there probably wasn't much more I could do. But often the police had multiple tasks needing their attention, and they might dismiss a teenager as a runaway and give the case only cursory attention.

Even if I only retraced old tracks, it was still better than cleaning the bathroom.

A couple of hours on the Internet found the basic details. Kimberly Fremont, known as Kimmie, was from Rhinebeck, New York.

It also filled in the usual sad details. When a thirteen-year-old goes missing and is not heard from again, the most likely ending is someday a hiker will stumble over a skull and she can be buried. Even her thirteen years didn't seem like happy ones. Her mother was getting divorced from her third husband. None of the articles mentioned Kimmie's father, so I guessed that he was long out of the picture. There didn't seem to have been a custody battle, which is the most common reason kids get snatched. The stranger in the raincoat is more prevalent in our fears than in reality; it's more likely to be the devil you know than the one you don't. It had been a messy divorce, the wife accusing her soon-to-be ex of pawing her young son. The older daughter claimed Kimmie had called her and said she was okay the next day, but she was charged with watching her younger siblings and hadn't let her mother know that Kimmie never made it home from school. The mother got in after her shift at the convenience store a little after ten and that's when she discovered her daughter missing.

I looked away from the screen. I wondered what had happened to them. The older daughter was only being a typical fifteen-year-old, but her moment of teenage inattention turned into a lapse with consequences that would haunt her. Maybe if she had noticed Kimmie wasn't there earlier, those hours would have made a difference. I wondered if she was still asking herself that question. She would be nineteen now. In college, trying to find a redemptive path in life? Or working at the convenience store like her mother, maybe already married, already with a child? The young son. He would be around ten now. Did he remember his sister? The mother, was she on her next husband? Or the next? Or had she given up? What happens to a family when a child just disappears?

I considered leaving it alone. If I was extremely lucky, the most likely outcome was that I'd find who murdered Kimmie and where the body was buried. I couldn't know whether living with the terrible hope that the child might return was better or worse than knowing for sure she never would.

I didn't want to talk to the family, although that was the logical place to start. They hadn't asked me to get involved and it felt like too much of a violation to call up and ask about their missing daughter.

I got up from my desk and walked to the window. Spring would come again, but today was sliding into a gray winter evening, light filtered through clouds that were coalescing into thunderheads. It would rain tonight.

Why was I looking for Kimmie Fremont? The bathroom wasn't a good enough excuse. Occasionally I take cases that no one pays me for. Sometimes because I have something to prove, or I'm angry at what I see as a wrong. Sometimes people can't pay me, yet they ask because they need the answer. Sometimes I agree with them and take on their search. Mostly I don't. Often what they need is something I'll never find for them—salvation, deliverance, forgiveness from someone who won't—or can't—forgive.

Was the banal and ignoble reason that I wanted to impress Ashley? Or the slightly better reason that this lost girl was *her* lost cause and I wanted to bring at least one missing girl home?

Four years gone. Maybe the family preferred hope. Maybe they didn't want to think about it. Maybe it was none of my business.

Or maybe I didn't want to focus on my life and the mistakes I'd made, ones that held no chance of redemption for me.

The rain started.

Time to go home. I needed to do something besides stare at the gray sky, watching it turn darker and darker.

CHAPTER EIGHT

B ut the change in location did little for my morose mood. It was still dark, still raining. Ashley hadn't called.

The cold air of the refrigerator wafted over me as I stared at the bare shelves wondering what to have for dinner. The three-week-old cottage cheese wasn't calling my name. Only the crab from last night was edible, but without a salad or ingredients to make crab cakes, it wasn't much of a meal. I finally shut the door.

You can break out of your self-imposed exile at any time, I told myself. Torbin called once a week—whether I wanted him to or not, as he pointed out more than once. He was now the special events coordinator for NO/AIDS Task Force, and it seemed about every week he was doing something and suggesting that I come along.

Danny had given up calling. Mostly because I never answered or returned her calls.

Joanne didn't call. I had screwed up our friendship in addition to everything else I had messed up. She and her partner Alexandra had struggled after Katrina. Alex fell apart; Joanne, a police officer, had stayed in the city and held it together. In one of their broken-up periods, Alex and I had gone out for a pizza. It was intended to be a friendly pizza, two lonely women trying not to be so lonely. I had a couple of beers and we flirted. We went back to her place and started to go beyond flirting, but like a cheap, boozy comedy, Joanne chose right then to drop by to return some books of Alex's.

I always wondered if she saw my car in front of Alex's apartment. In any case, Joanne wasn't happy and she chose to focus her anger (major pissed off would be more like it) on me.

I like to think Joanne realizing Alex might find someone else was the catalyst for them reconciling. A few weeks later they had started couples counseling and I had heard—via the message Torbin left at his last phone call because he'd run into Danny and she'd told him—Alex and Joanne were taking a long two-week vacation together out on the West Coast, starting in Napa Valley and driving up to Seattle.

I was happy for them, not that being happy for them did much for my wretchedness. I tried to console myself that if I lived the life most other people lived, everything would be okay. If Cordelia had stayed healthy, we'd be together. Or if…but there were so many ifs, so many twists and turns and possibilities that it really did begin to seem like one butterfly on the far side of the world determined our fate.

She had cancer. To get better treatment she'd gone to Houston, a seven-hour drive from New Orleans.

Had it only been last summer? Just barely past six months—how could so much change be contained in so little time?

The treatments were working, but there were setbacks, infections, adverse drug reactions, each threatening to swing a delicate balance between living and dying. Each one exhausting for her—and me—with worry and waiting.

One of her sisters came down to stay. Half sister, younger by a decade, certain how life should be lived. She believed in her god and had never really approved of me. Well, in truth, had never approved of having a sister who was a lesbian, but made it clear that she could manage a "tolerant" bargain if Cordelia could at least be with someone respectable, perhaps a tenured medievalist or at least a lawyer (civil, not criminal). The sister had married well, a husband who made money the old-fashioned way, screwing people out of it. She called it hard work and creating a business out of nothing, skipping over that the business was a chain of check-cashing stores in low-income areas in the Northeast.

She had the money and time to simply leave, rent a relatively nice residential inn, one with two bedrooms and a kitchen, near the cancer center and stay there. She thought there was something morally suspect about me running back and forth between Houston and New Orleans as if had I lived my life right—like she did—I would be able to stay with Cordelia the whole time. I think she lived her life to be superior to other people—better than Cordelia because she didn't have cancer and far better than me because she had cleverly arranged her life to be able do the right thing—the perfect little Lady Bountiful ministering to her ill sister. We were polite to each other—how could we not be, with Cordelia sick and unable to keep the peace between us.

In retrospect, I should have bitch-slapped her across the room and told her to take her self-righteous ass home. But in the way of the best manipulators she made herself useful. She provided the nice place to stay between treatments. She was there with Cordelia to fetch her water or alert the nurse if she was in pain. She took care of things, from returned phone calls to insurance paperwork.

The months of constant travel, too much work, too little sleep or decent food took their toll on me. I got sick, both too sick to get on a plane and too sick to spend time with someone as precarious as Cordelia. Instead of the trek to the airport, I collapsed into bed and stayed there from Friday night until Sunday at around noon. It was a luxury to rest, no plane to catch, and then recover enough to have a long afternoon to myself.

I hadn't talked about these things to Cordelia; didn't feel like I could. *"Hey, sorry you're fighting for your life and we have so little time to see each other, but flying in every week is exhausting me. Can I take a break? Please don't die while I'm not there."*

The reprieve was seductive. A small voice saying there was little I could do when I was there.

Except be with her and let her know I cared enough to get on the plane every week no matter how weary I was.

Then a client wanted her runaway daughter escorted back to Boston and was willing to pay very well. Well enough that it would cover the bills for the rest of the month so I could have a respite from worrying about money as well. The catch was that I couldn't fly back until Sunday so they could have time together before the husband flew off to Europe for business. He'd been delayed by Super Storm Sandy, so he needed to leave as soon as he could. To make up for it I'd fly out early Monday morning, spend the afternoon and the night in Houston, and fly home early Tuesday.

I needed the money and I convinced myself that a second weekend that cut our time together would be okay. I had gone there twelve weekends in a row. It would be okay to skip one and shorten another. I would take a long weekend for the next one.

I told Cordelia. She said little; she was tired and on painkillers. I felt guilty when I hung up, but I couldn't do everything and be everywhere. We had to make choices. When this was over, I'd make it up to her. At least that's what I told myself.

So I flew to Boston, first class even, escorting a sixteen-year-old child who had run away because her parents were mean enough to ground her and make her study more after she flunked two subjects. I found out everything I needed and more than I wanted to know in the airport wait and flight to be assured that she was not returning to abusive parents—far from it. The optimistic view was that she was going through an overwrought period of adolescence; the more realistic, that she was a spoiled brat who didn't think the world could tell her no.

We were not best friends by the time I handed her over to her parents because I told her no repeatedly. I was not buying her a beer, she could not kick the seat in front of her because she was upset, her parents were not Nazis (nor did she appreciate the deliberately long-winded history lesson I gave her on who and what the Nazis actually were and the ways in which being confined to her room were truly and meaningfully different from a concentration camp).

Then it was Saturday afternoon and my flight was not leaving until the next day. I went back to the hotel room and tried to call Cordelia, but her sister answered and said she was asleep. I left the message that she could call later if she felt up to talking.

Then I was by myself in a small hotel room with the bright winter sunshine beckoning me. I stuffed my cell phone in my pocket, bundled up, and went to explore Boston. I'd only been there a few times. First I played history tourist, checking out the Boston Common and Freedom Trail. I was in it mostly for the walk and to see the sites. I wasn't up to fighting the hordes of screaming school-age children to go into too many places. When I got cold, I ducked into the markets at Faneuil Hall. A bit touristy, but I was warm, could watch people and pass the time.

Standing in line for coffee, I chatted with the guys in front of me. We had quickly pegged each other as family in this family—different kind—of place. Once they found I was here on my own, they invited me along on their evening. They loved New Orleans.

Dinner turned into a piano bar. My plane was early, but not that early, so I had a drink. And then another. One of them was a Scotch fan, so we tried a couple of different varieties. They were both lawyers and insisted on paying the way, recompense for, as they said, "the sins of too many men making more money than too many women." The drinks were free; I didn't say no.

I got back to my hotel room after one in the morning. I could sleep on the plane. I felt guilty at having fun, but the small vacation from worry was welcome. In truth, I'd help no one by staying in my hotel room and glumly watching TV reruns.

When I took out my phone, I realized that the battery had died. I'd planned to charge it at the airport, but my young runaway needed her phone and therefore the one available public charger, and that was a battle I chose not to fight.

I plugged it in long enough to see that Cordelia had called. But no message. I'd call her when I got back to New Orleans. It was too late tonight and probably would be too early before I got on the plane.

That was all I managed. I'd had a fair amount to drink, enough to give me a pleasant buzz and make the hotel bed feel very, very welcome.

When I woke, I was confused, unsure of where I was. Then panic. I hadn't set the alarm and was supposed to be on a plane at 7:30 am. The clock beside the bed read 6:57. Damn, I had forgotten to set the alarm on my cell phone. I had gotten distracted with the dead battery and missed calls—and being drunk—and didn't do it.

Clearly I would not be on the plane. I gave myself an hour to snooze—and sober up—before calling to change my flight. When I woke again, a little after eight, the light had changed to gray. As I punched in the number of the airline, I looked out the window. Snow was falling. A dusting had already accumulated on the window ledge.

The airline people very politely told me that I was SOL. A major winter storm was moving in and the area was still recovering from Sandy. Within an hour planes would no longer be able to fly in or out for most of the rest of the day.

If I'd been on my originally scheduled flight, I would have made it.

The airline person told me to call back tomorrow, but her glum tone indicated this was a major mess. Already-scheduled passengers had priority. People like me were pond scum who missed perfectly good flights for no good reason.

I spent the next few hours finding a cheaper hotel; I couldn't afford what my client could. I tried getting one near the airport, but they were all sold out. The snow was pretty, but not when I was trying to schlep from one hotel to the other. They were ten long blocks away, but traffic was at a standstill and in the end the most efficient way to travel was the oldest way—walking. I left my bag at the new hotel, but they didn't have a room ready for me, so I found the closest coffee shop and settled in for a long breakfast.

When it was late enough in Central Time, I called Cordelia. I took the coward's way out and blamed the blizzard.

"I thought I'd see you today," she said, sounding cranky.

"I'll get there as soon as I can," was the only answer I had.

"You know we could spend my money and you could be here more."

"We need your money for medical bills. It can't cover everything."

"It could cover a week or two. You should take the time off and stay here."

I didn't answer quickly enough. I really didn't know what to answer. Some of it was money. But I was scared to give up my life, as exhausting as it was, my work was in my control and it was part of who I was.

"Never mind. There's nothing for you to do here. It's not a good time."

"No, it's not that…it's…we need the money and…"

"And you're not stuck here with a dying woman."

"You're not dying," I protested too loudly. Several patrons in the coffee shop glanced my way. "And I want to be with you. I'm just trying to find a workable balance."

"Let me know when you find a balance that works for you. I'm tired, I need to go."

"I'll call later. We can talk more."

"Yeah, later." She hung up.

I stared at my phone as if I could find an answer there. She was upset. I knew her well enough to know "I'm tired, I don't want to talk," was often her way of saying, "I'm totally pissed at you, but I want to calm down first." She'd been saying it more and more often.

Maybe she was right. Maybe I should take a week or two and stay in Houston. But I don't have a regular job where I can take two weeks' vacation. I'm a small business, the sole owner and, save for occasional jobbers, the only employee. If someone wanted to hire me to find a missing person, they weren't going to wait two weeks until I came back, they'd find someone else. And the next time they needed someone they'd call that person, not me.

Two weeks of not being available would be doable, if it didn't affect the weeks after that.

What's more important—your business or Cordelia? The answer to that was easy. Making that answer work, not so easy. I vowed when I got back to New Orleans I'd call in every favor anyone might suspect they owed me. I'd call Chanse and Scotty, every PI I had worked with in the past. And hope they wouldn't take advantage of the situation and steal my regular clients. I could do a lot from my cell phone and a laptop. I'd just have to get the beat-up old laptop in working condition so I could cart it around with me—another task to somehow find time for.

Maybe I'd try a week, see how it worked and what I'd need to adjust to stay longer.

I had thought that her sister—Linda, she does have a name, although I prefer Evil Stepsister—would have the decency to refrain from trying to break us up, but now I suspected she was getting in her little digs. *"If she really loved you, she'd find a way to be here. I did, after all." "Wonder what she's doing all the time she's back there without you."* Or maybe Cordelia wanted me there and not Linda, was tired of depending on the sister who was more family than friend.

Or maybe it was what had happened last summer. She got involved in a case and had to do something she swore she'd never do—fire a gun. She killed a man. His death shook her and although she claimed she'd do it again, I don't know if she ever really forgave me. She'd never get into those kinds of situations if she's been with a nice safe social worker or medievalist, like her sister wanted.

For the next few days my calls were either unanswered or the sister told me that Cordelia was in treatment or tired or asleep.

I was out in the cold both literally and figuratively.

I checked out of the hotel—even cheap places cost money—and camped out at the airport, hoping that I'd be more likely to get on a plane if they had to stare at my unwashed face instead of a disembodied voice on the phone. I spent the night there, but the next day—four days later than I'd planned, I got lucky—they could fly me to Dallas, if I was willing to go via Denver. It wasn't Houston, but once I landed, I could rent a car and drive there in a few hours.

Four hours to Denver, a three-hour layover, three hours back to Dallas, and the final flight delayed by forty-five minutes waiting for their crew got me in at around ten p.m. that evening.

I called again when I landed. No answer.

I drove for about an hour but was nodding off. I'd have to stop for the night anyway, otherwise I'd get there at around three or four a.m. I pulled up at the next cheap (but decent) hotel.

She'll have to talk to me if I'm standing in front of her, I told myself as I checked in. All I wanted was to be home in my own bed—with Cordelia healthy and there with me. The night in the airport hadn't been restful, nor had the nights in strange hotel beds. Instead I was at another nameless hotel, driving a clunky rental car through the middle of nowhere Texas.

But I'd screwed up, both in being drunk and missing the plane, but also in trying to hold too tightly to my life when Cordelia needed me to let go and be with her. I'd been blind to it, thought the material things—her sister there to fetch her water, take her back and forth—was enough. I hadn't made it a priority in my life to be there for more than a few days at a time.

I didn't sleep very well at the nameless hotel, a place to stare at the ceiling and listen to the whoosh of trucks on the nearby interstate. I fell asleep sometime after midnight and woke up before six. I was on the road just as dawn was a gray glimmer in the sky.

I called again when I stopped for gas. Again no answer. I wondered if the Evil Stepsister had hijacked Cordelia's cell phone.

By nine I was at the hospital. Today was a chemo day, so she should be there.

I knew something was wrong when the nurse looked at me and said, "What are you doing here?"

I managed to stammer out that I'd been stuck in a blizzard, had only been able to leave a few messages.

No, she wasn't dead. She was gone. Transferred to someplace around New York, to follow the doctor who had been treating her. It was also closer to her sister. They had left four days ago, flying out in the husband's company jet.

I was in a daze as I went to the airport, returning the rental car, getting a flight to New Orleans. Nothing felt real. I was so tired, had gone so many miles; somehow this still felt like it was all a bad dream, one I'd wake from.

But when I opened the door to my house, I knew it wasn't a dream and I'd never wake from it. They'd come by here, taken all of Cordelia's stuff. There were blank spaces on the walls where pictures used to hang. The cats were gone, taken with a brief note in strange handwriting saying she needed them with her right now.

"Do I get them back if you die?" I'd screamed at the empty house.

I tore through all the rooms, but the emptiness was the same.

Finally, exhausted, I headed to the kitchen to the liquor cabinet.

It was empty. She had cleared it out as if knowing once I realized what had happened, I'd take a drink. That was the match to the gasoline of my anger. Walking into our house and tearing herself out of it with no warning was a gut punch I'd never expected. Following it with this petty attempt at control was intolerable.

Like the local gas station around the corner didn't sell booze.

I threw my suitcase across the living room and stormed out.

By the time I got back from the grocery store and unloaded, there would have been a lot less alcohol in the house if she'd just left what was there.

"Guess you don't know me very well, do you?" I muttered as I put away the bottles.

All but one, a Scotch bottle that I kept with me for most of the night. It the morning it was sitting on my bedside stand with only half of the bottle left. I rolled over and went back to sleep.

The next thing I really remember is vomiting my guts out and not knowing if it was day or night. Once I'd thrown up everything I possibly could, I drank a little water and went back to bed. When I woke up, I stumbled to the kitchen and made coffee and toast. After that settled my stomach, I dared take aspirin.

When I finally looked up the date, I found I had lost two days.

After I'd been sober for a few hours, it occurred to me that it was probably the Evil Stepsister who'd thrown away the liquor. It was the kind of petty controlling thing she'd do. The note about the cats was probably her handwriting. Or whomever she hired to pack up Cordelia's life and take it from here.

I tried calling again, but my calls went to voice mail. After a week, the number was disconnected. Even after that, for three days I kept calling that number, as if in a nightmare and every sunrise held the promise I'd wake from it.

Finally, staring at the bright sun and hearing the mechanical voice tell me this number would never be in service, the creeping numbness of reality oozed into my bones. She had cut me out of her life with more decision and precision than the invading cancer. Her only mercy was a brief note telling me the cats were all right. Gone from my life, but safe with her—wherever that was.

The worst blows are the ones you never see coming. I wasn't prepared for this. She was ill, maybe dying. She needed me. She did need me, but she didn't need the half-assed compromise I'd come up with, me exhausted from travel, there for a few days and then gone. Only a visitor in her life. She needed a partner; I had stopped being one.

I poured alcohol into my wounds until I was finally brave enough—or numb enough—to call our friends. I left messages; I didn't really want to talk, I just wanted to know.

"If she dies, let me know. If she lives, let me know as well. Oh, and if the cats are okay," was the same message I left for them all.

I dragged myself through the days, working the cases I'd agreed to. They were the respite of things I could control, work I knew how to do, small successes of locating a person, finding the information, a reflection that I was still here. Surviving. I threw myself into work, volunteering for gritty surveillance hours that I normally would have avoided. Three hours here, an overnight there, slowly the days strung together.

Information I wanted and didn't need filtered back. She had moved to the New York City area near where the Evil Stepsister lived, following her doctor there. Finally her treatments seemed to be working, and she was getting better. One of the nurses caring for her had donated bone marrow, a nurse who had also moved from Houston to Boston; I didn't recognize the name, trolling in memory through the women in white who hovered around her. No face stood out, I could recall no extra kindnesses that portended what came. Maybe they were discreet; maybe they were only friends until after she cut it off with me. Maybe I was too blind, too immersed in my own sorrow to see.

The two of them moved in together after Cordelia left her sister's. Alex had tried to be kind: "I think they're just friends. It's expensive up there."

"Two lesbians. The cats will be okay," was my answer.

I started avoiding my circle of friends after that. I didn't want to know anything else. They knew I had failed, that I hadn't been strong enough or wise enough or caring enough to get us through this together, and I couldn't bear the reflection in their eyes.

Instead I stared at department store dummies, nothing except paint in their eyes. It was the holiday season; I took on security jobs for several stores in the area, desperate to fill every hour with mundane routines to drag the days by.

I lied to Torbin and said I was going to New York to spend time with my mother and lied to her to say I was staying here and would be seeing friends.

She had needed me; I hadn't been there, hadn't seen it. Thought I could balance things—no, called it balancing when what I was really doing was hedging my bets—if she died, I wanted a life to go back to.

It was my safety net, and I wasn't willing to give it up for her. The trips back and forth were a show of caring, theater to prove I was willing to make sacrifices, hoping to fool everyone, including myself, that I wasn't giving up anything truly vital.

Scotch and self-pity made me think that was too harsh an assessment. Maybe I was trying to find a path that worked for us both and got lost along the way. Or maybe if I'd been a nurse, earning a living while caring for her, instead of a PI who lived in a different city and had to give up my job to be with her we could have held together. I wasn't and we didn't. Maybe there was no way for me to have succeeded; maybe every path led to this same failure—I couldn't give her what she needed, and in the end she moved on to somewhere and someone else.

The days had passed and I was now here. I had to put my life back together. I just didn't know how.

I glanced at my watch. The evening was too young to sit here staring at walls that only reflected my haunted memories.

I grabbed my jacket and headed out the door. The streets—and bars—of the French Quarter were enticingly close.

CHAPTER NINE

I wandered around, a nod to doing the right thing, taking a stroll down Royal and browsing store windows of antiques I could never afford. I went all the way to Canal Street, then back along Chartres, pausing in Jackson Square to listen to a lone trombone player. I tossed a five into his hat and moved on as a noisy group of tourists ambled up and he started playing the kind of songs they expected to hear. I was way over my limit for listening politely to "When the Saints Go Marching In" if the Saints weren't playing.

I had told myself I wouldn't end up here, this time would be different. But I was tired, didn't want to go home, and the bar stool called my name. I found myself ordering decent, but not top-shelf Scotch. I choose different bars, all in the gay section of the Quarter, often called the Fruit Loop because there were gay bars on every corner. I didn't want to be hit on, at least not by straight men. Being in my forties helps in the daylight, but in dim bars and after enough alcohol, some men think any woman is fair game. This was a safe space, mostly gay men, a few straight women, even fewer lesbians and, most importantly, good bartenders.

Two drinks, nurse them, watch the crowd, then go home and to bed, I bargained.

I spotted two drug deals, an almost certainly underage boy plying his trade among the older men, and one person packing a gun who seemed up to no good, but he left without killing anyone, so it wasn't my problem. Professional hazard. I hadn't lied to Ashley when I said I couldn't turn it off.

I was just finishing my second drink, debating whether to stick to my bargain or have one more, when the bartender solved the dilemma by putting a fresh one in front of me.

In answer to my puzzled look he nodded down the bar, indicating the person who bought the drink for me. I looked at the amber liquid. He had poured it from the good stuff. I was reluctant to look, to ruin the daydream high-end Scotch offered. I wanted a tall, dark woman; reality would be a short, rotund straight guy who either hadn't noticed this was a gay bar or worse, had and wanted to get his lesbian fantasy jollies.

I took a sip. It was already poured and couldn't be put back into the bottle. Nice. Very nice.

But reality called. I turned to look down the bar.

A woman. Tall, dark, and handsome. Amazing blue eyes. Not that I could tell in this dim bar, but I clearly remembered them from our encounter this morning.

I took another sip. I might as well enjoy the booze. I wasn't going to enjoy the interrogation. I suspected Special Agent Emily Harris was more interested in asking questions than wild sex.

At least the Scotch was good.

I gave her a bare nod, but I'd let her make the first move.

It didn't take long. One more sip and she was standing next to me, wedged in close between the next bar stool.

"To what do I owe the honor?" I asked, raising my glass at her.

"A test. I have a theory that women who like good Scotch can't be all bad."

"Far kinder than dunking me underwater to see if I'm a witch."

"Ah, she knows some history, too. Very good." She set her drink down next to mine. Same amber.

"I occasionally stayed awake in school."

"Good thing since you went to one of the best ones in the country. Expensive to sleep through that."

Of course she'd checked me out, seen I'd gone to Barnard. "I was a poor scholarship student. Had to work or I didn't eat."

She nodded, then finished her drink and motioned the bartender for another one. Maybe she was off duty and harassing me on her own time.

She waited until he'd refilled her single malt, then said, "Yeah, me, too. The parental units weren't thrilled with a daughter who wanted to go into law enforcement."

"So you always wanted to play cops and robbers?"

"I didn't want to play, they were okay with playing. I wanted it to be real. They weren't okay with that. I buy you a drink, you're not supposed to mock my maudlin stories. Isn't that the way the game is played?" Her voice was controlled, but I felt the anger beneath. She leaned into me, her hip against my thigh, invading my space.

I didn't move away; I wasn't going to give ground to her. Admittedly, she had a point. I was being a jerk.

"It's very good Scotch. Thank you," I said. "So, we're two scholarship kids who went into law enforcement, albeit through very different paths."

"You think you're in law enforcement?" The anger was gone; she seemed to be asking.

"I usually wear a white hat—a proverbial one, anyway. Most of what I do is missing persons."

"Skip tracing?"

"Not often. I mostly stay away from collection agencies. Leaves a bad taste in my mouth. I will sometimes take deadbeat dad cases. Much of what I do is look for adult kids whose parents want to find them. The nineteen-year-old who rebels by heading to the opposite coast and not communicating."

"Divorce cases?"

"No, at least not often. My current one really is a favor to a friend. But those can be messy and nasty and only worth it if I need the money. If I have to do extra work, I take on security gigs."

"How is that law enforcement?"

"Hell, law enforcement can be selling dogs. Just think what would happen if no one put in an alarm system or had a dog or did neighborhood watches. Better to prevent crime than solve it. A lot of my missing persons work is stuff the cops don't have the time or resources for. A few times my search has led to a grave and the cops have an ID on their Jane Doe. Once they know who she is, they can figure out who her creep boyfriend who killed her is."

"Neat and simple?"

"Rarely, but sometimes it makes a difference."

She nodded, signaled the barkeep for another round.

I was only halfway through my current drink. "What made you want to get into it?" I asked. "Despite your parents." I took a large sip as the new drink was put in front of me.

"Probably watched too many cop shows as a kid. Thought it really would be law and order and putting the bad guys away."

My earlier sardonic comment was taking a toll. She wasn't going to open up to me. I reminded myself that I wasn't the only one with a hard life. I could wallow in self-pity or I could be a decent person.

I said quietly, "We don't fail when we can't find justice, we fail when we stop looking." I finished my drink, then picked up the new one in a salute. "Don't stop looking."

"Even if it means tracking down PIs like you and asking a bunch of obnoxious questions?"

"Even if it means that." She clicked her glass against mine and we drank a toast. "If you want, I can point you in the direction of a few who truly deserve the third degree."

She actually smiled. Maybe it was the alcohol, but she had a killer smile. Her teeth weren't perfect, a little bit of a gap, as if her parents couldn't afford braces in the teenage years when things like that mattered and she had decided not to bother as an adult.

"Are you single?" she abruptly asked.

"Sitting by myself in a bar, what do you think?" I took a large swig of the Scotch, relishing the burn and smoke of it.

"Could be avoiding the mother-in-law."

"Yeah, I'm single." Then I added, "How about you?"

"Same. Single. Moved here recently. You been single long?"

"Forever. It feels that way. By the calendar a few months. You?"

"Since I moved here. She said I put my career before our relationship. Guess there's some truth to that. She's back in DC, already moved in with someone else."

"Mine's in the New York area. Same thing, already moved in with someone else. But I don't want to talk about it."

"Neither do I. Why don't we get out of here?"

It was getting noisy and crowded, karaoke about to start. I nodded and finished my drink.

I stumbled slightly getting off the bar stool. She caught me, wrapping an arm around my waist. I'd had more to drink than I intended. Once we edged through the crowd and I was on solid ground, she let me go.

I couldn't read her. If I had to bet, it'd be we'd walk out of here, say our good-byes, and head in different directions. Her actions, buying me drinks and suggesting we leave the bar, would be in most cases an invitation to spend the night. But this wasn't most cases. And she was one of the last people I should sleep with.

The air was cool, a mist of rain haloing the lights. The wet chill kept people off the streets. Once we moved away from the noise of the bar it was quiet and we were alone. We were walking to the back of the Quarter. Long ago the mistresses of the plantation owners lived here,

Dauphine and Burgundy Streets, away from polite society. Now it was mostly residential.

We walked in silence, though it felt comfortable, like we'd talk if we had something to say and not waste time with polite chatter. At the corner of Burgundy we both turned and headed downtown.

A light rain started to fall. I turned up the collar of my jacket.

At the next corner, she motioned me left.

I shook my head. "Home is this way." I pointed straight ahead.

"I live this way."

"Need me to walk you to your door?"

"No. This is what I need."

She pushed me against a car, a hand in my hair. Then her leg was between mine and she was kissing me, hard.

I thought to fight her, but the thought never turned into action.

There were moments in my loneliness and despair when I wondered if I'd ever kiss or hold another woman again. If anyone would want me.

I let her kiss me, found myself kissing back, needing the touch of her hands—anyone's hands, the smoky taste of alcohol on our lips. More than the sex, I was desperate for the affirmation that someone still desired me. Emily Harris was an intelligent, attractive woman. I ignored every warning bell going off in my head and let her have me.

A car shushed by on the wet street.

"This way," she said, taking my hand and leading us to her house.

Halfway down the block she stopped, still holding my hand as if afraid to let me go, as she took out her keys and opened the door.

I stumbled up the stairs behind her. She didn't turn on a light, instead closing the door behind us. Then her hands were on me—no, our hands, we both had our needs. Roving and exploring, taking and conquering. Time and touch blurred. The charge of her cool hand under my shirt, then covering my breast. Pulling her hips into me, my hands on her ass, noticing the firm muscles. Kissing over and over again. Her loud groan as my mouth covered her breast.

Then she turned on a small table lamp, the one flare of light in the night, using the dim glow to find our way to her bedroom.

We had both drunk enough that our want was little impeded by thoughts of tomorrow. All I wanted was her to touch me and keep on touching me. What she wanted—I didn't know. Maybe the same thing I did. It was easy to think we both were recently broken up and needing the kindness of a stranger. In truth, it was easy not to think. To let our hands and mouths and bodies take the lead, take over.

I saw little of her bedroom, just where the bed, our destination, was; didn't see where our clothes landed.

Then we were naked and she was on top, her hand inside me, her tongue circling between my breasts as if she couldn't get enough. Our only foreplay had been the kissing on the street. I was wet, embarrassingly so, a talisman of how much I needed this and how much power my need gave her.

No, this was about sex. Two bodies meeting in the night.

She pushed my legs open as if she owned me. I let her. Let her push deeply inside me. Didn't stop to say no, not so hard, or touch me here. It felt good; I came easily and again, but I wasn't able to ask for anything, as if this unexpected sex was too fragile and anything could break it.

Only after she'd made me come twice did she let me touch her, guiding my head between her legs. No words, not even my name.

As she had, I pushed her legs open more, teased her by kissing her thighs, around her mound. If she wanted something else, she could ask. She didn't, letting me explore her with my tongue, set the pace, soft at first then hard and direct, making her jerk and moan. Making her come once and then again and again, until she rolled away, panting.

We curled in each other's arms. She murmured something. I like to think it was "Thank you."

We lay still for several moments, the only mark of time the beating of our hearts. I tried not to think, to sink into the warmth and closeness of her body, to let the stupor of alcohol and sex lull me into sleep. But a small part of my brain wouldn't let go, couldn't trust we were here for the same reasons, an animal want and need. I didn't know whether it was me or her not to trust the most.

She spoke first. "Now that we've fucked, are you going to come clean about what happened?"

"Is this your usual interrogation technique? Get your suspects naked and in your bed?" I countered.

She stiffened. "No. You know as well as I do that we shouldn't be doing this."

"So why are we?"

She slipped her arm from around my waist and rolled onto her back. "The usual reasons. I'm lonely, no sex since the breakup. You're an attractive woman. Throw alcohol on that and do something stupid."

"You think I'm stupid?"

She sighed. "No, not you. This. Us sleeping together. To be clear, you're not a suspect, at least not yet, but you are a person of interest in a case I'm working on. I don't think you were honest with me, but I can't tell if you're protecting a client and it has nothing to do with the case or withholding information that could be important."

"No possibility I was actually telling the truth." I rolled onto my back as well, staring at her dim ceiling.

"No, not much. There was a gas station about a mile down the road. You say you grew up down there and knew the territory. Why stop and charge into the bush on private property when there's a nice civilized bathroom not that far away?"

"Maybe I forgot about the gas station. Maybe I really had to go. Maybe the family who owned that land and my family didn't get along and I welcomed the chance to piss on their property."

"Maybe you're really good at telling tales. It comes with the territory, doesn't it?"

"Yes. But it doesn't mean I'm lying to you." I wanted to tell her the truth, wanted to relieve myself of the burden of seeing that red ledger and knowing those lines in ink were people. But I couldn't. Ashley had warned me. Maybe I could roll back into Emily's arms and tell her what really happened, but too many alarm bells were going off. Even if she wasn't the mole Ashley cautioned me on, she could still charge me on withholding evidence and perjury. If she was involved on the wrong side of the law, revealing what I knew could be my death warrant. FBI agents aren't paid minimum wage, but top-shelf Scotch at bar prices isn't cheap, nor is living in a fairly nice place in the French Quarter. Running into her at the bar seemed a coincidence, but she could have easily followed me there.

I wanted to trust her but I couldn't. Even worse, I still wanted to fuck her, and that was the most dangerous thing of all. I couldn't touch someone like we touched and keep lying as well.

"Perhaps not being untruthful, if you define withholding the truth as different from lying. You know, this is your chance. Tell me now while we're naked in my bedroom and I have to let it pass."

Her words were seductive. I could give in to her body, but I had to protect my soul. "Why were you at the bar? Were you following me? I'm an idiot for not thinking you'd be thorough in your check of me. You had to know I'd just broken up with someone I lived with for over a decade. That I'm a bit self-destructive and drinking my troubles away. Easy sex and information for you, win-win, right?" I sat up, looking down at her.

"No, it's not like that. Yes, I could have found out the information if we needed, but, frankly, you're not that important in the investigation for me to spend the time looking. I didn't know about your breakup and I didn't follow you to the bar."

"Just one of life's little ironies, right? Of all the gin joints in the world, we end up at the same one?"

"There aren't that many gay bars, and we both live in the neighborhood. Bound to happen."

"Ever so conveniently."

"Look, can we back up? I told you I got dumped because I was too involved in the job. Enough that I ask questions at the wrong time. We—I screwed up by letting this happen. I'm only making it worse by trying to question you."

"Will you drop it?"

She hesitated, a deep breath in and out. "No. I can't. But I'll keep my investigation to the proper times and places. And we can't do this again."

"No, we can't," I agreed.

"We can't do this again until the case is over," she said, her hand reaching over to cover mine.

No, we can't because I still wanted to trust her, to not believe that she might be mixed up in human trafficking. But I couldn't. Her hand squeezed mine.

"I should probably go," I said.

"It's the middle of the night. At least get a little sleep."

"Probably not a good idea."

"Why?"

"I still want to fuck you."

Her breath hitched and she said, "Then fuck me and fuck me hard."

I rolled on top of her, shoving my leg between hers. Hard, fast sex. I covered her mouth with mine, my tongue waiting for no invitation to enter her. She grabbed my ass, pulling me tightly into her.

This time was different. We had admitted what was unspoken the first time—we shouldn't be doing this and we both wanted it. The knowledge set free our desires. We both asked for what we wanted, demanded even. Faster. A little lower. Touch me here. Kiss me like this. Two fingers, three. Deeper. Harder. Make me come. Make me come now.

There was no fragility; it couldn't be broken. We both touched each other as if this was the last time, barely holding on to the slender thread that we might be free again once this case was over. Once we moved beyond the places we could not trust each other. But I know that wasn't likely, and I suspected she did as well.

Sweaty, gasping for breath, we finally rolled away from each other, a lingering kiss, until we had to break it off to breathe. From there I fell into a dreamless sleep, safe from answering questions and needing to trust.

CHAPTER TEN

The harsh jangle of a phone woke me. I struggled to wake up, reaching for it. Cordelia got the calls in the middle of the night. Why wasn't she answering it?

She's not here. And won't ever be again.

My hand found only air where the phone was supposed to be.

From the other side of the room I heard "Emily Harris."

I wasn't at home. Instead, I was in a bed I shouldn't be in, with a woman I knew only well enough to know I couldn't trust her.

A bedside lamp was turned on. I squinted my eyes at the sudden light. Emily was sitting up, her naked back to me, the sheets tumbled around her. Her voice was a contrast to the setting, cool and professional. Her side was mostly listening, with an occasional question like "How long ago?" and "Who called it in?"

Then she said, "I can be ready in fifteen minutes," and hung up.

I glanced at her bedside clock. It was a little past five in the morning.

"They work you early, don't they?"

"I'm going to have to be a cad and ask you to leave. My superior is picking me up in fifteen minutes. I can't have you here."

"He's not going to drop by for a social visit, is he?" The bed was warm and comfortable.

"I can't risk it. Please, do this favor for me." She was hastily throwing on professional clothes.

"Might be easier to hide me in the closet," I countered. "At least that way you don't need to worry about him seeing me walking down your street with my pants halfway on." I could see the worry in her eyes. He might not know she liked women. Even if he was okay with that, he certainly wouldn't be impressed to find me here.

"I'm really sorry, but please, get dressed and leave." Her voice had an edge. She wanted me out of here.

I wanted to stay, less to sleep, but this would give me a chance to check out her place, a possibility she seemed all too aware of.

"Love 'em and leave 'em, right?" I said as I rolled out of bed.

"I am sorry," she said as she headed to her bathroom. She almost sounded like she meant it.

I hastily grabbed my clothes and threw them on. She wasn't going to allow me unfettered access to her apartment. All I could accomplish by dragging my feet was to get her into trouble. Even if I couldn't trust her, I didn't need to piss her off. She wanted me gone, I would be gone.

I needed the bathroom myself, but decided I could wait the six blocks to my house. Her fifteen minutes were ticking away.

She emerged to find me fully dressed.

"Let me out and you're free and clear."

"Thank you," she said as she walked me to the door, turning on lights as she went.

It was a nice place, a kitchen with high-end appliances and granite counters, clearly renovated recently with the kind of period touches like antique doorknobs and molding that cost money. The furniture was also new and nice, luxurious matching leather couch and chair, custom bookcases, the walls decorated with artwork. She either had great taste or had hired a designer. Or had family money, since this was beyond most government salaries.

But she quickly walked me to her front door, and I had little time for more than a brief glimpse.

She put the key in her deadbolt, but before opening it turned to me and said, "This…wasn't planned…"

"Kicking me out before the larks have woken up and farted? I should hope not."

She managed a bare smile. "None of it." She glanced at her watch. Then she kissed me, very briefly, and opened the door.

"I am sorry," she said as I went down the steps.

"Yeah, me, too," I muttered, but the door was already shut.

It was still dark out. My way was lit by a few outside gaslights until I got to Rampart with its major streetlights. Few cars were out at this time. I walked quickly to signal that I wasn't drunk and wasn't a target, should any miscreants be lurking. But it was late enough or early enough that even they should have been in bed.

I considered doubling back around to see if someone really picked her up. I settled for crossing Rampart and heading up her street until a convenient tree from Armstrong Park gave me decent cover in the dark. This is why smart detectives never wear neon green—unless it's underwear and can't be seen in public. My black pants and dark jacket faded into the shadows.

I looked at my watch. It had been eleven minutes since the phone call. My bladder wasn't happy about the detour.

"Alcohol dehydrates, remember?" I muttered out loud. It would make me look crazy just in case anyone was considering a quick mugging. Robbers don't like crazy any more than the rest of us.

At fifteen minutes precisely, a big boxy black car turned down Emily's street. It stopped about where her house would be. I was too far away to read the license plate or glimpse more than a shape in the driver's seat.

Someone who was either Emily or her double got in the car. Even a good block away it was easy to recognize her stature and brisk walk. The street was one-way heading into the Quarter, so they wouldn't drive by me.

Still I headed farther into Treme, taking the side streets to my house, the last few blocks at a jog, more for the sake of my bladder than worrying about things going bump in the night.

I got home, quickly closing the door behind me, to make sure the cats didn't try and get out.

Then I remembered the cats were no longer here.

I hurried to the bathroom. I had spent years worrying about the cats getting curious and getting out the door. It was habit. One I'd need to break.

Once my bladder was empty, I guzzled water and took two aspirin, a standard when I've imbibed on the heavy side.

It was still dark out. The late-winter sun would stay hidden for another hour or so.

I stripped off my clothes, tossing them into the laundry basket. I didn't want to smell any lingering scent Emily might have left.

Then I flopped into bed, willing the oblivion of sleep to come.

Of course it didn't. Instead my brain rambled through everything, picking at old wounds. In my much younger days there were a few mistakes when I took the cowardly path of sneaking out on the woman (women, in a few cases) I'd stumbled home with, leaving in the early hours. But this was the first time anyone directly asked me to leave on such short notice.

What was her game? Could it possibly be as simple as she alleged? She was lonely, checked out a local gay bar, saw me there, bought me a drink on impulse, and let the impulse—aided by Scotch—bring me back to her bed? A seasoned FBI agent?

It was as likely as the tale I'd spun about needing to pee and pulling off the road in broad daylight.

The solution to Emily Harris was easy. Avoid her until the case was solved. Until I had some way of knowing what she was up to. Until I could trust her. If ever.

The only solace was the sex was good and she seemed attracted to me. It wasn't much, but I'd take what I could get.

That left me mulling on the other upsetting thing tonight, forgetting about the cats, forgetting about the phone. Cordelia was gone, not coming back. Why couldn't I get that through my head? She certainly had.

The reasons were obvious. She was the one who had chosen to leave, so she had more time to plan and accept it. She moved to a new place, so didn't run into memories everywhere she turned. And if the rumors were right, she had someone to spend her nights with, someone to fill the space she'd left empty for me. Ten years doesn't go away in a few months.

Maybe I should move.

Or at least redecorate.

Somewhere in trying to contemplate rearranging furniture, I fell into a fitful doze.

Chapter Eleven

I woke in the late morning, finally pulled from sleep by a bright sunbeam on my nose. I was groggy and grumpy. It was after ten. Other than bar peanuts, I'd eaten little last night. Emily had kicked me out before breakfast.

First order of business was caffeine. Coffee with toast, plain, as I was too lazy to find the jam. The coffee woke me up and the bread settled my stomach.

Then a shower.

Then I could sort my day.

Aided with more coffee and toast with the newly discovered strawberry jam, I sat down to scroll through the messages on my cell phone.

None. That was quick work.

Emily hadn't called to apologize for the hurried exit last night. Maybe she was still out fighting evil. She'd get twenty-four hours, then she was dead to me.

Ashley hadn't called either. She'd gotten me into the mess. The least she could do was keep me up to date on what was going on. Maybe Ashley could call the dogs off.

Cordelia hadn't called. But she wasn't going to.

Get dressed, go to your office. Muddle through the day, I told myself.

I threw a load of laundry into the washer before I left. I could put it in the dryer when I got back, the only way I'd have clean clothes tomorrow.

I took a roundabout way to my office, stopping at one of my favorite Mid-City po-boy shops. I got both roast beef and fried shrimp, plus a large order of fries. Perfect hangover food. I could microwave the roast beef this evening, and that would be supper.

I'd eat lunch while checking messages and email at my office. About two bites of it. There were no messages. Well, there were some, one wrong number, one call about donating to a cause I had no intention of donating to, and three messages from the wronged wife who had changed her mind and wanted me to go after her husband again.

Email was equally scintillating. Messages about erection pills—do they send them to everybody because they haven't yet noticed that half the population doesn't have a penis?—about half-price events that I wouldn't go to for free, more donation requests, and a reminder about my mortgage.

The exciting life of a PI.

I called the wife back, told her I was busy and couldn't retake the case for another three weeks. I left the name of a rival I didn't much like but who was dumb enough to think I might refer him business.

That left me at loose ends, waiting for phone calls that might never come.

I don't like loose ends, especially mine.

I scrolled through my computer, searching for what I'd been doing last. Ah, the girl Ashley had mentioned, Kimmie Fremont.

I looked back over the file I'd made on her from what I could find on the Internet. It wasn't much, but thirteen years of life didn't leave much of a trail, no graduations from high school or college, military service, marriage, children, the things that leave marks on paper.

I wasn't going to contact the family, not unless I found a solid lead. But in the initial newspaper article about her going missing was the name and number of a detective to call. He might hang up on me, would probably blow me off, but sometimes cops appreciated a private eye looking into cases like this, ones they didn't have the time or resources for. It was only four years out—he might still be around.

I dialed the number and asked for Frank Mullen. He wasn't in and I left a brief message, just that I wanted to talk to him about an old case.

Then I considered the women listed in the red ledger. Did their families wonder what happened to them? What kind of life do you have when it's reduced to cryptic numbers, one line each in a cheap record book? Who was looking for those women?

Not me, I told myself. Not my case, not my area.

Right. I finished my last fry and put my jacket on.

Drive around, ask a few questions. I knew people who knew

people who might know something. I need to be legal, but I don't need to be nice and legal the way Ashley and Emily need to be. If they had corruption in their ranks, that might make things even more difficult. Other than a few scars on my soul, I was pretty clean.

I had given Ashley and her crew the generic sin city tour, highlighting the places vice happened. But there were a few areas I had connections in.

Tulane Avenue—nowhere near Tulane University—was slowly being gentrified with new apartments and business, waiting for the completion of the new medical centers there, one for the VA and the new LSU one to replace Charity Hospital. There was talk of a Bio District.

But some of the hooker hotels held on. This had long been the stroll for women down on their luck and men who weren't too choosy. I doubted the red ledger women were in this area. It takes money and logistics to traffic women, and that meant they didn't offer ten-dollar blow jobs. But what happens to a woman when she's no longer young and pretty enough to command top dollar? Some of them get out of the life and some end up in places like my first destination.

The motel had probably never seen better days because it wasn't the kind of place that had ever been a beacon of hope. It had probably started out cheap and tacky and gone downhill from there. The paint was slapped on, the décor tacky, a small sign that was easy to drive by. You either knew what you were looking for or you drove right by and never noticed it. There were a few cars parked in the lot, a large pothole in the middle. My three-year-old bottom-of-the-line Mazda was the newest one in there.

In a few years this would be gone, taken over by businesses clustering around the shiny new hospitals and medical businesses. Where do the women at the end of the line go when their line runs out?

"Sorry, all booked up and we don't do business with dicks anyway," was my greeting on opening the door to the office.

"Be careful who you alienate, Chuck. I counted at least four code violations with my eyes closed."

"Alienate. You and your big words. What the fuck do you want, Knight?"

Chuck was not a friend, not even really an informant. I'd stumbled over him while surveilling a business and noticing that some of the employees were using the back storage room for marijuana bricks.

Chuck was small potatoes, but he went down. The only favor I did for him was vouch that he indeed was pocket change and not very bright pocket change at that. I got the impression that he felt if he was going to prison he wanted folks to consider him a kingpin, but his small role did reduce his prison sentence. He didn't consider that much of a favor, just enough that he couldn't pull a gun on me. I'd seen him shortly after he got out and prison seemed to have been good for him. He'd lost weight and gained muscle. His hair was a neat buzz cut. But that had been a few years ago. The weight had come back on, a double unshaven chin, and his T-shirt was snug over his stomach, his pants hidden below the bulge. His hair had grown out but was a straggly knot that only emphasized the growing bald spot at the top. His skin was the pasty white of no sun and too much fried food and cheap booze.

"The kind of info only a man of your talents might possess." Flattery goes a long way in Chuck's world.

"Bullshit. And I'm clean here."

"In this kind of hotel?"

"What, you desperate? Want me to fix you up?" He cackled a laugh that showed he had two missing teeth and one gold one.

"Soliciting? You know that's illegal."

"Hey, it's a joke. I'm as clean as a whistle."

One I'd want to dump in bleach and leave there for a week.

"You're in the clear. I'm just looking for information." I held out a twenty-dollar bill.

He snatched it out of my hand.

"What kind of information?"

"Trafficking." I quickly added, "Now, I know it's not happening here. But word gets around. Anyone here who might talk to me?"

He looked down at the register, looking for long enough that I started tapping my foot.

Finally he said, "Bianca. She's on the second floor. She should be up by now."

"Room number?"

He rubbed his fingers together.

I handed him another twenty. "If you're wrong I'm coming to get my money back."

"Twenty-four. When have I ever been wrong?"

Most of your life, but I didn't say that. Chuck was another person who would be left behind when the new shiny buildings came.

I hadn't been lying about the code violations, just prescient. One room had a heavy-duty electrical cord snaking out to power the chugging window unit in the room next to it. A trash can was overflowing with a stack of takeout pizza boxes on top, the stale grease smell tipping into rancid.

Room twenty-four was in the top tier. The stairs were a sturdy concrete, the iron railings rough from painted-over rust. They were probably slick in the rain, but would hold me long enough to get in and out.

I paused outside the room, listening. Chuck could be sending me here to discover a dead body. In which case, I would take my bribe back from him and include interest. Inside a radio was playing softly, a not-so-soft voice chiming in on the chorus. I waited for the song to end, then knocked.

The radio snapped off.

I knocked again. Forty bucks meant I wasn't going away easily.

"Please open up. I'm a detective and I just need some information. Once we talk I'll go away."

Silence. Then soft footsteps coming to the door. A distorted eye in the peephole.

"What kind of detective?" a muffled voice asked.

I pulled out my license and flashed it across the peephole.

A chain, then a lock and another lock were thrown and the door opened.

"Private. Why didn't you say you were a private dick?"

Bianca, in her six-foot glory, stood in front of me.

"Oh, Lordy, and you're a girl, too. Just like them TV shows."

She wore a red kimono with matching red slippers, clearly her lounging outfit. Her Adam's apple and large hands—in addition to her height—gave her away as trans. While it was obvious to me she had started life being called male, her face was androgynous, with full lips, eyes on the cusp between brown and green, startlingly light against her dark skin, and her high and full cheekbones giving her a long, regal face. Her hair was short and pulled back. I guessed she used a wig while working.

"Yes, ma'am," I said. "I am a woman, but real life is not as exciting as television."

"Since you can't arrest me, you're more than welcome to come in. Would you like some tea?" She stepped aside to let me enter.

It was the same sad room as all the others, but she kept it neat, the bed crisply made, her clothes put away, with a few hangings on the wall to hide the baby-puke-green color.

"Tea would be lovely," I said. There is never enough caffeine in the world for days like this, so I wasn't going to refuse any that didn't look like it would kill me.

She ushered me to the one chair in the room, then busied herself with pouring the tea. Paranoid as I am—or reasonably cautious—I noted that she had a pot and gave us both cups from it.

"What are we drinking?" I asked as she handed the cup to me.

"Boring Earl Grey, I'm afraid. It was on sale, and as you can see this isn't the penthouse at the foot of Canal Street. I'm a bit down on my luck."

"Down on your luck how?" I asked.

"Let's not play social worker. If you know how to find this place, you know what it is. Had a stint in jail. So not a good time. It was here and in the trade or sleeping under the Claiborne overpass and begging for jobs that require asking if you'd like fries with that. No one wants to hire a con with a record, even at minimum wage."

"I'm not judging."

"Of course you are. Look, honey, I'm judging, so you might as well join me."

"It's not an easy life and there are risks to it. Some men think of working girls as targets."

"When you're an ex-junkie con, nothing is easy, trust me. It's only bad choices or worse choices. I may be a working girl, but I'm not all girl, if you get what I mean. No money equals no hormones, so I've still got boy muscles."

"I noticed. But all the muscles in the world don't stop a bullet."

She pulled her robe open to show a scar on her thigh. "Got that when I was eight years old, playing in the courtyard at the Lafitte Projects. If being a little kid playing with dolls can't stop a bullet, nothing can stop a bullet."

"We all should be safe. Kids especially. I'm sorry."

"Don't be sorry unless you pulled the trigger."

"I can promise you it wasn't me."

"Good, 'cause otherwise I'd have to poison your tea. But you didn't come here to talk about my troubles."

"No, but it doesn't mean I can't listen."

She smiled. A chip in one of her front teeth, but a nice smile. "Okay, honey, the reason I drink on-sale tea and live in this dump is that I'm saving money. Going to hairdressing school during the day, working to make ends meet at night. Got a friend of mine who is the goddess of nails," she flashed me her long red nails with streaks of gold swirling in them, "and once I have enough of a nest egg we're going to start our own business."

"Great nails," I said, not that I'm an expert on these things. I think I used nail polish exactly one Mardi Gras, alternating gold, green, and purple. It wasn't a pleasant enough experience to repeat.

"Yes, indeedy. So, let's get to what brought you to my door. I have to start my makeup soon."

"Human trafficking. I'm looking into a case that involves people, mostly women, being brought here to unwillingly work the trade."

"None of us are willing, sugar. Like I said, it's bad choices and worse choices. I'm an ex-con, same as few others, and some of the other girls here are, let's be polite and say too dumb to do anything other than lie on their back. Broken families, drug use. Girls don't choose to end up here, they're here when they have no choice."

"I'm talking about the difference between bad choices and bad luck and being forced. Women who agree to come here to wait tables only to be locked in a room, repeatedly raped until they're broken and willing to turn tricks."

"Gotcha. Worse than a bad choice."

"Look, I doubt anyone doing this is working out of here. It's too low-rent to make it worth their while. But what happens to a woman after she's been used that way? Maybe she ends up walking Tulane Ave."

"Maybe, but most girls here sing the same sad song I do. Jail, no job, no hope of a job. A lot of drug use brought them here. But a big organized ring? Not that I know of."

"If you hear of anything…" I pulled the last twenty from my wallet and handed it and my card to her.

"You'll be the first one I call." She tucked the bill into her cleavage. "If you ever want a deal on your nails, you let me know."

I glanced down at my short, blunt nails. "Not a polish kind of girl."

"Dyke dick." She laughed again.

I'd heard the joke enough times that I merely smiled. "Thanks for your tea and time," I said as I let myself out.

"Drop on by next time you're in the 'hood," she called after me.

A big roach was crawling into the pizza boxes as I passed the trash can on the way to my car. Not likely I'd be back in this 'hood again anytime soon.

I sat in my car, thinking about the way life twists and turns you. What if I'd been a kid shot by a stray bullet, left to grow up in a world where it wasn't just possible, but had happened? I used legal alcohol as my drug of choice and managed to not fall over the edge. I drank, too much at times, but I sobered up for work, for the important things in my life. At least so far I had.

I stared at the motel, rows of tiny rooms, stinking trash, populated by people who made bad choices and worse choices.

I needed to be careful about the choices I made.

I started my car and pulled out.

Barely half a block down the road, my cell phone rang. I pulled over and managed to grab my phone before it went to voice mail.

To my hello a voice said, "This is Frank Mullen. You left a message?"

"Yes, my name is Michele Knight. I'm a private detective in New Orleans. I was interested in a missing person case. Kimberly Fremont? It was about four years ago."

"I'm not sure if I remember that one," he said. "I'll have to take a look in the files. It may take a day or two."

"I'd appreciate anything you can tell me."

He hung up.

It was about what I expected. He didn't tell me to go fuck myself, which was a plus. My bet was he was going to kick it up the ladder before he answered any questions. He either was a callous bastard or had memory problems if he didn't remember the case. No one forgets when a child disappears, especially if the case isn't solved. Maybe he'd call back, maybe he wouldn't.

I put my phone away, checked the rearview mirror, and pulled out.

One more stop and then I'd call it a day. The only problem was this one might cost more than money.

CHAPTER TWELVE

The storied madams of the French Quarter were mostly gone or had moved to more discreet and less clichéd locations. My destination was one of the remaining ones. I'd investigated a company worried about embezzlement. It turned out their chief account was cooking the books. Some of the money was going to an obscure business with a P.O. box address. The name of the putative company was Red Sky at Night. Of course the next line is "sailor's delight," referencing the weather. But this company didn't mean delight in any climate-related sense. Madame Celeste and her girls had been entertaining the accountant on the company dime for several years. They wanted to go after her, but I managed to negotiate a deal where they got a good portion of their money back in exchange for silence.

Madame Celeste wasn't happy about losing the money, but she merely sighed and said she'd earn less money if she and her girls were in jail.

No matter how high class, nothing can take the stench out of one person with greater power buying the body of another person. However, Madame Celeste protected her girls as much as one can and still make money off them. They worked out of an old house in the part of the Quarter that's partly residential, partly commercial. She kept a bouncer at the door, which was only unlocked for customers to enter or exit. If a john caused a problem, they weren't allowed back. Same if they left an STD calling card. Madame Celeste had a doctor—I suspected he got freebies—who checked her girls on a regular basis.

However, her kindness only went as far as the bottom line. She was smart and calculating and if I wanted something from her, I'd have to give something in return.

I parked in a pay lot off Canal Street. That way I'd have an excuse to not drink.

The late-afternoon light was waning, leaving shadows that were a blue chill. I tightened my jacket as a cold breeze blew off the river.

The house was as I remembered it, strategically in need of a coat of paint as if to say nothing valuable or important was here. But the boards of the doors and shutters were straight and true. They would hold against storms of any kind.

I tapped softly on the door. It was late enough in the day that they were open for business. I glanced up at the camera. It was well hidden behind ivy, but I knew there had to be one there. No one got through the door without being vetted. I wondered how many senators and captains of industry had stood here waiting just as I was.

The door silently opened, the hinges well oiled.

A big man in a dark suit looked down at me and said, "Can I help you?" His voice was a low rumble.

"I'm an acquaintance of Madame Celeste. My name is Michele Knight. If possible I'd like to talk to her for a few minutes."

"Please wait here. I'll see if she's available."

He shut the door in my face—softly, quietly. It wouldn't do to slam doors in this kind of business.

I waited five minutes. Then ten. She was in. She was toying with me, seeing what I'd go through to speak with her.

Fifteen minutes. It was cold and the sun was close to setting. Light and its promise of warmth would be soon gone.

Just as I was about to give up and decide her game wasn't worth playing, the door opened.

The voice rumbled, "This way, please."

The inside was very different from the outside. Fantasy reigned here. The walls were papered with rich reds and golds, lit with expensive and subtle lighting. The furniture was antique or well-done replicas. Everything to make sure the clients felt they were getting their money's worth.

Mr. Basso Profundo led me to a back parlor, one with a wide and deep dark leather couch and a well-stocked bar.

I wondered if she was watching me on the camera in the far end of the room. Knowing it was likely, I did nothing except stand where I'd been left. She'd get bored and come talk to me.

I didn't have to wait as long this time. Only five minutes.

Madame Celeste entered. In her late fifties, she was still a striking woman. She had been evasive when I asked, but I suspected she had once been a working girl herself, one who commanded a high price. She spoke French and Spanish and knew more about wines than most sommeliers. That didn't come cheap. She was tall, almost my height, probably five-nine. Her eyes were a startling green in a face that could have been any race or a blend of them all. Her hair was black and thick, worn loose to frame her face. She wore black pants with black suede boots, just enough heel to look me in the eye. Her top was a soft gray sweater, cashmere I'd guess. It accentuated the still-voluptuous curves of her body and draped gently over the areas that age had to have affected.

"Michele Knight, how pleasant to see you." She held out her hand as if we were old friends.

When I took it, she leaned in and kissed me on one cheek, then the other, Continental style.

"Madame Celeste, you are as beautiful as always." I returned her cheek kisses.

"Can I get you something?" She pulled a bottle of forty-year-old Scotch from a shelf in the bar.

It far eclipsed the twelve-year-old stuff Emily had bought for me.

It would be rude to say no. And stupid to turn down better stuff than I'd ever be able to buy.

"That would be lovely. Just a finger, I don't want to take too much of your time."

She ignored me and filled up half the glass. I didn't argue. She poured the same for herself.

"Cheers," she said, handing me the glass, then raising hers in a toast.

I responded by touching mine to hers.

"You brought me a lot of business."

"Oh?"

"Not intended, I'm sure. It seems some of the other executives of the company liked what they saw. And learned enough to not directly funnel company money to me."

"Glad to hear you made up the money you lost."

"I was never quite sure why you did that. Why not just have us arrested? You had the evidence."

"They don't arrest the men, only the women. I guess I don't think that's fair. Plus, I was hired to stop the embezzlement and get the money back. If you were arrested, the papers would have been all over it."

"Indeed, who doesn't love a good sex scandal." She took a drink and licked her lips.

"That would have made the company look foolish and they wouldn't have gotten their money back. In an imperfect world, we do the best we can." I took a sip. That was a mistake. It would be hard to go back to the usual stuff after sampling something this good. It was smooth and complex, smoke and fire in amber liquid.

"I appreciate how you handled that. As you might guess, I have little need for high-and-mighty moral types in my world."

"And here I thought they were your best customers."

She smiled and raised her glass in my direction. "True. I meant in business dealings like ours."

"In that we agree. I have little use for the pious hypocrites."

"They don't like either of us, do they?"

I hadn't specifically told her that I was a lesbian, but a woman over forty who's never married and works in a job like mine is an easy guess. "No, they don't. But I didn't come here to take up your time on this."

"Yes, but it's more pleasant than the real reason you're here."

I arched an eyebrow. "You know why I'm here?"

"The bodies they pulled out of the river early this morning."

I kept my face neutral. "What do you know about them?"

"Mostly what I need to know. Neither of them were my girls."

"Can you be sure so quickly?"

"None of my current girls. Once I heard, I immediately checked. None were missing or unaccounted for."

"What about former workers?"

"I don't think so. Of course, I can't keep track of all of them, especially the ones who've been long gone. But…it's not the kind of thing that happens to us."

By "us" I took her to mean her expensive and protected women, not sex workers in general.

"How much do you know?"

She smiled, not happy, but knowing. "Probably more than you do at this point. I have connections."

"Of course you do. Far better than mine, I'm sure," I said. Mostly because she could blackmail them with what they liked to do with her girls. I would never have that kind of power. "Why do you think they were working girls?"

"First, that my connections quickly alerted me. They thought they might be. Also from the details they gave me. The women were young, had been pretty before the fishes got to them. Dressed in clothing appropriate for the boudoir. Black lace corset on one, a red leather bra and panties on the other."

"There were two bodies there," I asked.

She eyed me. "Do you not know or are you testing me?"

"I don't know," I admitted. "I'm here on a case about human trafficking. I hadn't heard about the bodies dumped in the river."

"Human trafficking? You think that's happening here?"

"You think it's not?"

"You don't think I'm involved, do you?"

"No. I wouldn't be here if I did. But you probably know more about this world than anyone."

"Good, because I'm not. The girls that work here seek me out and they want to be here."

Bad choices and worse choices. Maybe an astronaut or a model or an actress, but no young girl dreams of growing up and ending up at a place like this. But I didn't argue with her. Not while drinking her good Scotch.

"True, which is why they're not likely to end up in the river. What else can you tell me?" I quickly amended that to, "Are you willing to tell me?" Madame Celeste would share what she chose.

"It has people upset. It's not good for business."

"No, I can see it wouldn't be." I kept the sarcasm out of my voice.

But she was an astute woman. "Yes, that sounds callous. Two young women are dead, they died horrible deaths. That's tragic, but there is nothing I can do about that. I don't know them enough to mourn. All I can do is go on."

"Which means you have to worry about business."

"Exactly. I have some control over that. The rest…there is nothing I can do." Briefly, a look of grief crossed her face, but it was quickly gone, replaced by her practiced expression, one meant to hide all feelings.

"How will it affect you?"

"The girls are scared. I can't blame them. So I'll need more security. Plus the extra scrutiny. Some official might take it into his head to crack down on vice."

"Could they be linked? The rumors of human trafficking in the area and what happened to these woman?" I asked. It was a long shot, but I wanted to see her reaction.

"I wondered about that myself."

"Why?"

"The way they died. It seemed intended to give a message. Escape or rebel and this is what happens to you. They were meant to be displayed."

"What do you mean?"

"Are you sure you want the details?"

"I'm never sure that I want to know. But imagination is worse."

"Their mouths were taped shut, their hands tied, and they were lashed together, back to back. They had a stake shoved into their vaginas and their stomachs were slit open. Neither wound was immediately fatal. They were alive when they were thrown in the water." She paused, sipping her Scotch as if she needed its flame. "They could kick their feet, but tied as they were, if one was up, the other had to be underwater. With the tape on their mouths they couldn't scream and could only breathe through their noses. The cuts were precise, enough to go through skin and expose their organs, letting the water in."

"That's a horrible way to die," I stated. If it was a message, it was one delivered by a sadistic fiend.

"The stakes were wooden, thick enough to…have hurt and long enough to pierce flesh, leaving two openings into…the body cavity." The practiced look slipped. She, too, was horrified, telling me the details as if she had to purge them from herself.

I took a slug of Scotch, finishing it.

"No identification on them," she said. "They were thrown in the river Uptown, probably the park on the river behind Audubon Zoo, which says they were meant to be found."

"Yes, it does," I agreed. They would have been carried by the current through one of the busiest parts of the river, some major shipping docks, the Algiers ferry, the Quarter with its walk along the bank. That was a message, all right. "Do you know when it happened?"

"Not many details yet. Sometime last night. They were found around four in the morning."

Ah, Emily's phone call. I'd have to say I got the better part of the bargain. The details were horrific enough; actually seeing the women would be a searing memory.

"The worst thing? One of them was still alive when they were found. She died just as they got her up the bank." Madame Celeste also finished her Scotch, a long swallow that had to burn.

I shuddered. The abstract lines in the cheap ledger. What if these two women had been in those sets of numbers? Had they fought back? Tried to escape? Been not pretty enough? Or randomly selected as a way to show all those other sets of numbers what would happen to them?

Or I could be conflating things. This might have nothing to do with sex trafficking or prostitution. It could be a maniac who liked to lure women to a dress-up party, then brutally kill them.

The only things I could be certain of were these women died a grisly death and that it was likely Emily's phone call was about them.

"But you said you didn't come about them?" she said. She went back to the bar and lifted the Scotch bottle, pouring another drink for herself. She looked at me questioningly. I held out my glass and she filled it.

"I didn't think I had. There could be a link. But…I don't want to see the wrong monster because it's convenient."

"Tell me about your trafficking case."

I wanted to be honest with her. As honest as I could. "It's rudimentary. I'm working as a local consultant with some Feds. They asked me about vice in the city. I've given them the tour. But we stumbled over something that makes it seem an organized group has moved in."

"What did you find?"

"Just numbers. A ledger with odd numbers. It could be a weird code, but they corresponded with numbers used to describe a person, a woman. Height, measurements, weight."

"Were all the entries like that?"

"I don't know, I only had a glimpse."

"Can you get a closer look?"

"Not likely. We weren't strictly supposed to be there and the owners didn't seem happy about it. The authorities might have it, but I doubt it stayed there long enough for a proper search to find it. Why, what do you know about this?"

"Nothing, it's just interesting," Madame Celeste said as she turned back to the bar to top off her drink. "It's not like we have conventions," she said over her shoulder, "and can compare best practices. Always interesting to see how others do it." Then she spat out, "Amateurs."

"Why do you think they're amateurs?" I asked.

"Numbers that can be deciphered at a glance. The violence. It's too horrific for just control. It's from someone who enjoys the torture. This is a business and they seem to have forgotten that. Coming back—coming here. New Orleans is not kind to outsiders who think they know us."

She covered well, but I caught it. She knew something, but I wouldn't get any more from her tonight. If ever. I was a lone-wolf private dick and she had connections far more powerful than that.

I took a long drink. It would be a shame to waste it. If I wasn't sober enough to drive, I was close enough to walk home and could get my car tomorrow, although twenty-four hours of parking in this area wouldn't be cheap.

"Would you like me to keep you abreast of what I find out?" I asked. My hope was that I could learn more from her by revealing more myself.

"That's very kind of you." She gave me a long, appraising look. "I have a better idea. Why don't I hire you?"

"Hire me? For what?"

"Security. Or let's be real, the theater of it. I can tell my staff that I have a PI checking up on us. Occasionally prowl the neighborhood, even if it's just walking to meet friends or go out to dinner."

"What am I looking for?" Hoping for a hint.

"Oh, the usual. Slobbering men in raincoats."

No, no hints. "I think they're all on Bourbon Street."

She smiled. "Keep me abreast on what you and your team find out. Be available—within reason—to do security theater here."

"What would that entail?"

"Nothing too difficult. Give my girls a briefing on security tips, make them feel something is being done. If some are especially nervous, escort them home or to their cars." She smiled on the word "escort." A very knowing smile.

I did *not* want to be a security guard for a whorehouse. Madame Celeste knew that. She also knew she was driving a bargain I couldn't refuse.

"I've got a fairly full case load," I hedged. "But I'll see what I can do."

"I can make it worth your while." She crossed to me, standing close enough for me to smell her delicate perfume.

"Money?" I said. But didn't move away.

She smiled. "Of course, money. What else would I mean?" She

went back to the bar, took an envelope from a drawer. From it, she pulled a stack of cash. I watched as she counted out ten one-hundred-dollar bills. I finished the last of my drink.

"An advance," she said as she held it out to me.

I walked close enough to put my empty glass on the bar and take the money. It was green, it would spend the same. She watched as she handed it to me, making sure our hands touched. Was she flirting or just playing? It didn't matter, it was all fire.

I folded the money over and stuffed it in my pocket.

"Oh, and a bonus." She capped the Scotch, pulled a wine gift bag from behind the bar, put it in, and handed it to me.

"A very nice bonus," I said, taking it from her.

"And this is mine." She cupped her hand around my neck, pulled me to her, and kissed me, open mouth, tongue darting between my lips.

Fuck my life. I kissed her back.

Then we both pulled apart.

"Nice," she said with an impossible-to-read smile. Nice kiss? Nice that I let her? Nice that she'd gambled and won? "Roland will see you out." She pressed a silent button behind the bar, summoning the help.

He appeared as quickly as if he'd been standing at the door—which he probably was. Madame Celeste would not see outsiders unless she was well protected.

"This way, miss," he told me.

"Thanks," I said, holding up the bottle to indicate the Scotch. I smiled, too, trying to make mine as enigmatic as hers had been. Hoping my confusion would pass for it.

I followed the tall man into the dark night.

CHAPTER THIRTEEN

What the hell had I gotten myself into, I thought as I sat in my car trying to decide if I was sober enough to drive. The cliché "when it rains, it pours" came to mind. The heavy flirting with promises of more from Ashley, the unexpected tryst with Emily, and now one of the top madams in the Quarter coming on to me. Whatever her game was, that was a major kiss and she seemed to have enjoyed it.

Six months ago this would have been easy. Six months ago I was in a committed relationship. I would have politely refused Madame Celeste's offer, knowing that Cordelia would not be at all happy to find out I was working for a house of ill repute. Especially this one.

But she was gone, and the moral core I used to have seemed to go with her. If she was here, I wouldn't be flirting with Ashley. Or have gotten myself involved enough in her affairs to want to help and therefore wouldn't have knocked on Madame Celeste's door. Nor would I have gone out to the bar just to get out of the house and run into Emily there.

I finally decided that I was sober enough to drive the twenty blocks home. Plus it was good Scotch; the good stuff doesn't make you as stupid drunk as the bad stuff, right?

I had just enough smaller bills in my wallet to get my car out of the garage. I couldn't very well use the hundreds Madame Celeste had given me. Going to the bank was on my list of errands for tomorrow.

It turned out that I was far more sober—or not as stupid—as other drivers on the road. One stayed stopped at a green light oblivious to the honks behind him until the light turned yellow and he finally moved. Two cars behind him ran the red. I was safely in the other lane, then got stuck behind someone who was either lost, stoned, or trolling for action in an all-too-obvious way. I puddled along behind, content to let his slowness force the crazy drivers to zoom past us. Guess they didn't realize they were about to pass the police station on Rampart.

When I got home, I grabbed the roast beef po-boy from the trunk—it was chilly enough that it should be okay. That would be my supper. Given the two drinks, I was glad I'd eaten a lunch of bread and grease. Nor did I forget the Scotch.

Gym tomorrow as well as the bank.

I stuck the po-boy in the microwave and then thought to look at my phone.

Ashley had called twice.

Had my life turned into a fucking Feydau farce, women behind every door?

I needed to eat before I called her back. While I had been sober enough for a short drive on familiar streets, I didn't think I was up for much else tonight. I also needed to sort out the events of the last few days before I met up with a woman I was…what? Seriously flirting with? Thinking about possibly getting involved with, assuming that she wanted the same thing? A passing fancy in my loneliness?

Someone to distract me from the mess I'd made of my life?

I brewed a pot of coffee, not that I needed the caffeine this late, but I did want to be awake and alert and was hoping that red meat and caffeine would do the trick.

No confessions, I warned myself. Ashley didn't need to know what I'd been doing these last few hours, at least the stuff not related to the case. We weren't a couple, I wasn't cheating on her. Maybe someday I'd tell her—years in the future. If we were together that long, if we weren't, then it didn't matter. *Two years, at least two years before you tell her anything.*

A large cup of coffee and the entire roast beef po-boy later, I was ready to call her back.

It went to voice mail. I'd wasted a cup of coffee and now would be up all night.

Two minutes later my cell phone rang.

I stared at it as if it were a strange creature. Then shook myself. *You're not an adolescent.*

I answered the phone. "Hello?"

"Micky!" It was Ashley. She sounded happy to hear from me.

"Yes, I'm sorry I wasn't able to answer your earlier calls. Was out working on a case."

"Oh? Anything interesting?"

"No," I lied. "Boring records search. Had to turn the phone off in the archives."

"I've been thinking about you."

"That's a scary thought."

"No, not really. I know it sounds strange, but I kind of miss not having you in my day, just hearing your take on things."

"We can find a way to fix that."

"I was hoping you'd say that. I'd like to see you…both professionally and personally."

"Your wish is my command."

She laughed, a little seductive, a little happy. "Can we meet tomorrow, no, wait, can't—as much as I'd like to—how about the day after—and talk about it? Can I take you to brunch?"

"Brunch?"

"For business. I still owe you a nice dinner."

"Brunch works. What time?"

"How about around ten thirty? Can I really impose and ask you to pick me up at my hotel?"

"Not a problem," I offered. "Maybe we should go ahead and schedule that dinner. Before it gets away from us."

"A great idea. After we meet and sort out the business schedule, we can fit in an evening on the town. Work before play, after all."

"Of course. I do understand that." A pause, then before we said good night, I said, "Can I ask what happened to the warehouse we were at?"

"What about it?"

"The police came in, right? What evidence did they find?"

"They're still processing it, but we're following along. Don't worry, we're doing what we can."

"Did they find a red ledger? One with lines of numbers in it?"

"They may have. I believe there was a lot of paperwork."

"This one was different from the others."

"Different? How? And how did it come to your attention?"

"You showed me a ledger, remember? Then left to check up front. I looked at that one and then started looking through the file cabinet. I found a different color one and glanced at it. It had numbers that could correspond to height and measurements, like thirty-six, twenty-four, thirty-two. It could be how they kept track of their human cargo."

"Why didn't you tell me about it then?"

"We didn't have a chance, remember? That was after you left… after we were separated."

"Oh, that's right. I'm so sorry, Micky. I don't blame you for forgetting about it. I really wish that hadn't happened."

"I think we can agree on that."

"I'll check with the ones running the scene and see if they found it. You could be on to something. I'm glad you remembered to bring it up."

I had done my duty. Now I could get the red ledger out of my head. It was someone else's problem.

Almost. "Let me know what you find out."

"I will if I can. I'm in a business where we can't always make promises. Except that I'll see you soon and we'll make a date for our night on the town."

I smiled at that, we said our good-byes and hung up.

The caffeine hadn't been wasted after all. I managed to do all the dishes—not many given my lack of recent cooking, but even cereal bowls can pile up—and sort through all the snail mail that had arrived, putting most of it, save for one bill, into the recycling.

Then I decided the antidote to the caffeine was the very nice Scotch Madame Celeste gave me. As much as I was tempted to keep it only for special occasions, its presence in my house was hard to explain. I couldn't claim to afford it on my own, especially now I was living off one income. And I couldn't very well enlighten most people where and how I got it.

I poured, limiting myself to two fingers.

It tasted good. But the first sip, and even the second, couldn't still my brain. It ran from the pleasant thought of seeing Ashley again to wondering what I'd gotten into with Madame Celeste. To remembering the feel of Emily's body against mine—and being hit with a jolt of desire. *Animal reaction*, I decided. Touching a warm and willing body feels good, that was all. The third sip made me wonder what it would be like with Madame Celeste if we went beyond our kiss. How could I want a woman who had had so many others? But why did that number matter? She had to know more about sex and pleasing her partner than any other woman I'd been with.

I shivered. From the cold, I decided. The chill of night was seeping through the floorboards.

Another finger of Scotch defeated the caffeine.

I woke in the middle of the night, clasped in sweaty sheets as if I'd been fighting demons.

"Never mix coffee and good booze so late in the day," I muttered as I stumbled to the bathroom. I walked carefully until I remembered the cats weren't here.

"Bitch," I said as I flushed the toilet. I wasn't sure who I meant. Cordelia, or Emily for the bum rush, or Madame Celeste for playing me. Or Ashley for making promises she might not keep.

Hadn't kept yet. *You've barely known her a week*, I reminded myself. I shuffled back to bed and didn't wake again until my alarm clock went off.

Somehow time passed.

Today I had set my alarm for earlier than usual. I wanted to be well awake for my date—my meeting with Ashley. In the bright of the morning, my confusion of the night was gone. Of the three women swirling around me, if I had to choose, it would be Ashley. Madame Celeste might be a thrill for one night, but that was all she could offer— all she could offer me; we would never be easy with each other's world. Emily was both raw and hard, as if she had something to prove. Maybe after she did, she'd have time for another person. That might be a while. Ashley seemed the perfect blend of the two. More settled than Emily, but not as jaded and willing to do anything as Madame Celeste.

I showered, giving myself a good scrub-down. Then another pot of coffee. At least *this* was the right time for caffeine.

I did a quick check of email. Nothing demanding my immediate attention.

I dressed carefully for our meeting: a decent pair of black pants, a gray turtleneck with a cobalt-blue sweater over it. If I bother with a mirror it's mostly to see if I have spinach in my teeth or to make sure my hair isn't too wild. Today I looked critically at myself. Nothing would erase the over forty years I'd been around. The hair was still mostly black, but strands of gray and silver were creeping in. It needed a cut—more a shaping given how curly it was. Genetics were on my side. My mother still has smooth skin, and mine was following her pattern. A few faint lines at the corners of the eyes. I also had her cheekbones, high, almost sharp, going into the strong chin of my father. Eyes dark brown, skin olive, also from her, tracking to her Greek heritage. Tall for a woman at five-ten. Some muscles from the two to three times a week I dragged myself to the gym. Maybe a little weight gain from my twenties, but it mostly went to my hips and bust, filling me out and giving me a bit more of a curve than I had in my skinny youth.

"The mirror isn't broken," I said to my image. "You're doing well."

The breakup with Cordelia, the messy, brutal breakup, one I had to acknowledge was mostly from my failures, had destroyed any sense that another woman could want me. Only now was I beginning to get it back, buoyed by the events of the last few days. As confusing as they were, it did my ego good to have three women interested.

Ashley was waiting for me outside her hotel as promised. The sun brought out the red highlights in her hair. *Too glossy and vibrant to be a dye job*, I decided as I pulled up beside her. She was nicely dressed, in hunter-green wool slacks and a rust-colored sweater that was both appropriate for the weather yet still managed to not hide her curves. The sweater had help from a dark-brown leather jacket that also did a nice job of not hiding her curves.

She got in. "Where shall we go?" she asked as she leaned over to kiss me on the cheek.

"What would you like?"

"Something I can't get when I leave here."

"That includes a lot of things," I said as I pulled out into the traffic. "Why do I suspect you won't like boiled crawfish for brunch?"

"Because you know me too well," she said with a laugh.

"I have an idea," I said, remembering a restaurant on Poydras. It had valet parking, and the last time I was there the food was excellent. I was pretty sure they had brunch, and it was right around the corner from Ashley's hotel.

As I pulled up in front, Ashley said, "Oh, this is where you meant?"

"Yes, is this okay? Don't tell me you've eaten here recently?"

"No, this is fine. Can't eat in places like this on a government salary."

"Trust me, I don't eat here often," I said as I handed the key to the valet.

"But I have to treat," she said once we joined each other on the sidewalk.

"Why? Is there a government rule?"

"I asked you to meet me."

We entered the hotel the restaurant was attached to. "Yes, but I chose the place. Let me pay."

She sighed. "Only if you let me pay for everything when we go out."

"Sounds like a good deal," I agreed as we presented ourselves at the maître d' station.

"Ah, welcome back," he said. "It's good to see you here again." It had been over six months since I'd been here. Torbin had gotten his new job and Cordelia was feeling well enough to go out, so we'd come here.

"You're mistaken," Ashley said. "I've never been here."

"I think he means me," I replied. "I've been here before, and it's excellent."

The maître d' smiled as if to say we were both right. Although we didn't have a reservation, they had a table open.

Once we'd settled and ordered, Ashley said, "Let's do business first." She added, "Then pleasure."

"Business it is, then," I agreed, taking a sip of water to hide the smile on my face.

"I wanted to update you on the warehouse. I checked with the people there and they said they didn't find a record book like you described. It may be well hidden."

"I threw it at him," I remembered.

"You what?"

"I was looking at it when the big tattooed guy surprised me. He didn't look friendly. I threw it at him to distract him so I could get away. It should be out in the open."

"Good thinking," Ashley said. "If that's the case, he probably took it with him. It might have been too valuable to leave around."

"Shit," I said.

"There wasn't much there to prove who's behind it, but at least they won't be using that site anymore."

"Did the locals shut it down?"

"They're still trying to sort all the pieces together."

"But you've talked to them and let them know the real purpose of that place, right?"

"It's more complicated than that. We can't bring in every local cop without risking they're on the take or just might mention something over beers to the wrong person, so we have to be very selective in whom we tell what's going on."

"Like me?" I asked.

She caught my meaning—how could she trust me and not actual cops? "Yes, like you. I know I can trust you, but even so I haven't told you everything. I'm sure you understand that. Also, our assumption was the warehouse was no longer being used. We didn't intend to stumble on an active operation with you in tow."

I nodded.

She continued, "So you became more involved than we planned. Clearly you're not a crook, and in some ways you being private helps. Cops don't make a lot of money and it's easy to tempt them."

"Us PIs aren't exactly giving Wall Street brokers a run for their money."

She covered her hand with mine. "I know that. But you do make enough to occasionally eat at a place like this. Own your house."

"The bank owns a good part of it," I interjected.

She smiled. "Yes, but you qualified for a mortgage and can afford to pay it."

The truth was Cordelia used her money to put a large down payment, close to half, on the house. She had more money than I did and felt—at least then—that she should pay more. We had split the remaining payments between us. Now I paid it on my own. I could manage it, but it did mean I had to skimp on other things. However, I wasn't getting into that with Ashley.

She was talking. "It's different when you have a family, wife, some kids and want to take care of them and realize that buying a house, any house, let alone the one you'd like, is far beyond you. Makes it easy to decide that playing by the rules is a sucker's game."

"Okay, so you trust me—even though you can't tell me everything—in a way you can't trust the locals. Where does that leave you in what you can do?"

The waiter brought our food. Ashley had chosen the white chocolate Belgian waffle. I went with a more traditional breakfast, eggs, bacon, grits and a biscuit. I needed something to absorb the recent extra caffeine and alcohol.

"Much as we'd like to capture every criminal, stopping a small-time gray-market operation is not our top priority."

"That's what you think was happening at that warehouse?" I took a bite. Grits can either be a lump of stone or a slice of heaven. These were on the latter side of the scale. If they didn't make my stomach right, nothing would.

"It's what we have proof for so far. Yes, we know it's more than that, but the challenge is to prove it beyond a reasonable doubt in a court of law."

"What about the women?"

"What women?" she asked, fork stopped in midair.

"The ones dragged out of the river."

"How did you find out about them?"

"I have contacts," I said. "Could their death be related?"

"Related how?" she asked, taking a bite that muffled her last word.

"A message to women who might try to escape. Being a forced prostitute is better than floating in the river with a stake in your vagina."

"Wow," Ashley said, wiping her mouth. "You have good contacts. I didn't think those details had been released."

"As far as I know they haven't. Back to my original question, can they be related?"

She took a sip of her coffee before answering. "Yes, they can. One of the things I can't tell you is how."

"Can't or don't know?"

"Does it matter?"

"Yes. Do you know or not?"

"We…suspect. But it gets back to having proof. That's the hard part."

"What do you have to do to get proof?"

"Catching them in the act is nice," she said with a wry smile.

"In the act of killing more women?"

"Before that would be best." She took the last bite of her waffle.

I chewed on some bacon.

"We're staking out what we think is his office."

"But you're not sure."

"Can't be unless we get in there, but can't go in without probable cause to do so."

"What if someone broke in? What happens if a petty thief breaks into a place where there is evidence of a major crime?"

"Evidence in plain sight is admissible," she said, then quickly added, "I can't ask you to do anything illegal."

"You're not asking me anything. We're just talking hypothetically."

"Hypothetically, of course. Just coincidence that someone happens on this particular location."

"Or there could be a connection," I said, finishing the last of my eggs. "Someone overhears something to make them think they might find money or drugs there."

"At times that's how things work out, we get a bit of luck and everything falls into place."

The waiter brought the bill. I didn't even look at it, just gave him my credit card.

"You're going to need to do surveillance on this place, right?" I asked. "I have a lot of experience."

"We are shorthanded. Could be helpful to have you spell the rest of the team. I'll run it by the others and see what they think. We could have you watch the building when we know no one is there. Just in case." She smiled.

I returned her smile.

"Now some other business," she said. "We need a better idea of the land here. Well, the land and the sea. How could women, goods, and drugs be smuggled in? Are you up to help us with that?"

"This place is a sieve. Waterways everywhere."

The waiter brought the check back. I added twenty percent and signed it.

Once he had cleared away our dishes and taken the check, she asked, "If you were going to smuggle something in here, how would you do it?"

"I'm probably not the model you want. If I were going to do anything it'd be something small like rubies. Tie a parcel to a crab trap and have someone else pick it up from there."

"Not a great plan for human cargo."

"No, and that's why asking me that question probably isn't a great help. I guess I can't conceive of hauling human cargo—*unwilling* human cargo around."

"Can it be done?"

"It obviously seems to be. There's a lot of water here, bayous, lakes, inlets."

"How about the river?"

"Not likely. Most of it has levees, and that means you need a dock for a boat. Plus it's full of river traffic and patrolled by the Coast Guard. Not to mention you need someone who knows how to navigate it. Commercial traffic has a bar pilot who meets ships at the mouth of the river, and the pilot, not the captain, steers the ship in because you need someone who knows the river."

"Interesting," she said. "Okay, how about a homework assignment. Can you come up with some possible ways to smuggle human cargo through here?" She stood up.

"I can," I said, also standing. I helped her with her jacket. "But for everyone I think of there are probably fifty more. It really depends on who their connections are. The bayou rats each know different areas. The ones I know may be different from the ones they do."

"Very good point. But what I'm trying to do is show my team how easy it is to do this here and why some of the bigger organizations might choose a smaller city like New Orleans for their home base."

"Okay, I'll put something together." We started to walk out of the restaurant. "You're going to check about the surveillance job, right?"

"I am indeed. I might even know something by tonight. Can you possibly be available on such short notice?"

I handed the valet my claim check. "Lucky for you, I have nothing pressing."

"I'll call you later today, then. We'll have to postpone dinner until we're done with the surveillance. But perhaps we can plan to meet tomorrow. Lunch?"

"Lunch would be great. I'll wait for your call."

"Thank you. This was a great choice. I'll see you tomorrow. I'm close enough to my hotel I can walk back. No need for you to chauffeur me." She leaned in and kissed me on the cheek, close to my lips.

I waited for my car. The sunshine felt good on my face.

The valet brought my car. I tipped him a five. Then had to squirrel around the one-way streets of the CBD to get going the way I wanted to.

I was heading back to my office. I would take Ashley up on her assignment, although I thought it would be less than useful. If they were trafficking here, it would be through the routes they knew best or had best access to. There was no way to know that unless we had more information on them.

But she had asked; I would do it. And wait for her phone call.

CHAPTER FOURTEEN

I took as my starting point the raided warehouse around the Jean Lafitte area. Even narrowing it down that much still left a lot of options. It would depend on what kind of boat they were operating, but unless it was something huge, they could get in multiple ways. And this was just from looking at the map. I knew the waterways around Bayou St. Jack, where I'd grown up, much better. *Or had known them*, I reminded myself. Wind and waves change everything. Hurricane Katrina and the smaller ones before and after had shifted where the water met the land.

"Nothing stays the same, does it," I said aloud, talking to myself, to the sun shining in through the window. I still owned the land out there, but it was wild now, nothing to mark it save for a rotten gate post and the property taxes I paid every year. Until Katrina, the house I'd grown up in was there. We'd occasionally go there to get away from the city, a weekend of fishing and sitting on the wraparound porch to listen to the crickets and bullfrogs. But it had been washed away, nothing left save for what the water brought from other destroyed homes.

Nothing stays the same. I glanced again at the map I'd marked up. My life hadn't. Nobody's life did. I wondered how Madame Celeste— not likely to be her real name—had come to where she now found herself. Maybe I thought of her because her journey seemed so far from my own. Had she chosen that life, or just done the best she could with the choices she was given? Like Bianca, except as a black man in a body that wanted to be a woman, she probably had far fewer choices.

Ashley, I could understand. Grew up in a family of cops, decided she wanted to do something besides birth babies, and found herself in law enforcement. Maybe because I was given her choices, similar ones, and not the choices Bianca or Madame Celeste had been given.

I looked again at the map. It would do. If Ashley wanted something more thorough, she could ask.

It wasn't until almost five when she called.

"Hey, glad I caught you," she greeted me.

"You said you'd call. I've kept my phone around."

"It's a go. All we're asking you to do is sit around in a chilly car and observe an empty building. If you see anything that seems suspicious or out of the ordinary, you call us. Deal?"

"Deal," I agreed. If I got bored and investigated further, that was all on my own.

She gave me the address. It was out in the suburbs, in the I-10 service roads. I hoped it wasn't a well-secured office building. Not impossible, but it would make breaking in harder.

"Are you part of the surveillance team?" I asked. I could hear traffic noise in the background.

"Yes," she said. "I'm handing it off to Jack shortly. You'll take over for him at nine. Sandy will relieve you around two a.m. Don't talk or act like you know each other. We want to be as careful as possible."

"Got that."

"Good luck and stay warm. I'll see you tomorrow."

We agreed to meet around one for lunch, as I would have a late night. The game was afoot. After that, I closed up my office and headed for the promised workout at the gym and then home.

But after I got there, I wondered why I'd bothered. It was just another place to pass the time in.

"Better kitchen," I reminded myself. Maybe it was time to cook an actual meal.

That would require going to an actual grocery store. I settled for rice with beans from a can, with some caramelized onions mixed in. I plopped myself in front of the TV to eat and to pass the time until I needed to leave. I'd be alone in the car, beans wouldn't matter.

I am getting too old for this, I thought as I peed one last time. Nine o'clock felt more like bedtime than time to head out into the night for work. It was a little after eight. I wanted to give myself plenty of time to get there and locate the exact address. I don't travel out in the suburbs much; I had no mental space for them, so I couldn't picture this location although I must have driven by it countless times.

When the sun went down, so did the temperatures. I was dressed warmly. Heavy black jeans, Saints long-sleeve T-shirt covered by a dark gray zip-up sweatshirt. If I got too chilly, I could always turn the car on. I had a full tank of gas as well.

Traffic was light and mostly sane.

Instead of heading straight to the parking lot where I'd find Jack, I drove around the area. I wanted to know the roads that led in and out. Due to the canals, a number of streets dead end. While I hoped it wouldn't be necessary, I didn't want to risk having to flee and finding my way blocked.

The location was just off one of the exits. Much of the area was residential, save for what fronted the part closest to the exit. In the last few years, they've built a long wall between the interstate and the surrounding area. The good news was that the place was protected by the wall, so no one driving by on I-10 could see. If a little B&E took place, that could be very useful. Not that I was planning to do anything tonight. Much as I wanted this to be over so Ashley and I could finally be free to spend an evening—and perhaps a night—together, I didn't want to rush into this. Another night or even two checking things out, even if it meant dragging myself out here this late, was a good plan. The dead women meant these guys didn't play around.

It was an older neighborhood, the small houses indicating most of them were built in the fifties or sixties, probably before the interstate bisected the neighborhood. The cars here were not the latest models; the streets were quiet, with few people out. The people who lived here worked and had to be in bed to get up in the morning. Good in that few inhabitants would be around; not so good in that this was the kind of place where a strange car or person would be noticed.

The actual office was, however, more commercial, next to a child-care center and pawn shop. Interesting combination. They were all located in a long strip mall. Even in the dark it was showing its age, had probably been built around the time of the houses in the sixties and meant to be torn down thirty years later and replaced with something better. But nothing better had come along, and it was still here. The putative Alligator Shipping and Export, Ltd. office was at the far end. On the other side of the strip mall was a pizza place still doing a decent amount of business, a closed nail salon, and a more permanently closed store with tattered Going Out of Business signs in the window.

There was a decently large parking lot for all the buildings. I drove around, spotting Jack in his car. I chose a spot about midway, close enough to the pizza place to look like I might be there, but not so close that I'd be quickly spotted hanging out in my car.

Jack was already pulling out before I turned my motor off. If he was smart he'd have waited a few minutes. But no one seemed to be paying any attention, and maybe he wanted to get back to Sandy. Or to pee.

I considered going into the pizza joint and buying something to give my being here a patina of reality, but rejected the idea. The place seemed to have mostly adolescent white boys as customers, and a middle-aged woman like me would stand out. The beans would do me fine and the last thing I needed was anything to drink.

If anyone asked, I'd say I had a fight with my boyfriend, had stormed out and needed some time to think about things.

Not that anyone asked.

The pizza place closed up around ten and even the cleaning crew was gone by ten thirty.

My car was getting cold. No, my car was probably fine; it was used to all kinds of weather. I was getting cold. I turned the car on, although I left off my headlights and moved about ten spaces closer to the office. I left the engine on long enough to get warm again.

I planned to case the building, but wanted to wait until after midnight to do so. The later it was, the fewer people were likely to be around. Boring as this was, sitting here for a few hours would give me time to watch the routine for the place. How many cars came past on the service road? Was anyone working late? There were still a few cars in the lot, but they were all back in the most well-lit area, like someone had left them there while out of town or this was where they parked.

I didn't do things like read or listen to the radio while on stakeouts. Not looking and not listening can cause problems. Yes, it's boring, but observing is what I was paid to do. Not that we talked about pay, but I trusted Ashley to be reasonable and businesslike about this.

I liked that she was taking her time. We were getting to know each other, not just through movie or dinner dates, but by actually working together. Much as my body relished the tryst with Emily, she came on too hard, no warning or notice, as if she was too focused on work to know how to interact with a human. I was also annoyed that she just assumed I'd say yes—and chagrined that's what I'd done.

I could use a little romance right now, not the hard sex Emily offered. I didn't want a fuck buddy, I wanted someone to go to the grocery store with and pick out food to cook for a special meal, to call when I was having a rough day, to make popcorn with, watch an old movie and snuggle afterward.

I wanted someone to replace Cordelia.

Maybe Ashley was that person. Or maybe she was the person who could help me find my way out of the fog, to be a person who might find love again.

In the distance a church bell tolled midnight.

I gave it another fifteen minutes. Some shifts might end at midnight. I didn't want to be prowling around the back of the building just as a neighbor was coming home.

At 12:16 a.m. I got out of my car. It was even colder outside than in. Feeble as it had seemed, my body heat had added some warmth to the car. The air was damp, adding to the chill. It would probably rain before morning.

I walked slowly to the office, taking my time, like a wronged girlfriend trying to clear her head. It was about twenty feet across, a tacky fake brick façade on the front, with a heavy wooden door and two windows on either side of it. I was able to press my face against the window and see there was an alarm keypad inside the door. The interior was dark and I could make out little. I had stuffed a small flashlight in my pocket but didn't plan to use it unless it became necessary.

Scanning the parking lot and seeing no one, I moved to the side of the building. Drat. It had one small window—why did I think bathroom—that was high and would be hard to reach. The silver lining was the property was marked by a ragged line of bushes. Like most of what was here, regular maintenance wasn't a priority, so they were tall and shaggy. If I had to come back with a ladder, they would give some cover. There was about two feet between the building and the bushes, the usual clearance to keep the bugs and mold away from the structure.

I slid quietly to the back. It was set up much like the front. Two windows and a door leading to an unkempt stone patio surrounded by a wooden fence. The fence, like everything else, was old, short enough that I could easily look over it. It wouldn't take much to remove a board or two.

Or even reach over and open the back gate, as I easily did. The small yard outside the fence sloped down to a drainage ditch. Memo to self—do not run hastily out of here without making a sharp turn. They've pulled alligators out of suburban ditches. And water moccasins.

I considered a quick look with my flashlight to see if any red eyes stared back at me, but decided against it. There were houses across the ditch and it wouldn't do for them to see a light where there shouldn't be one. This was more exposed, but the door and windows were old, and from the looks of it could easily be jimmied. That didn't solve the alarm problem, but maybe I could take care of that by cutting the wires. Most alarm systems had battery power now, mine certainly did, but the keypad looked old, so maybe the alarm was old as well. This was the suburbs, a safe area.

But I wasn't going to try anything tonight.

I made my way back along the side of the building, looking for the electrical box. It was near the front, high up enough that the bottom edge was about brow height. As a test, I tried to open the cover. Too bad I was right. It hadn't been opened in a while and might take work to pry open. Bring WD-40 and a sturdy screwdriver, I told myself.

I cautiously stuck my head out to scan the parking lot.

A car was driving this way.

I slunk back into the shadows, taking several paces back, then pushing into the bushes, using their mass to obscure my presence. They were thick enough that getting through the branches would be difficult, but it was a better alternative to the ditch.

The car was probably nothing, someone cutting through the parking lot on their way home.

I couldn't see the lot from where I was. I held my breath and listened. Car wheels on asphalt. Getting louder. Light slid around the side of the building. The headlights of a car.

Keep going, I told it.

The wheels stopped.

I pushed against the bush, trying to melt through it. It was too dense; I started pulling branches aside while still looking to the front of the building.

The engine turned off, but the lights were left on.

I had to be quiet; this was not the time for broken twigs. What the hell would anyone be doing here at this time of night?

Other than yourself?

Maybe this is when the crooks came out to play.

Doors slammed. Two? Three?

The sound of shoes on the macadam.

"This don't look like no drug den," a voice said.

I was no more than fifteen feet from the front of the building and therefore them.

"Shut up. We need to be quick." Another voice. Both male.

I had my cell phone with me but didn't dare use it. I tried to quietly step over twigs and into the bush, but a sturdy branch at my back wasn't moving.

"Cut the power," the first voice said.

Major, double shit. I pulled a branch in front of my face. If I was really lucky, they wouldn't bother to check out that someone else might be around. This is why I always wear black to events like this. Hiding in the shadows is never out of style.

What are the odds that someone else would break into the very place I was planning to break into?

I weighed my options. I could skitter as quietly as possible to the back, hope they didn't seem me, hope I could get out on the other side of the strip mall. But movement was a much more likely giveaway than staying still. I could try to shove through the bush and hope the branch at my back would give way without enough noise to alert them. Or I could stay as still as possible here, hope they wouldn't spot me and we'd all have a happy ending. If they wanted drugs, I was happy to let them pilfer drugs.

If they did see me, my options were about the same, shove through the bush—I wouldn't need to worry about making noise at that point. The branch binding me felt breakable, just not quietly so. That seemed my best option. On the other side was a street, and half a block would take me into the residential area. If they followed, I would start yelling "Fire," and that would get the populace out on the street.

"You cut the power. I don't know nothing about that shit."

"What kind of faggot are you, you can't flip a circuit breaker."

"The kind of faggot that doesn't like getting his fingers fried."

So far I'd heard only two voices.

"At least you know what to call it." A third voice.

"Yeah, whatever. Let's get this over with. It's fucking cold out here."

The beam of a flashlight shined down the side of the building.

I held my breath, trying to see what was going on and yet be as still as possible.

The light blinded me.

Then quickly swung away.

The patron saint of private detectives had been kind. He was only using the flashlight to find the electrical box and wasn't looking ten feet beyond it. Once he spotted the box, he turned the light on it, leaving me in relative darkness.

I took a shallow breath and looked at the man at the circuit box.

He was tall, heavyset, with several days' growth of beard. He wore a knit cap, so it was hard to tell hair color in the feeble light, but it looked either light brown or dirty blond. He had a weak chin, one that didn't help a face only a mother could love—narrow-set, beady eyes and a hawkish nose, crooked as if it had been broken a few times. His jowls were starting to sag, although he looked to be no more than late twenties or early thirties.

"Goddamn it," he let out as the covering failed to open for his scrabbling fingernails. "Give me a fucking screwdriver."

The light flashed across my face again.

Then away, again just random movements, not a search.

A second man came around the building. He was slight, skinny in an unhealthy way, his shoulders sloping. He had floppy brown hair in need of a cut and a smattering of stubble across his cheeks and chin as if he was trying to grow a beard and didn't notice he'd failed. "Here's your fucking screwdriver, bro."

"Fuck you very much," the first man said.

They laughed.

Meth mouth. They both exhibited the graying, rotted teeth of habitual meth users.

The first one, Mr. No Chin, took the screwdriver and jammed it under the lid, using it to lever the electrical box open. It came loose with a loud screech. They didn't seem to care.

Mr. Chinless jammed his hand in the box and flipped all the switches.

"Hey, you turned everything off," the third man from out front said.

"Who gives a fuck," Mr. No Chin muttered.

"The light at the day-care place went out."

"Like I said, who gives a fuck."

The light retreated. They went back to the front of the building.

Then a loud pounding. It sounded as if they were sledgehammering through the front door.

"Hurry, faggot," Mr. No Chin said. This sounded like a loosely organized gang and he was its loosely organized leader.

Another bang, then a splintering crash.

I used the noise to break the branch pinning me in and shoved through the bushes. It was no time to be careful; I was scraped in several places, including a rip in my pants. Damn, and they were my only pair of winter-weight black surveillance jeans.

Instead of being sensible and hightailing it to a quiet residential street, I crept behind the bushes until I could see as much of the lot as I dared. I wanted to know what these thugs were up to.

Mr. Third Man was also skinny, although he appeared as if he'd once had weight and been healthy, a hollowed-out man, still wearing a high school letter jacket that was now too large for his emaciated frame. His hair was a thinning, flyaway blond, a faint penumbra around his head in the far-off light from the interstate. He had once been handsome, I guessed, it was still barely visible in his concave cheeks, sunken gums, and eyes that seemed permanently dazed. He seemed capable of little more than watching guard in places that didn't need to be watched.

They weren't amateurs, but they were far from their prime.

It was time to fuck with them.

Mr. Third Man was mostly watching his friends inside the building. Perhaps he was being diligent and listening for the sound of sirens.

He certainly wasn't listening for stealthy steps around the dim edge of the parking lot. I carefully made my way back around to my car.

If they just got the drugs and ran, we'd all be happy. But it was possible there were no drugs there. It was also possible they'd find the drugs, but think there was more, and tear the place apart. Meth heads are crazy and I didn't want to have to wait around for crazy to finally decide their crazy was done.

My car was still parked more to the center of the lot. It had given me a wide view of the office and the parking area. And most blessedly was now behind where Mr. Third Man was looking.

I trotted when the noise was covered by what they were doing—which was most of the time. In about a minute I was at my car.

In the glove box I have a big, emergency flashlight, one with a red blinking light on the back. It's meant to be used in case of a breakdown on the road, to warn other drivers. Not the greatest theatrical prop, but it would have to do. I fumbled in the backseat and found the big road atlas, one I rarely use in these days of GPS. It would also do.

Show time.

I slapped the blinking red light on my dashboard, started up the engine, hit the headlights on high beams, and—this is why I love a stick—squealed my tires as I revved the engine. I charged halfway across the parking lot, then slammed on the brakes, taking care to leave the thugs a wide escape patch.

I reached across the passenger seat and threw open that door, then did the same on my side, so it looked like two people got out and were hiding behind the doors.

Using the rolled-up atlas as a bullhorn, I yelled, "Police! Drop your weapons and come out!" The high beams should be blinding enough they wouldn't see it was only a rolled-up map.

Then for kicks, I hit the horn, blaring a long blast.

"Police!" I repeated.

Yeah, this got their attention. Mr. Third Man was gaping, as if trying to understand how a cop car could be here without him having noticing it before now.

Mr. No Chin and Mr. #2 were not so philosophical. They charged out of the office and jumped into their car. I was concerned they were in such a hurry they'd leave Mr. Third Man, but he managed to jump in at the last moment.

"Police!" I yelled again and hit the horn.

They roared out of the parking lot, well over the speed limit when they got on the service road. At least it was late enough there was little other traffic about.

I remained in my car until they were well out of sight, only then parking it in a reasonable fashion and getting rid of the props. Then I grabbed a pair of gloves out of the stash I kept in my car and headed for the office.

I wasn't going to stay long, but I wanted a look around. At the warehouse I didn't have time to get more than a glance at the ledger, not enough to remember it. Ashley had implied someone was on the take, someone supposedly working on her side of the law. I didn't want anything to get lost because it fell into the wrong hands.

Misters 1, 2, and 3 had left the place a mess. The door had been shattered, left in pieces. Once inside, their method was to toss and destroy. I risked turning on my flashlight. The first area was bare save for one desk that was probably only there for show, given how little had been tossed from it.

But no reasonable crook would keep anything out here.

I quickly made my way to the back. But that was a small kitchen and break area.

Heading back to the front, I looked first in one office. It was torn up, but again not enough to suggest it was actually a working office. The next office was the same. The third office was also bare, but it looked like it had some use. There was a computer on the desk, some area maps, including nautical ones. It would be up to the cops to get into the computer. No way was anything I'd like to see not password protected, and I'd given myself ten minutes max to be out of here. I glanced at the maps, quickly taking photos of them with my cell phone. They might be a clue to the smuggling routes. But little else was there.

Seven minutes had passed.

One more door.

A janitor's closet.

I closed it.

Then opened it again.

There was a heavy-duty locked box on the top shelf. The Three Thugs hadn't even opened the door. I grabbed the box off the shelf and hurriedly carried it to the front office, where I put it on the desk. Before opening it I glanced outside to the parking lot. Saw nothing.

The Three Thugs had left their tools. I got the screwdriver and used it to pry open the locked box.

Drugs. Of course. A couple hefty bags of a white powder. I put those aside.

A red ledger, just like the other one I'd found. Maybe even the same one.

I opened it. No, not the same one, this one was barely started, less than a page filled. There were only ten entries. I took a photo. Below the last entry an odd message was scrawled: *Eula May, 9 at 11 on 18 up the bayou by the germans.*

I didn't know what it meant, but I took a picture anyway.

Tucked into the back of the ledger was a picture of a woman in a red leather bra. She was very much alive and her expression was one of terror. I swallowed my bile and took a picture of that as well.

Nothing else was in the box.

I put everything back the way I found it but left the box itself sitting on the desk up front.

Eleven minutes. Time to get out of here.

The parking lot was still empty. I trotted to my car, stripping off the latex gloves as I went. I got in and drove over to the end with the shuttered pizza parlor. It was almost one o'clock in the morning.

I dialed Ashley's number.

She answered on the second ring. "Micky? Where are you?"

"On the stakeout. Three crooks just broke in." I almost said "before I had the chance to," but we'd agreed to pretend I wasn't going to do that. "I managed to scare them off."

"What?" she said, sounding confused.

"Sorry, no time for a long story. They made a lot of noise and someone probably called the police by now."

"Oh, shit, you're kidding," she said. "Who the hell would break in?"

"Meth heads who thought they would find drugs here."

"Fucking amateurs," she muttered.

It was odd, but I remembered Madame Celeste saying the same thing. But about different people.

"Yeah, anyway, the place has been broken into. Once I'd scared them off, I did a quick check inside. To make sure no one was in there and hurt."

"Of course, makes sense."

"What do I do now?"

"What do you mean?" I'd probably woken her up; she didn't seem to grasp the situation.

"Do I call the police and pretend to be an innocent citizen who happened on this? Do I get out of here and hope someone else will call it in? Turn the power back on and let the alarm wail? What do you want me to do?"

"I don't know." Then she said, "Wait, give me a moment to think. It needs to be called in, but it's not a good idea for you to do it. Can you turn the power back on? See if that sets the alarm system on?"

"I can do that."

"Call me and let me know what happens."

"It may be a while. Once the alarm goes off, I'm gone and not stopping until I'm far gone out of here."

"That's okay. Just call and let me know."

I hung up. I needed to exit this place. The meth trio might have pooled enough brain cells between them to begin to wonder about the cops who didn't bother chasing them. It was still possible someone had called the police and they were dealing with more important crimes before making it here.

I drove back close to the office, not directly in front, but a short sprint away.

I hastened out of my car and went back to the circuit box, barely remembering to put my latex gloves back on.

At least the day-care place would get its power back. Hate to have the milk spoil for the kids.

I flipped the circuit breakers to the on position. An alarm started to wail.

I sprinted to my car, didn't bother taking the gloves off, and sped out of the lot. I was only briefly on the I-10 service road, heading back into the residential areas, a turn and then another turn before slowing to a sedate speed, as if I was someone coming home late at night. Nothing to see here, keep going.

Chapter Fifteen

I drove through the residential areas, slowly squirreling my way back to Veteran's, the main drag here in suburbia land, using that to get back to safety, aka Orleans Parish.

Once I was sure no one had followed me—and my nerves had calmed enough—I found a place to pull over to call Ashley. Before I called her, though, I emailed all the pictures I'd taken to my office computer. Back up, back up, and back up again.

Praise the fates for speed dial, I didn't think I could punch in digits and at two in the morning it's not nice to call a wrong number.

She answered on the first ring. "Where are you?"

"Where am I?" I looked out the window to get a clue as to where I was. "On the side of the road, Esplanade I think. Up near City Park. I came the back ways."

"You're away from the site? Did the police come?"

"I don't know. Probably. I turned the power back on and that set off the alarm. Didn't think it prudent to hang around and see."

"Okay, I'll check on it. Did you see anything? Find anything?"

"I didn't have much time, so it was a quick look around. Some drugs the meth heads missed. Another ledger."

"You found that? In not 'much time'?"

"Most thugs are only smarter than their thug buddies, and most thugs are stupid. There are standard places to hide things, like in the food pantry or the kitty litter. Places they think people won't look."

"So you found another red ledger."

"Yes, but this one was a new one, only about ten entries in it. Hard to think that they ran out of space in the first one and had to start a new one."

"Maybe they lost the last one and needed another. Did you take it with you?"

"No, I left it there, for the police to find as evidence."

"Of course, smart move. Why don't you come here?"

"Here?"

"To my hotel. So we can talk this over."

"It's late, you should get back to sleep."

"I can't sleep worrying about you. This is the second time it was supposed to be an easy assignment and instead something dangerous happened."

"I really am okay," I told her. "A little shaken up, but that's not the first time this happened."

"Just come here. Let's talk this through, okay? I need to debrief you and we might as well do it in a comfortable place with room service. Are you hungry?"

"I'm fine," I said, not that I'd thought about food until just now. "We don't need to take too long doing this."

"We'll take the time we need. You can crash here if you like or go home if you prefer."

"Thanks, I'll see you soon."

I was wired, still on an adrenaline rush and not likely to be sleepy for several hours. I put my phone away, buckled my seat belt, checked my rearview mirror, and pulled out. Late-night drivers are often less-than-sober drivers and I wanted to give the cops no reason to pull me over. That would be too much, the wrong people break in and I get caught for the wrong reason at the wrong time.

Most houses were dark; only a few distant headlights and an occasional streetlight pierced through the night until I got closer to the Quarter, the place where the city never slept. It did, however, stumble and weave drunkenly, especially the drivers. I slalomed around the slow-moving drunks on Rampart as I headed to the CBD.

I made it to Ashley's hotel in good time. Even the crazy French Quarter traffic didn't slow me down as much as it usually would.

I left my car with the valet. I'd need to check before I retrieved it that I have enough money on hand to pay for parking. Or maybe Ashley would cover it.

She'd given me her room number, so I walked purposefully through the lobby, the stride of someone who belonged here. Being female and middle-aged made me unthreatening, almost invisible. Besides, a hotel this close to the Quarter had to have seen its share of people coming in at all hours. This is a city where the bars never close.

I tapped softly on Ashley's door.

She was waiting for me and quickly opened it.

"Come in," she said, giving me a hug in the entryway.

She had a small suite. I'd entered into a sitting area with a table off to one side and a wet bar in the corner. On the table was a fruit-and-cheese tray and a bottle of wine.

She noticed my gaze. "Thought you might be hungry," she said.

"Thanks, but you didn't need to do that."

"I know, but it seemed the least I could do. Sit." She motioned to the love seat.

I obeyed, plopping myself into its deep cushions. It felt good to finally be at rest.

She brought the fruit tray and wine to the coffee table and took the overstuffed chair next to it. Our knees were close, but we could look at each other. Her briefcase was beside it, and she pulled out a notebook.

"Walk me through what happened," she said. She put her pen down on the coffee table and grabbed a few grapes.

Verbal report, I told myself and took her through the evening's events. She said little, scribbling a few notes in between eating the grapes. Halfway through my recitation, I realized how tired I was. Usually I have enough warning about late nights that I either sleep late or take a nap so I'm not exhausted. I hadn't had a chance this time. Plus the hangover and the added dehydration from too much alcohol.

"Thirsty?" she asked as I faltered. She started to open the wine bottle.

"Water?" I asked. Avoiding the need for a bathroom on a stakeout doesn't do much for hydration.

"Sure," she said crossing to the bar and retrieving a bottle of water from the small fridge there.

I took a long swig, then finished telling her about scaring them away.

She opened the bottle of wine. "Can't let it go to waste," she said. "What did you find inside?" She poured herself a moderate glass of wine.

I took another sip of water, then described the office and what I'd seen.

"The janitor's closet," she said when I told her where I'd found their hidden box.

"Like I said, crooks are dumb. Once you don't find things in the likely places, go to the most unlikely, as that's where they'll try to hide things."

"Good trick. I'll have to remember that."

I told her about the drugs, said, "I took pictures," and pulled out my phone.

"Let me see." She leaned in to me, close enough I could smell her perfume mixed with the wine.

I also got a decent view of her cleavage.

Then quickly looked back at her face.

Not quickly enough. "Thanks, but you're exhausted, sweetheart. And so am I, for that matter." She leaned over and kissed me on the cheek. "Show me the pictures."

I scrolled slowly through them, back and forth several times.

"They make no sense," she finally said.

"Could the numbers be women? Their measurements?"

"Maybe," she said with a yawn, "but that would be a stupid way to keep track. What do you do, measure every time you need to know who it is?"

"Might be easier than names. These women are probably from Eastern Europe and have the kinds of names Americans can't pronounce."

"They can just give them American nicknames—Gigi, Susie, whatever." She yawned, then added, "They don't care about their lives, they certainly don't care about their names."

"I guess," I admitted.

"What do you think of that weird note?" she asked.

I looked at the photo on my phone. *Eula May, 9 at 11 on 18 up the bayou by the germans.*

"It sounds like a meeting place," I said after reading it a few times.

"Really? Why do you think that?"

"Nine people are arriving at eleven o'clock—could be a.m. or p.m., if they're doing military it would be the morning—on the eighteenth of the month."

"Hard to know. It could be code. What the hell else could Eula May be?"

"A boat," I answered. "A lot of boats, especially the shrimping and fishing boats, are named for women. It could be the vessel they're using for smuggling."

"Okay," she said slowly, taking a sip of wine. "But what about the rest of it? It makes no sense."

I stared at the words, then admitted, "It sort of makes sense, but not very useful sense. 'Up the bayou' could be anywhere given all the bayous around here. I'm guessing it's a known place and what they call it. As for 'the germans,' that might be who they're meeting and it's how they know them. Again, not helpful. People could be German because they're from Germany or because they like bratwurst."

"That's plausible," she said. "But I'm still betting it's a code. One that sounds like it's a real message so people think it is and act accordingly. We can have our people look at it. You need to delete those photos."

"Delete them? Why?"

"Too risky. It ties you to the scene."

"But who's ever going to look at my phone?"

"I don't know. But it is hard evidence you were there. Don't take the risk. Delete them now."

"Don't you need a copy?"

"We'll get it through legit channels, from the police evidence." She put her hand on mine. "I don't want you to end up like the women in the river."

I didn't want to end up like them either. I had to trust Ashley on this one. I deleted the photos one by one while she watched.

I didn't mention that I'd already emailed them to myself. I was pretty sure I'd covered the rest of my tracks well or at least blended them in with the meth heads so they'd be blamed.

"Thank you," she said. "Now I feel better. Is there anything else you can think of about tonight?"

I shook my head.

"Okay, your part is done." She poured me a glass of wine. "I have to send in a report of what happened—you were doing surveillance and saw someone breaking in. It needs to be on a desk in the morning." She got up and went to the table where she had a laptop.

"What do you want me to do?" I asked.

"Eat something and enjoy the wine. You're off duty now."

I was hungry, I realized, mixed in with the fatigue. It had been well over eight hours since I'd last eaten. I cut a couple pieces of cheese and grabbed crackers to go with them. The wine was white and in the real world probably about a ten-dollar bottle, in the hotel world probably about thirty, which was generous considering Ashley's government salary. But I'm not much of a white wine drinker and this wasn't good enough to make me change my ways. I managed to finish my glass and another half one in between eating cheese and fruit. And sipping water.

After I finished eating, I tried to stay awake. Ashley had to, after all. But with the hunger gone, it left only the exhaustion.

"Are you sure there's nothing I can do?" I asked her.

"I'm sure," she said. Then smiled at me, a wistful smile like the last thing she wanted to do was the report in front of her. Like she wanted to be with me instead.

I put my head back. I would just close my eyes for a few minutes.

"Hey, your neck is going to hurt in the morning if you don't get to bed." Ashley was standing over me, gently shaking my shoulder.

"I was sleeping?"

"Yeah, you're been out for over an hour. Crash here. I'm going to be up for a while longer so you might as well use my bed." She took my arm, pulling me up and leading me back to the bedroom.

"There's a couple of extra toothbrushes in the bathroom," she said.

"I don't want to kick you out of your bed."

"You're not. Like I said, it'll be a while before I get there and you may be awake by then. Plus it's a king, we'll both fit."

This wasn't the romantic night I had hoped for but it was almost better. Much as I wanted touch, I also reveled in being taken care of, having someone worry about whether or not I'd eaten and how tired I was.

"Thanks," was all I could think to say.

"Sleep well." She went back to the other room, gently shutting the door.

I did a quick run through the bathroom routine, taking advantage of the free toothbrush, then turned out the light and went to the bedroom. The king bed did look lovely to my tired body. I usually sleep naked, but that seemed a little too friendly. I settled for stripping down to my T-shirt—taking the bra off, of course—and underwear.

I gratefully slid into the bed, my eyes shutting as soon as I hit the pillow.

Then one nagging thought. I didn't remember telling Ashley the ledger was red, yet she called it red. Maybe I had. Or maybe that was one of the we-can't-tell-you areas.

That was my last nagging thought.

Later, late enough that the dark was turning to gray, I felt someone get into bed. A soft rustle of blankets, then silence. I started to fall back to sleep, then there was a rustle again. Ashley quietly rolled to my side of the bed and gently put her arm around me, snuggling together.

We fell asleep that way.

CHAPTER SIXTEEN

I woke by myself, wondering if it had been a dream. But then I rolled out of bed and noticed our two pillows next to each other.

The next thing I noticed was the smell of coffee.

Good coffee.

That got me up.

Bathroom first. The hotel provided robes, so rather than searching for my clothes, I put that on over my ratty T-shirt and underwear.

"Good morning," Ashley greeted me as I entered the sitting room. She was also in a robe, just showered, her hair still wet. "I took a guess and ordered room service for us both."

It had clearly just arrived. She was pouring her first cup of coffee, careful with the carafe as it was so full. Two covered plates promised food.

"This is wonderful. I could get used to it." I sat down beside her and she poured me a cup before first sipping from hers.

"Milk? Sugar?" she offered.

I took a sip. "Nope. I do it the old-fashioned way." Another sip. My brain was joining my body.

She removed the covers from the two breakfasts. One was French toast and the other was a standard eggs and bacon. There was also a fruit tray and pastry basket.

"You get to pick," she said.

"Either is fine."

"Same here. Which is why you get to pick." She'd gotten the waffles when we'd gone to brunch, so I guessed she had more of a sweet tooth than I did. I pulled the eggs my way.

"Great choice," she said with a smile, taking the French toast for herself. She sighed and said, "I have to be in a meeting in an hour."

"So we'd better eat."

"We don't have to speed eat, but we can't linger either." She added, "This time."

That was good enough for me. "It's pretty nice having coffee and food magically appear. You can't make the entire world go away."

She smiled and we ate. Once we were finished, she said, "I need to get ready. Which means I'm going to have to throw you out." She gave me the wistful smile again.

"I'll stay out of your way," I offered. "And I can take you where you need to go."

"It's just a few blocks away, I'll walk. And…you're a distraction."

"That's a bad thing?"

"It is when I can't be distracted." She stood up, took me firmly by the hand, and led me back to the bedroom. "You have to get dressed and out of here and I have to get ready for my meeting." She let go of my hand.

I did as I was told, finding my clothes and getting into them. One advantage of the winter months was that yesterday's clothes weren't crusted in dried sweat. Never attractive. Ashley went back to the other room while I was dressing. That way neither of us could be a distraction to the other.

Once I was finished, I rejoined her. She was standing by the arm chair, putting her notepad into her briefcase, still in the bathrobe. It had loosened slightly, showing the pale skin of her neck, leading to the soft mounds of her breasts. She was wearing nothing under it.

But we couldn't be distracted. "Have you seen my phone?" I asked. I had thought I'd brought it to the bedroom with me, that's my usual habit, but it wasn't there.

"Your phone? I don't…oh, wait, there it is." She picked it up off the side table by the love seat.

I took it from her and stuffed it in my pocket.

We walked to the door.

"I'm sorry to run you out like this…"

"It's okay. At least you fed me first."

She looked down, then up at me. "I shouldn't do this," she said. She put her arms around me tightly and kissed me.

I kissed her back, embracing her. She smelled fresh and clean from the shower, her mouth a mix of sweet and coffee, riveting and intoxicating.

She pulled away. "I…we…you need to go." Her voice was shaky. Adding more firmly, "I need to be in meetings most of today, and meetings that I need to pay attention to."

"I'm going," I said. "But I'd like to come back."

She opened the door. "I'd like that, too."

I stepped out. She blew me a kiss and closed the door.

I headed for the elevator. Yes, I was tired. Last night hadn't been a long, restful sleep, but I was also happy in a way I hadn't been in a long time. The world had become new and filled with possibilities and second chances.

The mundane did pop up as I had to stop at the lobby ATM and pay the outrageous fees to get enough money to spring my car from the valet parking. I kept the receipt. After all, this had been *mostly* business.

It was a little after nine o'clock when I pulled out of the hotel. My first task was to go home, shower, and change clothes. I hoped I hadn't scheduled any morning appointments. I didn't remember any, but given the multiple distractions of the last twenty-four hours, I didn't trust my recall to be perfect.

I cut through the French Quarter. I was early enough that most people should be sober, and the ones who weren't had probably stumbled home around sunrise to sleep it off.

My route took me near Madame Celeste's place. On a whim, I turned to drive past it. I wished I'd never agreed to do security theater for her. *But the case isn't solved yet*, I reminded myself. Plus I might do some good by providing her working girls with info—and a few soft body parts to hit—that might prove useful. At least I could tell her I'd driven by.

All was quiet, as befit the workaday morning hour. It looked like what it wasn't, a historic building, probably residential where the residents couldn't quite manage the upkeep. The only telltale signs were that the sidewalk was clean and swept, no go cups left from the night before, and the small, discreet camera pointing at the doorway. This appeared to be a sleepy block, one few tourists visited.

My duty done, I headed home.

The shower and clean clothes were good. More coffee was even better. I'd only had time for one hotel cup earlier. My coffee cup holds a lot more than theirs do.

I pulled out my phone. I probably needed to charge it, but wanted to check my calendar.

The wrong view came up. The main view I use is a mostly blank one, with a finger swipe to get to the one with all the junk—apps, files, etc., on it. Now it was coming up to the cluttered view. I darkened the screen and brought it up again. Same thing. The last time I'd used it was showing Ashley the photos. I have a four-digit password. She had been close enough to see as I entered it to get to the pictures.

She'd hacked my phone.

"Do you trust anyone?" I said out loud. I quickly scrolled through to see if anything was missing or changed. I was annoyed.

Why would she trust me? Certainly she'd done a background check by now, probably accessed most of my phone records. I know enough about security to know that if it's written down, collected, stored anywhere, someone can get a hold of it.

Maybe she needed to be sure I really had deleted the photos. Maybe she needed to be sure she could trust me, and that required either time spent together in the kind of situations that show what a person is really like, or finding out as much as you could as quickly as you could.

She had kissed me after she'd checked out my phone. Maybe that meant she hadn't found anything to make her wonder about me. Most of my photos were of our cats or food. There were probably some of Cordelia still stored there, but I didn't want to see her, so hadn't bothered to delete them.

"If you can't trust me, you can't kiss me," I said to the now-darkened screen. But the words were more a dare than a truth. If I got the chance I knew I'd kiss her again. Did I trust her? What does trust even mean? I'd certainly trusted Cordelia, and one of the things I'd trusted was that she would never intentionally hurt me. Maybe what she'd done hadn't been intentional—at least not about hurting me. It was what she needed to do to survive and get through the dark and scary place she was in. But I'd been hurt, was still hurting, still thinking about her too much.

Did I trust Ashley? She genuinely seemed to care about me. She was attracted to me—as I was to her. I trusted her as much as I could given the situation. I'm too old and scarred to easily jump into love and wouldn't call this anything close. Yet. It was a beginning, a road that didn't seem to say dead end. I trusted her enough to take a step and maybe another step to see where they would lead.

I'd ask her about the phone, not because there was a right or wrong answer but to see what she'd say, see if she was honest or would deny it. Every step would be a little more trust. Or a little less.

I shook myself into the present. *Deal with what you can deal with.* I checked my phone calendar and was relieved to find that I hadn't missed anything.

Much as I wanted to go back to bed, I'd skew my body clock if I did that and woke up in the afternoon. That meant plowing through the day until something close to a reasonable bedtime. And that meant going to my office, with no tempting bedroom ever so near. I sighed, a long, loud sigh for a long day.

I also filled a travel mug with coffee.

At least the sun was still shining. A rainy, gray day might have been too much to stay awake through.

Once there, I forced myself to attend to the usual boring tasks, answering email, returning phone calls, only to leave a message that would have to be returned in turn, filing—oh, I hate filing—sending out bills, another hated task, but one that occasionally brought in money. My schedule had hit a bit of a lull, fortunately for my groggy head. I had just wrapped up a bunch of cases. A few were in a holding pattern—initial reports in and I was waiting for my clients to see what they wanted to do next. Several security installations were up and running and would only need an occasional check now and then.

While it meant I wasn't going to mess up anything critical due to my tired state, it also left me with no compelling tasks to pull me through the day.

I made a pot of coffee, the travel mug long empty. I bargained with myself that I would caffeinate until mid-afternoon, then wean myself off to be able to sleep tonight.

I wondered how Ashley and her meetings were going. She had been up even later than I had. Although when I had called she sounded like she was sleeping, so maybe she managed some shut-eye while I was chilling out in the parking lot.

After lunch—a sedate and healthy turkey sandwich—and just as I was sipping the last of the coffee, my buzzer sounded.

Flowers. Someone was sending me flowers.

I buzzed the woman in, then headed down the stairs to meet her. Partly out of kindness—my office is on the third floor—and mostly out of caution. I could look over the stair rail and make sure it was indeed

J.M. Redmann

a flower person and not someone using the well-worn ruse of gaining entry with a claimed delivery.

She was skinny and young and carrying a bouquet of flowers.

I met her on the second-floor landing; she handed them off to me and scampered back down the stairs.

How sweet of her, I thought as I carried the cheerful yellow, gold, and crimson bunch back to my office.

I found a vase for them and then put them on the side of my desk so I could smell the fresh floral tang.

Then I opened the card.

I'm very sorry for kicking you out so early in the morning. I'd really like to talk. EH.

EH?

Emily Harris.

Shit. I had assumed they were from Ashley. The woman who'd only kissed me, not the one I'd slept with. Or I wanted them to be from Ashley and for Emily to ever so conveniently disappear out of my life.

The phone rang. I stared at it for a moment, afraid it was Emily wanting to talk.

I roused myself and answered it. I was a big girl; if I made a mess, I needed to clean it up.

It took me a moment to recognize the rumble as a human voice and another moment to place it. Madame Celeste's assistant. What was his name? Roland. He was asking if I had some time late this afternoon or early evening to come over and talk to his "coworkers," as he called them.

Remembering the very good Scotch, I agreed. After all, I had said I would and taken her money. Ashley had meetings all day, plus she had to be tired from last night. Much as I wanted to spend time with her, we hadn't made any arrangements and I wasn't going to be a high school girl waiting around for her to call. I knew I'd need to talk to Emily, but had no clue what I wanted to say. Sending flowers wasn't exactly a message that said, "Sorry, it was a mistake, let's forget it ever happened." I felt like I should choose but didn't know enough to make a choice. Yes, probably Ashley, but she was on temporary assignment here, and much as we both seemed to like each other, one passionate kiss isn't a relationship.

Nor is spending one brief night with someone. Brash as she was, I also liked Emily. If Ashley weren't around, I'd be a lot more interested in her, probably be happy at the bouquet and her wanting to see me again.

"I hate this fucking romantic stuff," I told the flowers.

They just looked pretty and said nothing.

I decided to go earn my Scotch—and the money—Madame Celeste had already given me.

I printed out info on self-defense and made ten copies. They could make more if they wanted. Vice is a business, after all, and most businesses had copy machines.

Shortly after that I left my office and headed home. I wanted to change clothes. While there seemed no fashion rule as to what to wear to a whorehouse to talk about self-defense, the old jeans and baggy sweater I had grabbed this morning didn't seem up to my sartorial standards. Plus, it was a nice night, which meant parking in the Quarter would be impossible. I could leave my car at home and walk in.

Black jeans, dark gray boots, deep purple V-neck sweater, and my black leather jacket. Not a motorcycle one—I'm not that hardcore. I stuffed my handouts into a messenger bag—also black to fit in with the overall theme of my ensemble—as well as other things like my gun. Not that I was planning to use it, but you never know.

I headed out the door. It would be about a fifteen-minute walk. Ten, if I hurried.

The evening was perfect, a golden sunset, cool temperatures that made walking easy. I took Burgundy, a mostly residential street and one with fewer tourists.

I hoped the brisk air and movement would help clear my head, but the only thing that came to me was to let things play out. I could talk to Emily and hear what she wanted to say. I could go out on the town with Ashley and see where we ended up. I could make decisions when I had to make decisions.

I turned on the street of Madame Celeste's establishment. It was quiet, the gaslights of a few places on, adding gold to the blue of the evening.

Roland opened the door just as I knocked. He must have been watching. That was probably his job, watching.

"Good evening," he greeted me. "Please come this way."

I returned his greeting and followed him. He led me a different way from the last time, to the other side of the building. Madame Celeste had her space and the "coworkers" had theirs.

Just pretend they're Girl Scouts, I told myself. This was one of the more unusual places I've done talks like this. I couldn't let what I might be thinking show on my face, all the conclusions I've been told to have: They were wrong; they shouldn't be in this business. It was dangerous. If they wanted to be safe they could work in a bank.

I could afford to make moral judgments. I'd never been faced with the bad choices and worse choices that brought a woman here. Minimum wage or a thousand a night? An abusive husband or nameless johns? Get caught on the wrong side of the law and find it too hard—many places won't hire convicts—to get back to the right side. Or even a prudent business decision? Spend a few years making a lot of money; use it to go to school, set up a business—like Bianca and her dreams of a hair salon.

Roland led me to a lounge area with comfortable couches on one side, a TV on the wall, and a small kitchenette on the other side with a long table and enough chairs to seat eight. The furnishings were nice, the couches leather, the table a well-made solid wood, and all the chairs matched. If it was a cage, it was a comfortable one.

Several women were sitting on the couches. It could have been any break room in any company except these were some of the most gorgeous women I'd ever seen. While some of them were in jeans and T-shirts, a few of them were clearly dressed—or not so dressed—for work in teddies and lingerie. Three of them were blond, probably one natural and two from the bottle, judging from their skin tones and eye color. One was a redhead, probably also from a bottle, although she had the green eyes to make the real thing possible. One was a brunette, subtle highlights probably also gotten at a hair salon instead of the beach. Two of the women were dark-haired, natural since they were also not white like the others. But their olive skin was hard to read, Hispanic, Mideastern, very light black, or some combination. Beautiful, yes, but also exotic. Madame Celeste catered to a variety of tastes. I noticed there were no truly ethnic woman here, no black women or clearly Latina or Asian. Maybe they worked at different times. Or maybe they weren't what the customers wanted. Beauty is in the eye of those who pay for it.

I took a brief glance. It's hard not to stare at a woman in a low-cut silk bra in leopard print whose breasts were from either great genes or a skilled plastic surgeon.

One of them—the blondest one—looked up at me. "Roland didn't say you'd be a girl," she said.

"Does it matter?" I answered. "As long as I know what I'm doing?"

The woman next to her answered. "No, it's kind of cool you're a woman." She emphasized "woman" just enough to make her point.

Roland did introductions, but the names he gave were clearly their working names—Destiny, Ginger, Eva, Ramona, Antoinette, and Bordeaux.

Show time.

I don't like to lecture, especially to a group of six people. I grabbed one of the kitchen chairs and used it to complete a circle with the couches. Asking questions, I led them through most of my suggestions. Pay attention to your surroundings. If possible travel in pairs or groups. Wear practical shoes and clothes so you can run if you have to. Trust your instincts. If a situation or person feels not right, get out of there. Stay in well-lit, well-traveled areas if you can. Carry a whistle or something else that can make a lot of noise. If you're attacked, yell and make noise if you're in an area where people are around. Yelling "fire" will often get people out when things like "help" might not. Know your route and places you can go for safety.

We talked through some possible scenarios. The blondest woman was my problem child. She came up with unlikely possibilities, as if her goal was to stump me. "But what if it's three big guys and you're in high heels?" or "What if you're in the middle of nowhere and you don't know anyone?"

Some of the other women rolled their eyes at her. I kept calm and answered as best I could. "Each situation will be different. Always look for how to escape. Don't fight unless you have to. If you do have to fight, your goal is one killing or incapacitating blow. Eyes, groin, whatever you think you have the best prospect of hitting very, very hard."

When I got the chance I asked if any of them knew the women who had been killed. They all said they didn't, some indicating and Blondie right out saying they didn't hang out with that rank of girls. They were high-class, expensive women, working behind secured doors. Other women, especially those out on the streets, were far more at risk.

I nodded and didn't argue. Maybe they were safer. But I knew no one was truly safe. Nothing builds an impenetrable wall that can keep all danger out.

We'd been talking for just about an hour, and time was money here. I told them if they heard or saw anything that worried them to call me and handed out cards.

Roland led me back to the main hallway. Just as we got there, the door opened and a man in uniform came in. I recognized him. He was Joanne's boss's boss's boss, high up in the cop world. He was a tall, distinguished man; a thick head of gray hair and the lines on his face gave his age. He noticed me, and cop that he was, knew that I knew who he was.

"It's not what you think," he said.

Roland left us, presumably to find Madame Celeste.

"I'm not thinking anything," I replied.

"You're the PI who's friends with Joanne Ranson," he said. "Thought you looked familiar."

"Joanne is a good cop," was my reply. He must have paid attention to know that.

"Yes, she is. What are you doing here?"

We were both in a whorehouse. He could be thinking the same thing about me I was thinking about him. Except I wasn't important enough to get it for free.

"Security. Talked to the staff about how to keep themselves safe coming and going from here."

"Celeste told you about the murdered women?"

"Yes, and asked me to do what I can to keep things safe."

"She thinks her girls are at risk?"

"No," I admitted. "But they're worried and she wanted to reassure them."

"Believe it or not, I'm here for the same reason."

"No reason not to believe."

"We go back a long way. I busted her a few times in my rookie cop days. Liked her enough to be glad she got off the street. Do I like this? No. Do I think I can stop it? No. Better to have a place like this than kids in the streets doing anything and some of them getting killed."

"So you turn a blind eye to what's going on?"

"Yeah, more or less. Maybe I'm jaded, but there are more important criminals to go after."

"This is a victimless crime?"

"There are always victims. We can't save them all. Do I save the next woman who might be dumped in the river? Or bust this place?"

"I think we can agree on that."

"And Celeste sometimes helps out. She lets me know things I'm not going to find out any other way."

"Like what senator is visiting here?"

He shook his head, annoyed at my sarcasm. "No, like if a new gang is muscling in, someone we need to look out for."

"Is that what's happening here?"

"That was just an example. She's a smart woman. When you see Joanne, I'd appreciate it if you didn't mention me being here."

"She's on vacation, out on the West Coast. I doubt I'll talk to her anytime soon."

He nodded at me.

Roland and Madame Celeste entered.

"Ah, Micky, my staff said you were very helpful."

"Glad to hear that," I said. Maybe I was, but her staff hadn't had enough time to report to her. *What game is she playing*, I wondered. Had she planned for the two of us to "accidentally" run into each other? If so, why?

To him, she said, "Joseph, it's so good to see you again. As you can see, I did take you up on your suggestion and bring in someone to talk about self-defense."

"Glad to see you occasionally take my advice," he answered.

"Please come back this way, if you have a few minutes. I have one or two things to mention to you." To me, she said, "Micky, thank you so much for doing this."

"No problem," I said. It was time for me to leave. "I'll continue to come by at random times and check on things like you asked."

She smiled at me, understanding my meaning and seemingly appreciating that I wasn't playing along quite as nicely as I was supposed to. Or else she was far too practiced at smiling for me to know what was going on behind it.

I followed Roland to the door. I didn't look back to see where Madame Celeste took him. I wanted to think the Scotch she'd given me was special.

Roland watched me as I left. He, too, was on guard, protective of anyone who came through those doors, as if his watchfulness could keep the evil away.

Maybe it could. I wanted to think something could help protect the woman who didn't have great choices in life.

It was cooler now with the sun gone and only a wan new moon in the sky. I zipped up my jacket and wished I'd brought a scarf to keep the wind out of my throat.

I could hear the occasional noise from Bourbon Street two blocks down, horns honking, an occasional shout or drunken singing. But it was mostly quiet here. I chose to walk back on Burgundy, although Rampart with its higher volume of traffic and businesses would be what I'd advise the women to do.

I'm tall and have a gun. That allowed me to prefer the quieter street, lit by the dim glow of scattered porch lights. Save for the parked cars, I was walking the same streets of a century ago. I liked feeling the history, the whispers of the past the night brought out.

I heard footsteps behind me.

I lengthened my stride so whoever it was wouldn't catch up with me.

A car slowly drove past.

Once it was gone the footsteps sped up.

It was one person.

I cut to the other side of the street.

The footsteps followed.

I adjusted my jacket and brought the messenger bag in front of me. I stuck my hand in and found my gun.

Most likely it was someone who lived here hurrying home. Or a lost tourist trying to catch up to me to ask directions. It was early in the evening for criminals to be out.

The steps were getting closer.

I held off looking back; that would give away I was aware of the person behind me and worried enough to be spying on them.

Not a small person, but I couldn't tell if it was a man or a woman.

I had passed a small grocery store a few blocks back, but I didn't think there were any more down this way.

This was a dark area, the next light a good twenty feet away.

The steps were closer, only a few paces behind me.

I suddenly stopped and turned, my hand firmly on the gun. If I needed to—and I certainly hoped I didn't—I could shoot through the bag.

I was pushed against a wall, a hand on my throat.

"Be careful, Knight, you can get in trouble walking by yourself."

Emily Harris.

"Bang. You're dead," I said, shoving the bag hard enough against her to feel the barrel.

"You have a permit?" She was still holding me against the wall, her hand loosened, a gentle grip.

"Of course I have a permit. I'm one of the law-abiding people, remember?"

"Really? What are you doing coming out of a house of prostitution?"

"Are you following me?"

"Would I tell you if I was?"

"No."

"So answer my question."

"Are you interrogating me? Is this part of your official investigation?"

"Not yet."

"Security."

"Security? What do you mean?"

"Even houses of ill-repute need security."

"Seriously? You expect me to believe that?"

"No, but then you do seem to have a problem believing me."

"You're telling me Desiree Montaigne hired you to provide security?"

"Who?"

"Desiree Montaigne, the owner of record on the property."

That had to be Celeste's real name. "Oh, sorry, that's not the name of my contact. But yes, they seriously hired me to help with security."

"Who's your contact?"

"My clients pay for confidentiality."

"Right."

"I spent about an hour talking to the, ah, workers there about how to protect themselves when walking to their car or home."

"Not in the place?"

"Quit interrupting."

"Yes, ma'am. You're sexy when you take charge."

Damn. I was doing my best to ignore her body against mine, pinning me to the wall. The hand on my neck had now turned to a caress.

Focus, Micky. "They're well protected there. But my contact was worried about them outside. The working girls were spooked after hearing about the women dumped in the river."

Emily tensed. "How did they hear about them?"

"I don't know." I did know, but it was hearsay, and that was close enough to "don't know" for me. "I once worked an embezzlement case that involved services on that property. I worked out a deal where no arrests were made and they got a good portion of their money back."

"So the embezzler can do it again at another place?"

"I'm not the police. My client hired me to get the money back."

She snorted. "Okay, go on."

"So my contact knew who I was. Once she heard about the murders, she wanted to do everything she could to protect her girls."

"Her business, you mean."

That was too close to the truth for me to admit. "Either or both. Anyway, I was hired to talk to the women about ways to protect themselves, things they need to think about on the streets. Also to occasionally drive by or walk around."

"By yourself? That could be dangerous."

"Remember bang?" I said, waggling the bag against her. I'd let go of the gun. It would be downright unfriendly to keep my finger on the trigger. "Besides, my contact admitted that it's mostly security theater. Her workers are nervous and she wants them to feel more secure."

"So Desiree hired a hot PI like you to help out?" Emily worked her thigh between my legs.

"I told you, we knew each other from a previous encounter. And I never said my contact was Desiree."

"You said 'she,' and the only she in charge is Desiree."

Shit. I hadn't meant to give that away. "There's a car coming."

"Is it black and boxy?"

"No, a small red Mini Cooper."

"Not to worry, then. It's not one of ours."

"But it could be homophobic assholes."

"In a Mini? Get real. Besides they'd have to be stupid enough to take on two armed woman who are well trained in taking care of ourselves."

"Even guns don't always protect against other guns."

"So you just happened to get hired to do security theater at one of the high-class hooker hotels in the city. Think you're being set up?"

"No." I tried to pull away from her. But I didn't try very hard.

She lifted her other hand up and held my face between her hands. "I don't know how much you know, but you don't want to get involved with this. These are dangerous, brutal people, ones who will stop at nothing. I really don't want to drag you out of the river."

"Not in my plans. Not at all in my plans."

She kissed me, very softly, a whisper of her lips against mine. As if she really did care.

I let her kiss me. It seemed safer than talking. Then I kissed her back. That wasn't safer than talking, but at this exact moment, safety wasn't on my mind.

I wanted her. I wanted not to think, not to worry about the next moment or the next day. To be held and kissed, to take in the intoxicating scent of desire. I wanted everything to melt away to two bodies touching each other, pleasure and warmth, like we were new people and had just found each other.

Another car drove by, its headlights piercing the shadowed envelope we were in.

We weren't new people; we were the women we had become, all the years and scars and hurt places and fears, and there were always consequences and the morning would come.

We pulled away.

"Why don't you walk me home?" she said.

"Yeah? So who walks me home?"

She took my hand, holding it as we walked. A claim, one I let her have.

"I can if you want."

"But then I'd have to walk you back to your place."

"Like an Escher print," she said, assuming I knew enough about art to recall his print of never-ending staircases.

"We can leave it at one walk."

"Next time I'll be the one left alone," she said, as if seeing a future.

We were silent for half a block, I said, "Emily, what are we doing?"

"You're attractive and I'm trying to save your life. I can't speak for you."

"This is complicated."

"Understatement, my friend."

"Complicated, messy, we don't trust each other. You're risking your career."

"I'm risking getting sent to Peoria, but not my entire career. At least I don't think so. If it turns out you play a major role in this, then I'll be scrubbing toilets in Duluth."

"You think I might be the kind of killer who mutilates a living woman and dumps her in the river?"

"No, I don't think that." She hesitated. "But I can't close the door on your being involved in ways you're not being honest about. Oh, and how did you get that little detail? We certainly did not release that to the press."

"I have connections in law enforcement."

"Who?"

"Can't tell you."

"Figured. That's annoying, you know."

"That I won't tell you?"

"That you don't trust me enough to let me help sort this out."

"It's not trust"—although it was—"but my clients pay me to keep my mouth shut."

"Even around murder?"

"I wouldn't protect a murderer. I make it clear up front I'm not the cops, and if they cheat on their taxes it's not my concern. But if I stumble over a major crime, murder, diddling kids, major theft, I'm not going to cover it for them." That was my standard spiel. I'd never put it to the test, mostly because I rejected clients I suspected of wanting me to cover for them.

"Glad to hear it."

We turned down Emily's street.

"Hey, thanks for the flowers."

"Felt guilty about sending you out without breakfast."

"You were called to the river, weren't you?" I asked quietly.

"Yeah, we needed to be at the scene."

"Do you think it was a message?"

"Message? What do you mean?"

"To the other women. Don't act up, don't try to escape."

"Maybe. It's hard to know. My best guess is that if it was a message, it was to the other gang."

We stopped in front of her house.

"Other gang?"

"Keep it confidential. We think two groups are fighting for control. They both think New Orleans, especially with all the events coming up, is golden for making money off the sex trade. One side killed the two women because they had been brought in by the other side. It wasn't a message to the women—they're expendable. It was a message to their rivals."

"What evidence do you have for that?"

"Sorry, no one-way streets. That's all I'm giving until you give me what you know."

"Everything?"

"Everything."

"I know it's cold, Mardi Gras will be in a few weeks, the earth isn't flat—"

"Not that everything," she cut in.

"Can't," I said, wishing I could. She had named the stakes, brutal murder. I couldn't trust her yet. I didn't want to end up in the river. Or send Ashley there.

"I wish you'd come clean with me. I can help," she said quietly. She would be good in the interview room. She sounded like she really meant her words, really meant she would help, get you a better prison, a lighter sentence for cooperating, rehab.

"I don't need help." I added, "Really, I don't. I'm only involved as much as giving working girls tips on walking home."

She sighed. "Much as it's not useful, I admire that you won't break your code of ethics."

It was a genuine compliment, not what I'd expected from her. Like the flowers. "Yeah, uh, thanks. As annoying as it is, I admire your persistence."

"Bullshit, no, you don't."

"Okay, I don't. Actually, I do, but there's more annoyance than admiration."

"Fair enough." She looked at me. "Do you want to come in?"

I looked down. "Want to? Yes. But…it's not a good idea."

"Probably not," she agreed and let go of my hand.

"Okay, see you around." I started to walk away.

"Hey, Knight. Call me if you need me."

I turned back to look at her. "I will." I started walking away again.

"You can call me even if you don't need me," she said softly, as if it didn't matter whether I heard it or not.

I turned again. "Yeah, maybe I'll do that." I had to walk away, otherwise it would be too easy to leave the cold and enter her warm house. My so-called code of ethics was frayed and ragged at the edges. Waking up next to her, her head on my shoulder would make it too tempting to tell her what she wanted to know, to believe she wasn't the corrupt one Ashley had warned me about or the too-trusting friend who told her coworkers everything.

"Damn, damn, damn," I muttered as I crossed Rampart.

She was too tempting, and I didn't need that kind of temptation.

I hurried, from the cold and away from her lure.

Who did I trust? Ashley? She was the one who'd warned me about the snitch in her ranks and she was the one most at risk. Maybe Emily didn't know or maybe she was part of it. If she did know, she didn't trust me enough to tell me.

"Complicated, way too complicated," I muttered. The case *and* my life.

Once back at my place, I occupied myself with finding something to eat. And drink. I allowed myself to nurse a glass of the good Scotch while I threw together dinner, a stir-fry of everything still edible in the fridge. Well, not the milk.

I let the food—and the alcohol—burn off the edge, make everything seem solvable or at least okay to wait until tomorrow.

Maybe that was how I'd let too many things slide until tomorrow, a day that never came. I'd worried about Cordelia in Houston, me here. But the nights would come and I'd tell myself I'd think about it the next day. Or the next. I'd find some way to be there for her and not abandon my life. But the next day held no answers, only the bustle of life from the demands of work, groceries, the bank, arrangements for the next trip there. Not a future, just the days slipping away. Until they were gone and I couldn't call them back.

The saddest thing is I only knew the wrong answer, not the right one. Maybe if I'd been there, maybe if I'd pushed her to talk more and knew her despair better, maybe…but I *needed* to work for the money to cover our expenses. She had enough to get good medical care, but much of what she'd inherited had been locked away in the foundation she started to support a clinic for those who needed care. As the months dragged on, complications, different treatments, had soaked up money like a black sponge. I took over the mortgage, all the bills, cable, power, food, the trips there we'd formerly split.

I poured myself another inch of Scotch.

Maybe if we had talked more…

But that was hard when she wasn't feeling well, nauseated and weak from the chemo. I tried to keep it cheerful, with funny pictures and videos of the cats, updates on friends. Had I shut her out instead? Made it too difficult to talk about the hard things? I don't know that I ever mentioned my work covering as much of the bills as it had to. I didn't want her to worry when she had so much to worry about and endure.

The choices I made were the wrong ones. Maybe the other choices were just as wrong. Maybe there were no right ones. I wanted so desperately to have been a better person. Even now, when I didn't matter, I wanted that. But I didn't know how.

Except maybe not drinking my life away.

I took another sip, let the smooth burn glide down my throat, as if an essential warmth could be found in the amber liquid.

Then I put the glass down and picked up my phone.

I dialed Ashley.

She answered on the second ring. Maybe she was hoping I'd call.

"Wanted to check on you and see if you survived your meetings."

She laughed. "I seem to have. The real challenge was to not die of boredom."

"That's always the challenge."

"True. Look I was about to call you. I wanted to update you on a few things and…schedule a time for us to go out. If you still want to."

I heard the hesitation in her voice, as if scared I might say no. "Yes, I'd like that very much," I reassured her.

"Oh, good. That makes me happy."

Me, too. I said, "Yes, how about tomorrow?"

"Tomorrow would be great, but I can't. How about later this week? Friday? I can pretty much promise that will be free for me. Plus I don't have anything on Saturday, so we can stay out as late as we want."

"Sounds perfect."

"Meet me at my hotel at around seven? Dress for a night on the town."

"Still sounds perfect."

She laughed again, a deep throaty laugh, one of anticipation. "Now that we have the important things settled, how about some updates?"

"Sure, what do you have for me? Did you get access to the ledger I found?"

"Yes, we did. The locals have been pretty cooperative. Oh, and you did a good job. They're totally convinced the only people there were the meth heads."

"Good to know. Much as I like you, I don't think I'd want to end up in jail for you."

"Not going to let that happen."

"What about the message? Did you crack it?"

"My team is still working on it, but like I said before, our best guess is a code, the words are meaningless."

"Okay, that's your specialty, not mine. What about the murdered women?"

"What about them? I mean, in what way?"

"Are they connected?"

"You're asking the tough questions, aren't you?"

"Sorry, it's an occupational hazard."

"What do you mean?"

"It's probably the same for you. Much of what I do is seek information, and I get a lot of it by asking questions, until I find what I need to know. Guess it's a habit."

"It's not one you have to have with me. Look, I have to finish another report. We can chat some tomorrow, maybe around lunch. And see each other on Friday."

"Don't work too hard."

"I'll make up for it when we go out."

We hung up.

I picked up my Scotch and bargained with myself—I wasn't ready to give up alcohol yet, but I would cut back and buy one really good bottle at a time. The price would be enough to make me slow down.

I went back to my cubby of a home office, taking the final few sips in the glass with me. I didn't want to think anymore, at least not about my life. I needed to do something with the photos I had emailed to myself, the ones I assured Ashley I'd deleted.

I wasn't quite ready to get rid of them. But I could obscure where I got them. I downloaded the photos, deleted the emails I'd sent from my phone, emptied my deleted file, and defragmented my computer. While that was running in the background I stared at the photos, especially the one Ashley said was a code.

Eula May, 9 at 11 on 18 down the bayou by the germans.

Maybe it was a code, but it seemed more like a straightforward message to me. Why code something in a book when you're supposed to be the only one looking at it? It wasn't meant as a message that could be intercepted. But maybe Ashley was right, it was disguised to look like a message so no one would think it was a code, thereby making them try to understand the message and not decode it.

That sounded way too Cold War spy for an operation that so far hadn't impressed me with its brains and sophistication.

Down the Bayou Road.

A childhood memory. Driving with my dad to look at a boat. Him commenting, "This is one of the most imaginative road names ever. Down the Bayou Road." We'd both laughed and then come up with other names—The Road Here Road, The Road There Street, Going Home Road, Road That Doesn't Lead Much Anywhere Road.

There was really a road—at least there had been—named Down the Bayou.

The Germans. Des Allemands.

A small fishing town about an hour from New Orleans. It was named for the German immigrants who lived there, part of the German coast. Des Allemands, French—or Cajun—for "the Germans."

What was the likelihood that a coded message could actually hit on actual places that made sense as a straightforward message?

I pulled up a map on the computer to see if my memory was right.

Down the Bayou Road, just off Highway 90 in Des Allemands. It ran, as its name implied, right next to the bayou. It was a small fishing town, probably hit hard by the recession and the BP oil spill. It also fit in with the warehouse we'd found. These were locations known by someone who was from here and knew the ins and outs of the bayou country. For a fisherman who knew his—or her—way, it would be easy to get from there to the Gulf. Meet a boat out there at night, transfer the cargo, come in through the back way bayous and bang, you're on the old state highway that leads directly into New Orleans.

It made too much sense for me to ignore.

I picked up my phone and dialed Ashley.

"Hey, what's up?"

"I'm sorry to bother you, but I was thinking"—caught myself from saying "looking at"—"about that message I saw in the ledger."

"The one in code?"

"I don't think it's code. There is a town called Des Allemands— The Germans, and it has a street named Down the Bayou Road."

"That…sounds weird."

"Think about it. A boat named *Eula May* will deliver nine women at eleven o'clock—probably at night, otherwise it's too obvious—on the eighteenth of the month. Tomorrow. It makes too much sense to ignore."

"That's clever, but you've got to be wrong. Our info indicates they're coming in by truck on the interstates."

"The warehouse. Someone has to know the area to think to put it out there. We're dealing with someone local, someone who knows the bayous. There are no state troopers back in the bayous, no one to stop you if your boat has a missing starboard light."

"Hey, look, Micky, I appreciate you thinking about this, especially after all the trouble we've put you through, but this seems unlikely. Like I said, our info is that it's an overland route being used. The back waterways are too risky. Only a few people would know how to navigate them. These organizations survive by having disposable people. Anyone can drive a rental truck. It makes them easy to replace. But someone who has a boat and knows the back channels? That's not a safe person to have around."

"But they've clearly got someone like that. No outsider could have come up with where to put that warehouse."

"All right, I see your point. This is the kind of stuff you don't want to get involved in. It gets dangerous. Let us handle it."

"Isn't it as dangerous for you as it is for me?"

"Yes. I mean, no. I have a whole team for backup, big guys with guns. You're one lone private eye. Big difference."

She had a point. "Will you at least consider it?"

"I'll pass it on. But I really think, while it sounds good, it's not the right message. Maybe meant to lead us astray."

"Okay, I'll trust you on this one. But please, at least consider it. I grew up out in the bayous. It's a hard time out there now. Hard times open a lot of doors."

"Yeah, hard times do. Listen, thanks for passing this on. But please, stay out of trouble until I see you for our night out, okay?"

"I'll do my best."

She put down the phone. I heard it click off.

Perhaps she was right. It's easy to see the world through what we know. I'm familiar with the bayous, lived there until I was ten. My ego wanted to be smart enough to figure out what was stumping the federal boys—I didn't want to be Robin; I wanted to be Batman.

I took another sip of Scotch. My last one. I got up to refill it, then remembered my bargain with myself. I put the glass down.

Then I buried the pictures deep among boring photos of the last renovation of the kitchen.

I was tired. Another day with nothing solved, nothing changed, and all I could do was think about it tomorrow, the day that never came.

Chapter Seventeen

By the second cup of coffee, I again found myself looking at the maps. The morning only made me more certain that I was right. Why would someone scribble down a coded message in an offhand scrawl like that? It seemed more like what you'd do when taking down notes while talking on the phone.

Maybe I was right, but Ashley was telling me I wasn't because that was one of those areas she couldn't talk about with me.

This was frustrating.

I could call Emily and see what she thought. Except how would I explain seeing the message without coming up with an explanation even *less* believable than needing to pee and wandering off in the woods?

Or I could contact Madame Celeste and ask her to pass it on to her contacts. She might listen. But it was too early to call or drop by her place. I wondered what official whorehouse hours were. "Please press one for information. We're open from twelve noon for the lunchtime quickie until four a.m. for all your evening's pleasures." Or maybe customers had to schedule in advance.

I again filled the travel mug full of coffee, telling myself I was headed down to my office.

Instead I crossed the bridge over the river and caught Highway 90. *It can't hurt to look around*, I told myself. It would just be coincidence that I'd be there around eleven in the morning.

The day was cool and crisp. A perfect day for smuggling. I shuddered at the thought. What would it be like? Promised a decent job and instead forced on a terrifying journey? There would be no escape from the boat, no chance to jump out at a gas station. Just miles of green water winding into swamps, tight bayous edged with thick brush. No sign of humans save for your captors on the boat. Even at your destination, it would be desolate, a small insular town, one that would believe a local boy over women babbling in a strange accent.

It took me a little under an hour to get there. The town seemed to have changed little from my memory of it. Maybe older, showing its years and the wear of a life lived clinging to what could be taken from the water.

I drove around, found Down the Bayou Road. It became Up the Bayou Road on the other side of 90. It was, as I remembered, next to the water. While some of the houses on the side across from the bayou looked cared for, there were several that weren't in good shape, possibly abandoned. Two of them were next to each other near the end of the road. Rusted chain-link fence corralled the front yard of each. And each place was guarded by a large dog. The dogs prowled the fence, pacing me as I drove by.

I wondered what they were protecting.

I drove back into town and found the one place that seemed to be the local gathering spot.

Time for more coffee. And a bathroom.

"You're not from around here, are you?" was my greeting as I settled at a small table in the corner.

"New Orleans now," I answered. "But I grew up in Bayou St. Jack."

She nodded. Set a coffee cup in front of me without even asking and poured. It looked black enough to put tar on my tongue. I took a sip. Smiled and nodded. You don't get information when you dis the coffee.

"You the owner of this place?" I asked her.

She looked around mid-sixties, but could have been younger and lived in the sun and the salt for many years. Her hair was still mostly black and she had a face that had softened around her lines, like dough with creases in it. She was stout, with muscled forearms from lifting heavy coffeepots all day.

"Naw, just work here. Married to the brother-in-law of the owner."

I ordered a shrimp po-boy. It was on the early side for lunch, but that seemed the safest choice in a place like this, even though I hadn't had breakfast yet and this wasn't my morning meal of choice. I doubted this place did brunch.

"What brings you here?" she asked after taking my order. Strangers are fair game.

"I'm looking for someone my family used to know. My dad ran a shipyard in Bayou St. Jack and we had a friend of the family who owned a boat called the *Eula May*."

She made a face.

"You know the family?"

"Not much of a family, if you ask me."

"What do you mean?"

She refilled my coffee up without my asking. I do coffee black, but I usually don't do tar-paper black. "Probably not the people you're thinking of. Just moved here not that long ago."

"About how far back?"

"Hard to remember. No more 'an ten years. Bought the boat with cash. Then a year or two later couldn't pay the bills. Two brothers, near as we can figure."

Ten years was a short time around here. It usually took about two generations to be considered not recent arrivals. "They married? Have wives?"

She cleared her throat in a dismissive manner. "Wives, no. Women around 'em, yeah. Seems a new one every time we see 'em. Which ain't much, let me tell you."

"Why not? Where else do they go besides your place?"

"They ain't real welcome here. That couldn't pay their bills thing. They don't much hang with folks from here. Heard they grew up around Lake Charles. Not very friendly. The rumor is they make their money running drugs."

"Really?"

She poured more coffee and went to the kitchen to fetch my po-boy.

She returned and plopped it in front of me. I wasn't sure I could do this much fried with the coffee toxic sludge in my stomach.

"Really," she continued. "Know they don't do much shrimping 'cause they only occasionally show up with anything. Not enough to make ends meet, even if they don't pay regular. But they both have nice new trucks. How do you get those if you always have the smallest haul?"

"Doesn't make sense to me." I took a bite. The shrimp was good. It would be a war with the coffee in my stomach. I hoped the bread would be my secret weapon. "Anyone see them do anything bad?"

"You know how rumors work. It's more what we don't see. New trucks and no shrimp is what we do see. Plus they're not nice people."

"Not nice how?" I took another bite. So far things were at a standoff.

"Not friendly. Just packed up their stuff and got the hell out when Isaac headed this way. Didn't bother to offer to help anyone else. Drove right by a boat in trouble, like they didn't see 'em."

"You seen them lately?"

She started to pour the coffee and I waved her off. "A few days ago, heard they loaded up that boat of theirs and took off early in the morning. Not in good weather, so it doesn't make sense they're out there."

I took another bite. The coffee fired the first warning shot.

"What kind of boat do they have?"

"Shrimp boat."

"I know that. What kind of shrimp boat? Is it fairly large? Painted white with blue trim?"

"Pretty big boat. Made it all the more funny they paid in cash. White with red-and-black trim."

"You're right, that's not the same people—well, the same boat— we used to know. What's their name? Do you know?"

"The Guidry brothers. One is Sam, I think, and don't know the other one. You sure you don't want any more coffee?"

"I'm sure. Doctor told me to watch my caffeine intake. But it sure is good." I chewed down a hunk of bread to appease the coffee. "How long have they been gone?"

"'Bout three, four days now. Why you so interested?"

"Sound like the kind of people to avoid. Have to know about them enough so if I see them coming I can get out of the way. Like knowing what snakes to watch for."

"Yeah, they're like snakes, all right. They mostly stay away from us as well. Look for tattoos. They're covered in 'em."

"What kind of tattoos?"

"Don't know. Never got close enough to look. You want some apple pie?"

I got it to go. More to be polite—and keep the chatter going—than any possibility it would end up in my stomach.

Once I left there—after a long enough stop in the bathroom to ascertain the tar coffee and fried shrimp hadn't decided on an exit strategy yet—I again drove Down the Bayou Road. It was a little after 11:30 a.m. If the morning was the appointed time, the boat should be back. But the docks were mostly empty and I didn't see a white boat trimmed in black and red anywhere. Only the prowling dogs, watching my car as I slowly drove past.

I headed back to New Orleans. I'd been noticed, but I was hoping only noticed in the way that any new face would be. Hanging around here until the late night would get me noticed in ways I'd prefer to avoid. Plus, I had a sneaking suspicion at some point I was going to want to spend uninterrupted time in a bathroom. I headed back the quick way, catching 310 at Boutte and then I-10 back to the city.

If my reading of the cryptic message was right, then the delivery would be tonight. Nine? Women? Bundles of pot? Exotic reptiles?

I had learned a few things. A boat named *Eula May* did exist and it docked in Des Allemands. It was owned by two brothers whose means of support wasn't easily visible. At one point they'd certainly had wads of cash, enough to buy a boat. Shrimp boats aren't luxury yachts, but they're not a dinghy either. People out here didn't have that kind of money. Like the man I'd encountered at the warehouse, they had tattoos. Maybe he was one of the Guidry brothers.

Not a smoking gun, perhaps, but they all added a number of checks to the possible column.

Once in town I headed to my office. The bathroom there is easier to clean.

I called Ashley but only got her voice mail. I left a message asking her to call me. I wanted to talk to her about this instead of dumping data at her.

I drank a lot of water and ate another two slices of bread. That seemed to help my roiling stomach.

I spent most of the rest of the afternoon on a consult with a Dallas firm on a missing person case in this area. I think I was helpful, and they paid well.

That, and waiting for Ashley to call me back.

Which she did just as I was getting up to pee for the fourth time since I'd gotten here. Water in, water out.

"Hey, what's up?"

"I have some more info for you."

"Really? What?"

"I drove down to Des Allemandes this morning."

"You did what? Didn't I tell you this is dangerous?"

"Don't worry, the only danger was roadside coffee that had been brewed to the essence of a tar pit."

She sighed. "Still, you really need to let us handle this."

"Which is what I'm doing. There *is* a boat named *Eula May*. It left several days ago even though the weather wasn't great. It's owned by two brothers who are known around town for their tattoos, not being friendly, and having no visible means of support. Gossip is they paid for the boat in cash but ran into money troubles."

She was silent for a second, then said, "Wow, you found out all that in a morning?" She sounded impressed.

"I'm pretty good at what I do."

"How do you get that much info so quickly?"

"I'm from out in the bayous. I know how to ask the right questions and fit in."

"That's all interesting, but…we intercepted another message this morning."

"You did?"

"Yes. Just like we thought, coming in via the roadways."

"But could it be two different shipments? Two gangs? How do you know we're both not right?"

"Look…there are things I can't talk about. Our intelligence is the human trafficking is via the roadways. What you've probably stumbled on is drugs. Yes, it's important to stop, but we don't have the manpower to bust everyone who brings in a kilo of marijuana."

I started to talk, but she cut me off.

"However," she said, "I'll bring it up to them again. See if they want to do anything or at least kick it to the locals. It can't hurt to have all bases covered. You've done a great job of information gathering. Maybe you should come work for us."

"Naw, I'm not good with rules."

She gave a throaty laugh. "I've noticed. I have a fond spot for women who don't always play by the rules. Maybe we can break a few tomorrow night?"

"Any rule you want."

"Alas, right now I have to think about playing within the rules and doing my job. Look, I'll call you tomorrow and let you know what happened."

Then she was gone.

Let them take care of it, I told myself. Ashley sounded like she was willing to believe me, but others were less receptive. They had their intelligence and were sure they were right just like I was. They would ignore what I had found. I didn't want to get Ashley caught in a pissing match between her superiors and me.

But I didn't want scared young women dumped into a brutal system, either.

Joanne was out of town.

And wasn't speaking to me.

Danny was here, but it would take too long to explain everything to her. Especially given how sporadic my contact with her had been lately. I knew her well enough to know she would not approve of my borderline-legal activities and to know she'd hound me with questions until she got the answers she wanted—which would reveal those activities.

Take a walk. Talk to Madame Celeste and see if she could pass something along to her connections. That way I could keep my hands sort of clean. Or at least clear of questions I couldn't really answer.

I took the needed trip to the bathroom and headed home. It was time for another walk in the Quarter.

This time I took Rampart. It was busier, but I was hoping this was not the route Emily would take to walk home.

The bracing night air and the walk helped dislodge the last of the tar sands. I was finally beginning to feel normal as I turned down Madame Celeste's street. To do part of the job she'd hired me to do, I walked around the block, looking for anything suspicious, but few people were out; the cold was doing a good job of keeping them in the bars.

I again approached her place, watching to see who might be watching.

I knocked on the door.

Roland answered it. "Come in," he told me, taking my arm to help me up the stairs. He, too, scanned the streets, as if looking for something.

"If possible I'd like to speak to Madame Celeste. Briefly."

He bolted the door.

"Has something happened?" I asked, but he was already leaving the room.

He wasn't gone long when he came back and beckoned me to follow him. He again led me to Madame Celeste's private chambers.

This time she was dressed in a silk robe of rich emerald green. It was cinched tight at her waist, showing her curves, the high, full breasts, the rounded hips tapering to voluptuous thighs. She smiled as I entered. The smile didn't reach her eyes.

"Has something happened?" I asked again.

"You're perceptive."

Roland quietly left, closing the door behind him.

"It's part of what you pay me for."

"Come, sit," she said, motioning to an intimate arrangement of a love seat flanked by two chairs. "Would you like something to drink?"

"Water," I replied. Good alcohol would be wasted on the tar in my stomach. I sat in one of the chairs.

She brought two sparkling waters and put one in front of me. She sat near me on the love seat. "They are more clever than I thought."

I took a sip. "In what way?"

"A nice gentleman came in this afternoon. We check, we have to. They must provide a credit card and name. We ran it. His came up clean. We provided the usual service. Once he was done he told the girl he was giving her a tip—if she didn't want to end up like the women in the river, she needed to get out of town now."

"What? Was he just playing a sick game?"

"He provided details. Ones not put in the paper, nor have I told them. It scared her."

"Understandably. Can I talk to her?"

"She called from the airport."

"Ah, he scared her away."

"Yes, and he slipped by my guards."

"We can make it harder, we can't make it perfect."

"He's taunting me."

"Who is he?"

"The one who came this afternoon? No one. Part of his operation. Someone who could deliver his message."

"What is his message?"

"He'll win this time." She shook her head, looked close to crying. Then she took a drink of water and it passed. "I wanted it not to be true. Here in New Orleans, we're not cutthroat. Oh, yes, we have our rivalries, like any businesses. About five years ago, someone from New York tried to move in. They undercut prices, advertised heavily—as much as one can and not have every vice cop in the vicinity on them. A few pimps died. They did well enough in the low-class end, but couldn't crack us. Our customers are loyal and they pay for our discretion. I had to tip off the police a few times. They finally gave up. But I got a card in the mail saying it wasn't over."

"Why do you think it's them?"

She looked down at her drink. "Because the card...described

what would happen to me when they came back—a stake would be put in my vagina—not the word they used—and I'd be left to float downstream."

"They killed the women to send a message to you?"

"To us. I'm not the only one they wish to take over."

"Who else?"

"I can't tell you."

"Can't or won't?"

"Both. And it doesn't matter."

"You've told your police contact?"

"Yes. At the time, I showed him the card."

"What did he do?"

"Nothing, they were gone. We dismissed it as an empty threat." She took a sip of water, her hand shaking faintly.

"And now?"

She shook her head, almost in despair. "Now…how much protection can the police give to a place they're supposedly trying to shut down? I can't very well ask them to do background checks on all my clients."

"Don't take any new clients, let only the ones you know and trust in," I suggested.

"Mardi Gras, the Super Bowl? I'll lose a lot of business."

"Isn't that better than losing your life?"

She shook her head again, this time as if clearing it. "I am down one girl. Maybe a few others will leave as well." She gave a bitter laugh. "Anything can be broken down to business, can't it?"

"No, it can't," I retorted. "That's what they're doing. This is just business for them. Murder, rape, trafficking. Anything to make money. You care about your workers. You've given them a safe place, comfortable surroundings, pay them well, look out for them as best you can."

"You make me sound like a saint."

"No, you're not. But you know that. I'm pointing out the difference between what you do and what they do. I don't know that I approve of either, but if we can't get to a world where women don't have to sell themselves, I'd rather it by your way than theirs."

She reached out and took my hand. "Thank you, I think. Somewhere in your disapproval, there is a compliment."

"Somewhere. I've fallen too many times to judge others who also fall. I will do what I can to help you and save my disapproval for when we live in a perfect world."

She raised my hand to her lips, softly kissing my fingers, leaning slightly as she did, giving me a better view into cleavage that was already far too distracting.

Holding my hand next to her lips, she said, "We are all human, aren't we? With our messy needs and desires."

I shivered.

She led my hand to her neck, pressing my palm against her throat.

I said nothing.

She slowly pulled my hand down, over her collarbone to the rising flesh.

I shivered again.

Then stopped my hand. "I have information I need you to pass to your contacts."

We were still, my hand warm against her soft skin, then she again brought my hand to her lips, another soft kiss, and she placed it back in my lap. "What information do you have?"

"You can't ask how I got it."

"I understand. No questions."

"I saw a message indicating a boat might be arriving in Des Allemandes at eleven tonight. It will be carrying nine of something, possibly women. The boat is named the *Eula May*. It's white with red-and-black trim and owned by two brothers named Guidry."

She got up and crossed to the bar, got us both another bottle of water and herself a notebook. "Eleven tonight," she said as she wrote, "Des Allemandes, *Eula May*. Guidry brothers. I'll pass it on."

"Maybe getting busted will distract them."

"This is war. I welcome any weapon I can get." She glanced at her watch. "I must call, make arrangements to serve only regular clients." She stood up. "When will I see you again?"

"Soon," I hedged. "Let's see what happens tonight." I got up.

She walked me to the door of her chamber. "Soon," she said, and kissed me very briefly on the lips.

I found my way to the front door. Roland first checked through the peephole before opening the door and letting me out.

He stood in the doorway, watching me as I headed down the block.

I strode home, as if the exertion could exorcise my jumbled desires. I wanted to be the kind of woman who clearly went for good-girl Ashley. She was the safest, sanest choice. But I had liked sex with Emily and I liked the idea of sex with Madame Celeste. I was all too aware that only fragile circumstances kept me from sleeping with each of them.

Too dangerous, I repeatedly told myself. Too fucking dangerous. I was clueless how to safely navigate my jumbled and contradictory desires.

The cold and exercise helped calm me down, but offered no answers.

At home I was too agitated to eat. I finally forced myself to make a sandwich, using the dregs at the bottom of a jar of indeterminate jam, peanut butter hidden in the back of my cupboard, and hastily defrosted pita bread that was shoved in the back of the freezer, probably from last summer. I ate half of it.

I started to pour the Scotch.

Then put the glass away.

I needed to know what happened tonight, if I was right. If the kinder, gentler prostitution would survive—at least for a few women, those with the looks and the charm to be kept in a safe cage. Chuck at the hooker hotel wasn't going to run interference for Bianca. She'd be lucky if he'd call 911 if she was beat up and bleeding.

Madame Celeste's contacts were not a two-way street. Maybe she would find out and maybe she would tell me. If I slept with her.

That's a neat trick, convince yourself you'll only get the information you want by sleeping with her so you can claim you weren't doing it because you wanted to, but because you had to.

It sucks to be self-aware enough to know what bullshit that was. I'd sleep with her because I wanted to. She'd give me the information if she knew it. All I'd have to do is ask.

I looked at my watch. Almost eight o'clock.

You can be a bystander. Watch and see what happens. As if I hadn't been planning to do that in the back of my head all along.

I changed into my standard "hang out and blend in" outfit: black jeans, charcoal-gray long-sleeved T-shirt, black hooded sweatshirt. This time I remembered a scarf. Deep blue was the darkest I had; I needed to buy a black scarf for nights like this. Plus heavy socks and black sneakers, an old pair in case I had to muck around docks. Also, my usual surveillance gear. And my gun.

You're not going to do anything except watch, I told myself as I got in my car. No matter what happened, the most I'd get involved was to call 911 and hightail it out of there. My plan really was to find a reasonably hidden place and observe what happened. Even if I had to watch nine women being led in chains from the boat to a waiting truck, I would not get involved. Ashley was right, these were dangerous men. I needed to make sure no one would see me there.

I was out my door around 8:30 p.m. I wanted to get there early enough to check things out well before anything suspicious took place, at a time on a night when people were out and about. I'd be someone living in the area visiting friends.

I took the quick, mostly interstate, way and was there a little after nine.

The town was quiet; not even being this close to the weekend livened up the streets much. It was dark this far out in the country, the few lights from curtained windows and an occasional porch light. Traffic was light, as most people were either home or where they planned to be this evening.

The gods of surveillance were with me. Partway into Down the Bayou Road a party was taking place. I drove just far enough past to make my car look like I could be parked for their event. If I was lucky they would party until midnight and be the perfect cover for extra cars here.

Plus this gave me an excuse to play with one of my toys, night vision goggles. They look like binoculars and can increase magnification. They give me about two hundred feet of view into the dark. Not perfect, but better than plain old eyesight. With them I could see the houses with the prowling dogs as well as the dock on the bayou near them. The dogs were still there, mostly still although occasionally pricking their ears at a burst of noise from the party.

The dock was empty.

I settled in to wait.

I'd been smart enough—or experienced enough—to stop at a gas station at the last exit off the interstate and make a pit stop. I'd gotten a small bottle of water, which I would judiciously sip, and a bag of trail mix.

I wasn't hungry, but telling myself in ten minutes I could open the trail mix was a way to make the time pass.

Which it did slowly.

The party got louder, probably drunker, as the evening wore on, until a little after ten a neighbor from down the road drove up, honked his horn for a good loud pull, and shouted at them to quiet it down.

Making noise to tell people not to be noisy didn't seem like a winning strategy to me. I was proven right by how quickly the noise level returned to its previous boisterous pitch.

Another ten minutes, a little more trail mix. At the half hour I allowed myself a sip of water.

At around 10:30 I saw the lights of a boat coming up the bayou. Using the night vision goggles I looked at it. It was a smaller boat, not big enough for more than the two people—oh, wait, man and woman, and they were clearly close friends—in it. The Cajun variation on the backseat of a car. They headed past me, presumably back to the homes where they didn't have as much privacy.

More trail mix. Hold on the water.

I had also been watching to see if law enforcement was going to do something. So far I hadn't seen anyone or any car that looked like it might be here for the same reason I was. Maybe they had positioned themselves farther down the road and gotten here before me. Or they were waiting at one of the intersections closer to the highway. I was guessing the homes with the prowling dogs were the site, but I could be wrong. Maybe the party was going to get wilder at eleven with the arrival of a bunch of chained women. Possibly the police were spread out.

Or they weren't here.

At five minutes to eleven a large van rumbled past me. I let it get about fifty feet farther before picking up my night vision binoculars.

No license plate. It looked like a delivery van, but nothing was written on it and the only windows were in the cab. The kind of van your mother warned you about.

It stopped next to the dock across from where the dogs were. They picked up their ears and came to the fence but didn't bark.

A figure dressed in dark clothes, a man I guessed, got out, trotted across the road, threw something to the dogs—something edible from their reaction, snuffling on the ground and chewing. He hurried back to the van. He wore a dark ball cap low on his face. I had the impression of a scruffy beard and a paunch, but couldn't get a good look at him.

Though it was cold, I rolled down my window. It made the party louder—no wonder the neighbor was complaining—but it let me hear the other sounds of the night.

A soft wind in the trees. The far-off bark of a dog.

The approaching chug of a boat, faint, in the distance.

I couldn't yet see it even with the goggles.

I glanced at my watch. A minute or so after eleven.

Another minute and I could make out the ghostly green of the boat. It was large, the right size. Its running lights were off. Without the aid of the goggles, I wouldn't be able to see it.

Maybe it wasn't human trafficking, but it was something shady. This time of night, no lights on the boat, no license on the van.

I kept watching, mesmerized by the boat's slow progress to the dock. I put the night vision goggles down. Without them, it disappeared, only a vague directionless rumble of a motor. I only heard it because I was listening and listening intently. Behind closed doors it wouldn't register. Outside, the noise of the party masked it.

I picked up the night goggles again. The boat reappeared, closer now, slowing to come to the dock.

Again, only because I was listening, I heard the soft thunk of the boat as it nudged the dock. Someone jumped off it bundled against the cold of the night and the water. The figure was tall enough to be a man, but the heavy clothes told me little else. He quickly tied it off.

I tried to gauge his height against the boat. Tall, either had ten layers on or he was sturdy or stocky. But like his compatriot in the van, he also wore a cap pulled low with a sweatshirt hood over it.

Another man also got off the boat. Same deal, dressed for the cold and to be hidden. He was a little shorter than the first man.

I heard the sliding door of the van open. It was facing the dock, so I couldn't see it.

This was about the time the cops should show up, if they were going to show up.

I heard a crash and drunken yell from the party and then raucous laughter.

Someone was leaving the boat, smaller, slighter than the other figures.

Then another.

A horn blared.

I looked in my rearview mirror. The peeved neighbor was back, this time an even longer blast of his horn. He slammed on his high beams, casting a harsh light down the road, catching my car and most of everything down the bayou.

Two more figures were hustled into the van.

I put down the night goggles. I was visible to anyone looking.

Sitting in a car, maybe. Sitting in a car with funny-looking binoculars would be noticeable, and not in a good way.

With his light, I could just make out the boat.

In the rearview mirror, I could see him yelling at one of the partygoers.

Then he got out of his truck, leaving it in the middle of the road.

I lost count of the women—I was guessing they were woman—being taken off the boat. Two, three more?

The angry man starting shoving and pushing a party person. Then a punch was thrown. I could only make out a slice of the action from my mirror.

Sirens. Then very clearly in the mirror, flashing lights.

The cops. Where they here for the party or the boat?

I was able to see at least three pairs of lights. Had to be for the boat.

But they were stuck behind the truck. This was a narrow lane, and for two cars to pass, one would have to pull to the side. With all the party cars parked, it made it impassible, no way to edge around the truck in the middle of the road.

Shit, shit, shit. Oh, make that major shit.

Were all the women off the boat?

With all the hoopla from the fight, I hoped no one would notice me grabbing my goggles.

One small person was standing on the dock, one of the bigger men holding her arm. She jerked it free and started running in the direction of the lights and sirens. Toward me.

Two of the men started after her.

The truck hadn't moved yet. The cops were still stuck behind it.

I broke my promise that I would just watch.

Turning on my car, I slammed on the high beams, catching both the woman—and she was clearly a woman—and the two men chasing her. I squealed out of my parking place, heading toward them, yelling out of the window in my most butch voice, "Stop! Police!"

The woman kept running in my direction.

The two men turned back to the boat, sprinting away from the lights.

The van driver jumped out and started to untie the boat.

The only way out was by water.

A shot rang out.

I couldn't tell if it was from the boat or the cops.

Didn't matter. I was between them.

I reached the woman. Stopped my car and flung open the passenger door.

"Get in," I yelled.

She looked at me, then behind her.

Another shot.

She jumped in and said something in a language I didn't understand, not even well enough to guess what language it might be.

The two men ran to the boat as it was pulling away from the dock, its engines revving. The slower one had to take a running leap to make it aboard.

It was in reverse, not willing to take the time to turn, but going as fast as it could away.

I heard the sirens move. The truck had finally been cleared.

I pulled over, out of their way.

The woman in my car was sobbing, crying in a language I couldn't comprehend.

"It's okay," I said, doing my best to calm her. "You're safe now. You're free."

She couldn't understand me either. I took her hand. She was cold, trembling.

The cars sped past me, only to jerk to a stop at the van.

A number of officers got out, guns pulled, demanding whoever was in there to come out with their hands up.

By my count only the women were still in it.

The woman in my car saw the guns and started screaming. She jerked away from me. But as she fumbled with the door lock, I jumped out and dashed around to her side. I grabbed her before she ran into the cops.

I held her tightly, what I hoped she'd understand as protectively, and we slowly walked to the van.

"Hey," I called. "Three men jumped onto the boat. I think it's her and her friends in the van."

One older cop looked back at me.

"Who the hell are you?"

"Just a bystander. Was leaving the party and saw all this mess. This woman," I pointed to her, "looked like she was trying to get away from them, so I let her in my car."

"Who is she?" he asked me.

"I don't know. I can't understand her language. Eastern European, maybe?"

"Tell 'em to come out," he instructed.

"If you lower your guns, they might get the message," I said.

He looked at me, at her, at his gun, at the other cops surrounding the van.

The boat was out of sight.

In the silence, we heard women crying, coming from the van.

He looked at me again and holstered his gun.

I felt the woman beside me let go a held breath. She called to the van, what sounded like names.

Several other cops lowered their guns.

"It's probably locked from the outside," I suggested. "They might not be able to get out."

The older cop looked at me, then one of the younger ones and nodded at him. The younger man cautiously approached the van, his weapon still in his hand, but pointed down. He carefully opened the side door.

For a second nothing happened, then women piled out. They were all dressed like my friend, cheap clothes not warm enough for the temperature.

The woman beside me pulled away, running to one of the other women, grabbing her in a fierce hug. They looked enough alike to be sisters. They also looked young, the one who ran to me maybe eighteen, the one she was holding no more than fifteen.

Bastards. Fucking bastards.

But for these women, their ride in horror was over.

If it weren't midnight, I'd ride off into the sunset.

I slowly stepped back, away from the van and the cacophony of languages. What little information I had, they could easily get. Anyone and everyone in this town would quickly tell the same tale my coffee-pushing waitress told me.

I didn't need to be anything more than a chance bystander.

I counted the woman. Nine.

That was all I needed to know before quietly turning away and getting back in my car. The night was cold, and I'd done what I could do.

Chapter Eighteen

Much as I wanted to blow town, the narrow street defeated me. Between the cop cars and the former partygoers, now a gawking crowd, there was no way to move my car. At least not without drawing a lot of attention to myself by asking about twenty people and three police cars to get out of my way.

Other than being a little cold, I was okay. As long as I didn't desperately have to go to the bathroom, I could stay here until it had cleared up enough for me to leave without being noticed.

I closed my windows, zipped the sweatshirt, and wrapped the scarf tightly around my neck. Then I let my seat back and shut my eyes, hoping for a nap blessedly long enough so I could wake and head home.

Crack!

Something slammed against my car.

Groggily, I sat up.

Then noticed a hand against my door window.

A hand holding what looked like an official shield. The metal banging against the glass was what made the noise.

I blinked my eyes.

Read the badge.

FBI.

Read the name.

Emily Harris.

She rapped sharply with her knuckles. "Open the door, Knight," she said, her voice muffled by the closed window.

I half obeyed and rolled down the window.

She leaned in, her eyes flashing. "What the fuck are you doing here?" she demanded.

"Scenic drive."

"Bullshit," she growled. "Bringing in some trade for Desiree?"

That woke me up fully. "No," I retorted. "Not even remotely close."

She strode around to the other side of my car and attempted to yank the passenger door open. It was locked.

I had enough sense to unlock it before she shot her way in.

Even so she almost tore the door off opening it.

"I am so not standing in the fucking cold, fucking rain, fucking talking to you," she informed me.

A drizzle was coming down my windshield. Must have started while I was napping.

"It's not what it seems—" I started.

"It never is with you."

She had a badge and I didn't have a good excuse for being here. "I heard a rumor—"

"From where?"

"Let me get through it. Then you can ask your questions," I said in as calm a voice as I could muster.

She curtly nodded.

I started again, "I heard a rumor. Talked to someone I know in law enforcement, but they blew it off. It nagged me. Made perfect sense to me to smuggle goods—and people—through these bayous. So I came here to watch. To see if I was right or not. That's really the story."

"Okay, if that's your story," she said, her voice so tight the words were clipped. "First, let's start with the rumor. Where did you hear that?"

I pondered what to tell her. The truth, that I'd after-burglared some burglars, wouldn't be wise. That left me with the very weak "I can't tell you. I have to protect my sources."

"That's giving me no reason not to arrest you right now."

"It happens to be true. And…"

"And what?"

Go for it. See how she reacts. "And my source thinks there's a leak, a corrupt cop. They don't want their name brought up."

"So now it's our fault?"

"I can't prove her wrong. Can you?"

Emily turned to me and grabbed my chin in a hard grasp. "I have worked with several of these people for most of my professional career. I trust them with my life. Could some cop somewhere be on the take?

That's always possible. But no one in our inner circle. No one who would know information that could put anyone in danger."

I pried her fingers from my face so I could answer. "I'll go back and talk to my source and tell them what you said. But I can't reveal a name right now."

She sighed, an angry sigh. "What did the rumor say?"

"The information was cryptic." I wondered what I dared tell her. What if she was wrong? Or lying? "It mentioned the name of a boat, the *Eula May*." The cops could easily find out who docked here. "Then numbers, nine at eleven on eighteen."

"That was enough to lead you here?"

"No. It also mentioned down the bayou by the Germans."

"Ah, that's what led you here?" she challenged.

"Yes. I know you don't believe me, but I grew up down here."

"I believe that. We pulled your birth records. Lived in Bayou St. Jack until you were ten. Metairie after that."

The words seemed too small to sum up those years, my father's death, living with Aunt Greta and her rules, never accepted by my cousins, Uncle Claude lost in TV and a life that had defeated him. I cleared my throat. "Yes, so I remembered being here once and my father commenting on Down the Bayou Road. How original a name it was. I also know this is referred to as the German coast, and Des Allemandes is French for 'the Germans.'"

"How did it get that name?"

"A number of German immigrants settled here, farming and fishing. They did a lot of trade with New Orleans back when it was owned by the French."

"I'm supposed to believe that some unnamable source dumped those choice nuggets of info in your lap rather than go to law enforcement?"

"I did what I could to pass it on," I argued. "Clearly someone listened, otherwise you wouldn't be here."

"Did you happen to notice they got away?" The sarcasm dripped.

"Yes, I did manage to see that. But how is that my fault?"

"You warned them."

"Fuck you," I said, and realized she was deliberately goading me. I took a breath. "That's crap and you know it. If I were going to warn them, I'd warn them to change their plans. Show up at a different time. Clearly they didn't do that. They got away through dumb luck. And your side not thinking to have a boat ready to go after them."

She looked away. I got her on that one. She broke the silence. "It's not a good thing you're here. I didn't believe your first story, but I let it slide because it was possible—just possible—your reasons for lying weren't relevant. I don't believe you now either. And it's getting harder to think your lies can have an innocent explanation."

"I'm not involved with selling women into sex slavery. Any women, but especially ones as young as these were."

She stared at me for several seconds, then said, "I hope that's true. But if it's not, I'll put the handcuffs on you myself." She got out, slamming the door hard enough to make my car shake.

I sat still, not looking after her.

What had I accomplished here? Madame Celeste had passed on my information to someone who listened. The cops were here and they probably would have been able to arrest the men on the boat if they hadn't been blocked at the crucial moment by the truck. All it took was two or three minutes to give them enough time to get back on the boat and pull away. That would have happened if I was here or not. All I managed to do was let Emily spot me at the scene of another crime.

The woman who'd run. What would have happened to her if I hadn't let her in my car and acted like police? Had that made them decide to abandon the women and jump on the boat?

Maybe. And that was the best I could give myself.

It was after one a.m. The party had ended and even the gawkers were gone. Clear enough for me to do a three-point turn and head back up Down the Bayou Road.

I was careful to do the speed limit the entire way back.

Once I got home, I poured myself some of the not-so-good Scotch, chugged it in a few swallows, and went to bed.

As I had hoped, the alcohol helped me fall asleep.

It didn't help me stay asleep.

Emily swore no one in her inner circle, the ones investigating this, would be corrupt enough to work with the bad guys. Ashley claimed someone was. They couldn't both be right. Madame Celeste clearly had contacts in law enforcement, but was it as benign as they claimed? Had she arranged for me to meet her contact so he could spin an innocent story? Emily said there were two rival gangs. Ashley implied there was just one. Madame Celeste said one that had tried to move in after Katrina was back again. She was in the business; Ashley and Emily weren't. But Celeste was by now a wealthy woman, if she'd been wise with her earnings. Unless she was truly greedy, she had no reason to want to be part of a larger gang. It might make her more money, but she'd lose control. My instinct was that was more important to her. But if she hadn't been careful with her money, the lure of more might be too hard to resist. What better way to get me off track than by concocting a story about another rival gang?

Ashley was staying in a decent hotel, but that was on the government dime. From our trip to Café Adelaide, she didn't seem the type to head to the fancy places. Emily, on the other hand, lived in a nice place in the French Quarter. Those don't come cheap. She was a grunt FBI agent, probably near the bottom of their pay scale. Not minimum wage by any means, but not enough to live the lavish life. Still, she might have had money in the family, or a friend who liked her and gave her a deal. Then I wondered about the second voice I'd heard out by the warehouse—a woman with a low voice? It wasn't Ashley; she was gone by then. Emily's voice was the same range. So was Madame Celeste's.

Emily knew my car was there. I'd thought I got away before the cops arrived. Had a helpful neighbor seen my car and reported it? The thugs out there drove past it as they escaped; they had to have seen it. Maybe they called their pet cop and asked him—or her—to check it out?

Who should I believe?

And should I believe anyone?

Dawn brought light, but no answers.

CHAPTER NINETEEN

Somehow I did manage to fall asleep, as I woke up with the light of late morning across my bed. *At least I slept*, I thought as I slowly got up. This last week with its late hours hadn't been kind to my getting the proper amount of rest.

After a long, hot shower and a reasonably healthy breakfast, whole-wheat, oatmeal pancakes also pulled from the freezer behind the pita bread, which probably meant they had been there since last summer—and a lot of caffeine—I decided to do what I'm supposed to be good at, detective work.

Even though I really wanted a day off, I headed down to my office—travel mug of coffee in hand—as that was where I had the better computer and the bookmarked search engines.

It wasn't likely I'd find anything truly revealing via online searches. Only the young and dumb leave a trail that wide. But I could find crumbs, and those could give me clues as to what I was dealing with.

First up was Madame Celeste aka Desiree Montaigne. For her career path, it seemed like Desiree might be a perfect name—unless it was her real name and for obvious reasons, she decided she didn't want to use her real name.

Emily had been right about the property; Desiree did own the building, free and clear even. Her taxes were all paid. She also owned a smaller building next to it, listed as a private residence. At current market prices those properties were probably close to two million. For her business, she had it listed as a private club. That probably allowed her to skate on the legal line. Of course, charging money for sex is illegal, but they had to catch her at it, and it seemed the local cops weren't interested in doing that.

It took searching, but I was able to find an arrest record for her. It went back almost forty years, her first arrest coming when she was eighteen. She'd gotten arrested a few more times until she was about twenty-five, charges associated with prostitution such as "crimes against nature," which could be charged for oral sex and was often used as it was a felony instead of the misdemeanor charge of soliciting. From the court record, she had spent a stint in jail of about six months. She never went back after that.

What leads a woman to a life like that? Probably not a happy childhood. Sexual abuse as a child? What happens to kids when staying at home is a bad choice? Parents or guardians so chaotic and unstable that it's impossible to study or have a chance of graduating even in the bottom of your class. Where do those kids go?

They get arrested for prostitution when they're eighteen.

A lot of them turn to drugs to survive the pain and hopelessness. They get arrested like Bianca and go to jail, and that narrows their options even more.

A few, a very few, find ways to survive and do as well as Desiree. Even so, she lived an illegal life, one that could crumble at any time.

Much as I searched, I could find little to crack what I knew of her story. She seemed to be what she presented herself as, a successful madam who'd worked her way there from being a working girl.

To have survived and thrived as she had meant she was smart, savvy, and willing to do what it took. But the Internet search gave no indication of how far she would go. Could she be as ruthless as her competition, or was the face she put on for me, someone trying to survive as honorably as she could in an ignoble system, the real one?

That took a good part of the morning.

Next up was Emily Harris.

She bought her property in the French Quarter for cash. I found that out by cross-referencing the address and chancing on a social media post from the seller bragging about getting asking price and in cash. He didn't mention her name, but the address was the same and the time was about right.

Did her family have that kind of money?

She was born in a suburb of Boston. From the census data I looked up, not one of the snooty ones, more a solid middle-class to solid working-class one. Went to the University of Massachusetts. Again, not an indication of money. It was a decent school, but also her state one. After that she went to law school at the University of Michigan.

But from the dates, it looked like she took a few years off between. Yes, I got lucky and found a résumé she'd posted on a job search website. It was old. She'd worked for about a year at a law firm in DC, then became a good girl and worked for a nonprofit environmental law organization, one that, at least from their current website, did lawsuits about environmental racism—fighting putting belching factories in the poor communities and the like. That was the last job listed in the résumé and that was about six years ago. No indication of when she joined the FBI or what caused her to go from fighting big companies taking advantage of poor people to fighting crime at an elite level.

Property records indicated she bought a place in DC during her first year there, while working at the law firm and probably making decent money. She sold it about six months ago to a woman named Susana Parker. A little more digging found that the two of them had lived there together for four years. The record of sale was for about half of what the property was worth, indicating that Emily's ex had probably bought her out. If she put that directly into the New Orleans property, that would have covered about two-thirds of the cost.

It was past lunchtime, and nutritious breakfasts only go so far. I hadn't brought anything with me because I hadn't gone to the grocery, which meant I had nothing at home to make lunch with. I had gone through all the archeological layers in the freezer. While debating whether to chuck my search and do a proper grocery run, my cell rang.

I didn't recognize the number but answered it anyway.

"Yeah, this is Frank Mullen," the caller answered.

"Who are you calling?" I asked.

"You called me, remember? About the Kimberly Fremont case?"

Now it came back to me, the case Ashley said haunted her. "Yes, thank you for calling me back. What can you tell me about that one?"

"What do you need to know?"

"I have a friend who's an ICE agent and she said it was one of the cases that bothered her. I'm a private detective who specializes in missing people, so I told her I'd give it a look if I have the time."

"Why?"

"I know it's a long shot, but to see if I can find her."

"Find her? Whoa, she's not lost. Showed up about two months after she went missing."

"What?" Damn, I'd only searched the immediate time period.

THE SHOAL OF TIME • 185 •

"Yeah, you know, the usual thing, teenage girl meets one of those older creeps, he promises her the moon, she falls for it. Took her one and a half months to figure out he was a horny creep who only wanted to get in her panties. She came back. We busted the pervert and he's still in jail."

"Well, that's good news. Guess my friend missed out on that part."

"She shoulda called. Coulda sorted this out a long time ago."

"You're right. Guess she got caught up with other stuff and assumed that it didn't have a happy end."

"Yeah, happy enough, I guess. Kimberly wasn't the brightest light on the Christmas tree. Last I checked she was doing okay, in the local community college studying medical records. What kid her age falls for 'the older guy madly in love with her' crap?"

"Someone who wants to believe the love stories will happen to them."

"Guess you're right. Wife loves those romance books. When I complain, she reminds me she's a football widow."

"Go Saints."

"Giants. May the best team win. Say, who's your friend? One of my former coworkers' daughter is now with ICE. Met her a few times. Real impressive gal."

"Ashley West."

"Bingo, that's her. Tell her Frank, the football nut her dad worked with, says hi."

"I'll do that."

"Huh, how the heck did she not ask him about Kimberly?"

"You know how family can be, last people you want to ask."

"Guess so, although I thought they were close. Oh well, done now."

"Thanks a lot, Mr. Mullen. Good luck with the football season."

"You, too." He got out another "Go Giants" before we hung up.

I could at least tell Ashley that the kid she wondered about had come home. Plus I'd talked to someone who knew her and seemed to think highly of her. Nice, all in all.

But my stomach was still grumbling.

Given that I was meeting Ashley tonight for dinner—with hints we might spend part of tomorrow together—the grocery store could wait.

I ran to the Food Co-op on St. Claude and got a salad. And some chips, but healthy chips, mind you. I didn't want to be starving for dinner tonight.

Instead of going back to my office, I headed home. A couple hours of cleaning was beyond needed. I wasn't planning to bring her back here—I was trying not to plan anything except a pleasant meal with a smart, attractive woman. But a clean house is always a nice thing, and this way I was prepared for whatever might happen. Including coming here alone afterward.

I took another shower to get off the dust and sweat from my housework.

She had said to dress for a night on the town. I'm not a night-on-the-town kind of girl and my wardrobe reflected that. If I needed a dress, I usually borrowed it from Torbin, since he had a closet full of drag queen clothes.

I did have a few dresses all of my own for those times I didn't want something that had appeared on stage in a French Quarter drag show, but that meant panty hose, and I wasn't up to that, nor was it likely I had an intact pair in the house.

I settled for as femme as I could be in pants with a gray suit of a light wool material, a white V-neck cashmere sweater, a birthday present from my mother, and actual girl pumps, black with about a one-inch heel. I didn't want to tower over her. Silver earrings and necklace completed the look.

I gave my hair a good brushing to make sure no rats were living there.

"It'll have to do," I said to the mirror.

One last mouthwash rinse and I left.

Traffic was the usually drunken, tourist-besotted insanity in this area. I like living near the French Quarter, but it does make driving all too interesting in the Chinese curse way.

I got to her hotel just at seven and valet-parked my car.

She was waiting for me in the lobby. She was dressed in a green flowing jumpsuit, made of what I guessed was silk. It was cinched in the waist in a way that showed off her figure. The green brought out the green in her eyes and contrasted with the red in her hair. She had on a gold necklace with a small, tasteful emerald hanging from it, perfectly matching her outfit. Her shoes were classic black heels, an inch higher than I would have wanted to try, but they looked great on her. She'd even put on a discreet amount of makeup. I was buoyed she'd taken the time and trouble for me.

"You look great," she said as a greeting.

"Not as good as you." I half bowed to show my appreciation.

She smiled a warm radiant smile.

This was what I wanted, needed, more than the raw sex—and mistrust—offered by Emily. The quiet moments of connection, each of us taking the time to dress for each other, a smile when she saw me, going out to dinner to enjoy each other's company.

"You're too kind," she said, but her smile told me she appreciated the compliment. She tossed a dark-green wrap across her shoulders, then linked her arm through mine. "Ready for your night on the town?"

"Only if you are."

"I've been looking forward to this for a long time. I'm sorry it's taken us this much time to finally get there."

I was, too, but just smiled. Part of my wish was to keep things simple and clean, no longing for women I shouldn't want.

As we walked out of the lobby, she continued, "We have reservations at the Palace Café. White chocolate bread pudding strikes me as something one should try while in New Orleans."

"Yes, you definitely should."

"Not all by myself, you'll have to help me."

"I could be persuaded."

She laughed again, a warm welcoming sound. "Are you okay to walk? Or should we take a cab? It's about six blocks."

"I'm fine walking if you are."

Still a little chilly, but a nice enough night for a stroll. We walked for about half a block in silence, her arm still tucked in mine.

I broke it by saying, "You heard about my little adventure last night?"

"Your what? No, I don't guess I did. All I heard was…there were some problems. What happened?"

"I went to Des Allemandes, to see if anything did happen at eleven."

"After I warned you?"

"Not to do anything, just watch. Maybe call 9-1-1 if needed."

"But the police had been tipped off, right?"

"Yes, they were there."

"Were you the one who told them?"

"No. Well, not directly."

"How do you indirectly tell the police?"

"I have a friend who has contacts. I told her my worries and what I thought. I don't know if she passed it on or not, but it seems she did."

"Ah. So tell me what happened."

"Everything would have been fine, except there was a party. A complaining neighbor parked his truck in the middle of the road and got into a shouting match with the revelers at the wrong time. He blocked the cops from getting to the boat. It gave them just enough time to pull away from the dock and get away."

"Wow, that's bad luck," she said.

"Yeah, lousy timing. The cops might have gotten them if they'd had a boat available. But at least the police know who they are and the name of their boat."

"Really? Can you be sure they have the right ones?"

"It's a small town, people notice things."

"So you think they'll find them soon?"

"Maybe not soon, they can probably hide in the bayous for a long time. But eventually. Plus they've lost what seems to be their preferred smuggling route. That means they have to find a new route, one they're less familiar with."

"So all you did was watch?"

I sighed and delayed answering. We crossed Canal Street, thick with tourists, six lanes of traffic, and streetcar tracks in the middle.

She left the silence, so I knew I'd have to answer.

"I didn't want to get involved, but one of the women broke away and two of the brutes started to chase her. The real cops were still stuck behind the truck, so I pulled my fake cop act again, driving at them, yelling, 'Stop, police.' It seemed to work, they stopped chasing her and headed back to the boat."

"So they might not have gotten away if you'd let them keep chasing the woman?" Her tone wasn't harsh, just questioning.

"They could see the road clearly. As long as the truck wasn't moving they were safe. I think if I hadn't acted they would have recaptured her and maybe had enough time to reload the other women."

"The women get away?"

"All nine of them."

"Did they say anything to you?"

"Lots of things, all in a language I didn't understand."

"The police saw you there?"

"I claimed I was just a bystander, leaving the party. I think they believed me."

"Smart move."

"Yeah, it would have worked if that FBI agent I tangled with before wasn't also there."

"Which one?" she asked as we arrived at the restaurant.

I delayed my answer while she announced us at the reservation desk. When she was done she turned back to me with an expectant look.

"The same one who questioned me about reports of my car being out by the warehouse."

"What did you tell her?"

"The truth. As much of it as I could. I claimed a client I couldn't mention was the one who gave me the info. And that I came out only to watch what happened."

"Do you think she bought it?"

I had to admit, "No, not very much. I think she believes I'm involved. You told me there was a mole, so I've been very careful about what I've told her."

We were led to our table, pausing our conversation while we were seated and ordered drinks; she got a dirty martini, I went traditional with a Sazerac.

Once the waiter left, Ashley said, "That's good that you've been careful."

"The problem is it's contributed to her not believing me."

"Have you mentioned me? My team?"

"No, I haven't. Like I said, very careful." I took a sip of water. "It would help if I could. She promised that no one in her inner circle would be on the take."

Ashley sighed. "It's always the people who promise you can trust them that you shouldn't trust. What is her name?"

"Emily Harris."

She looked at the menu for a moment, then at me. "There are things I can't tell you. And some things I shouldn't tell you, but I don't want you to get hurt. Be very careful around the FBI."

"Are you saying she's the traitor?"

"We don't know for sure, but you really can't trust her."

"I'm not planning to have anything more to do with her." Not that

I'd planned our last two encounters, but intentions should count for something.

"Good, keep it that way." Ashley put her hand on mine and gave it a lingering squeeze. She let go as the waiter brought our drinks. She took a sip of her martini and said, "I need to apologize to you. You were right about what the message meant. I should have pushed it more with the higher-ups."

"No apology needed. You did the best you could. It's not your fault that others get stuck in what they want to believe."

"Still, it would have been better if we had been there—and you hadn't. Now I'm worried you're too involved in this."

"I made my choices, you're not responsible. Besides, it's only a matter of time before they catch them and this is over."

Ashley shook her head. "That's not good."

"Not good that they're caught?"

"No, sorry. Of course it's good they'll be caught. It just means… I'll be leaving here."

"Then let's enjoy the time you're here. Besides, planes leave and arrive every day."

She smiled at me again. "You are one very smart, resilient woman. I have to say I've been pretty impressed with how you've handled things."

"Thanks," I said, hiding my pleasure in her compliment by sipping my drink.

The waiter hovered to see if we were ready to order. We both took the hint and looked over our menus. We agreed to share the crabmeat cheesecake and a spinach salad. I got the catfish pecan and she opted for the duck.

Once the waiter left she said, "You were persistent in following through on that lead. And knew enough about the area to make sense of the clues—why we hired you in the first place. I always say it's dumb to not pay attention to the local people."

"Like I said, it's not your fault. You can only do so much."

"I still should have done a better job. It's not often I stumble over very smart, good-looking women along the way. I should do a better job of taking care of those I do find."

"You've done a fine job. This is a very nice thanks for everything."

"Just a meal."

"I'm including your company."

She smiled.

I returned it.

"Can you tell me how you managed to get the info to the authorities?" She looked away and said, "Sorry, can't seem to quit working."

"That might be something we're both guilty of." I took a sip of my drink. "Keep in mind I'm a private detective, not the police. A while back I worked on an embezzlement case in which some of the money went to high-end call girls. The company I worked for was more interested in getting the money back than prosecution. I brokered a deal with the madam to return most of the money and the company wouldn't make a stink."

"Okay, makes sense. Well, it does if you're not in law enforcement."

"The madam appreciated my efforts. So when the dead women were found she hired me to basically do a safety one-oh-one with her staff. Which I did." I watched Ashley's face to see how she would react to this. So far she didn't seem particularly upset.

I continued, "The woman in charge has been around for a while and has a lot of contacts. So I asked her if she would pass it on."

"That's clever," she said, sipping her drink, so I couldn't fully read her face. "Use one house of prostitution to take down a rival. You could be pretty sure she'd pass the information along."

"It's more complex than that," I said, feeling I needed to defend Madame Celeste. "I think she had it in more for this particular rival than others."

"You're okay with prostitution?"

"I have a lot of issues with women—and men—selling themselves to the highest bidder."

"But you worked with her?"

"I'm realistic enough to know nothing is going to change anytime soon. If it's going to go on, I'd prefer it be done by women who were former sex workers, who do things like hire private detectives to provide safety tips, than men who dispose of unwanted women by ramming a stake in their vagina."

"So, you're okay enough with it to take money from a woman who runs a whorehouse?"

"Ouch," I said.

Our salad arrived.

Ashley put half of it on a plate for me. "Sorry, I'm just trying to find where you draw the line."

I took a bite of the salad. "I'm not sure where I draw the line. It may depend on the day and the person. I'm not perfect and I've slipped and fallen a few times. I've just never fallen far enough to consider selling my body to survive. I try not to judge those who do."

"True, I'm not perfect either. I've done work that's taken me close to, if not over, some lines. I'll follow your lead." She speared a pecan, chewed, then said, "Look, I can't make any promises. When and if this thing blows, it may blow big, but I can try to steer them away from your friend. Keep the arrests and jail time for the kind of men who murder women."

"I know you can't make promises, but anything you can do would help."

"Who is it?"

"Who?" I was in the middle of a mouthful of spinach.

"Your friend? Or should I say client?"

I swallowed. "Client. She goes by Madame Celeste. I believe her real name is Desiree Montaigne."

"Okay, thanks. I'll do what I can."

The crab cake came. Ashley also split that between us.

"You don't get food like this anywhere else," I said after taking a bite. "So you'll have to come back to New Orleans often."

"I'd like that, I'd like that a lot. This is divine."

"One more work piece, then we ban it for the rest of the evening," I said. "I remembered the picture you showed me, the missing girl."

"Oh, yes?"

"I called the precinct where it happened and talked to the detective on the case. He said she returned about a few months later."

"She what?" Ashley coughed. "Shell," she said, grabbing her water.

She coughed again and I waited until she recovered. "I'm okay," she said, her voice raspy. She nodded at me to continue.

"She returned. He said it was the usual thing, an older guy cooing love songs to her, she believed him, then figured out he was a creep and came home. They arrested the guy and he's still in jail."

Ashley cleared her throat, then said, "Really? Wow, that's good to know."

"I thought you'd like to find out she hadn't been lost forever. Even better, it turns out the guy I talked to knows you. Said he worked with your dad."

"Wow, you have been busy. What else did he say?"

"To say hi from Frank, the football nut friend. Said you were a real impressive girl."

"Well, that was nice of him. And nice of you to track it down. I should have done it myself. Yeah, Frank, the football nut. I remember him now. Nice guy." She coughed again.

"Are you sure you're okay?" I asked.

"Fine. Just went the wrong way." She finished her martini and said, "Now, no more work talk. Are you a cook? And if so, what kind of food do you cook?"

It turned out we both liked to cook. I talked about seafood and she went on about Italian. That got us through the main course and to dessert, where we talked about other restaurants and made a bucket list of places and things to eat before we died. Yes, she did have the white chocolate bread pudding. I was kind and only took a few bites, leaving most of it for her. We lingered over after-dinner drinks as if the night was infinite and wouldn't end until we wanted it to.

Full and happy, we left the restaurant.

Once we'd crossed Canal Street and left the bustle of the French Quarter behind for the quieter streets of the weekend CBD, she slipped her arm through mine.

A gust of wind, cold with the night, blew through the street, causing her to huddle against me for heat.

I liked the feel and warmth of her against me. I still tried to place no expectations on the night, to enjoy the moment.

In the next block, after a car passed and there were no more behind it, leaving the street to us, I turned to her and softly kissed her on the lips.

"Thank you," she said, when we pulled away. "I was hoping you would do that."

"You're welcome. I was hoping you'd want me to do that."

She slid her hand down my arm until we were holding hands.

Gentle and effortless, we moved to openly being a couple. It was so easy, it made me wonder why I'd torn my heart open on the unsure ones, wasting time in messy ambivalence. Falling in love could take the route of a good dinner, an aimless walk, and holding hands. Cordelia and I hadn't managed it; it had taken almost a year of fits and stumbles, wondering and worry before we finally got together. This was so much easier.

We walked, silent for much of it, enjoying the warmth of our entwined hands, comments on the weather, the food. The night seemed made for us. We were meandering our way back to her hotel, a block out of the way here and there. When no one else was around, we stole quick kisses, building for more to come.

We found ourselves at Lafayette Square, quiet in the evening hours. This is the legal area, with the Fifth Circuit Court of Appeals on the south edge of the square. We took a detour by it, then headed up the square, again moving in the direction of her hotel.

Halfway down the block, she stumbled against a tree root, tripping, and would have fallen if I hadn't caught her.

"Damn," she said as she took a step. Her uneven gait signaled the problem. She'd broken a heel.

After four lopsided steps she stopped. "Double damn. This isn't going to work." She was right. It was about three or four blocks to her hotel, but that was a long haul with a broken shoe.

"Let me run back to Poydras and get a cab," I said.

"Great plan," she said, blowing me a kiss.

"If you can hobble to St. Charles"—half a block away—"that'll help. Otherwise he has to go around the square."

"I'll do my best hobble; you do your best hail."

I trotted away, to St. Charles, then turned for the half block to Poydras, a major thoroughfare in the area.

I don't know what made me turn back and look; maybe I wanted to check how fast Ashley was moving. Maybe I heard the echoing footsteps.

A stray shaft of light caught his arm, covered in tattoos, his pace an assured stride as he closed the distance between them.

"Ashley! Look out!" I yelled as I raced back to her.

My warning was enough for her to swing away from his first blow.

His second sent her crashing down to the pavement, a low groan as she hit.

His third blow would have done even more damage but I threw myself at him, tackling him with a shoulder to his stomach.

He was a big, muscled man, but I was strong enough to shove him into the iron stanchions on this side of the park. One caught him on the thigh. He howled, less in pain and more in outrage. He hadn't planned on having a real fight on his hands.

I was enraged, furious and scared that Ashley had been hurt. I needed to end this fight so I could see to her.

He swung at me, but I ducked below his punch. He had the muscle and weight advantage, but his bulk made him less mobile.

I slammed my palm against his groin, then grabbed and twisted. His jeans were thick and tight, so my grip wasn't as effective as it might have been, but it was enough to force him to defend the jewels instead of attacking.

With his hands covering his crotch, I was able to land a solid blow to his nose, a satisfyingly loud thunk in the night.

He howled again, this time as much from pain as rage.

He lifted his hands away from his crotch to throw a punch and I took advantage to land a kick there.

"Hey, what's going on?" someone shouted from across the park. There are bars and restaurants here, though the evening wasn't as busy as the day.

"A mugger," I heard Ashley say.

Two young guys started running in our direction.

The tattooed man realized he was outnumbered. He threw back at Ashley, "Next time it'll be a stake in your cunt."

Then he ran as fast as he could away from us and the cavalry coming to our rescue. He jumped into a truck that roared away, another person in the driver's seat. I couldn't tell if it was a man or a woman.

I was kneeling by Ashley's side. "Are you okay?"

Her nose was bleeding and there was a cut on her cheek. She grabbed a big wad of tissues from her purse and dabbed the blood away. "Yeah, I'll be okay," she said, "More scared than hurt."

She put her hand out, for me to take and help her up. I did, although she had to lean on me when she was upright. I was still worried about her.

The two young men reached us, their dates trailing a safe distance behind.

The taller one asked what happened. Ashley stuck with the story that it was a random mugger.

One of the trailing dates did the sensible thing and went to Poydras to hail cabs for all of us, while the men assured us that we were safe with them and didn't need to worry about any muggers.

Ashley kept the tissues to her nose and said little. I followed her cues and didn't enlighten the stalwart young men that if a federal agent and a licensed-to-carry PI could be mugged, their masculinity wouldn't protect them.

Lucky for all of us, the sensible woman was good at hailing cabs. They let us have the first one.

The driver was a young man and he spent the entire five-block ride wondering why anyone would come into a city as crime-ridden as New Orleans. He lived out in the suburbs and never had to worry about crime.

As I was paying him, I said, "Wait, isn't that the area where the serial killer is still active? You might want to be careful as well."

Ashley made a snorting sound. I couldn't tell if she was laughing or coughing through the mass of paper at her nose.

"Are you sure you don't want to see a doctor?" I said as we walked across the lobby. She was leaning heavily against me to make up for the ruined shoe.

"No, no doctor. I'm okay."

I shook my head but obeyed her wishes.

When we got to her room, she kicked off her shoes, then stripped off the pantsuit, tossing it on the bed. "It's silk, I don't want to ruin it," she said with a wan smile and headed for the bathroom. I followed her.

Yes, I did notice she was wearing a low-cut black lace bra and high-cut matching panties. However, this was not the moment to do more than notice.

She was looking at her face in the mirror.

I turned on the water, running it until it was hot. Her nose didn't look broken, but it was still trickling a small stream of blood; her cheek wound seemed to have stopped bleeding. She'd have a major bruise on her face in the morning.

"Are you going to call the police?" I asked as I got a washrag and gently cleaned her face.

"No, I don't want to do that. At least not yet."

"That wasn't a random mugging," I pointed out.

"No, it wasn't," she said. "That's why I don't want to go to the police."

"That makes no sense."

"Yes, it does." She grabbed my wrist. "Look, someone set this up. It's likely linked to whoever is working on the inside. They're getting desperate to throw us off their tracks. Let me and my team handle it. It'll be safer that way. For both of us."

"Okay," I said. "You're the law enforcement pro. But you are pretty banged up. At least let me go downstairs and get an ice pack and some aspirin."

"I'll survive. I've had worse happen to me."

"This isn't a competition. Let's take care of how you're hurt now, okay?"

She turned to look at me. Then put a hand on my cheek. "Okay. Thank you for being here."

She started to cry.

I put my arms around her and held her. She lifted her head for a moment, got a towel, and put it over my shoulder so she wouldn't bleed on my suit. Then she relaxed into my arms. I just held her, trying not to notice how little clothing she had on, the places my hands covered warm skin.

Finally she pulled away. "You're right about the ice and aspirin. Can I ask you to be discreet?"

"There's a grocery store close by. I'll run there and get the stuff."

She bent forward and softly kissed me. "Thank you."

I hustled out, half jogging most of the way there and back. I got two kinds of anti-inflammatory drugs, aspirin and an alternative in case it upset her stomach, and an ice pack for later, as it needed to be cooled. I picked up the old standby, frozen peas. Some Band-Aids and healing ointment. Also some dish towels—we could wrap ice from the ice machine in those.

Oh, and chocolate. Two really good chocolate bars.

When I got back to her room, she was sitting on the sofa and just getting off the phone. Most of her end was listening. Finally, she said, "We can deal with it tomorrow. I need to put some ice on my nose."

She'd put on one of the robes provided by the hotel, but underneath was still wearing the black lace bra and panties.

She blew me a kiss as she hung up.

I handed her the frozen peas and the aspirin and its alternative. I got the ice bucket and went and filled it.

"Thank you," she said as I returned to the room.

"No problem."

"I'm used to…dealing on my own. If you're a woman in this business, you have to be tough. No crying. Or admitting to pain."

"Doesn't seem right. Even big guys can feel pain."

"Right isn't always how it works. My dad made my brother's life hell because he wasn't strong enough. We didn't say it then, but he was clearly one of those boys who was going to grow up to be gay."

"Your dad didn't like that, I'm guessing." I wrapped ice in a towel and handed it to her to replace the unwrapped frozen peas. I put them back in the bucket of ice to keep everything cold.

"Hated it. Hated it when any of us cried or acted what he called weak. I didn't want to be my brother, so I learned never to look fragile or ask for anything."

I got her a glass of water. "That's a hard way to grow up."

"It was harder on my brother. I was a girl, so I got a pass. My dad made it so hard on him and let the other kids beat him up as well, he finally gave up." She stared down at her drink.

I finally prompted her, "What did he do?"

"Got drunk and jumped off a bridge."

"Did he survive?"

"It was the middle of winter. He landed on ice. The cops called him a broken rag doll."

"I'm very sorry."

She took a sip of water, then brushed her hand across her face. "So I'm not used to someone running to the store when I have a bloody nose. It was always my responsibility to clean it up."

"Not when I'm around," I said, angry for the little girl who had to clean her own cuts and had lost a brother because he didn't fit in the proper male mold. I sat down next to her, on her uninjured side.

She put her hand on my thigh and rested her head on my shoulder. "Thank you," she said softly. "Don't be too nice, otherwise I might get used to it."

"Get used to it. I'm not going anywhere." I put my arm around her shoulder, holding her gently.

She snuggled into me. "This isn't the night I planned."

"Not your fault. I wish you hadn't been hurt."

"It's stupid, but I'm kind of glad I did. It showed me what kind of person you are. The kind who's willing to fight for me. And take care of me afterward." She slipped her free arm around my waist.

"You'd do the same."

"I'd like to think I would. You've proven it." She kissed me on the cheek and put the ice pack down, using that hand to cup my cheek.

It was cold; I turned to kiss it, to warm her palm and fingers.

She let me, then pulled my face to her, a deep, more intense kiss than we'd shared so far. Holding the kiss she moved on top of me, her knee between my legs. She undid the robe so it fell open.

I let her kiss me, reveled in it. I finally said, "Hey, I'm enjoying this, but you need to take it easy. We don't want you to start bleeding again."

She stroked my cheek. "Thank you for worrying, but this is what I need right now."

We were kissing again, her tongue exploring my lips, in my mouth.

I wrapped my arms around her, underneath the robe, her skin hot under my hands. I let them roam, from her shoulders down to her thighs and back again.

We kept kissing, lips, neck, cheeks, only avoiding her injured area.

I slipped my hands under the hook of her bra, unfastening it.

She whispered in my ear, "You are a bad girl, aren't you? You have me mostly naked and you haven't taken off a thing."

"We can change that."

"Let's."

She stood up, flinging off the robe and her bra, leaving only her panties. She grabbed my hands and pulled me to standing, then started hastily pulling off my jacket to throw it on the pile of clothes. My sweater quickly followed, then my bra.

We embraced and kissed, our breasts hard against each other.

I kicked off my shoes and she quickly pulled both my pants and underwear off.

"You are so beautiful," she said as she looked at me. "My hero."

Then she was kissing, my neck, my throat, my breasts.

The focus became our touch, everything went to the background.

Soon we were on the bed, both naked.

She was fierce in her passion, as if it had been a long time since anyone had touched her with caring and kindness.

We made love once, then again and again, hands, mouths, bodies, touching and tasting, exploring as if the night would end too soon and we had to take in as much pleasure as we possibly could.

Finally, exhausted, we fell into a sleep of twisted sheets and entwined bodies.

I woke briefly at dawn, a faint morning light through the window. Ashley was lying next to me, one arm draped across my chest.

This wasn't a dream was my first thought. I lay awake, watching the sun rise, enjoying the feel of her against me. Remembering the night before. Her vivid green eyes as she leaned in to kiss me. Her moan of pleasure as I touched her, made her explode into orgasm. The softness of her breasts as my lips explored them. The way she held me, arms so tight as if she was afraid she might lose me. The way she took me, ardent, passionate, touching everything where she thought might give me pleasure.

I gently kissed her forehead, not wanting to wake her, much as I wanted her company again.

Somehow I fell asleep again.

CHAPTER TWENTY

I woke again when Ashley stirred.

"Wow, what time is it?" she asked as she rolled away from me.

I looked at the bedside clock. "Around ten. In the morning." I gave her a wicked smile.

She smiled back, but got out of bed and headed to the bathroom.

I also got up; I needed that destination as well.

"We're going to take a shower together," she announced when she was finished.

She was already under the running water by the time I finished peeing.

I joined her. It was partly a shower and mostly lovemaking.

We paused long enough after the shower to order a room service brunch. Caffeine and food were necessary to keep the sex going.

Which we did after eating. The bed was in a high state of disrepair by the time we were finished.

"We need to let the maid in," I pointed out after a second, more prosaic shower.

She agreed and we got dressed.

I was still in what I'd worn the night before, wrinkled and dirty from the wear and the fight. I stopped long enough at my house to get changed and grab an overnight bag with extras in case I didn't make it back before tomorrow.

We spent the day together the way people falling in love should. Lunch at a hole-in-the-wall barbeque joint. A drive across the lake to take advantage of the bright sunny day. We ambled around in the park up there, took a drive along the lake as the sun set. Had dinner at the Abita Brew Pub.

We drove back across the lake, holding hands, the stars bright in the sky.

As we got close to her hotel, I asked, "Do you want my company or should I drop you off?"

"Are you getting tired of me?"

"Not in the slightest. But I don't want to overstay my welcome."

"Not a chance," she said, running her hand up my thigh to the V in my legs.

"Careful, I'm driving," I said.

"Then we'd better get to my hotel room."

We did and again made love most of the night.

Had Sunday in the same pattern, a lazy morning, brunch and the papers, a walk in Audubon Park, a late lunch up around there, followed by a drive up the river by the plantations. She was here; she should at least get a glimpse. After that a nice dinner close to the hotel and back to her room for another night of lovemaking.

I woke in the early dawn; Ashley snuggled beside me, her face relaxed in sleep. One cheek did have a big bruise, but the rest of her face was peaceful, happy. Or perhaps I wanted to see that.

Maybe because I was happier than I had been in a long time. Maybe even happier than I ever thought I could be. Ashley appreciated me, seemed to see the person I wanted to be, could see enough of the good to forgive my sins. She had called me her hero, words I'd been yearning to hear for a long time, words that proved I could be better than I'd been.

How could I have considered Emily with her distrust and hard questions? She was the past. I'd never kiss her again, or even consider it. This investigation would be over; she would learn that I wasn't involved, indeed was on her side the entire time. But it would be too late.

Even Cordelia was past. Now I had a future that didn't include her, didn't need her. Was wiped clean of the mistakes I'd made with her.

Ashley stirred, sleepily leaned in and kissed my breast. She shook herself and said, "What time is it?"

"Just before seven, the sun's just coming up."

"Damn," she said. "It's Monday, isn't it?"

"Yep, sorry, but it is."

She rolled out of bed and headed to the bathroom. I gave her a few minutes, then went in to take care of my own needs.

"I'm sorry, I'm going to have to work today," she said.

"Don't be sorry. It's the way life is. We can meet in the evening," I said. "If you want."

"Of course I want." She put her hand between my legs. Played just long enough to make me moan when she pulled away. "I'll finish that tonight," she said with a playful grin.

After that we behaved; I'd only brought so many pairs of underwear, after all.

She had a breakfast meeting at eight, so I left her to the workday and headed out to forage on my own, fortified only by one small cup of hotel room coffee.

Since I knew there was nothing to eat at home, I did the necessary run to the grocery store, hitting the one in the CBD. It's not as big as others but has enough to provide the necessities—coffee and enough food to get me through a few days.

From there I went home and had a proper eggs and sausage breakfast with freshly ground and brewed coffee.

It was also Monday for me, albeit a kinder, gentler Monday since I was my own boss and made my own hours. I would never be foolish enough to schedule a meeting for eight on a Monday morning.

A little after ten, I left and headed to my office. This time I even remembered to bring a turkey sandwich for lunch.

Ah, Monday, you cruel bitch, you.

A small black car was parked outside my office. I considered driving past, but she'd clearly seen me, was getting out of the car before I'd even parked.

My favorite FBI agent had a few more questions.

The sight of her pretty much did in my post-sex high. *You can get it back this evening*, I reminded myself.

"About time you showed up," she said.

"I work for myself, I can make my own hours. You can call and make an appointment, you know."

"I do know. That only works if you actually answer your phone."

Oh, yeah, I had turned it off, I remembered. To her I said, "Sorry, put it in my gym bag and forgot to take it out."

"So you didn't answer your phone at all? And here I pictured you seeing it was me and throwing it across the room."

"Nope, not the case. There are very few people I'd destroy a cell phone for. You're not one of them."

"Can we get out of the wind and go inside?"

"Why? This is going to be a brief conversation. I told you everything on Thursday night."

"Did you talk to your source?"

"My source?"

"Yeah, the one who gave you the information about the delivery of the women. You know, that human trafficking thing."

"I did. And she—" Damn, I had slipped up. "And that person wasn't willing to risk it. Sorry." I moved to go past her.

"She, huh?"

Double damn, she had caught it.

"Maybe. But she's a transman, and I slipped and used the gender I used to know her by."

"Bullshit. Let's go inside and talk about this." She put her hand on my back, guiding me to the door.

I tried to pull away from her, but she kept close.

"Nice perfume," she said as I put the key in my lock. "Didn't think you could afford something like that."

Triple damn. Some of Ashley's fragrance must have transferred to me in our passionate good-bye.

"You must be mistaken. I'm not the kind of girl to wear perfume. A homeless person bumped into me outside the grocery store, and she had on what smelled like gallon-a-dollar toilet water."

I turned the key in the lock, opening the door. I had to let Emily through before I could close it, but I did what I could to keep her far enough away from the lingering scent of Ashley on me.

"I know the fragrance," she said as she followed me up the stairs. "My ex, the law partner, used it all the time."

"Maybe it's you, then. Perhaps it's lingering on your clothes." I was hustling up the stairs trying to keep ahead of her. It wasn't working very well, given how in shape she was.

"Not a chance," she said, "it was one of the bones of contention in our relationship—how much she'd spend on things like that. I grew to hate the smell."

I had to stop at my office door to unlock it.

She easily caught up with me, leaned in, and took a good whiff of my hair. "Yes, definitely the same perfume. You been cheating on me with someone else?"

I opened the door and strode into my office, crossing behind my desk before turning to her. "I'm not *cheating* on you because we're not in a relationship. We both admitted it was a drunken moment of weakness. And it's over."

She didn't let her lips move, but her eyes held a smile. She'd intended to provoke me and she'd succeeded. I needed to be cool and calm and it was hard to do that with such recent memories of Ashley and my need to protect her—and us—from the criminals and the corrupt officers who abetted them.

"Very true," she said. "You're allowed to come to work smelling like the woman you spent the night with."

"And you're allowed to be bitter because the best you can do is manage a drunken one-night stand that we both regret."

That took the smile out of her eyes. She shot back, "Smells like the kind of perfume your friend Desiree Montaigne would wear. Is that where you spent the night? Getting paid in something other than money?"

"Fuck you. I'm not the kind of girl who..." Who would sleep with a woman like that? Like sex workers are trash and I'm better than that? "I don't pay for sex," I finished.

"Okay, so you got it for free. Desiree is not a bad-looking woman. She could probably teach you a few tricks."

Don't go there. "What do you want, Harris? I have things I need to do."

"Trying to crack a case. As I'm sure you know, the boat disappeared into the night."

"I didn't know that. Why would I?"

"Anyone who's part of the gang would."

"I'm not. I do know enough about the bayous to know how easy it is to hide in them. Which is why you needed a boat to chase them. Which you didn't have."

"Where did you meet the Guidry brothers?"

"I haven't. Nor do I want to."

"Really? But you passed their name on to the cops."

"I investigated, like good private eyes do. Found out that was the name of the owner of the *Eula May*, the boat my source mentioned. That's all I know about them."

"That so? You mean you had no clue they also owned the warehouse where you so desperately needed to pee?"

"What?" That was news. "No, I didn't know that."

"Like you said, you grew up out there. Maybe you're the connection between the city slickers and the bayou boys."

This was not going well. Given the evidence she was mounting against me, I might think I was guilty if I didn't know myself so well.

"No, that's not what happened. I'm not involved, not the way you're claiming."

"Oh, yeah? How's a one-person operation like you have over fifty thousand in a bank account?"

"My ex…had money. She left me some." Cordelia had cleaned out all the accounts that were hers, even the ones that had my name on them so I could access them if I needed to. But the savings and checking account we shared, she'd divided in half. I'd just left the money sitting in the savings account. "You can check and see that it's been there a long time."

"Trust me, I will."

She pulled a pair of handcuffs from her belt.

"No," I said. "Not unless you want to drag me down three flights of stairs."

"I might enjoy that. You're looking pretty guilty to me. Enough to bring you in to ask you a lot more questions."

This day had gone from riches to rags all too quickly. I did not want to spend the afternoon, evening, day, or fates forbid, the entire night being questioned. The challenge was to finesse telling her enough to get her off my tail and not telling her anything that would reveal too much.

"Okay," I said. "I still do have to protect client confidentiality. Can you at least understand that?"

"I understand it," she said, crossing her arms, the handcuffs dangling in one hand.

"I'm working with someone who knows something about this case through the ICE agents she knows." She had to know all the agencies who were involved, so I didn't think I was giving much away.

But Emily looked perplexed. "ICE isn't working on this. They're not involved yet."

Of all the things you said you can't tell me, Ashley, you could have told me this. I covered by saying, "Not that they're working the case, but they've heard a few things. She—they mentioned it to my client. And my client is…worried about how this might affect her."

"Desiree?"

"Yes," I lied. "She wants to know who they are and if she and her establishment are in danger."

"Why does she think she's in danger?" Emily asked. "Certainly in this city with Mardi Gras and the Super Bowl coming up, there should be plenty of work for everyone."

"It's personal. She thinks it's a gang who tried to move in here a while ago, failed, and are trying again. They took their failure personally."

"Sounds a bit over-the-top."

"She told me a customer warned one of her girls. Said she needed to get out of town, otherwise she'd end up in the river like the other girls. And to pass the message on to Desiree."

Emily looked at me. "Why the hell didn't she come to the police? A description of that john would have been useful."

"It's not easy for a madam to come to the police and complain about a threatening john," I pointed out.

"Okay, I get that. But in the future if you find out things like this, can you come to me and let me know? I can't turn a blind eye to crime, but I can focus on the important things like putting a brutal murderer and trafficker behind bars."

"We can both agree on that."

She put the handcuffs back on her belt. "Warn her—and yourself— no one from ICE is assigned to this case. There are no women ICE agents in the area."

"Did I say 'she'? I meant my client. I have no idea who the ICE agent is." I looked at her, keeping my expression neutral. She had to be lying. Didn't she? "I'm just the go-between. I don't know who my contact knows," I repeated.

"Tell your client to stay out of this. And by her staying out of it, I mean you. If she's just running an establishment of good-time girls who choose to be there, she's not part of this and we'll leave her alone. If she's involved, she's in trouble. And so are you."

She walked around the desk to face me. She was close enough that I could smell her shampoo. "I'd like to believe you," she said.

"Why? Because we slept together?"

"I don't think you're that kind of person. I only slept with you because I thought that, not the other way around."

"Nice of you."

"I could be wrong."

"Not so nice of you."

"I like to think my instincts are good. Doesn't mean I won't check and double-check them."

"Check all you want."

"I will." She put her hand on my cheek.

I didn't move.

"I really liked kissing you."

"Not going to happen."

"No, it's not," she agreed, turning and walking back around my desk.

"I'll call you if something comes up, okay?" I said.

"You'd better. Better yet is to take a long vacation and stay away."

She again looked at me as if gauging whether I was telling the truth. I kept my face as blank as I could. Let her read whatever she wanted to on it.

"I'll think about that."

She left without saying anything more.

I sat at my desk, just staring. Then quickly got up and locked my door. I had really liked kissing her as well. With Ashley in my life, she should be gone from my brain. I was annoyed that she wasn't, that I could easily recall the softness of her kisses, her body against mine, and feel the heat.

I'm going to become the kind of private dick who only searches for lost poodles. This was getting beyond complicated. Ashley was ICE, but Emily claimed there were no female agents around. Ashley had warned me about Emily and now Emily was warning me about Ashley.

Not enough coffee, vodka, and aspirin in the world to help sort this one out.

To distract myself, I did the usual routines, checking email and voice messages, but nothing truly distracting was to be found. In desperation, I started to clean my coffeemaker.

My cell phone rang. I answered it without looking at the number.

"Hi, this is Bianca. Or that's the name I gave you. I doubt you remember—"

"Of course I remember you. Great tea," I said. "What's up?"

"You said to call if I noticed anything, right?"

"Yes, what's up?"

"There's a girl two rooms down. I know they look younger every day, but she's too young to be doing this."

"You don't want to call the cops? That might be the best solution."

"I don't consider the police my friend. They might decide to bust

me as well. Plus she's shadowed by a big, tattooed muscle guy and he
doesn't look friendly to the likes of me."

"Have you tried inviting him in for tea?"

"One of the tattoos is a swastika. I don't invite those kinds in."

"Ah. Got you."

Muscles and tattoos rang a lot of bells, none of them good.

"Where are they now?" I asked.

"Sleeping off last night, as near as I can tell."

"What's the number of the room?"

"It would be twenty-six if the numbers hadn't fallen off."

"Okay, thanks. I'll do what I can."

"Let me know if the police might be visiting. I'll make myself
scarce."

"I'll do my best."

Time to head for the low-down hooker hotel.

This go-around I will just watch, I told myself. But I wanted some
photos. I hadn't gotten a great look at the man who jumped us in the
CBD, but I'd recognize him if I saw him again. I took my best high-
powered camera and car cell-phone charger. It's never good to have a
low battery when you might have to call the police.

And my gun.

I got in my car, carefully looking for anything that might be FBI
or other cops. I'd told Emily I'd stay out. I just didn't say it wouldn't
be very far out.

Midday traffic was light. I was there in about ten minutes. I parked
in the street, but in a place where I could see into the courtyard. The
garbage looked like it still hadn't been taken out.

How long do I wait here, I wondered, after looking at my watch
for the third time. It was a little after twelve. Of course, I'd left my
turkey sandwich back at the office. Ashley and I had burned a lot of
calories in the last few days, and my appetite noticed.

Another half hour passed. I was about to take a lunch break when
the door to that unit suddenly slammed open.

A young girl stormed out. Bianca was right; she couldn't be much
more than fifteen.

She was followed by a muscled, tattooed man.

Not the same as the one who attacked Ashley. He was a little
shorter, a bit of a paunch, and he had scraggly hair in a half mullet that
had gone out of style years ago (and never should have been in style in
the first place) with facial hair that was either half a beard or someone

who forgot to shave three days in a row. His T-shirt was half hanging out of his jeans, with an open wrinkled shirt hastily thrown on for the cold, and he wasn't wearing shoes. He either seriously needed a bath or the dark splotches showing at his wrist and neck were tattoos that had seen better days and/or younger skin.

He grabbed her arm, jerking her back his way. She struggled against him, but he was bigger and stronger. She slapped him, but he slapped back, a lot harder.

So much for just watching.

I jumped out of my car and ran in their direction.

He was too drunk, high, or stupid to notice me until I had climbed the stairs, skittered down the walkway, and was only a few feet away.

"Let her go!" I bellowed. I backed up my bellow by pulling my gun and pointing it at him. The lack of shoes hinted that if he had a gun, he had neglected to bring it with him.

"Yeah, let me go!" she yelled in very American English.

He looked from her to me back to her, then back to me again before finally dropping her arm.

"That hurt," she said as she pulled away. "You promised me we'd go to Bourbon Street and I want to go now."

"How old are you?" I asked.

"Who wants to know?" she said.

I pulled out my PI license and flashed it in front of her face far too quickly for her to read it.

"It's legal for me to go there. Just can't go in the bars," she said.

He was still looking between her and me as if watching a confusing and slow-motion ping-pong ball.

"How old are you?" I asked again.

"Sixteen. In a few months."

"Fifteen, in other words. Way too young to be here and doing this."

"This isn't fair," she wailed. "I want to go to Bourbon Street and hang out. You promised," she screamed at the man. "You said if we made some money, we could—"

"Shut up!" he yelled. "Don't say nothing."

"He's forcing you to have sex?"

"I don't know," she said. "I get real sleepy and wake up with money."

"Liar," he yelled, "you're awake and you like it."

"Do not! 'Specially since we ain't gone to Bourbon Street yet. The men like me, not you!"

"We'll go right now. Just let me put my shoes on," he said.

"What do you do with the men?" I asked.

"Nothing, just talk," he answered.

"Have fun with 'em," she said, taunting him. "Real fun."

"Blow jobs or real sex?" I asked, using the terms they might know.

"If they're nice enough to me, we can do whatever they want," she said, sticking her tongue out at him.

"Anal sex? In the butt?" I asked.

"That's disgusting!" she said. "Just blow jobs mostly."

"She's lying," he said.

"Who are you?" I asked.

"Why do you want to know?"

"Which one of the Guidry brothers are you?" I guessed.

"I'm the cousin. I don't mess with them."

Well, hot damn. Bingo. "Where are they now?"

"Don't know."

"They'd take me to Bourbon Street. They always got money," the young thing chimed in.

"Bobbie Sue, you just hush now," he said.

"You learn from them? They do the high-class women and you do the low-class ones?" I asked.

"I'm not low-class," she whined.

Despite the cold and his bare feet, he was sweating. "Don't know what you're talking about," he said in a tone that told me he did. "Bobbie Sue's my cousin and she just wanted to come to town and have a good time. That's all."

"Bobbie Sue, how long have you been here?"

"'Bout three days."

"Real good time in this cheap hooker hotel, right?"

"It's just what we can afford," Bobbie Sue said. "Ain't that right, Dwayne?"

"Dwayne Guidry?" I guessed.

"I don't hang with my cousins, okay? Not into what they're into, okay? I'll take Bobbie Sue back out of here. Don't want no trouble, okay?"

I decided to hold off telling Dwayne that in the big city we frowned on prostituting our younger cousins. "Tell me what you know about your cousins and maybe I'll let you off," I said. And I would. The police wouldn't.

"I don't hang with them," he said defensively. "Much."

"Tell me what you know," I growled, taking a step closer, my gun still trained on him.

"They did the usual stuff for a long time, little booze, dope, you know, nothin' real illegal."

I nodded as if I agreed with him.

"Then 'bout two years ago, they started doing real well. Lot of money. I asked if they needed help, so they sometimes let me. I'd be at the dock and meet the boat. Help them load and unload. You know, stuff like that."

"Unload women?"

He hung his head. "Yeah, but Sam said it was okay, they were leaving Commie places and wanted to come to America."

"In handcuffs."

"Yeah, Sam said it was to protect them. Keep 'em safe. If they got caught, make it look like they didn't want to be here."

As stupid as Dwayne clearly was, I didn't think he was stupid enough to believe that. It was a lie they could hide behind so the Dwaynes of the world would be willing to make the money and ignore the monstrosity of what they were doing.

"They come up with this on their own or were they working with someone?"

"I don't rightly know," he said, betraying that he did.

"You want me to jog your memory?" I took another step closer.

He looked at the barrel of my gun. "I don't know, but I seen a few things. Big fancy car with New York license plates. Had a pile of money in the trunk. They handed a big stack of it to my cousins. Said there was more to be made if they had the balls. Not what they said, if they were brave enough."

"What did those people look like?"

"All white. Two men and two women. Classy looking, nice clothes. You know, like in the TV shows."

"Young or old?"

"Both," he said. "I mean, one man and one girl were young. The others older."

"The young dude told me that if I ever came to New York, he'd show me a good time," Bobbie Sue cut in. "Said I should call him."

"Did he give you his number?"

"No," she pouted. "Said to have my cousins get in touch."

"What was his name?"

"Jack."

"Did he give a last name?"

"No, he just said Jack."

"What the hell were you doin' running around with them?" Dwayne cut in.

"Having a good time, unlike with you."

"How long ago were they here?"

"'Bout six months ago," Bobbie Sue answered.

"Where did they meet?"

"At their place on the North Shore," Dwayne answered.

"Where's that?"

"Outside of Covington."

"Outside of Covington, where?"

"I don't know the address. Down a road and then another road. Out where there aren't many other folks around."

"Not the place in Des Allemandes?"

He looked at me, scared I knew that. "No, no. They didn't tell them New York folks about that."

"Why not?"

"I don't rightly know."

Oh, yes, he did. "A little on the side?" I guessed. "Trying to cut out the top dog and take it all?"

"No, nothing like that."

"Bullshit."

"Yeah, maybe. I just helped. Loaded and uploaded stuff."

"Take it to the secret warehouse down around Jean Lafitte?"

"Shit," he said. "I didn't know it was illegal. Just stuff they were bringing in."

"He got a real nice TV, big as his wall," Bobbie Sue chimed in. "I ask for one and they just laughed at me."

"Bobbie Sue, you hush now," he pleaded. Stupid as he was, he was still smart enough to see the hole she was digging for him. The desperation showed on his face.

"Where are they now?" I demanded.

"I don't know. I really don't know. After the mess-up and losing those girls, they had to hide. Back in the bayous somewhere. They don't tell me shit."

"You drove the van, didn't you?" Another guess.

Another right one. "I didn't know what they were loading up. Thought it would be more TVs."

All he thought about was making money. He had no idea what the cargo was. Worse, he didn't care.

He continued, "They dropped me off in the middle of nowhere, left me to call my sister to get a ride home. Told me not to talk to anyone 'bout anything. To act like I never knew them. They even accused me of letting it slip 'bout the landing."

"You're in trouble, you know that?" I told him.

"I know my cousins are mad at me, but I really didn't tell no one."

"It's not just your cousins you need to worry about," I said.

Light—very dim—seemed to dawn. "I didn't do nothing, not really. Helped out my cousins, brought Bobbie Sue to town for a good time."

"I'm going to call for backup now," I said. "Do yourself a big, big favor. Tell the cops who take you in everything you just told me. Don't even wait until they ask. Tell them as much as you can."

"But won't my cousins be mad at me?"

"Maybe. But you have to take care of yourself now. With your tattoos"—Bianca was right about the swastika—"you don't want to spend a lot of time in Orleans Parish Prison. Lot of the inmates won't appreciate the artwork." I made a circle with my thumb and forefinger and ran it up and down the barrel of my gun. He got the message. Fear glistened on his face.

I felt dirty using his racism against him—terror of being raped by big black men—but damn, it was effective.

"Okay, okay, I will," he stammered.

"Tell them everything," I said backing away from him.

"What about me?" Bobbie Sue said.

"You'll be okay. Do like your cousin and tell them everything you know. They'll let you go."

"And I can go party on Bourbon Street?"

"You sure can," I totally lied. "Both of you go back into the room and stay there."

She was cold enough to hurry back in. He followed her but kept looking over his shoulder at me.

As their door snicked shut, I tapped on Bianca's door and said softly, "Time to go buy more tea."

"Bless you, honey," she called from inside the door.

I hastened down to my car and got in. I didn't want to be here when the cops came. I picked up my cell phone, pitched my voice high, and called 911. I claimed I was a social worker and had seen a girl far too young to be at this hotel. I gave them the room number and a description of both Bobbie Sue and Dwayne. I said I didn't want to be involved and hung up.

Greed gets you in the end. The cousins got away with it and got away with it and started to think they'd always get away with it. They bring in their dumb cousin Dwayne to help—he's family and can be had for some beer and an extra TV—because they're sure they won't get arrested. They forget he's stupid enough to bring his wannabe party-girl cousin to town and think he could make money off her, just like his cousins make money. Only Dwayne is a dimwit and gets caught. The weak link breaks the chain.

I drove away but took a swing around the block, dallying just long enough to see the flashing lights in the distance and to make sure Dwayne wasn't smart enough to make a run for it.

To ice the cake, I made a stop in the upper French Quarter.

Madame Celeste wasn't in, but Roland took the message. "Pass on to her contacts they want to question a lowlife just arrested at a Tulane Avenue hotel. His cousins are the Guidry brothers." I also asked if they had any surveillance footage of the john who had threatened her. Roland said he'd see what he could do.

I went back to my office and my very well-deserved turkey sandwich.

This would be over soon. If the Feds were lucky they'd break the entire thing open and get the head honcho. Worst case was the Guidry brothers, along with their stupid cousin, would go to jail for a long time.

Ashley would return to New York, but we could work something out. I'd gone to college there and knew the city. New Orleans had always been home to me, but maybe there were too many ghosts here, too many bad memories, and it was time to try somewhere different.

It was frustrating to sit in my office distractedly looking at my computer screen when I knew things had to be happening. By now Dwayne was getting the third degree of third degrees, maybe even raids to the place on the North Shore. But I was a civilian, outside the loop. I could only hope this evening I could get an update from Ashley.

My hopes were dashed when she called around four.

"I'm sorry, I can't talk long. Things have changed and I'm going to be working tonight."

"Call me when you can. Even if it's late."

"It'll be real late. We can talk tomorrow. I'll call you then," was her good-bye.

This is your fault, I thought as I packed up to leave the office. The case was breaking open, thanks to my convincing Dwayne Guidry he needed to tell the police everything. Ashley might be working very late. Maybe they would even capture the mole. I was hoping it wasn't Emily, only that she had been fooled by someone she trusted.

When I got home, I switched on the local news, but the stories were about a traffic accident that blocked the interstate or the upcoming Super Bowl.

Maybe they'll have something on the ten o'clock news, I thought as I turned the TV off.

Or maybe I wouldn't find out anything until tomorrow.

Or maybe the cops had forgotten something as important as a boat and they'd escaped again.

I wandered the house, too distracted to want dinner.

Madame Celeste might know something. I could at least go there and do some of what she was paying me to do and patrol the place, even if she wasn't available.

A drizzling rain had started, so I decided to drive the ten blocks rather than walk. By the time I got there and was parked, the rain had stopped, but the damp made the chilly night even colder. I had on a jean jacket, not enough for the cold. I was glad my walk was only a few blocks and not the length of the French Quarter.

A cold, wet Monday night had emptied the streets. I was the only one foolish enough to be out here at this time. I glanced at my watch. It was almost nine. Even the after-work happy-hour drunks were long home by now.

I turned onto the block for Madame Celeste's. It was darker than I remembered.

First I thought it was the night and the rain, but then I noticed missing lights. I felt a crunch of glass under my feet and looked up to see a broken streetlight.

Then I saw a small pool of light coming from a door that had always been closed before.

I hurried my steps.

A shadow sidled from between Madame Celeste's place and the one next to it.

First just a shape, but as I got closer I could see it was a man, tall, bundled in black against the cold. He was holding something.

He was splashing liquid around the building.

In the faint light of the door I could now see Roland, inside, on the floor, one hand stretched just over the threshold. His head was bleeding. I thought he was dead until the hand moved, trying to close the protective door.

The man walked past him as if he wasn't there.

The smell of gasoline hit my nose.

He's going to torch the place.

I couldn't shoot him. That might be enough of a spark to set the fire.

All the lights were on in the house. The women were in there. They'd burn alive.

He was being careful to not get any of the gas on himself.

The hat pulled low over the face made it hard for me to see him, but there was a dark spot on one of his hands, like a tattoo.

He put down the can and stepped back.

I charged him.

He heard my footsteps and turned to me. He had a match in his hand.

I could see his face. He wasn't the one who'd attacked Ashley, but they were related. Probably brothers. He looked like the man I'd seen at the warehouse.

I slammed into him, shoulder at his chest. He stumbled backward but remained standing. He swung at me, hitting my shoulder.

We grappled, my shoulder against his torso. I shoved my foot behind his, trying to unbalance him. He stumbled again but still didn't fall. He knew what I was trying to do.

He punched me in the throat, making me gag.

Ignore the pain, I told myself. If he pushed me down in the gas, all he needed to do was toss the match.

I punched him as hard as I could between his legs. Then again.

He groaned.

A risk, I bent farther down to reach my hand to the back of his knee and pull hard.

With my other hand I punched his balls again.

He stumbled, teetered.

I pushed with my shoulder in his stomach, yanking his calf to me.

Finally pulling him down.

He held on, taking me with him.

I struggled to stay on top, trying to let him soak up as much of the gas as I could. If he was covered in it, he wouldn't dare light the match.

He swung at my face.

I turned aside just enough that his blow clipped my chin.

I slammed my palm into his nose.

Did it again.

He was big and strong. Eventually he would win.

I had to end the fight before that.

"Fire!" I shouted. "Call the police! Fire!"

Someone had to hear me even behind all those closed doors.

Fire is a fear in the French Quarter. The old buildings, many of them wood, are close together, wall touching wall. A blaze could quickly spread.

He struggled, rocking violently to throw me off.

I used a knee to pin his arm, rubbing his sleeve in a pool of the gas.

He used the other arm, swung; hit me in the stomach, rolling me off him.

Now he was on top of me.

I deliberately raked my hand through the gas, then flung the droplets at his face.

Instinctively he closed his eyes and reared away from me.

It was a small opening, but I took it.

Punched him as hard as I could in the solar plexus. Left hand, then right hand.

He groaned in pain.

I shoved him off me, back onto the gasoline-covered sidewalk.

He hadn't been trained as a fighter, had relied instead on being big, strong, and menacing with his tattoos.

I knew the soft, vulnerable places to hit. The groin, the solar plexus, right at the base of the throat, the nose.

I pummeled him, hitting one spot after another, throat, nose, lifting up and letting my weight fall with my knee into his balls.

I paused once or twice between blows to smear gas on his chest, his throat and face.

The second time I slammed my knee into his groin, I realized he wasn't fighting back, feebly moving his hands to protect himself.

I stopped punching, but stayed on top of him.

Voices, shouting. The sound of our fight had drawn a crowd. The street exploded into a cacophony of sirens, both police and fire.

I got off him, suddenly aware of how much my body ached. He had landed blows and they took their toll.

"There's gas everywhere," I shouted to the first uniform I saw. I pointed to the man in the street. "He was trying to burn the place down. He's covered in gas."

"So are you," a fireman said as he pulled me to the side.

I was exhausted, the fight and the fear draining me. I let the cops and the firefighters take over.

I kept my statement simple. I saw him trying to burn down the building and stopped him.

Roland was packed into an ambulance.

The firefighters were putting down something that looked a lot like cat litter on the gasoline.

Madame Celeste—now Desiree Montaigne, owner of the building—joined us. She was dressed in jeans and a sweatshirt, a business owner after hours. I didn't see any of her staff or their clients. Probably a back door somewhere.

She added to my story, saying I was a private detective—I showed my license—and she had hired me for extra security.

"You need to get out of those clothes," she said to me. She held up a robe and led me to a dark end of the street.

I quickly stripped of all but my bra and panties. Even my shoes and socks. They were ruined anyway. One of the firemen took my gun and holster, to make sure there was no gas there. My wallet, license, and cell phone were in a deep enough pocket to have only a slight odor.

Desiree took charge of those for me.

Once we were finally able to leave—I got my gun back, but the fireman suggested a new holster—she led me back to the smaller house she owned and directly to the bathroom.

"Shower," she instructed. "A very long shower."

I let the water get as hot as I could stand. Standing in the cold drizzle barefoot had chilled me, especially as exhausted as I was, no reserves to keep warm.

I washed my hair three times and conditioned it twice. Then I scrubbed and rescrubbed every part of my body, from between my toes to the backs of my ears.

I finally had to back off on the hot water but still stood under the stream for several minutes, letting it flow over me. Then I turned the water off, too exhausted to keep standing.

When I opened the shower curtain, Desiree was there with a towel.

I took it from her and wrapped myself in it, at first too enervated to even dry myself.

"Let me check you," she murmured. She leaned in and smelled my hair, then my neck and arms to the fingers. "No hint of gasoline," she assured me.

I nodded and started tiredly drying myself.

"You're bruised," she said, gently touching the one on my back, then my chin.

"Yeah, but you should see the other guy," I said as I finished drying. With nothing else to wear, I draped the towel around me.

"I did see him. A man who could do that—you should have hit him harder."

I looked down at my bruised and scraped knuckles.

She followed my gaze. She took my hands and gently kissed them. "But he didn't light the match, and justice will deal with him." She let go of my hands. "Let me find you a robe. You can leave the towel hanging here."

I left the towel and followed her, too tired to think I was naked until we were standing in her bedroom. Even then I was too tired to think much about it.

"Here," she said, handing me a heavy robe. "Socks?" she asked, pulling a pair from a drawer. "You seem to be cold." She looked at my breasts, the nipples erect.

I nodded acknowledgment and put on the robe and the socks.

She smiled at me sitting on her bed, reached for my hand, and said, "Let's go to the kitchen and talk."

"Any chance I can get a snack?" I asked. Hours ago I hadn't been hungry and had skipped dinner. Now I was ravenous.

"Anything you like."

This was where she lived, the furnishings expensive but not in the showy way of those at the other place. There were antiques, mixed with well-made wooden pieces, the drapes and walls muted, soft colors. Many of these were the colors and styles I might have picked.

Her kitchen was homey, clearly used with copper-bottomed pots hanging on a rack near the stove, pot holders with faded stains on them from long-ago spills.

"Soup and sandwich?" she asked as I sat at a comfortable stool at her kitchen island.

"Anything short of shoe leather sounds divine."

She threw together toasted cheese sandwiches and heated up a bowl of ginger-butternut squash soup she'd made the day before.

I devoured half a sandwich in two bites. That took the edge off and I could eat in a more civilized manner after that.

As I was eating, she said, "I need to thank you for saving my life. And possibly the lives of everyone who works here. Roland was hit in the head and has a concussion, but he'll be okay."

I swallowed and said, "Everyone else got out the back way?"

"Yes. No one saw anything of importance, so there was no point in getting them involved."

"They could have gotten away from the fire, then?"

"Possibly," she said slowly. "It involved unlocking a back gate, climbing over another wall, and escaping through someone's back garden."

We both nodded. A gas-fueled fire can rapidly spread. Some probably wouldn't have made it. The horror of being burned alive was haunting, so narrowly missed.

"It should be over soon," I said. "Or at least a good chunk of the body bitten off the snake. They hired some locals, the Guidry brothers, to smuggle through the swamp. They got greedy and stupid. One of them is in jail right now, smarting from having a woman beat him up." I told her about Dwayne and what he was probably spilling to the cops. "In fact, I was coming over here to see if your contacts knew anything. The waiting to hear was driving me crazy."

"I was waiting to hear from…my contact. I received another threat."

"You did? Why didn't you tell me?"

"I told my contact. I thought of telling you, almost called, but decided you were one person and I worried about the danger."

"What kind of threat?"

"Pretty much the same. A stake in a delicate place if I passed on any more messages to the cops."

"How could they know it was you?"

"I don't know. I talked to only one person. Someone I trusted to be discreet with what he hears from me."

I'd told Emily.

"What's wrong?" she said.

"Damn, I may be the problem." I told her about Emily and her questioning. I didn't tell her I had lied, using my work for her as a cover to protect Ashley.

She put her hand on mine. "You didn't know. Couldn't know. And as you said, it's almost over. One of the brothers is in custody, the other will be soon. Even if he isn't, he's been too weakened to attack."

"True," I said, hoping it was indeed so. "He might do better in custody than answering to the big boss in New York."

"Think about it. They've lost access to their smuggling route. Now one of the brothers is in jail and he'll stay there a long time. A snitching cousin is also in custody. If the other brother isn't caught it will only be because he got a plane ticket to someplace with lax extradition treaties."

"The one brother in jail might rethink his loyalties. He's in lock-him-up-and-throw-away-the-key territory unless he helps get the ones they really want. Certainly the mole will be exposed."

"Even if they get away, it's not likely they'll be back here." She smiled at me. "Now finish eating."

I had stopped eating when I remembered telling Emily. I started again. I was hungry. My watch had been thrown out with my gas-soaked clothes, so I had no idea of the time.

Once I had finished, she asked, "Anything else?"

"This will sound stupid, but do you have any hot chocolate?"

"Not stupid at all."

She had the old-fashioned kind you make with real milk. She made us both a cup. Without asking, she poured a shot of cognac as well.

"I had a fire going in the fireplace," she said, leading us into her living room. "Perfect place to drink hot chocolate."

We sat on a comfortable leather sofa in front of the dying embers.

"Will your contact tell you what's happening?" I asked.

"If I ask. If he can."

"I talked to an ICE agent as well. I might be able to get information from her."

"Did you tell her about the message?"

"Well, yes. But she knew about it before I passed it on to you. Besides…I trust her." I had told Ashley as well as Emily. But I did trust Ashley. I also trusted Emily in an odd sort of way. I just couldn't trust the people she might have told.

I was too tired and it was too complicated. It was easier to let my head roll back against the couch and close my eyes. I felt her arm go around my shoulder. It was so comfortable to rest my cheek there.

I must have dozed because I felt Desiree take the half-drunken cup of hot chocolate from my hand.

"You need to go to bed."

"I can crash here on the couch."

"You're too tall for it. Come to bed."

I didn't argue, I just wanted to keep sleeping.

Until I realized that she had only one bedroom and I was naked under the robe.

"I'm very tired," I hedged.

"I know, all we're doing is sleeping." She kissed my cheek, then undid the sash on my robe.

"And…I'm involved with someone," I stumbled out.

She smiled a sad smile as if understanding the real reasons for my rejection. "It's okay," she said softly. "Just sleep."

"It's true," I answered. "If I weren't…it would be different."

I bent in and softly kissed her on the lips. I had made no promises to Ashley, but still they seemed implied. Even if I hadn't made them to her, I'd made them to myself. I wanted to find a path that wasn't as twisted and turning as what I'd been on. But underneath my exhaustion was a giddy joy at being alive, the noxious smell of gasoline and what might have happened still so close. I wanted to be held and hold, to do what I'd almost lost to the flicking of a match.

But not tonight, not with Desiree, despite our sharing the danger. I would wait for Ashley.

She held the kiss, put a hand on my chest, down to my breast, and gently cupped it.

A moment more, then we both pulled away.

"Sleep," she said. Then she turned from me and pulled back the covers.

I took the robe off and slid into bed, my back to her, and fell asleep within minutes.

Chapter Twenty-one

I woke in the morning with the utterly mundane thought of wondering where my car was parked. Would Emily spot it and notice it was close to where one of the Guidry brothers had been caught?

You gave your name to the police. All she needs to do is read the police report to know you're involved once again.

I felt something warm against my back. I carefully turned over, leaning up on my elbow. Desiree was next to me, on her side facing away. Her ass had been against mine as we slept. She had thrown off most of the covers in the night. We were both naked.

She was gorgeous, her body still sculpted and generous, ample breasts, hips and thighs a perfect curve.

I wanted to turn her on her back and climb on top of her. Banish the terrors of the night with the pleasures of the morning.

But I turned away, quietly got out of bed, and went to the bathroom.

When I emerged, Desiree was awake, chaste in a white flannel robe.

"Did you sleep well?"

"Yes, thank you." I remembered to ask, "Did you?"

"Yes. It was…comforting to have you here. I woke up several times, afraid he might come back. Was reassured to find you here."

"I'm not protection against a madman like him."

"You've done well so far." She smiled her half-sad smile at me. "You saved us, that's good enough for me. I want decent human beings, not heroes."

"I'll do my best to be decent. Speaking of, do you have any clothes I can borrow?"

"Yes, let me see what I can find." She dug through her drawers and found a baggy pair of sweatpants and sweatshirt, socks, and a pair of slip-on shoes that I could get my feet into. Not a great ensemble, but it would be enough to get me to my car and home.

"Coffee?"

I was tempted. Her coffee was probably as good as her Scotch. But there were too many other temptations here. I needed to be gone. "Thank you, but no. I should head home and deal with whatever today is going to bring."

"I understand," she said as if she was used to people leaving her. She led me to her door.

"Let me know if you hear anything from your contacts."

"I will." She took my hand. "Again, thank you, Micky, for your courage last night. I don't think anyone…has ever done that for me."

I looked down at the ground. I couldn't meet her eyes or I might get lost there. "I just did what I had to do. I couldn't let him burn you or anyone."

"Will I see you again?" she asked.

"Yes," I said quickly. "I have to return your clothes."

"They're not important."

"Yes, you will see me again."

She opened the door.

I walked out. Turned and looked back. Waved good-bye.

She still had the smile on her face, the one that never let the world know what she was truly thinking. She couldn't be just a person, instead always seen as a fallen woman or a sex worker, or a temptress. Her sexual history blotted everything else out—once a prostitute, people, including me, saw only that. I'd thought she was a game player, but maybe what she wanted—and couldn't ask for since she'd been rejected so many times—was to be seen as a person, a woman not that different from me and you.

I needed to call Ashley, to remind myself she was not a dream, but a real, breathing person, one I could be happy with.

Luck was with me. My car was parked in a No Parking Eight AM to Six PM zone. It was just after eight and the meter maid was already on the block, but hadn't made it to my car yet. I managed to drive away before she was close enough to see my license plate.

I was home quickly and the parking gods were kind enough to give me a place right in front of my house.

I had remembered to retrieve my phone, wallet—needed my driver's license even for the short drive home—PI license, and gun. I wiped them all down with a damp, soft cloth, trying to get rid of any lingering gas scent. The fireman had disposed of the bullets in the gun. No, not a good idea to fire bullets soaked in gas.

One of the first things I did after the fuel cleanup was look at my phone. Ashley hadn't called. Maybe she'd had a long night and was now sleeping.

I took another shower, only washing my hair twice this time. Then changed into real clothes, jeans, a T-shirt covered by a sweatshirt and fixed the all-important coffee.

I checked the local news and they had picked up the story but had few details other than a man had attempted arson in the French Quarter.

I kept waiting for my favorite FBI agent to come harass me, but maybe both of the Guidry brothers were in custody by now and she had her hands full with real criminals.

I stayed at home, didn't feel like going to the office, but kept my phone charged and near me.

Lunch came—another turkey sandwich, I had to use the turkey before it went bad—and went and I still hadn't heard from Ashley. I was beginning to worry.

Finally around two in the afternoon, I called her, but only got voice mail.

The crooks had been caught, everyone was busy. I should be glad. I could take it easy, let my bruised spots heal, and justice would be taken care of while I sat with my feet up.

At four I called Ashley. Still got voice mail. I left a message again, just to let her know I was thinking about her. I have to admit I also wanted her to know what a big hero I was. Maybe have her take care of me for a bit.

Just as I was contemplating what I might cook, my cell rang. Ashley.

"Hey, I've been wondering about you," I greeted her.

"Sorry," she said. "It's been a crazy day." There was noise in the background. I could barely hear her.

"Where are you?"

"Sorry," she said again. "I'm in New York."

"What?"

"They called us back. I wanted to call you, but it all happened so quickly."

"You're in New York?" I said stupidly. "Like New York City?"

"Yes, we just got in. I'm waiting for my baggage. This is the first chance I've had to call you. I'm sorry. I wanted to call sooner."

"That's okay. I know it's been crazy lately. I'm glad you called when you got a chance."

"I can't talk long. I know I shouldn't ask this, but can you come here?"

"You want me to fly up there?"

"Yes. Can you?"

"Yes, of course. I'm not sure how soon I can get a ticket."

"I'll pay for it. Can you come this week? Tomorrow even?"

"I'll try," was all I could offer.

"Please try hard. I have to go. I'll talk to you later."

"I'll call you—" But the phone was dead.

I stared at my phone. I felt bereft and alone. I had wanted to see Ashley, was looking forward to being with her, telling her about my brush with death and have her hold me. Not this. She was a thousand miles away and didn't tell me until she was already there.

Stop whining, I told myself. If she was there, maybe it meant that someone in the Guidry family was spilling on the higher-ups. Maybe they'd soon have their man and Ashley would be up for some time off.

I was a good girlfriend and looked up flights. There were several left and the prices, at least on the ones that made several stops, weren't too bad. I tried to call Ashley but only got her voice mail. I texted her a couple of the options to see what she thought.

About an hour later, I get a reply. *Love to see you. Whichever works for you.*

I went ahead and booked the flight that had the best combination of inexpensive and reasonable flying time. I texted her the info but didn't hear from her.

Okay, I'm on a plane tomorrow. To tidy things up, I headed for my office, picking up a shrimp po-boy on the way. I could eat salads in New York City.

After the all-important eating, I changed my voice mail to indicate I'd be out for a few days and my email to an autoreply that I might be slow in responding. I'd left the return trip open. Once I actually talked to Ashley, we could sort that out.

Emily's words came back to me. She trusted me, but she was going to check and double-check.

Don't lose your heart to a woman until you've at least done a criminal background check. I had checked both Emily and Desiree, but other than my phone conversation with Frank Mullen, hadn't looked into Ashley. Ashley West isn't an uncommon name, so the usual searches weren't so helpful. I found about forty Ashley Wests. The kids on Facebook I immediately dismissed. I found an Ashley West from New York state, but she was a six-one African American basketball player. Or had been about seven years ago. Although it was evening, I called a friend in the Justice Department in DC. A simple favor, could he verify someone named Ashley West was an ICE agent? And also that Emily Harris was an FBI agent. I promised a Sazerac bar tour next time he was in New Orleans—and to introduce him to the man of his dreams. We both laughed at that.

I had told both Emily and Ashley about Desiree being the one with the police connections to go after the boat in Des Allemandes. I wanted to dismiss Ashley, but I told myself I needed to be a hard-nosed private eye all around. She would check out, but the only way to be sure was to check her out. Given the cost—what had almost happened to Desiree—I had to cover everyone, no matter how much I dismissed the possibility.

What about the people she was with? I only knew their first names. John, the older man; Jack, the younger one; Sandy, the young woman with Jack; and Cara, the older woman. Another man had been with them at the restaurant where we first met. That was the only time I saw him.

A memory slipped in. In the pizza place where we first met, the man introduced as John had been called Mel.

No big deal, people often have nicknames.

Bobbie Sue of the Guidry family said one of the crooks was named Jack and he had flirted with her.

Still no big deal, a lot of men are named Jack.

How had they lost me at the warehouse? Ashley said the tattooed man must have entered through a back door. But I hadn't seen any back door. Maybe it was on the other side.

Emily was sure no one on her team was working as an informant. Ashley was equally sure. What if Ashley was wrong? It was her boss who quashed the information about the boat, insisting the trafficking route was overland.

I picked up the phone again and called Desiree.

She has such a beautiful voice, low and sultry.

"Can you do me a favor? You have surveillance outside your door, right?"

"Yes, of course."

"The john that threatened you. Can you send me a picture of him?"

"Yes, I can. Roland was working on that for you, wasn't he?"

"He was. Any word on how he is?"

"Doing much better than expected. I was just with him a little earlier. A big headache. But he's awake and complaining about wanting to get out of the hospital. Thank you for asking."

"Tell him to take care of himself."

"He's more familiar with the video equipment, but I'll see what I can do."

"Thanks, I appreciate that."

Just as I hung up with her, my DC buddy called back.

"Yep, Ashley West is an ICE agent. She'd been in NYC but was just transferred to Seattle. As for Emily Harris in the FBI, so far nada. She new? Anything else you need to know?"

"She could be," I answered.

"I'll keep looking," he promised. "I love me some New Orleans cocktails."

I thanked him and promised the Sazerac of his dreams, if not the man.

Seattle. That was pretty damn far away. Maybe she could get transferred back to New York. Or down here.

I did the same searches on Ashley West that I'd done on Desiree and Emily, but found no property for an Ashley West that seemed to fit this particular Ashley West. I didn't know what to make of Emily not showing up. The ID she'd shoved against my car seemed real enough. Maybe she was new and not in the database my friend had access to yet.

Finally, around ten p.m., I closed my computer. I had confirmed that she was an ICE agent. Emily had to be wrong—or not informed—about her being here. Or maybe Emily was deliberately misleading me, claiming ICE wasn't involved.

Time to go home and pack.

CHAPTER TWENTY-TWO

I was up early to finish packing. Since I wasn't sure how long I was going to stay, I wanted to pack smart and light. If I flew back in two days—Ashley with me, I hoped—I didn't want to have two weeks of clothes.

If I stayed, well, New York had plenty of stores.

As I closed my overnight bag, I mused there was one advantage about having lost the cats in the divorce. I didn't need to worry about them if I went out of town.

One last check. I took my PI license with me because it's always useful to have. Also my passport since the time I'd forgotten to get my driver's license renewed and spent an entire week wondering if they'd let me fly back home on an expired license. I wore my black leather jacket. It was too heavy for here, but I'd need it in New York. An extra pair of jeans, one decent pair of black pants. And enough underwear to get me through heavy sex. That kept my bag small enough so not only was it carry-on, but I could easily tote it around. We hadn't arranged a place to meet, so I could see hanging out for a while until we got together.

I hadn't heard from Desiree but assumed she was either busy or not familiar enough with the video equipment to get a picture.

I called a cab to take me to the airport. I was so used to having one of my friends—or Cordelia—drive me that I hadn't used a taxi in years. But I didn't want to explain to the friends I'd ignored for the last few months that I was flying to New York to be with a woman I'd just met a few weeks ago.

The cab will do. It'll get me there to see Ashley.

Once I was there and through security, I sent her a text message. She messaged back, *See u soon.*

Okay, I'm old-school and actually spell out words in text messages. But maybe she was busy and skipping two letters saves time.

But still, as they started the initial boarding call, I texted, *About to board. See you as soon as the planes get me there.*

She didn't answer.

Just as I was about to turn my phone off another text message came through.

It was from Desiree. *Sorry this took so long. Had to talk to Roland this morning to figure it out.* Under the message was a grainy black-and-white photo.

Jack.

I stared at the photo as I boarded the plane.

I needed to tell Ashley. I thought of forwarding her the text, but didn't. She could be with him right now. If he saw it, she could be in danger.

She was in New York, probably surrounded by all sorts of law enforcement. He couldn't do anything to her there—unless he got desperate because he knew he'd been uncovered.

I'd see her in a few hours. Best to do it face-to-face when I knew she wasn't near him.

I debated whether I was doing the right thing the entire time I waited in the Atlanta airport to change planes. Stuck to my original plan: tell her in person.

While up in the air, I cursed myself for not doing a better job of vetting her associates. Ashley had a winning smile; I hadn't looked much beyond that in agreeing to work for them. I should have asked more questions, at least gotten full names.

Other than my frantic worry, the plane trip wasn't bad, mostly on time and the screaming kids were on the other end of the plane.

Then I was in New York City, the Queens airport part of it, staring at my phone. Ashley hadn't called and left any messages. I called her, got voice mail. I texted that I had arrived.

I followed the crowd in the direction of baggage claim and ground transportation, but I needed to know where I was going to go anywhere. I didn't want to go into Manhattan if it turned out she lived in Queens, three subway stops from the airport. I was at the point of mentally grousing the sex wasn't good enough to strand me in an airport when she texted me back.

I was to meet her in a hotel in the Times Square area.

That settled, I headed for the appropriate ground transportation. I decided to do it the cheap way and take the subway. Given that it was just about four in the afternoon, going below ground would be faster than anything above ground.

I was glad I had packed light. I could sling my overnight bag across my chest and let it rest under my arm and carry it easily that way. I had to walk to the airport train, which took me to the E train and from there into Manhattan.

I got off at the Fiftieth and Eighth Avenue station. The hotel Ashley had directed me to was on Forty-sixth Street between Seventh and Eighth.

It was a small, boutique hotel. The lobby was on the second floor and barely big enough for more than three people with luggage. On the first floor was a restaurant and bar. I settled in at the bar, ordered a beer, and texted Ashley.

A few minutes later I got a reply: *I'm on my way.*

I had a cold beer, had reached my destination, and my girlfriend—I was starting to think of her that way—would be here soon. Couldn't ask for much more.

She arrived before half the beer was gone.

I saw her first, walking down the street. The last glow of the sun caught her hair, bringing out the gold and red in it. She was dressed in dark-brown suede pants, deep-green boots, and a matching leather coat. Under it I got the hint of a black turtleneck sweater.

When she looked through the window and saw me, a big grin split her face.

I grinned in return.

She quickly came through the doors and embraced me, settling for a kiss on the cheek in this public place.

"More later," she whispered in my ear. "Do you want to finish your beer? Or come up to the room?"

I could see she clearly favored the latter.

As did I. The beer was left behind.

I followed her to the elevator. She used her key card to access it.

Once the elevator doors closed, she pulled me to her and kissed me, holding it until the doors opened on our floor.

She led me to a corner room and keyed us in.

It was a suite, with a small living room and bedroom. The outer area had a large TV, plush crimson couch, coffee table, and desk with a chair.

She kissed me again when we were inside, a deep passionate one.

"Let me show you the bedroom," she whispered.

"Yes, I want to get to that," I said. "But I have something I need to tell you first."

"What? That you missed me?" Her hands slid inside my jacket, then under my shirt.

"I did miss you," I said, enjoying the feel of her hands. "But this is important."

She pulled away, took off her coat, and tossed it over the sofa. "Okay, what?"

"How well do you know Jack?"

"Jack?" The question surprised her. "Well enough, I guess," she said offhandedly.

"He's working for the traffickers."

"Really?" she said, but she didn't seem as shocked by it as I had been. "How do you know that?"

"He was the patron who threatened one of the women working for the place in the French Quarter."

"Can you be sure?"

"They have video surveillance in the front area. It caught him." I took out my phone and showed her the picture.

She looked at it, bit her lip, but said nothing.

"I know this is hard to believe, but the corrupt cop is part of your team, not the FBI," I said as gently as I could.

She finally looked up at me. "Yes, I know."

"You know? How long have you known?"

"Look, this is one of the things that I couldn't talk to you about." She took my hand. "Much as I wanted to."

"But you kept implying the informant was part of the FBI."

"Please understand, I couldn't be honest with you."

"Can you be honest now? Has he been arrested yet?"

"No, he hasn't. Not yet. It's not time yet."

"Can you be honest with me now?" I asked again.

"Yes, I've always wanted to be honest with you. I just…couldn't." She brought my hand to her cheek and nuzzled it.

"The FBI agent in New Orleans said that ICE wasn't involved in this case."

"You believe her over me?" Ashley put her arms around me, looking searchingly into my eyes.

"You just said you haven't been honest with me," I pointed out.

"Couldn't be honest. There is a difference. I wanted to, but couldn't be."

"So what are you doing about Jack?"

"We're going to use him to lead us to the people in charge."

"How?"

"I can't really tell you our operational plans." She kissed my neck.

"But how did he get to be an ICE agent?"

She sighed. "I desperately want to make love to you. Can we hold the questions until later?"

"I want to make love to you. You've gotten me caught up with this. I need to understand what's going on."

"I know. I feel guilty and selfish for getting involved with you. I should have waited until this was all over. Except...I'd be back here and it would be too late. Can you forgive me?" She rested her head against my shoulder.

"Yes, of course. It's not about forgiveness, it's about you being safe, okay?"

She lifted her head to kiss my neck, then my chin, the corner of my lips. My lips, soft, then not so soft, then firm and demanding. A hand went down my pants, teasing me.

I couldn't think of any more questions to ask.

We made love for hours, until hunger drove us to get dressed and go out before everything closed.

Ashley was happy, laughing easily. So was I. We were perhaps not so young, but falling in love, in a magic city. We deliberately didn't talk about work or the case. I didn't mention my fight with one of the Guidry brothers. That could come later. Right now, I wanted the ease of being together with all our cares aside for the evening.

After dinner we grabbed a cab and went to a lesbian bar downtown. Being a weeknight, it wasn't very full, but we had a few drinks and, more importantly, danced a few slow dances.

Then back to the hotel where we again made love until we both were too tired and needed sleep.

Chapter Twenty-three

In the middle of the night, I woke up—no, it was closer to almost dawn than deep night. I needed to go to the bathroom. Alcohol, wine with dinner, and drinks afterward do that.

And it had been a while since I'd been this sexually active. Cordelia and I had simmered along nicely, once or twice a week, until she got sick, then only on the rare occasions when she felt well enough and interested enough.

That was something else I might have done, shown more physical affection. I'd left it to her to take the lead; she might have read it as my withdrawing from her, unwilling to touch a sick woman.

Too late. It's broken and can't be fixed and I'm in bed with another woman.

I looked at Ashley as she slept, her hair flung across the pillow, her lively eyes closed and at rest. I watched her for a moment more, then quietly made my way to the other room. The late dinner and alcohol made my stomach feel unsettled. Sitting upright for a few minutes might help things move along as they were supposed to.

Enough light came through the window that I didn't need to turn any on. The city that never sleeps also always keeps lights on.

Ashley's purse was sitting on the coffee table. It looked like the same leather as her coat and boots. I ran my fingers against it. Then rubbed the coat still flung over the coach. Yes, the same, a very supple leather. I picked up the purse. It was heavy. A gun? That would make sense. I reached in to see if I could touch the heavy metal.

I felt a barrel. I'm not a gun fanatic. I carry one because every once in a while it comes in handy. But I do have a professional interest. I carefully lifted hers out. The safety was on. It was a Sig Sauer. Nice. The Feds clearly had a better ballistics budget than I did.

I hadn't brought my gun. They're a pain to check and I know that New York has sane laws about carrying guns. Not to mention I wanted to give it a very good cleaning before using it again.

Just as carefully, I put it back in.

My hand brushed against a heavy leather case. Her badge?

Curious to see what an ICE badge looked like, I lifted it out. It wasn't a badge; instead it was a leather portfolio with several IDs in it, credit cards, frequent flier cards, hotel cards. I looked at one.

Janet Fielding.

I looked at another. Denise Fisher.

I closed the case and put it back, trying to leave it exactly where I found it. I put the purse back on the table. Why did she need cards with different names on them?

Yes, I do it. I have several fake business cards, with personas that help me accomplish what I need to do. But it's just cheap business cards. My credit cards are all in my name.

Doubt began to creep. How well did I really know Ashley West?

Well enough to have verified she really was an ICE agent. Well enough to sleep with her, well enough to think I might have a future with her. *There's probably a reasonable explanation. It's not hers, it belongs to a coworker, or is part of evidence, or something I'm not thinking of because it's late and my stomach is upset.*

I found my phone and played the latest stupid game for about ten minutes. My stomach felt better and I went back to bed, curling around Ashley and thinking how good she smelled.

I woke in the morning to the aroma of coffee and Ashley's voice in the other room. I started to pick up my watch to see what time it was but remembered it didn't survive being doused in gas. I rolled the other way to look at the bedside clock. Just after nine a.m.

I got up and went to the bathroom. There were bags under my eyes. It had been a long, late night.

When I came out I heard Ashley say, "It's not what it seems. I'll handle it, I told you. You need to trust I know what I'm doing. I haven't let you down yet." A pause as if someone else was talking, then, "I'll be there. I said I would. About two hours, depending on the trains."

She saw me, smiled, then grimaced at the phone. She repeated, "I told you I'd be there, okay? Yell at me when I'm not there, not before I've even left. I have to go. Room service is at the door."

She was still in a robe, her hair tousled from sleep.

"Good morning," she greeted me. "Coffee and pastries."

A room service tray was on the coffee table. Her purse had been moved to the floor.

"Yum. Caffeine is necessary today." I poured a cup and took a bite of a croissant. Bread might help my stomach. I sat down beside her. "Did I hear that you have to be somewhere soon?"

She looked at me. "Oh, you did listen to that? Yes, there's always more work to do. I'm sorry."

"Don't apologize. You have a job, an important one. I'm just happy you didn't need to be there at the crack of dawn."

"You and me both." She took a long sip of coffee.

I considered being honest and bringing up that I'd dug in her purse last night, but I chickened out. Instead, I picked it up as if to move it out of the way of my feet and accidently upended it.

"Damn, I'm sorry. Clumsy without my coffee." I dropped it away from her so she would have to reach over me to help put things back.

"Careful," she said. "I can do it." She stood up.

I was quicker. I picked up the leather case, flopping it open as I did. "Who's Janet Fielding?" I asked. "Or Martha Fleming?" Another name.

"Please give that to me," she said, coming around to take it out of my hand.

"Sure." I did. "Ashley, what's going on here?" I handed her the gun.

She stuffed everything back in the purse, then sat back down.

"I shouldn't tell you this. I'm undercover. That's why I know who Jack is. He thinks I'm part of the gang."

"What? Are John, Cara, and Sandy agents or are they also part of the gang?"

"I really can't tell you much more, okay? I shouldn't have told you this." She bit her lip.

"Tell me what I need to know to know you'll be safe."

"I'm safe. Watched every step of the way."

"Like now?"

"No, I can have some privacy. Don't worry, our activities of last night aren't on tape. But it's one of the reasons I didn't call you yesterday, only brief texts. They monitor my cell phone calls." She cupped my face between her hands. "This will be over soon and we can go away somewhere, okay?"

"Yeah, okay." She gently kissed me, coffee and mouthwash.

"That's why I have those different cards. I got them through the gang."

"But you're really Ashley West, an ICE agent?"

"Yes, you know the real me. The woman who adores being with someone as smart and brave as you are. Not to mention sexy." Another soft kiss.

I felt like an asshole for not trusting her and for the dumped purse ruse. If she was being honest with me, even when she shouldn't be, I should be honest with her. Not that I confessed, but in the future, if I had questions, I would ask them.

"Hey, you're the sexy one," I said, "I'm just responding to you."

She smiled, then glanced at her watch. "I have to get moving."

"Yeah, I overheard that part of your call."

"I'll try and get back this evening," she said, standing up.

"What should I do in the meantime? Can I help in any way?"

"No, not that I know of. Just enjoy a free day."

She went into the bathroom and turned on the shower. I followed her.

"Can you call me and let me know what's going on?"

"That might be hard," she said as she stepped under the streaming water. "They monitor my calls."

"Just text me to let me know what time you might be back."

She nodded and started washing her hair.

I put on one of the hotel robes, left her to her showering, and continued my caffeinating.

When she emerged, she quickly dressed, gave me a lingering kiss good-bye, and left, taking her purse with her.

I took my time showering and dressing, having another cup of coffee and finishing a second croissant and a blueberry muffin.

My day felt unanchored. This was a whirlwind trip; my only purpose here was to see Ashley.

But obviously she was in the heat of an investigation and limited in her free time. I was touched and happy that she needed to see me enough to say the hell with the usual practicalities. We should have waited for the plane fares to be cheaper, until we could actually schedule time together, instead of these small windows available now. I gave her the benefit of the doubt on asking me to come here while she was working undercover. It might be that she knew the arrests were imminent, it might be done today and we could celebrate tonight. Or at least she could rest in my arms and we would celebrate tomorrow.

I left the hotel room around eleven without much of a destination in mind. I did replace my watch, eschewing the great deal on Rolexes from a sidewalk vendor and settling for a cheap one at the drugstore. I debated buying more clothes in case we stayed here longer but decided to hold off. More clothes would require another suitcase, which was more money.

Ashley had said she'd pay for the airline ticket. I would take her up on half of it so we shared the cost equally. Plus I hadn't yet been paid for the work I'd done for her. But had I been working for her and the Feds or her as part of the gang? Even if it was the latter, I trusted that she would make it right.

But until that happened, better to err on the frugal side.

I wandered around Times Square for about half an hour but quickly got tired of the tourists. I headed over to the High Line, the new elevated walking path. I had to zip my jacket up and shove my hands in my pockets against the cold wind from the Hudson River but enjoyed the walk, floating over the streets and the traffic below.

I walked all the way to the end, despite how cold my nose was. It was interesting and didn't cost anything and would pass the time until Ashley could rejoin me.

I hurried to the subway stop and the warmth of underground. It was close to one o'clock and I was getting hungry.

Once I exited the subway near the hotel, I contemplated my options for lunch. Just when I had decided to hit a grocery store and go back to the room, my phone rang.

Ashley.

"Hey, what's up?" I said as I moved to a quieter part of the street.

"I need you to do me a really big favor."

"Sure, whatever you need."

"I need you to join me up here and drive a truck to another place."

"Um, sure, I can do that. How big a truck? I've only got a standard license."

"Not a problem," she said. "It's about the size of a typical moving truck."

"Where are you?"

She gave me directions to one of the wealthy communities to the north of the city. I could catch a train from Grand Central. She even had the train schedule for me. I had about an hour before the next one.

I had a lot of questions, none I could ask over the phone. I settled for, "Should I bring my stuff? Or will we come back here?"

She paused for a second, then said, "You can bring your things. It might be hard to make it back." She added, "I have to go. See you soon."

I could hear voices in the background. Then they were gone as she hung up.

Abandoning my lunch plans, I headed back to the hotel to pack. Given how little I'd brought, that took about five minutes.

I hiked across town to Grand Central, getting there with enough time to grab a sandwich to eat on the train.

The train ride was about an hour and I got there just before three p.m.

Ashley was waiting for me on the train platform.

Jack was standing behind her with another man I didn't recognize.

I would take my cues from her.

She smiled when she saw me, so I smiled back.

When I got to her, she gave me a quick kiss on the cheek. "Thanks for agreeing to do this. It means a lot to me."

"No problem."

"You remember Jack?" she said, turning to him.

I am enough of a Southern girl to do polite and do it well even when I want to spit in someone's face. "Yes, of course. How are you? How does Yankee food compare to New Orleans?"

"Makes me miss it," he said easily, shaking my hand in a friendly manner.

"And this is Luke," she said about the other man.

"Hi, Luke, good to meet you," I said, shaking his hand.

He just nodded and returned the handshake as briefly as he could. He looked like a central casting goon, heavyset, two days of dark beard, small beady eyes.

I had to do everything I could to resist the urge to grab Ashley and run back on the train.

Luke and Jack were both carrying guns. Their winter coats hid the bulge well, but I was looking for it.

I had to trust Ashley, that she knew what she was doing. In a perverse way, I was gratified she had enough confidence in me to know I'd play along.

I followed them out of the train station and to a black SUV, the gangster's vehicle of choice.

Luke and Jack got in the front, Ashley and I in the back.

Once we pulled out of the parking lot, she took my hand, then said very softly, "They know about us."

I squeezed her hand to let her know I'd heard, but didn't do anything else. Luke, the driver, could see us in the rearview mirror.

She continued, "So I said you were cool and could help. All you need to do is drive a truck for a couple of miles and park it. Then it's all over."

I squeezed her hand again but said nothing.

The drive was short, a mile at most from the train station. I was closely paying attention to the streets, the intersections, landmarks.

Luke turned from the main road to a back lane. It was narrow, barely big enough for one car, a ditch on one side and a sharply sloping up hill on the other. We were on it several minutes before the lane led to a massive gate. It had once been beautiful wrought iron but had been ruined by black sheet metal backing it, blocking anyone from looking in. Jack hopped out and hit a button on the intercom.

"We're back." There was a burst of static that I couldn't make out to which he said, "It's Jack and Luke with the girls, okay? Let us in." Another squawk of static to which he answered, "The password for today is fuck you for being an asshole. We just fucking left."

That seemed indeed to be the password, as there was a click and Jack was able to push the gate open.

Once we drove through, he closed the gate and jumped back in.

Interesting that they didn't seem to have a camera there.

A winding drive with mature trees lining it brought us to the front of the house. Many of the trees were evergreens, welcome color in the bleak winter landscape. The trees and the curves hid the dwelling from the gate. The house had once been a beautiful manor, Georgian style or possibly even original, made with red brick faded in age. It was three stories, a large rambling house. Vines were growing up to the roof, now bare strands of brown. Some of the shingles on the roof needed replacing, and the windows sagged as if the wood was old and tired. The driveway hadn't been kept up, with ruts and potholes in it.

"That's the truck over there," Jack pointed out.

At the far side of the asphalt area in front a large white truck was parked. As Ashley had said, it looked like it might have once been a moving van, about sixteen feet long.

"Where do I drive it?" I asked.

"Got a map," Jack said. He pulled a piece of paper out of his jacket and handed it to me.

I studied it. I was to drive it to the next town up the river, a much larger one than this, to a parking lot at a bank in the center of town. That seemed easy; the burning question was why.

"Here's the keys," he said, handing them to me.

"Can I get a bathroom break first?" I asked. I really did need one, and I was curious to see the inside of the house.

He sighed, then said to Luke, "Go show her the powder room."

I had hoped to get Ashley to take me. I wondered if they were trying to keep us apart.

Having no choice, I followed Luke.

The front door stuck as he opened it and he had to give it a yank.

The inside was like the outside, beautiful, but not kept up. Dust covered the baseboards and several of the lights were out.

I could hear voices, all male, coming from back in the house, but Luke led me to a small half-bath under the main stairway.

I quickly did my business; there was nothing interesting in the bathroom. And what was interesting, where the voices were, wasn't a place I'd be allowed to go.

When I came back out, Jack was futzing with a combination lock, with Ashley holding a heavy chain.

Lucky for me, my eyesight is still good. I paid close attention as he spun the dial. Especially lucky for me, he had to try several times before he got it open. By the time he was done, I had a fairly good idea of what the combination was. This kind of attention was habit. This was a dangerous situation; I had no idea what might come in handy. They could lock Ashley up with that lock and if I knew the combination, I could free her. Or maybe they would lock a toolshed and it wouldn't matter. Same thing with the streets and what I could gather of the layout of the house. One scrap of information might be vital. I just didn't know which.

"Ready to go?" Jack said as he slung the lock and chain over his shoulder.

"Sure," I answered.

We all, Jack, Ashley, and Luke, walked together to the truck. Jack looped the chain through the back handle.

"What's in there?" I asked.

"Some computer stuff, junk like that," he said, not looking at me as he cinched in the chain and spun the lock.

"What do I do after I get there?" I asked.

Jack looked at me as if he hadn't thought about that.

"Give me a call," Ashley said. "When you're parked, all you need to do is call." She looked at Jack and he nodded.

"Okay, about how long? Why not have someone follow me?"

"You'll be much slower in the truck. It'll save time to just come and get you then," Jack said.

"It's taken care of," Ashley said. "Let's go." She walked with me around the truck to the driver's side.

Mercifully Luke and Jack didn't follow.

She kissed me quickly, then said very softly, "You are special. You made me feel like I deserved to be taken care of."

"You do."

She held her face still, but her eyes were shining as if saying *this is dangerous and we might not see each other again.*

"We'll be together soon," I said.

"Yes, we will," she said, taking my hand, then letting it go and turning away.

I got in the truck and started the engine.

It was an automatic and I had to remember not to shift gears. This truck had seen better days—the brakes almost sank to the floor before engaging and the engine whined as it tried to pick up speed.

I took my time driving to the gate, getting used to the truck in the safe confines of a private road. I was also checking out the grounds. As far as I could see, a red brick wall about eight feet tall encompassed the large yard. Halfway down one side there was a small pedestrian gate that led to the back lane. The main gate was built into one of the corners, leading to an intersection of the back lane and another small road. Close as this was to the train station, it was still isolated and hidden from view. The grounds, like the house, hadn't been cared for in a while. Even in bare winter it seemed overgrown, hedges unkempt, tangles of dead vines marking disappearing paths.

Once I got to the main gate, I had to get out of the truck, reach around to the intercom, and ask to be let out. No static greeted me, only the buzz of the gate lock. I swung the iron gate into the road, drove though, then had to get out and close it again.

Not a great system, I thought as I got back into the truck. It made me wonder if this was a secondary location. Maybe Ashley was right, this would be over soon. The traffickers were on the run, having to make do with backup locations because the main ones were too hot. An operation this big and sophisticated should have much better security.

I started down the back lane when my phone rang. I looked at the screen.

Ashley. "Where are you?" she asked.

"Just outside the gate. Takes a bit to open and close it." I pulled to the side of the road, which was mostly the middle of the road considering how small it was, but no other traffic was around.

"Okay, good. About how long until you get there?"

I looked down at the map next to me in the seat. "Maybe half an hour? Depends on traffic and the roads, this truck is not a speed demon."

"Okay, keep me posted, let me know when you're close."

I took a chance. "You can't talk, can you?"

"Not really. I'll call you in a bit." She hung up.

Before rolling again, I pulled up a map on my phone and had it give me a time estimate. It said about thirty-eight minutes and gave me a more direct route, one that bypassed the main drag through the town. I didn't know if the truck was a signal, so I would stick with their directions. Perhaps a beat-up white panel truck passing Road X would be the sign for the Feds to move in.

I started driving again. There was no traffic back here, a sparse area of big houses with extensive lawns. It was slow going on this small lane. I needed to be careful not to get my tires caught in the ditch. My half an hour was turning into closer to forty-five minutes.

I turned on another road that led to an intersection with an actual stop sign. Hard to believe I was only an hour out of New York City. Just past the intersection, there was an out-of-business fabric store.

It was close to four o'clock and would be dark in an hour.

Curious, I pulled into the parking lot. It would be an extra two minutes, but I wanted to know what was in the truck, now, while there was still light. I also wanted to know if I was unwittingly carting something illegal.

I fumbled with the lock in the cold. Once, twice, a third guess. It didn't open. One more try, then I would give up. I spun the dial.

The lock clicked open. I shoved open the truck gate.

And stared at the monster in the truck.

CHAPTER TWENTY-FOUR

It was loaded with explosives. I'm not an expert, but I know enough to recognize a pile of pressure cookers, big plastic garbage bags, and timers. At a guess, it wasn't a sophisticated bomb, instead something thrown together in a hurry.

I was to drive this to the center of a town, the largest one in the area.

I very carefully closed the truck gate. I didn't bother with the lock and chain.

A school bus drove by. Few kids were on it.

I broke into a cold sweat at the thought of what this could do.

What game are we playing, Ashley? I silently screamed. Did she know? Could she?

I recalled the haunted look on her face as we said good-bye. Was it for me?

The Feds needed to swoop in right about now.

The school bus was gone, no one else on the road. I'd seen no one, not even a supposedly innocent repair van on my way out.

I called Ashley.

"Where are you?" she asked. "Are you there yet?"

She had me on speakerphone. They were listening in. "No, it's slower going than I'd hoped. This truck barely makes it out of third gear."

"Okay, just let me know when you're close."

The line was dead.

I walked down the road away from the truck. What was a safe distance?

What did I really know about Ashley West?

I scrolled through previous calls until I found the number for Frank Mullen.

He answered. Relief. There was no time for voice mail.

"Hi, this is Michele Knight, the private investigator from New Orleans. Can I ask you a few more questions?"

"Sure. Not likely I'll have the answers."

"For these you might. You said you worked with Ashley West's father."

"Yep, sure did."

"How would you describe her?"

"Huh. She looks a lot like those tennis players. Can't think of their names."

"Current ones? Retired ones?"

"The sisters."

"Serena and Venus Williams?" My heart sank.

"Yes, that's them."

My heart bottomed out. "She pretty tall and played basketball?"

"Yes, that's her," he said. "Is that all you wanted to know?"

"That answers a lot of questions," I said, keeping my voice steady. "One more question. Do you remember a suicide in your area? A young man who jumped off a bridge onto ice? Supposedly his father wasn't happy that he wasn't the butchest of men."

"That's a question from out in left field. But, yeah, we had something like that happen here a while back. Sad case. His father owned the adult stores in the area. We got called out to them on occasion. He was, pardon, my language, a bastard. Angry at everyone and everything."

"Do you know if he had a daughter?"

"He had three daughters. Two of them ended up pregnant before they graduated high school, always in petty trouble until the kids kept them at home."

"What about the third one?"

"She was more trouble than the other two, brought her in several times myself, but as much as her father was mean, she was smooth, could talk her way out of everything. She was pretty enough and could always say the right thing. The judges always took pity on her and let her off with things like community service."

"Would she be in her thirties now? Reddish-brown hair? About five-five? Green eyes?"

"I don't remember the eye color, but the rest sounds about right. Why are you asking me this?"

"Because she claims her name is Ashley West and she's an ICE agent."

"Oh, wow. Sad thing is I'm not surprised."

"Do you remember what her real name is?"

"Yeah, Martha Fleming. She came back here now and then to help her dad with the business. She didn't blink an eye at the things going on in those stores."

"Thanks, that's been very helpful."

"Okay. She need to be arrested?"

"Probably, but I think the Feds are hot on her tail."

And I was about to be. I thanked Frank Mullen and hung up, then went into my phone and turned the GPS off. Just in case they were tracking me, I didn't want them to know I wasn't following their route.

I got back in the truck and carefully turned it around. Ashley, or Martha, had used what she knew, leaning on her past and background. She wanted to pretend to be a federal agent, so she took a name she knew would check out. Few people would know Ashley West was really a black woman, as pictures would be hard to find for someone like me. She probably had a different ruse for anyone with the authority to look up her credentials.

Traffic was still light, so I broke the law and used my phone to look up current events in the town I was ostensibly headed for. Today was the founder's day parade and festival. Right in the center of town. I would be driving by school bands and cheerleaders, moms and pops out with their kids.

What if a massive task force is breathing down your tail, about to arrest everyone all the way to the top?

Distract them with a terrorist bombing. Every person vaguely involved in law enforcement would be diverted.

"You are not going to get away with this," I muttered. I pushed the truck, making the engine strain.

Ashley or whatever her name was had lied to me. I was expendable. Had been at the warehouse. I had been smart enough to get away then. I might not get away this time, but I would bring her down and her scum-sucking fuckwads with her. Rape and torture women to make money. Blow up a town to get away. Human beings don't come more evil than that.

Why had she slept with me? Just another kinky thrill? Fuck the sacrificial goat?

Was there possibly still a piece of the young girl who had to take care of herself hidden in the hardened woman? Maybe that young girl had actually cared for me?

Or perhaps I didn't want to think I had been so utterly fooled by her.

My phone rang.

Ashley.

"Are you close yet?"

"Getting there. This truck goes down to about ten miles per hour on hills and there are a lot of them around. Plus the school zones. It wouldn't do to get a ticket. I'll be about another twenty minutes."

"No, don't get a ticket. Can you describe where you are?"

"Yes, I...gotta go, a cop. Can't talk on the phone." I hung up on her. "Bitch."

I again had to be careful on the narrow back lane. I didn't want to strand the truck anyplace likely to get innocent bystanders.

The ugly iron gate loomed in front of me. It was the only exit, at least for vehicles, out of the compound.

"Should have installed a video camera," I said as I pulled beside it. I backed the truck so it was across the gate, completely blocking it. Even if the explosion went off, the wreck of the truck and the twisted metal of the gate would bar the way.

I got out of the truck and threw the key as far away into the underbrush as I could. I grabbed my overnight bag—I wasn't going to give up my good pair of jeans unless I had to. I also took the lock and chain. I had a use for them. I trotted down the lane along the brick wall, finally hiding them behind a bush.

My phone rang. Ashley.

"That was close," I said on answering it. "Cop almost saw me talking on the phone."

"We don't need to talk long. Just tell me where you are."

I pulled the map they had given me out of my jacket pocket. "I'm coming down Short Hill Road, about two blocks from the turn onto Main St. Then the ten blocks through town to the bank parking lot. Almost there. Fifteen at most."

"Good, good to hear. Call me as soon as you're parked."

"Are you going to come get me?"

Her voice hesitated. "Yes, yes, of course. We'll be together soon."

"Okay, talk to you in a bit."

I went back to the truck and very carefully edged open the back lift gate.

And just as carefully took two of the timing devices. They were both attached to what looked like smaller explosives, ones that would start the conflagration. I counted another four timers still in the truck. They were going to make sure it was a big explosion. I didn't bother closing the back of the truck.

I carefully strode down the lane to the small gate.

It was open, the lock rusted through. Another security mistake. They probably never used it and never checked to see what time and wear did to the lock.

I could be at the house in about a minute, easily hidden by the overgrowth.

As I slid through the gate, a rational voice in my head told me this was one of the stupidest things I've ever done. I should be hightailing it out of there and calling Emily Harris to give her the address.

Hell hath no fury like a woman betrayed. This was personal. I wasn't going to walk away to be left to hear what happened on secondhand newscasts or let the Feds forget to bring something like a boat and mess things up.

I kept to the edge of the trees lining the driveway, still carefully balancing the bombs. The late-afternoon sun was low on the horizon, sliding into twilight. The dim light would help.

As I got close to the driveway I heard voices.

I put down the bombs long enough to switch my phone to vibrate. Leaving the devices on the ground, I crept closer to the voices.

Luke and John—he must have been one of the men I'd heard in the house—were loading suitcases into a car. It and the SUV were the only two vehicles here. It was cold enough to keep the others inside.

"Careful with that," John told Luke.

"Why? It's just a fucking briefcase."

"Full of money."

"Shit," was all Luke said.

"Put the suitcase on top of it," John instructed.

My phone vibrated. I ignored it.

Wondered if the bombs would go off when she didn't hear from me.

"How much more we got?" Luke asked.

"Two more small cases. Some gold to add to the money. As soon as they're ready."

They turned and went into the house. My phone stopped vibrating.

Either do it or run like hell out of here.

I picked up the two bombs. As quickly as I could, I edged through the trees and underbrush to the driveway. Crouching low I ducked behind the SUV, using it to block me from the house.

One bomb went under its back tire.

I duck-walked to the car, placing the second bomb under its same tire.

The low sun was behind me. I would be hard to see in the glare. On my knees I leaned around to the trunk.

Somehow I doubted I was going to get paid for all the work I'd done for them.

I pushed the suitcase off the attaché with the money. They were lazy, thinking no one else was around. Why lock something if you're going to open it again soon?

From my position, it was a long reach, but I was able to flip open both the catches on the briefcase. It contained piles and piles of money.

I snatched four bundles and stuffed them in my pockets.

I sidled back into the trees, moving in a low crouch until I thought I was far enough away from the house to be hidden by the underbrush.

Then I flat-out sprinted as quickly as I could, running along the overgrown trees, jumping tangled vines, heading madly for the unlocked gate.

My phone vibrated again just as I was at the gate.

This time I answered it.

"Yeah?" I said, then holding the mouthpiece away so she wouldn't hear my heavy breathing.

"Where are you?"

"Almost there. Sorry it took so long. It's been slow with some parade and big festival in town. Cops everywhere. I had to be careful about answering my phone." I covered the phone mic with my hand to take another breath.

"Are you near the festival grounds yet?"

"Close, another block. Then two more to the bank. Maybe you should be on your way to pick me up."

"Soon. I promise, soon."

I quietly let myself out of the gate. I didn't want her to hear a squeak.

The phone went dead.

I crossed to where I'd put the chain, hastily taking it back to the gate. I wrapped the chain around the iron bars, doing what I could to make it difficult to reach through the gate and get to the lock.

Once the lock clicked shut, I again ran, just remembering to grab my overnight bag out of the brush. I crossed the narrow lane, then climbed the hill on the other side of the road to get my bearings. Off in the distance I could see the Hudson River. The train station would be right next to it.

I continued along the hill. Cutting through the trees slowed me down, but I didn't want to be close to a road for fear part of the gang might drive by.

I punched in the number for Emily Harris.

She answered on the first ring.

"Just listen," I said. I gave her directions to the house, the streets I paid such attention to. "There are a bunch of men there who are about to get away. And a few women. In a minute or two you're going to have plenty of reason to go in and raid the house."

"What's going on? Where are you?" She had to hear my heavy breathing, the sloshing through fallen leaves.

"Someday I'll explain. There's no time now."

My phone buzzed. Another call. "Someday," I echoed. "You were right, there are no female ICE. agents involved."

I hung up and answered what I knew had to be Ashley's call.

"I'm right across from the festival now. Still going slowly," I said, looking down at the house. The hill was high enough I could see over the brick wall. In the summer the trees would block the view, but the bare branches of winter revealed the unkempt lawn and faded bricks. I kept walking, looking back over my shoulder.

"Okay," she said slowly. "Micky, thank you so much for everything you're done for me. It's," then very softly, "you deserve the kind of woman I wish I was."

I heard a note of longing in her voice. It told me that some of it had been real. It also told me she knew what was about to happen.

"Yep, almost there," I lied. But I wasn't lying; we were almost there, just not the destination they intended.

I kept the phone open, hoping at the last minute she'd yell at me to get out of the truck, to run.

Instead she said, "Good-bye, Micky."

"I'll see you again in a half hour," I replied.

She hung up. Those were her final words.

The world erupted, a roar followed by louder roars, gold and flame leaping to the sky. A huge blaze at the main gate, smaller ones near the house. I swear I saw bills floating in air, wafting over the ruins of the cars.

I powered down my phone and starting jogging down the other side of the hill.

CHAPTER TWENTY-FIVE

Going between a slow jog and a fast walk, I made it to the train station in about twenty minutes. It was rush hour, so the trains came at frequent intervals.

One was just pulling into the station as I bought my ticket back into the city. I paid with cash from my wallet, not the stacks now hidden at the bottom of my bag.

I put my phone in there as well, leaving it safely off. Otherwise I might call Emily and ask if they'd raided the place yet. Or Ashley and scream every vile name I could think of at her.

Silence was better, safer.

I had made a fool of myself. This was the year of bad decisions, wrong choices, dead ends. Ashley West was a shimmering mirage, playing the perfect woman because I desperately wanted someone to reflect me as I wanted to be, not as I was. Emily or even Desiree would have been better choices, but they were real people, Emily with her distrust, Desiree with her past, honest enough to show me their flaws, honest enough to not make promises from desires.

I suddenly had a stabbing longing for Cordelia.

Bid time return, call back yesterday.

But I couldn't. Time is relentless, the past unchanging. I couldn't go back and fix what had been broken.

I was on a train with no real destination. I'd go back to New York, of course, but I had no purpose there. My mother lived in the city, but I was too broken and ashamed to want to see her and her partner and confess my reason for being here—I followed a woman who lied to me. Time might give me the will to talk about what had happened, how deluded I'd been, going from destroying a love of long term to lurch into a fantasy affair.

That left me on a train in the night with no answers for the morning.

Still, we arrived in Grand Central and I had to go somewhere. I wandered down Forty-second Street until I found a hotel that would let me pay in cash. I made up a story about trying to get away from an abusive partner and not wanting to use a credit card that he could trace. It helped to pay up front. The money came from the bundles at the bottom of my bag.

After that I found a liquor store and bought the best Scotch they had. I also picked up something to eat. I wasn't hungry now, but I would be eventually.

Then I went back to the hotel room and cried into my Scotch. It seemed the fitting end to the day.

The next morning I woke with a hangover, no surprise.

It was a beautiful clear winter day. I hadn't been blown into scraps of flesh nor burned alive. The explosives in the truck had been used against those who would have killed innocent people with them. There were things to be thankful for. Breakfast and coffee also helped.

I also had sixty thousand dollars in cash. I carefully checked a number of the bills; they seemed real, and I couldn't see any way they were marked except for a fifty that read "gay money."

I went shopping, buying new clothes and the suitcase to carry them in. I bought some really nice tea, stuffed five thousand into one of the tea boxes, wrapped it in several layers, and addressed it to Bianca at her Tulane Avenue address. *Thanks for the tea, maybe this will help you get started in business* was the note I put inside. I didn't include my name or a return address. I also bought a new tablet to use instead of my phone. I didn't get an account but would use it when I could find wireless Internet. I wanted to be as hard to find as possible.

It's not as easy to spend money as it looks. I went to two different banks and set up checking accounts of just under ten thousand dollars, to avoid them being reported to the IRS. I lied to both and said I'd been very lucky in Vegas.

In the afternoon I chanced turning on my phone. Emily had called five times. Ashley hadn't tried once. I quickly turned it back off.

The explosions and subsequent arrests made the news, front page (below the fold) even in the *New York Times*. The article said a number of people had been arrested. I saw John's picture and those of several others, the kingpins, but nothing on Ashley. My guess had been right; the FBI had identified their main operating location, and they had hurriedly relocated to the property I'd seen. They were packing up to leave there and spread to the four winds, plane tickets already in hand.

They had to know I'd been the one to screw up their plans. Between the FBI and the crooks, if any had escaped, it wasn't a good idea for me to hang around.

I spun the globe and picked a place to run off to.

Melbourne, Australia, sounded like about the right distance. I wanted a city big enough to disappear into, and I was lazy enough to want some place where they spoke English. My French is poor and more Cajun than anything in Paris.

It was stolen money—or money that came from the wrong places, so I didn't care how quickly it went.

I found a travel agent—how I love the density of New York—and booked my flight for the following day. I splurged on business class. I managed to pay in cash by claiming I'd gotten it in a divorce settlement and I didn't want to put it in a bank, otherwise he might try to get it. He was a cheap bastard—my fictional boyfriend/husband was coming in handy.

I wasn't truly fooling myself; I knew the travel was a distraction, motion to keep me going through the days. But the exigencies of arranging everything, getting a visa, easy enough for Americans, gathering enough clothes and toiletries to get me through for a while. Emailing Chanse and Scotty to see if they could take on any pressing cases while I was away. All the activity kept me busy, away from my demons. And the Scotch.

I felt I could legitimately keep the money I would have earned had Ashley paid for everything she said she would pay for. The rest needed to be burned in spending, to get it out of my pocket and into other people's, one who would use it to buy school clothes for their kids or a new stove.

My phone stayed off, in the bottom of my suitcase.

This time I took a cab out to JFK to catch my late-night plane out of here. I'd change planes in Hong Kong, then on to Melbourne. I got there a little after ten p.m. My plane left at one thirty a.m. This time of night was a slow point at the airport. I got through security more quickly than I expected and headed for my gate.

I was browsing the latest bestsellers in a newsstand when I caught sight of a glint of red hair.

A green coat.

I followed her. She was walking quickly, in a hurry. I hastened to catch up, to be sure it wasn't my imagination playing tricks.

It was the same purse; I recognized it.

I waited until she passed the stores with the few people around in them before speeding up enough to catch her.

When I was just behind her, when she had to have heard my footsteps, I called, "Martha! Martha Fleming!"

She turned and stared, then started to run.

I grabbed her arm.

"How did you—?" she started.

"Know your real name? I'm a detective. Finding out things is what I do."

"You must know I didn't want that to happen."

"You mean you didn't want me and scores of other people to be killed by a bomb? Really? You fooled me into thinking you did because you didn't do a goddamn thing to stop it."

"No, it's not like that. I couldn't. They would have killed me."

"Yeah? We could have escaped at the train station."

"They had guns."

"That they would have used in a bunch of people ensuring their immediate arrest."

"I hoped to get away. And you did. You saved the day."

"You would have let me die. Maybe if it was just me for you, I would have even offered, but you wanted to make it look like a terrorist attack, killing many more people. That I can't forgive."

"That's not what I wanted to happen." She bit her lip in the little-girl fashion she had perfected.

"What did you want to happen?"

"I desperately wanted to get away from them. That's why I asked you to come to New York. So we could get away together."

"You should have let me in on that."

"There wasn't time."

"If we'd had one less orgasm there would have been time."

She looked down and said contritely, "I know. But...it was so good to be with you. I thought we'd have more time, but they didn't trust me and were watching me. They must have suspected I wanted to get away. They ordered me to get you involved. I kept hoping for a miracle, some way to avoid what they were doing. But they had a gun on me the entire time."

She was lying. I was tired of her excuses.

"What was going on in New Orleans? Why where you there?"

"We—they had hired the Guidry brothers to run their operation down there, but they were overstepping and we—John, Jack, Cara, and I were sent down to straighten things out. My role was mostly to take notes and arrange logistics."

"Secretary to the mob. Why get the cops out to their warehouse?"

"The brothers weren't supposed to be doing that. We wanted to send them a warning."

"The plan was to leave me there and take the blame, right?"

"It wasn't my plan. I didn't know John had that in mind."

She was good, just the right quiver in her voice, her eyes direct and holding mine. One of the best liars I've even encountered.

"Who killed the women? The ones dumped in the river."

"The brothers," she said too quickly for me to believe her.

"Why would they do that?"

"They were psychopaths. They wanted to scare the other women they had from trying to escape."

"Were you there?" I asked.

She looked at me. "No, of course not. I…it was the brothers. They did it."

That was all I'd get from her. John and Jack were probably the murderers, and it was meant as a threat to both the brothers and Desiree.

"Why did he attack you?"

"Payback. They weren't going to quietly tuck in their tails and say 'yes, sir.' I was their message." Then she put her hand on my face. "Micky, I know I'm a terrible person, but please know I wanted a new life with you, to start again and be someone better. That was the only reason I asked you to come up here. I was…was falling in love with you. That's not something I let myself do. You were the one who took care of me. I so wanted that as a future…not this."

Even though I knew she was a self-serving liar, I wanted to believe part of that was true, that somewhere in her tangle of lies, she did care for me.

"Where are you running to?" I asked.

"Somewhere far away. I'm not safe from the law or Jack if he finds me."

"He got away?"

"I think so."

"I'm supposed to just let you go?"

She looked down. "I know I have no right to ask this, but give me an hour. Give me one more chance." She leaned forward and gently kissed me.

"All right. One more chance."

She smiled, the radiant smile that had so bewitched me. "Thank you. I'll never forget you." She started down the concourse.

"I'll never forget you either," I called after her.

She turned and blew me a kiss.

I watched until she turned a corner and was out of sight.

I dug into the bottom of my carry on and found my phone. I turned it on and called Emily.

"Knight! Where are you?"

"Don't ask. That's not important. JFK in Terminal 7. The woman who called herself Ashley West and claimed to be an ICE agent is there and about to get on a plane. Her real name is Martha Fleming. She's part of your trafficker gang."

"Shit, Knight, for making my life easy, you're making it hard. This is the second tip out of thin air that I'm supposed to pass on."

"I was right on the first one."

"True."

"Just tell them…it's from someone who trusts you."

I ended the call.

One hour?

Fuck you, you lying bitch.

Chapter Twenty-six

I loved Melbourne, a friendly, fantastic city, a walkable center and streetcars that remind me of New Orleans. Great food from all around the Pacific Rim. And seafood. It was a port city, after all.

After getting here, I'd found a spot with wireless and written Emily an accounting of what I'd done. I left out taking the money but was honest about everything else, even my messy affair with the woman I still thought of as Ashley West. After enough time for her to have bounced it to the higher-ups, she'd replied that I was in the clear. I'd saved people from being burned in the French Quarter and prevented a horrible attack on innocent civilians and in such an ingenious way that it stopped the real criminals from getting away. They weren't giving me a medal, but they weren't going to lock me up, either.

They had caught Jack. And John, Cara—the sister of the kingpin—Sandy, all the voices I'd heard in the house. Broken the back of a monster.

They hadn't caught Ashley. Yet.

I also wrote Desiree with much of what I told Emily.

Her reply was kind, saying she hoped to see me before she left. She was closing the business, tired of the life and its risk. She planned to sell her French Quarter property, now a hot market, and move somewhere out west, maybe a small Oregon town on the coast. As different a life as she could imagine herself in. I hoped I'd see her before she left, too.

About a week after I got here, Ashley sent me a brief email: *I knew you'd call. You're that kind of person. An hour was too much to ask. I left the airport and am trying to find a different life. One you might respect me for.* Maybe. Or maybe she was a liar to the end. No matter how much she changed, gave up her lying, I'd never trust her, never believe her again.

I'd be back in Melbourne in a few days.

At the moment, I was sitting on a bluff just off the Great Ocean Road. I'd found some mates, Lindy and Chell, and together we were on a road trip. First we'd gone to the Barossa Valley, one of the great wine-producing areas of Australia, sort of like Napa Valley with kangaroos.

We were coming back via the Great Ocean Road, a place that had always been on my bucket list. Cordelia and I had talked of it, our runaway plan. I was sad she wasn't here with me—she'd have to get to this part of the world on her own—but happy I was on this seared umber bluff, seeing the great sculpture of rock and waves carved by nature.

I was slowly learning to forgive myself. I had tried to be a decent person, had tried to do the right thing. Had failed and failed again, but even so, tried to learn from my mistakes. I couldn't ask for perfection, only that I tried—and kept trying—to do the right thing.

I was writing postcards and letters to all my friends. Torbin and Andy, Danny and Elly, Joanne and Alex. Telling them what great friends they had always been to me and how much they meant, the things I would have regretted leaving unsaid if I'd been blown into the sky. Telling them I had taken a break, needed some time to think things through, the usual clichés.

But it was true. I needed to see the vastness of the world, to remind myself of the possibilities in it, how small my troubles were in comparison.

I sent a postcard to Cordelia, to our address in New Orleans with a request that it be forwarded. I didn't say I missed her, although I did. I just let her know I'd finally made it here, was sitting on a sandy bluff watching the startlingly blue waves crash against this slowly eroding cliff.

The world can be a beautiful and savage place.

Today it was beautiful.

About the Author

J.M. Redmann is the author of a mystery series featuring New Orleans private detective Michele "Micky" Knight. Her latest book is *Ill Will*, which made the American Library Association GLBT Roundtable's 2013 Over the Rainbow list. Her previous book, *Water Mark*, was also on the Over the Rainbow list and won a *Foreword* Magazine Gold Medal for mystery. Two of her earlier books, *The Intersection Of Law & Desire* and *Death Of A Dying Man*, have won Lambda Literary Awards; all but her first book have been nominated. *Law & Desire* was an Editor's Choice of the *San Francisco Chronicle* and a recommended book on NPR's *Fresh Air*. Her books have been translated into Spanish, German, Dutch, Norwegian, and Hebrew. She is the co-editor with Greg Herren of three anthologies, *Night Shadows: Queer Horror*, *Women of the Mean Streets: Lesbian Noir*, and *Men of the Mean Streets: Gay Noir*. Redmann lives in an historic neighborhood in New Orleans, at the edge of the area that flooded.

Books Available From Bold Strokes Books

Love and Devotion by Jove Belle. KC Hall trips her way through life, stumbling into an affair with a married bombshell twice her age. Thankfully, her best friend, Emma Reynolds, is there to show her the true meaning of Love and Devotion. (978-1-60282-965-7)

Rush by Carsen Taite. Murder, secrets, and romance combine to create the ultimate rush. (978-1-60282-966-4)

The Shoal of Time by J.M. Redmann. It sounded too easy. Micky Knight is reluctant to take the case because the easy ones often turn into the hard ones, and the hard ones turn into the dangerous ones. In this one, easy turns hard without warning. (978-1-60282-967-1)

In Between by Jane Hoppen. At the age of fourteen, Sophie Schmidt discovers that she was born an intersexual baby and sets off on a journey to find her place in a world that denies her true existence. (978-1-60282-968-8)

Under Her Spell by Maggie Morton. The magic of love brought Terra and Athene together, but now a magical quest stands between them—a quest for Athene's hand in marriage. Will their passion keep them together, or will stronger magic tear them apart? (978-1-60282-973-2)

Scars by Amy Dunne. While fleeing from her abuser, Nicola Jackson bumps into Jenny O'Connor, and their unlikely friendship quickly develops into a blossoming romance—but when it comes down to a matter of life or death, are they both willing to face their fears? (978-1-60282-970-1)

Homestead by Radclyffe. R. Clayton Sutter figures getting NorthAm Fuel's newest refinery operational on a rolling tract of land in upstate New York should take a month or two, but then, she hadn't counted on local resistance in the form of vandalism, petitions, and one furious farmer named Tess Rogers. (978-1-60282-956-5)

Battle of Forces: Sera Toujours by Ali Vali. Kendal and Piper return to New Orleans to start the rest of eternity together, but the return of an old enemy makes their peaceful reunion short-lived, especially when they join forces with the new queen of the vampires. (978-1-60282-957-2)

How Sweet It Is by Melissa Brayden. Some things are better than chocolate. Molly O'Brien enjoys her quiet life running the bakeshop in a small town. When the beautiful Jordan Tuscana returns home, Molly can't deny the attraction—or the stirrings of something more. (978-1-60282-958-9)

The Missing Juliet: A Fisher Key Adventure by Sam Cameron. A teenage detective and her friends search for a kidnapped Hollywood star in the Florida Keys. (978-1-60282-959-6)

Amor and More: Love Everafter, edited by Radclyffe and Stacia Seaman. Rediscover favorite couples as Bold Strokes Books authors reveal glimpses of life and love beyond the honeymoon in short stories featuring main characters from favorite BSB novels. (978-1-60282-963-3)

First Love by CJ Harte. Finding true love is hard enough, but for Jordan Thompson, daughter of a conservative president, it's challenging, especially when that love is a female rodeo cowgirl. (978-1-60282-949-7)

Pale Wings Protecting by Lesley Davis. Posing as a couple to investigate the abduction of infants, Special Agent Blythe Kent and Detective Daryl Chandler find themselves drawn into a battle over the innocents, with demons on one side and the unlikeliest of protectors on the other. (978-1-60282-964-0)

Mounting Danger by Karis Walsh. Sergeant Rachel Bryce, an outcast on the police force, is put in charge of the department's newly formed mounted division. Can she and polo champion Callan Lanford resist their growing attraction as they struggle to safeguard the disaster-prone unit? (978-1-60282-951-0)

Show of Force by AJ Quinn. A chance meeting between navy pilot Evan Kane and correspondent Tate McKenna takes them on a roller-coaster ride where the stakes are high, but the reward is higher: a chance at love. (978-1-60282-942-8)

Clean Slate by Andrea Bramhall. Can Erin and Morgan work through their individual demons to rediscover their love for each other, or are the unexplainable wounds too deep to heal? (978-1-60282-943-5)

Hold Me Forever by D. Jackson Leigh. An investigation into illegal cloning in the quarter horse racing industry threatens to destroy the growing attraction between Georgia debutante Mae St. John and Louisiana horse trainer Whit Casey. (978-1-60282-944-2)

At Her Feet by Rebekah Weatherspoon. Digital marketing producer Suzanne Kim knows she has found the perfect love in her new mistress Pilar, but before they can make the ultimate commitment, Suzanne's professional life threatens to disrupt their perfectly balanced bliss. (978-1-60282-948-0)

Trusting Tomorrow by P.J. Trebelhorn. Funeral director Logan Swift thinks she's perfectly happy with her solitary life devoted to helping others cope with loss until Brooke Collier moves in next door to care for her elderly grandparents. (978-1-60282-891-9)

Forsaking All Others by Kathleen Knowles. What if what you think you want is the opposite of what makes you happy? (978-1-60282-892-6)

Exit Wounds by VK Powell. When Officer Loane Landry falls in love with ATF informant Abigail Mancuso, she realizes that nothing is as it seems—not the case, not her lover, not even the dead. (978-1-60282-893-3)

Dirty Power by Ashley Bartlett. Cooper's been through hell and back, and she's still broke and on the run. But at least she found the twins. They'll keep her alive. Right? (978-1-60282-896-4)

The Rarest Rose by I. Beacham. After a decade of living in her beloved house, Ele disturbs its past and finds her life being haunted by the presence of a ghost who will show her that true love never dies. (978-1-60282-884-1)

Code of Honor by Radclyffe. The face of terror is hard to recognize— especially when it's homegrown. The next book in the Honor series. (978-1-60282-885-8)

Does She Love You by Rachel Spangler. When Annabelle and Davis find out they are in a relationship with the same woman, it leaves them facing life-altering questions about trust, redemption, and the possibility of finding love in the wake of betrayal. (978-1-60282-886-5)

The Road to Her by KE Payne. Sparks fly when actress Holly Croft, star of UK soap *Portobello Road*, meets her new on-screen love interest, the enigmatic and sexy Elise Manford. (978-1-60282-887-2)

Shadows of Something Real by Sophia Kell Hagin. Trying to escape flashbacks and nightmares, ex-POW Jamie Gwynmorgan stumbles into the heart of former Red Cross worker Adele Sabellius and uncovers a deadly conspiracy against everything and everyone she loves. (978-1-60282-889-6)

Date with Destiny by Mason Dixon. When sophisticated bank executive Rashida Ivey meets unemployed blue-collar worker Destiny Jackson, will her life ever be the same? (978-1-60282-878-0)

The Devil's Orchard by Ali Vali. Cain and Emma plan a wedding before the birth of their third child while Juan Luis is still lurking, and as Cain plans for his death, an unexpected visitor arrives and challenges her belief in her father, Dalton Casey. (978-1-60282-879-7)

Secrets and Shadows by L.T. Marie. A bodyguard and the woman she protects run from a madman and into each other's arms. (978-1-60282-880-3)

Change Horizon: Three Novellas by Gun Brooke. Three stories of courageous women who dare to love as they fight to claim a future in a hostile universe. (978-1-60282-881-0)

Scarlett Thirst by Crin Claxton. When hot, feisty Rani meets cool vampire Rob, one lifetime isn't enough, and the road from human to vampire is shorter than you think... (978-1-60282-856-8)

Battle Axe by Carsen Taite. How close is too close? Bounty hunter Luca Bennett will soon find out. (978-1-60282-871-1)

Improvisation by Karis Walsh. High school geometry teacher Jan Carroll thinks she's figured out the shape of her life and her future, until graphic artist and fiddle player Tina Nelson comes along and teaches her to improvise. (978-1-60282-872-8)

For Want of a Fiend by Barbara Ann Wright. Without her Fiendish power, can Princess Katya and her consort Starbride stop a magic-wielding madman from sparking an uprising in the kingdom of Farraday? (978-1-60282-873-5)

Swans & Clons by Nora Olsen. In a future world where there are no males, sixteen-year-old Rubric and her girlfriend Salmon Jo must fight to survive when everything they believed in turns out to be a lie. (978-1-60282-874-2)

Broken in Soft Places by Fiona Zedde. The instant Sara Chambers meets the seductive and sinful Merille Thompson, she falls hard, but knowing the difference between love and a dangerous, all-consuming desire is just one of the lessons Sara must learn before it's too late. (978-1-60282-876-6)

Healing Hearts by Donna K. Ford. Running from tragedy, the women of Willow Springs find that with friendship, there is hope, and with love, there is everything. (978-1-60282-877-3)

Desolation Point by Cari Hunter. When a storm strands Sarah Kent in the North Cascades, Alex Pascal is determined to find her. Neither imagines the dangers they will face when a ruthless criminal begins to hunt them down. (978-1-60282-865-0)

The Gemini Deception by Kim Baldwin and Xenia Alexiou. The truth, the whole truth, and nothing but lies. Book six in the Elite Operatives series. (978-1-60282-867-4)

I Remember by Julie Cannon. What happens when you can never forget the first kiss, the first touch, the first taste of lips on skin? What happens when you know you will remember every single detail of a mysterious woman? (978-1-60282-866-7)

Scarlet Revenge by Sheri Lewis Wohl. When faith alone isn't enough, will the love of one woman be strong enough to save a vampire from damnation? (978-1-60282-868-1)

Ghost Trio by Lillian Q. Irwin. When Lee Howe hears the voice of her dead lover singing to her, is it a hallucination, a ghost, or something more sinister? (978-1-60282-869-8)

The Princess Affair by Nell Stark. Rhodes Scholar Kerry Donovan arrives at Oxford ready to focus on her studies, but her life and her priorities are thrown into chaos when she catches the eye of Her Royal Highness Princess Sasha. (978-1-60282-858-2)

The Chase by Jesse J. Thoma. When Isabelle Rochat's life is threatened, she receives the unwelcome protection and attention of bounty hunter Holt Lasher who vows to keep Isabelle safe at all costs. (978-1-60282-859-9)

The Lone Hunt by L.L. Raand. In a world where humans and Praeterns conspire for the ultimate power, violence is a way of life…and death. A Midnight Hunters novel. (978-1-60282-860-5)

The Supernatural Detective by Crin Claxton. Tony Carson sees dead people. With a drag queen for a spirit guide and a devastatingly attractive herbalist for a client, she's about to discover the spirit world can be a very dangerous world indeed. (978-1-60282-861-2)

Beloved Gomorrah by Justine Saracen. Undersea artists creating their own City on the Plain uncover the truth about Sodom and Gomorrah, whose "one righteous man" is a murderer, rapist, and conspirator in genocide. (978-1-60282-862-9)

Every Second Counts by D. Jackson Leigh. Every second counts in Bridgette LeRoy's desperate mission to protect her heart and stop Marc Ryder's suicidal return to riding rodeo bulls. (978-1-60282-785-1)

The Left Hand of Justice by Jess Faraday. A kidnapped heiress, a heretical cult, a corrupt police chief, and an accused witch. Paris is burning, and the only one who can put out the fire is Detective Inspector Elise Corbeau…whose boss wants her dead. (978-1-60282-863-6)

Cut to the Chase by Lisa Girolami. Careful and methodical author Paige Cornish falls for brash and wild Hollywood actress Avalon Randolph, but can these opposites find a happy middle ground in a town that never lives in the middle? (978-1-60282-783-7)

More Than Friends by Erin Dutton. Evelyn Fisher thinks she has the perfect role model for a long-term relationship, until her best friends, Kendall and Melanie, split up and all three women must reevaluate their lives and their relationships. (978-1-60282-784-4)

Dirty Money by Ashley Bartlett. Vivian Cooper and Reese DiGiovanni just found out that falling in love is hard. It's even harder when you're running for your life. (978-1-60282-786-8)

Sea Glass Inn by Karis Walsh. When Melinda Andrews commissions a series of mosaics by Pamela Whitford for her new inn, she doesn't expect to be more captivated by the artist than by the paintings. (978-1-60282-771-4)

The Awakening: A Sisterhood of Spirits novel by Yvonne Heidt. Sunny Skye has interacted with spirits her entire life, but when she runs into Officer Jordan Lawson during a ghost investigation, she discovers more than just facts in a missing girl's cold case file. (978-1-60282-772-1)

Blacker Than Blue by Rebekah Weatherspoon. Threatened with losing her first love to a powerful demon, vampire Cleo Jones is willing to break the ultimate law of the undead to rebuild the family she has lost. (978-1-60282-774-5)

Murphy's Law by Yolanda Wallace. No matter how high you climb, you can't escape your past. (978-1-60282-773-8)